SWEET LIES

Eden's face grew crimson with rage. "I never did any such thing! Shamus was my husband. I loved—"

Damon broke off her heated words by pulling her toward him. "No need to tell lies to me," he whispered, his words fanning her face like wanton flames. "I just want to taste those sweet lips which lie so expertly."

Before Eden realized what was going on, Damon had wrapped his arms around her. He brought her so close against his body that she felt his heart beating against her breast. Then his mouth crushed hers.

Desire shot through her like an electrical current, sapping her resistance to fight. She leaned into him, simultaneously defeated and triumphant. Never had she felt this way or had any idea a man's kiss could be so thrilling. Men had kissed her before, but never like this. Now, for the first time, she was willingly surrendering some of herself to another human being, and glorying in that surrender . . .

ZEBRA BOOKS

are published by

Kensington Publishing Corp.
475 Park Avenue South
New York, NY 10016

First printing: November, 1990

Printed in the United States of America

Wicked, Wild Eden

Lynette Vinet

ZEBRA BOOKS
KENSINGTON PUBLISHING CORP.

Chapter One

New Zealand, 1870

Eden Flynn wiped the fine sheen of perspiration from her brow with the back of her hand. The bodice of her gown was damp and wisps of reddish-gold hair clung to the sides of her cheeks. She couldn't wait to get back to her hotel room and indulge in a cooling glass of iced tea. New Zealand was much too warm during the height of summer for her liking.

Shamus hadn't told her about the weather. He'd often elaborated about the Remarkables, the mountains in the distance which rose like protective giants above Queenstown. Nearby Lake Wakatipu, whose watery surface resembled dancing diamonds and sapphires in the sunshine, contrasted sharply with the Neolithic mountains. Modern paddle steamers and various other craft plied the waters daily, sometimes crisscrossing at such odd angles that Eden wondered at such folly. Luckily, there were never any serious accidents.

Queenstown, a Maori settlement until the 1850's when

white settlers arrived, was now crowded with miners and people who had caught gold fever. She could almost hear Shamus's voice in her ears now. "You'll be thinkin' you're still in San Francisco," he'd assured her many times.

Eden sighed. She wasn't in San Francisco any longer and she missed it. Homesickness assailed her, and the summer sun so drained her of energy that she felt as wilted as a plucked dandelion. And her mood wasn't the best. With each passing day and no sign of Damon Alexander, Shamus's nephew, Eden grew more apprehensive and agitated.

As she left the mercantile store near the river, her arms loaded with packages for the journey she was about to undertake, she wondered at the foolhardiness of her actions. Perhaps she shouldn't have left America for New Zealand. She didn't know anything about mining, and the little she'd learned about it from Shamus had convinced her it was hard work. But he had insisted she come, begging her to promise she'd claim her share in Thunder Mine after he'd gone. She'd promised only as a means of keeping him quiet, but in the end she'd done as he wished. After a long and miserable sea voyage, she was here. Now she must contend with Damon Alexander—if he ever showed up.

Eden crossed the dusty street which led to her hotel. The bottom of her fashionable gown—a red taffeta creation with tiny black bows at the cuffs and high neckline, designed by one of the most sought after seamstresses in San Francisco—dragged the ground. She was used to walking on cobblestones or hiring carriages to convey her to her destination. Shamus hadn't mentioned Queenstown was still rather primitive in some

6

respects. Eden doubted she'd be able to find a suitable carriage in the whole town, so she opted to walk. She now doubted the practicality of the gown she'd chosen to wear for her shopping sojourn that day. The ladies in the mercantile had looked enviously at it, and Eden noticed their own gowns were much plainer and not made of such fine material. In truth, she would rather have worn a simple black dress—she was still in mourning—but Shamus had insisted she wear colorful gowns and not hide her beauty.

She hated drawing attention to herself and felt conspicuous. Lusty leers and less than gentlemanly comments were hurled her way by men lounging against storefronts or passing her on the street. Anything could happen to her, a woman alone in a foreign country. For the hundredth time she cursed herself for listening to Shamus. She hated experiencing that horrible, gnawing feeling of insecurity again. She thought she'd overcome that when she married Shamus, but she knew that wasn't the case when she began to hurry back to the safety of her hotel room.

Stepping from the street onto the wooden planks which served as a sidewalk, the many packages in her arms obscuring her view, Eden didn't see the man leaving the saloon. She felt him, however, when she plowed into him.

The wind gushed from her lungs. With a startled and painful cry, she fell backward into the dusty street. Her packages flew into the air and fell hither and yon around her. She had no idea that her gown was pushed up to reveal the ruffled hem of her chemise or that her silk-stockinged legs were all too visible to the staring bystanders. At first she thought a huge boulder had pinned her to the ground. It was only when awareness dawned upon her did she realize the punishing weight atop her came from a dark-haired man.

Like a heavy counterpane he lay sprawled over her, crushing her breasts with his powerful chest. She heard him inquire if she was hurt, but she could barely speak from the breath being knocked from her and the hypnotic effect this man's face held for her.

He was swarthily handsome, possessed of a finely made nose and full, sensuous lips, lips which now were turned up into a genuinely concerned smile. He stared down at her with eyes so blue they resembled the calm waters of the nearby lake. Within their sapphire depths were tiny, golden pinpoints of molten fire. Eden had never seen a more handsome man—or been more embarrassed.

Despite her discomfort, she almost found herself enjoying the pressure of his body atop hers. It had been so long since a man held her or touched her that she almost gave in to the inclination to push her body into his, to dissolve into his sensual warmth.

But she grew frightened of her own feelings, the odd sense of intimacy this stranger induced within her. What was wrong with her to think such wicked thoughts, to actually like it when she felt the hard-muscled arm draw her closer to him? He had nearly killed her and here she was aching for something so wanton she started to blush.

The spell broke and she came to her senses when she smelled liquor on his breath. Her proper upbringing rose to the fore; her eyes flared like greenstone and her lower body bucked. "Get off me, you drunken fool!"

His head reared backward, but his gaze never left her face. "Drunken fool, am I? Is that any way to speak to a person after you nearly trample him to death?"

"Trample you? You've nearly killed me. I can't breathe. Get off me before I knee you."

The arrogant man smirked; but even then he was handsome. "I thought you were a lady, but I was wrong."

"What do you mean?" she asked, seeing that people milled around them and all too aware of the suggestive scene they must make on the ground together.

"Ladies don't knee men and ladies don't push themselves hard against a man," he whispered. "How long has it been since you've had a good tumble with a gent?"

She sputtered in outrage, unable to think of a scathing retort except to demand he get off her. The man flashed her a smile, but did as she asked. He extended his hand to her, a hand she refused to take, but he grabbed her by the elbow and unceremoniously hauled her to her feet. A woman in the crowd came forward and began dusting off the back of Eden's gown. Eden smiled gratefully at her, pretending she didn't notice the handsome man who stood only inches from her. She willed herself not to look at him, but she found herself taking covetous glances nonetheless.

He was taller than she realized, taller than Shamus. Eden took note of his shirt, which was the same blue as his eyes. When he bent down to retrieve the large-brimmed hat he'd lost during the fall, the thin material strained with the effort, leaving no doubt as to the broadness of his shoulders. From the tight-fitting denim trousers he wore, the brown boots which were mud-caked and in need of a polishing, he was definitely all male. And a randy one at that, Eden decided. She could spot one a mile away, and even in New Zealand, men were the same. They always wanted one thing from a woman.

Except for Shamus, who'd been the only decent man she'd ever known other than her father.

Eden averted her gaze and pushed down the odd sensation which flooded her to realize he was watching her in an openly appraising fashion. Never had she noticed a man in such a wanton way and felt guilty for doing so now. Shamus had been gone for such a short time.

"Are you all right?" he asked her again.

"Yes, I believe I am, at least I seem to be in one piece," she said curtly, though her body already ached.

"I'll escort you home."

"I can manage quite well by myself, sir. I need no help from you." She knew she sounded shrewish, but something about this man bothered her. She started to collect her packages when a small brown-skinned Maori boy appeared and assisted her. He spoke to her in his native language.

"He wants to carry them back for you if you'll pay him," the stranger interpreted for her.

Eden nodded at the child and smiled. "Tell him I'd be most pleased."

The man spoke to the boy and he grinned his understanding while he waited in silence for Eden. "I would have done it for nothing." The man's deep voice followed Eden when she turned to walk away.

Eden whirled to face him. "I doubt that. Men usually want something for their trouble."

"Ah, miss, you wound me with your suspicion." His eyes gleamed with amusement when he put his hat on. "You're a Yank, aren't you?"

A Yank? Eden stared in outrage, her blood boiling to be called such a despicable name. She knew that to this man with the Irish lilt to his voice, her accent was clearly American. And she also knew he probably lumped all Americans together. Her reaction to his question was ridiculous, but she couldn't help herself. She was a southerner. The war had left too many scars for her not to be offended. "I'm no . . . Yank." She could barely say the hated word.

"Sorry, thought you might be. Would it trouble you to tell me your name, miss? I'd appreciate knowing it."

"My name isn't your business, sir, and anyway I'm a *Mrs.*" Eden waved her hand at him. The large gold wedding band caught the sunlight.

"My mistake then, Mrs. Whoever you are. I apologize for any discomfort I caused you. Good day to you."

To Eden's surprise he walked past her as if she didn't exist for him any longer. She watched him until he turned a corner of a nearby street and felt foolish over how she'd acted. What had gotten into her to be so rude to him? It wasn't like her to be insulting and ill-mannered. Perhaps she should run after him and apologize? She discounted the thought almost as soon as it surfaced. The man might misinterpret her apology and expect something else from her—something she'd give to no man—especially that one.

Taking some of the heavier packages from the small boy, she made it back to the hotel with his help.

Gazing down at the street below her, Eden Flynn twisted the wedding band on her left hand. Where was Shamus's nephew? He should have come to escort her to Thunder Mine by now. She'd been in Queenstown for ten days, having sent a message to Damon Alexander upon

11

her arrival. The hotel clerk assured her that the note had been delivered, the distance to the mine being no more than four days' travel both ways. If that were true, then she should have heard something by now. She hoped nothing had happened to Damon. Shamus had been so fond of him.

Thinking of Shamus caused Eden to finger gently the outline of the heart-shaped locket beneath her bodice. It seemed only yesterday that Shamus had placed the golden locket around her neck. She found it hard to believe a year had passed. His lilting Irish accent still echoed in her ears. She could still feel the warmth of his eyes upon her when he opened the locket to reveal a small tintype of himself. "So you won't be forgettin' me when I'm gone," he had said before kissing her cheek.

"As if I could forget you, Shamus," she had told him, and now found herself whispering the same words to the empty hotel room. There was no laughing response this time, no answering hug. A sob rose in Eden's throat. His death was fresh in her mind, nine months later. The pain of losing him all too real.

Shamus had commanded her not to grieve, but she couldn't help herself. He'd given her so much in their brief time together as man and wife. It wasn't only the gifts he bought for her, the wealth he bequeathed to her upon his death. He'd been kind and concerned for her well-being and she'd been powerless to save him. Despite her caring for him, her willing him to live and grow stronger, he'd died just as he'd predicted.

The picture in the locket was how he wanted her to remember him. His image looked as healthy and robust as he himself had been the day they met at LaRue's Pleasure Palace in San Francisco. He'd told her that no matter the thirty-year difference in their ages, he didn't want her memory of him to be of the weak, gaunt-faced creature he'd become at the end.

Eden poured a glass of tea and fanned herself with a lace handkerchief. She found it hard to believe Christmas was but a month away, and she grew homesick not for San Francisco but for the many Christmases she'd shared with her parents on their Georgia plantation before the war.

"I won't think about it," she mumbled when her mind drifted to her family and the happiness they'd shared. Even to remember the good times pained her because she couldn't relive them or bring back her parents. Nothing of her former life was left after the South was defeated. The plantation house had been burned to the ground during Sherman's march to the sea. The invading Yankees had swarmed through the house and across the grounds like marauding fire ants, stealing what they could carry away and burning what they couldn't.

Her father had been bayonetted by a murderous Yank like a sacrificial lamb when he attempted to defend his family and home. Eden's mother went wild at his death and tried to stab the soldier with a knife. Her end hadn't been swift and merciful . . .

It was here Eden always stopped her thoughts, unable to dwell upon Lila Prescott's rape and death. Eden had witnessed all the horror from the inside of a child's treehouse, hidden from view by the shielding leaves of the giant oak. Her father had sent her there when news came of approaching troops. She'd been fifteen at the time, and had not climbed into the treehouse in three years. She tearfully clung to her father, crying she didn't want to leave him. For the first time in her life, her

13

father's gentle face hardened into an iron mask and he forbade her to leave the tree under any circumstances. Always an obedient child, Eden did as she was told and she later knew that her father had saved her life.

But the memories of that day would be with her forever.

After the Yankees departed, one of the Prescott's neighbors found her aimlessly wandering the road in apparent shock. With his help she made her way to her father's sister in Atlanta. Her aunt had fared little better, having grown old and sickly before her time. The family home was barely habitable, but the two women made do. Eden cared for her aunt until she died two months after the war's end.

With her aunt's passing, Eden had no one and nothing to call her own. She knew she must put her former life behind her and make a new start. She decided to do what many people were doing then. She'd head west.

In Savannah, the captain of a whaling ship hired her to tutor his two little girls. Eden's job ended some months later when the ship reached the busy city of San Francisco. She'd earned enough money to allow herself time to decide what sort of job she'd enjoy doing. Tutoring was rewarding, but it didn't pay enough, so she steered clear of newspaper ads for tutors and governesses.

By chance she made the acquaintance of an older man in her boarding house. He told her he had resigned his bookkeeping position at LaRue's Pleasure Palace. His health was failing and he was going to live with his daughter. Eden, who'd always had a head for figures, discreetly inquired about the salary, and learning it was much more than she'd earned as a tutor, decided to apply for the job.

14

She had no idea what a pleasure palace was, but upon seeing the red-and-gold furnishings and the number of scantily clad young women, she quickly understood LaRue's purpose. Before the war, she'd have been thoroughly shocked and sickened to consider entering such a place, much less working there. But the war had changed her. When LaRue herself hired Eden as a bookkeeper, Eden warmly thanked her.

From the money LaRue's took in, Eden decided vice was most profitable indeed. Strangely, she didn't dislike the women who catered to the customer's baser needs. They made a living at what they knew best, and like Eden, all of them were survivors of their pasts.

After Eden had worked at LaRue's for three years, Shamus Flynn entered her life. He'd thought he'd been overcharged on the meal he'd ordered and insisted on seeing LaRue. She had been away but because the big, rough-looking Irishman was making such a fuss and disturbing the other patrons, Eden was asked to intervene.

She hadn't liked Shamus at first. He seemed a typical Irishman to her—boisterous and swaggering. But after she'd calmed him down and seen to the bill, he apologized with so much charm that she forgot her original impression. He invited her to share a glass of wine with him, and Eden never regretted her acceptance for one second. Beneath Shamus's florid exterior was a shy, gentle man. He was the first man she allowed into her prim and proper existence.

After about a month, Eden came to know a great deal about Shamus Flynn. Shamus loved to talk about his boyhood in Ireland, the land he'd left over twenty years ago, during the Potato Famine. Taking his sister's

15

orphaned son with him, they had headed to New Zealand, where he thought he could make a new start for himself and the boy. He worked at various jobs until he decided to try his luck at finding gold in the Otago area. After six months he struck it rich, and Thunder Mine transformed him into a wealthy man.

Damon Alexander was now his partner in the mine. Shamus loved him like a son, but he confided to Eden he was still lonely sometimes. Shamus's eyes twinkled when he took Eden's hand in his. "At least I was lonely until I met you, pretty Eden." He gently touched the reddish-gold strands of her hair and smiled nervously. "Would you consider becoming my wife?"

She never thought Shamus would want to marry her. In fact, she'd never considered him as a husband. She cared for him, was more than fond of him, but she didn't love him like a potential wife should love a husband. Before she could refuse, Shamus's face grew very serious. He told her he didn't expect their marriage to be a "normal" one. It couldn't be. He was ill, and had come to San Francisco to meet with a doctor he thought might be able to help him. But the doctor had told him his illness was progressive and he didn't have much time left.

Shamus looked so healthy and robust that Eden was shocked, unable to believe such a diagnosis, but he assured her it was true. He was going to die, and he didn't want to die alone.

"I know I'm asking a lot of you, Eden, but I love you and I think you care for me. We've both had our share of grief in the world, so we understand each other. I don't expect to be a husband in the biblical sense to you," he'd hastily blurted out. "I wish to heaven that I could, but, well . . . I'd be content just to have you near me. I don't

16

trust anyone but Damon or you. I'll never see Damon again, and . . . and I don't want anybody else caring for me but you." His warm, laughing eyes suddenly grew misty. "I'd be most grateful if you'd consider looking after me until the end. As my wife, all my wealth will be yours. And my part in the mine, too." Shamus squeezed her hand. "I know what it is to want something of your own, Eden. I can give you that."

Eden's lips turned pale. "You're making it sound like a business arrangement instead of a marriage—as if you're buying a wife who's waiting for you to die. I can't, Shamus. I won't."

But in the end she changed her mind because Shamus needed her. She never regretted her decision. He became her whole existence, replacing the family she'd lost. More than once he'd grab her hand at the times she knew he felt most ill and would shoot her a warning glance. "Don't be gettin' too attached to me, my darlin'," he'd advise with a wink. "Promise me after I'm gone you'll head to New Zealand to claim your share. Do that for me." He'd become so agitated that Eden always assured him she would do as he asked.

His end was peaceful. She held up well through his burial. It was only weeks later, after she'd written to Damon Alexander telling him about her marriage to Shamus and Shamus's subsequent death and informing Alexander she'd be departing for New Zealand to claim her part in Thunder Mine, that she truly realized Shamus was gone.

LaRue, who had become her friend, paid a call and found her weeping. The woman comforted her when Eden told her through blinding tears that she hadn't done enough for Shamus. He'd left his wealth to her and she didn't deserve it. LaRue gave Eden a motherly hug. "Don't be silly, dear. Shamus knew what he was doing. I knew him on and off for fifteen years and found him to be a sensible man. Believe that he wanted you to have his money and the mine. Why else would he be so insistent about your going to New Zealand to claim your share?"

Eden wondered about that, too. She could easily own part of Thunder Mine and enjoy its yield without having to travel thousands of miles. But she'd promised Shamus, and suddenly she wanted to go. She was glad she'd written Alexander of her imminent arrival. Something tangible waited for her in New Zealand, something which belonged to her, and she was bound and determined to claim it.

She went ahead with her plans to leave, not giving an extra thought to what Damon Alexander would say.

Chapter 2

Damon Alexander had a great deal to say about Eden Flynn, and none of it was complimentary. He sat in the Greenstone Saloon with Nick Patterson, a middle-aged miner friend of Shamus's, while his arm hugged the waist of a comely creature named Bella.

To Damon, women like Bella, who wore rouge on their faces and dressed in skimpy, cheap gowns, were good for only one thing. Having been at Thunder Mine for months, he felt the need to indulge in good whiskey and the stirring kisses of a bought woman when he came into town. When he left, he'd put the doxy from his mind—until the next time. But while he was here in town, he wanted a good time and was not about to stop his fun to escort his uncle's widow to the mine. From what he'd learned about Eden Flynn, she was no better than Bella.

"You're being unfair to the lady," Nick admonished over the high, whining notes of the player piano. "Mrs. Flynn has been in Queenstown for two weeks, waiting for you to fetch her, and here you've been for five days, not lifting a finger to see her. Shamus would be ashamed of you."

Damon did feel ashamed of ignoring the Widow Flynn, but he swallowed his shame with a large swig of whiskey. "I told you what she is."

"What is she?" chirped Bella, playfully squeezing the bulge in Damon's trousers.

He hadn't thought Bella was following his conversation with Nick and he was irritated. Women like Bella should do only what they were paid to do and not interrupt or offer opinions about other matters. "Nothing you need to know, love. Be a good girl and get me another whiskey."

Bella applied more pressure to his crotch and smiled. "Why don't you join me upstairs instead?"

Damon nodded, more than aroused and ready for Bella's pleasuring. However, he knew he'd have to finish his conversation with Nick.

Both men watched Bella walk away from the table, their eyes following her well-proportioned figure. Nick whistled. "That one's a wildcat all right."

"Aye, but like all whores, maybe she only pretends to like it."

"That's the reason a man pays for the likes of her," Nick sagely pronounced with a knowing smile. "Decent women aren't supposed to like it, so with the naughty ones there are no surprises and lots of fun. But, Damon, my lad, Bella and her kind aren't deaf and certainly not mute. You'd best be careful what you say and how you say it."

Damon's eyes glinted like blue frost. "Bella's a whore just like that bitch my uncle married. I told you one of Shamus's mates saw the woman with him in San Francisco in that place she worked. LaRue's. If not for that information, I wouldn't know anything about the gold-digging tart. Shamus didn't see the need to write and tell me he'd gotten married." Damon clenched his hand into a fist. "He was probably too humiliated to admit he'd made a mistake."

"I doubt that. Shamus and I were friends for many years, and he wasn't one to be taken in by a pretty face."

"No? Then explain why she's staying in one of Queenstown's fanciest hotels, paying her way with money she wheedled out of my uncle by marrying him. She wants to collect her share of Thunder Mine, which should have been all mine but for that fortune huntress."

"You're jumping to conclusions, lad."

"Hah!" Damon spat out with such a vehemence that Nick jumped. "The bitch is young enough to have been his daughter. Tell me she married him because she loved him!"

"Maybe she did. You're letting your past experiences color your reason. Why don't you just go introduce yourself to the lady?"

Rising suddenly, Damon knocked over his chair. Beneath the wide brim of his hat, his dark hair hung in shaggy strands on his forehead. "Because she's as much of a *lady* as the whore who's waiting upstairs for me. And you're right in saying my past is coloring my reason. I'm an expert when it comes to whores."

"Tessa's gone, Damon," Nick reminded him. "Forget her and live your life. Find a good woman—"

Damon's painful laugh interrupted Nick. "Aye, mate, I'd do that if one existed, but a woman might seem to be virtuous, might claim she loves you, but like all women, she's after only one thing: money. I learned the hard way, and I won't be learning that same lesson again."

21

"What are you going to do about Mrs. Flynn?" Nick persisted when Damon started to walk away.

Not halting his stride up the stairs, Damon called over his shoulder, "She'll wait until I'm ready to see her."

Stroking the gray stubble on his chin, Nick mumbled under his breath. "Not if I have a say in the matter."

"Begging your pardon, Mrs. Flynn, but I'm Nick Patterson, an old friend of your husband's. Do you mind if I join you?"

Eden gestured to the chair next to hers in the hotel dining room. Nick Patterson wasn't dressed as elegantly as some of the men seated around them, but Eden found herself instantly liking him. He mopped his furrowed brow with a red-checkered bandanna. "Been mighty warm lately," he noted and smiled.

Agreeing that indeed it had been warm, Eden ordered an iced tea for him and quelled her urge to laugh when his first hesitant sip produced a screwed-up face. It was evident that Nick wasn't a tea drinker. "Perhaps you'd rather have a beer or a whiskey, Mr. Patterson."

"Oh, no, ma'am. This is just dandy."

Eden knew he was lying, but let the matter pass. "So, you knew my husband . . ."

Nick's face brightened. "Aye, I did. A finer man I've never met. And may I say that old Shamus did right well by you, too. You're the prettiest thing Queenstown has seen."

Eden was used to men telling her she was pretty, but Nick's compliment was so clearly heartfelt, her cheeks dimpled. "I'd say I was the one who did well, Mr. Patterson. My husband was an extraordinary man. I still miss him, even more so since my arrival in Queenstown. He spoke so often about the town that I feel as if I've seen it many times."

"Queenstown was Shamus's favorite place," Nick agreed. "Except for Thunder Mine. I never saw a man take to mining the way Shamus did. He had a natural-born instinct for it, almost as if he could smell gold. His nephew does, too. That's why they made such a good team."

At the mention of Damon Alexander, Eden stiffened. "I sent word to Mr. Alexander of my arrival but so far he hasn't responded. Am I to assume he's ill?"

Nick shifted uncomfortably in his seat and sipped the tea. "No, ma'am. Damon's well and hearty."

"Then you've seen him. Did he receive my message? The hotel clerk assured me he had."

"Aye, he got the message. The fact is, I delivered it to him."

Eden assessed Nick's troubled face. "Mr. Alexander isn't coming to Queenstown for me?"

"Oh, he intends to take you to Thunder Mine, truly, he does. Why, he's been here for a number of days, but pressing business—"

"Please don't make excuses for the man's rudeness," she interrupted. "It's quite clear that I'm being ignored. Except for you, Mr. Patterson, I'd wonder if all men in Queenstown were so ill-mannered." She couldn't help remembering the man who'd knocked her down earlier that day. She found herself trembling from Alexander's slight, unused to being purposely ignored. Her voice possessed a brittle edge when she asked, "Where is he staying?"

"Uh . . . you don't want to know that. He knows

23

you're here and he'll be coming—"

"Where is he?" she persisted.

Perspiration popped out anew on Nick's brow. This wasn't what he'd had in mind when he'd decided to find Eden Flynn. He felt he needed to look after Shamus's wife, to let her know Damon hadn't slighted her—which the young pup surely had, though there was no need for her to know that. But he could see she was on to him. He could also tell she was a proper lady, nothing like what Damon believed her to be.

He couldn't stop the mischievous grin which tugged at the edges of his mouth. Maybe this was one female Damon should meet, and meet soon. She wouldn't be so easily wooed with his good looks; and since she didn't appear to be the whore Damon had described, then she wouldn't jump into bed with him, either. Maybe the arrogant fellow would finally meet his match. "He's staying at the Greenstone Saloon," Nick told her.

Eden threw down her napkin on the table and stood. "Will you be so kind to escort me there?"

Nick shook his head. "I'll tell him I saw you. You don't want to go there, Mrs. Flynn."

"Why not?"

Licking his lips, Nick found his mouth had gone suddenly dry. "It's not a fit place for a lady."

Eden laughed. "If you mean it's a brothel, sir, then I assure you that I've worked at the notorious LaRue's in San Francisco. Whorehouses don't bother me." Nick's face fell, prompting Eden to take his arm. "I trust my nephew will be pleased to see me," she said in a silky southern accent as she led a tongue-tied Nick away.

Damon Alexander wouldn't make a fool of her! If he thought he could keep her cooling her heels while he

24

bided his time with a Queenstown whore, he was sadly wrong. *He probably believes I won't hunt him down,* Eden thought, digging her nails into Nick's arm.

"Ow! You're hurting me," Nick complained.

"I'm sorry."

"This is a bad idea, Mrs. Flynn."

"No, it's a good idea, Mr. Patterson. Damon Alexander won't dictate to me. I won't let the man insult me."

After walking down the dusty thoroughfare for almost three blocks, they crossed the street to stand at the back entrance of the Greenstone Saloon. The whining notes of the piano mingled with the boisterous voices of the men inside. "I'll go fetch him for you," Nick offered.

Eden halted him with a gloved hand on his arm. She looked very much the lady in the prim blue bonnet and matching gown she'd changed into after that afternoon's mishap with the obnoxious, insulting man. "I'm going with you. I refuse to wait out here."

"Begging your pardon, Mrs. Flynn, but you don't want to go inside, either. There's no telling what you might see. Go back to the hotel while I speak to Damon."

"I assure you that I've seen quite a bit in my time and won't be shocked. Now take me to Mr. Alexander."

Nick's eyes narrowed and he said thoughtfully, "Maybe Damon was right."

"Right about what?"

"Nothing." Nick shrugged, and gestured Eden toward the back stairs.

A wooden door at the top of the stairs opened with a creak. Eden found herself in a darkened hallway with doors on both sides. The heat was stifling. Perspiration trickled between her breasts from the warmth and her own daring. What was she doing in this place anyway?

Had her good sense fled along with her pride? Why did it matter if Damon Alexander snubbed her? But somehow it did and the snub hurt. She needed to prove to him that she wouldn't be placed in the position of helpless female. She owned part of Thunder Mine and Damon Alexander would have to accept that.

"Which room is his?" she asked Nick, who followed closely behind her.

Nick stopped before a closed door.

For a second, Eden hesitated to knock. Perhaps she should follow Nick's advice and have him speak to Alexander while she returned to the hotel. On the verge of leaving, she changed her mind when a deep male laugh, followed by a feminine squeal, wafted through the wood paneling.

It was as she'd thought. Alexander was playing while he'd kept her waiting for days. Her supple and soft mouth grew hard and rigid. She wasn't about to leave.

Knocking hard upon the door, Eden at first wondered if anyone had heard. "This is a mistake," Nick mumbled in agonized tones. "I shouldn't have let you come here."

"I'm here, and Alexander is going to answer if I have to stand here all day." Once again, she pounded resolutely upon the door until the laughter ceased.

"Who in bloody hell is it?" demanded a masculine voice from behind the door.

Eden took a deep breath, the sweetness of her own voice belying her anger. "It's Mrs. Shamus Flynn, Mr. Alexander."

She heard a sudden and strained silence, then a vicious curse accompanying the thudding of feet hitting the floor. When the door was thrown open, Eden couldn't help but gape at the powerfully built man whose naked

26

chest glistened with sweat, a sheet unceremoniously draping his lower body. Dark tendrils of hair fell wantonly across his forehead. Eyes filled with blue fire swept angrily over Eden before widening in stunned surprise. A frown turned down the corners of his sensual mouth. "Dammit! It's you."

Eden found herself taken aback, not only by the man's nerve in answering the door draped in a sheet but by who he was—the very man who'd knocked her down earlier that day. She nearly groaned aloud.

"Watch your language, Damon," Nick scolded before she could say anything. "Mrs. Flynn is a lady."

"So, she's gotten to you, too," Damon mumbled. "You're as hopeless as my uncle. Why did you bring her here, Nick?"

"Don't blame Mr. Patterson." Eden quickly came to Nick's defense. "I insisted he escort me here to see you, but if I'd known you were Shamus's nephew, I'd still have come." The defiance shining within the depths of her eyes hid her embarrassment at finding him in a state of undress. "I've been in Queenstown for some days, as you well know, sir. I'm ready to leave for Thunder Mine and wait only for you to take me there. And to be frank, I think you've been incredibly rude to keep me waiting."

He tilted his head to the side. His eyes perused her from the top of her hat to her slippered feet, then up again to linger a bit too long on the gauzy white lace which primly covered the valley between her breasts. "Ah, a true lady you look to be," he noted, and fixed his gaze on her face. "Such a well-spoken and polite lady you are in your anger. And you *are* angry, aren't you? But you're not going to say you are—just like all 'proper ladies.'"

27

Eden didn't like the derogatory way he spoke to her. It was evident that Damon Alexander disliked her, and she wondered why. She sensed he *wanted* to offend her. Could it be he didn't want a woman as a partner? She knew many men didn't think women belonged in business. But she wasn't just any woman. She was Shamus Flynn's wife, part owner of Thunder Mine and a woman with a good head for business. Damon Alexander would have to accept her, whether he wanted to or not. Still, he unnerved her with the strength of his partially nude body and the way his eyes raked over her. She clutched her reticule, willing herself to meet his insolent stare and get on with her mission.

"I shall expect you at my hotel this evening, Mr. Alexander. We have a great deal to discuss concerning our journey."

"I'm sorry, but I may not be able to make it tonight."

"I insist you do, sir!"

Damon opened the door wider and allowed Eden to see into the room. On the sheet-rumpled bed reclined a woman who didn't appear the least bit bothered over her nudity. During her days at LaRue's, Eden had seen undressed women and didn't think a thing about it, but now she was suddenly embarrassed to realize that this woman was waiting for Damon Alexander's lusty lovemaking. And for the flash of a second, Eden envied the woman Damon's caresses—going so far as to imagine herself on that bed awaiting that man. The thought caused her face to redden with such intensity she felt her face might explode. "As you can see, I'm occupied," she heard him finish.

She took a deep breath and willed herself to speak. "I suggest you . . . complete your business as soon as possible."

"Some things can't be rushed, Mrs. Flynn. A woman like yourself should know that."

The horrid man was actually smirking at her. His words were clearly meant to insult her, but she wasn't certain how. "I'll be waiting, Mr. Alexander. Good afternoon."

Eden turned away, rushing blindly down the hallway, unaware if Nick Patterson followed behind her. She wished only to escape the image of Damon Alexander's very masculine body draped in a sheet, to get her thoughts in order. But her mind was jumbled with pictures of Alexander taking the woman in his arms. She distinctly saw his hands stroking the voluptuous flesh, clearly heard the woman's moan of pleasure . . .

Eden stopped dead-still on the street and clutched her throat in dismay; the moan she'd heard had come from her own mouth.

Chapter 3

"Traitor!" Damon hissed at Nick after Eden's abrupt departure. Not giving Nick the chance to reply, Damon slammed the door. The veins in his neck jutted out; his mouth hurt from gritting his teeth so hard. Raking tanned fingers through his tousled hair, he barely glanced at Bella. His attention was still fixed on the mental image of Eden Flynn.

She'd looked so much like a proper lady, so perfect in her manners and deportment. He recalled how wisps of golden-red hair peeped from beneath the blue bonnet, how her long golden lashes framed the most incredibly beautiful green eyes he'd ever seen. She was more beautiful than he'd expected. Perhaps that was the reason he'd purposely bumped into her on the street earlier that day.

He hadn't intended to knock her down, only to nudge her so she'd notice him. Instead, he had tripped over his own feet at the last instant. He'd felt like a big lummox, which was exactly what Eden must have thought. At the time Damon hadn't known she was Shamus's gold-digging widow of course. He'd wanted to meet her when he first spied her heading toward the saloon. Her arms had been loaded down with packages, nearly obscuring her face—a face he hoped would be the counterpart in beauty of her curvaceous form. And she hadn't disappointed him. She was beautiful, a perfect lady.

At least he had thought she was a lady until she'd threatened him with her knee. But now he knew without a doubt that Eden Flynn was the whore he had anticipated. No woman of quality would have marched inside the Greenstone as she had done. And she'd barely flicked an eyelash at his state of undress, a clear indication that she'd seen many a naked man in her time. A gnawing sensation started in the pit of his stomach when he wondered how many men she'd seen that way.

Shamus had been one, and now she'd snared Nick into her wanton web. "Well, she won't claim me with her fancy ways," Damon mumbled, then realized with a start that Eden hadn't given any indication of being interested in him. Quite the opposite actually, and for a man who was used to women finding him attractive, this realization stung his male ego.

"What's the matter, love? You're not tired of playing with me already, are you?" Bella's sultry voice from the bed drew his attention to her. Damon cast the sheet aside and joined her. Here was a woman who knew what she was and didn't pretend to be something she wasn't. In her own way, Bella was honest—unlike Eden Flynn.

Damon nuzzled the valley between her large breasts, then his hand strayed to the spot between her thighs. "I'm never too tired for this," he assured her.

Bella giggled, but began to moan with pleasure when Damon's fingers slipped inside her and worked her to a frenzy. "I just love when you come into town," she

31

whispered, allowing his tongue free rein over her body. "You're the only paying gent who thinks to give me some fun."

Bella had told him this before. He found himself wondering if things had been that way for Eden, too. He didn't want to think about her and forcefully pushed the image of her from his mind. He felt almost grateful to Bella at that instant as she opened her legs to him, inviting him to plunder her. Happily he did so, but his release never came. For the first time in his long experience with women, he couldn't perform.

"Aw, Damon, don't feel bad now." Bella stroked his hair later, after it had become all too clear to both of them that none of Bella's whore-tricks would work, either. "Sometimes this happens. Take it from me."

"This has *never* happened to me before." Damon bounded from the bed and took a cheroot from a box on the bedside table.

"You're not blaming me, are you? I did my best, but you . . ."

"Aye, aye, Bella. I'm knowing you did. I don't blame you."

"You're not thinking of making me give you back some of what you paid me, 'cause I won't and you can't make me." Bella folded her plump arms across her bare breasts and glared at him.

Damon couldn't help but laugh. Beneath the painted face and whore's body, Bella was like any other astute business person. He'd always known what she was, but he liked to think he was special in some way to her. Maybe that was why he always took care to make her climax. It set him apart from the other men. Though he'd long suspected her mercenary heart, it still hurt to learn it firsthand.

He lighted the cheroot and took a deep puff. A dusky purple sky settled above the Remarkables in the distance and reminded him of Thunder Mine. He ached to go home. If not for Eden Flynn, he wouldn't have been thinking about her with other men when his mind should have been on Bella's pleasuring. He had also worried about the mine's future and what would happen to his own life if Eden pursued her claim. Despite his rugged existence, his life was well ordered and there wasn't any room in it for a woman, as a lover or business partner. Yet her very presence in Queenstown was proof that she did intend to claim her share. The wench was not only intent upon ruining his business, but his personal life, too. She was clearly the reason he couldn't perform with Bella.

The solution to his problem was quite simple, and one he'd intended from the very first. He couldn't have a woman messing up his life in any way. Tessa had left too many scars for him to allow Eden to inflict wounds. He knew what to do now, and like the gold-digging wench Eden was, he was certain she'd agree.

Damon started to dress. "Where are you off to?" Bella asked, yawning.

"I've business to attend to. Get your wrap on and be on your way."

"But you bought me for the night." Her eyes accused him.

"Aye, I did, and I won't be asking for a refund. Just get yourself out of my bed and my room. When I return, I'd like a lengthy sleep." He hoped his problem with Eden would be over then and that he'd finally be able to sleep in peace.

She watched him from beneath her long, silky lashes.

Every now and then she'd lift her eyes to him, drinking in his powerfully built body as he paced the floor of her hotel room. Eden found it difficult to swallow, to even breathe at times. Damon Alexander's masculinity was so blatant and self-assured that she could barely concentrate on his words. When she made the attempt to understand what he was saying to her, her gaze fastened on his mouth, lingering on his sensual lips. She wondered how it would feel to be kissed by those lips, but her own wanton imaginings caused her to shiver both in anticipation and dread of her own wicked response to this man whom she determined to dislike.

And from what he was telling her, it was more than obvious that he disliked her.

"That's what I propose, Mrs. Flynn," she heard him say. He stopped pacing and stood before the sofa, looking down at her.

She found it difficult to speak, so totally mesmerized by him that she was forced to shake herself from the trance his very presence induced within her. "I . . . I fail to see the value of your proposition, Mr. Alexander," she finally managed.

Damon blinked, apparently baffled. "I don't see how you can't."

Eden stood, feeling the subservient position put her at a disadvantage. She steeled herself for the outburst she was certain would follow upon her refusal. Alexander didn't want her as his partner and was determined to send her packing. She was just as determined to claim her share of Thunder Mine. He didn't know how resolute she was, or how stubborn. "Your offer to buy out my share is more than generous, but I must refuse."

Until this point, he'd been almost amiable. Now his

eyes darkened to a stormy black. "So it's more money you'll be wanting. I should have guessed."

"No, no, sir, you're not listening. I don't want your money. No amount you can offer will make me change my mind. I intend to be a working partner with you."

"Over my dead body, Yank."

Eden winced. Alexander truly didn't want her, and not only because she was a woman. There was something else. But what?

Alexander's height dwarfed her, but she couldn't allow him to realize she felt even a tad intimidated by him or that since meeting him, she was unsure of her own position as Shamus's heir. His dislike of her was evident, but she wouldn't let him take advantage of her by doing her out of her inheritance. Owning part of Thunder Mine meant the world to her. She needed something of her own again, some bulwark against an uncertain future. Damon Alexander wouldn't deprive her of the security she so desperately craved. Not now, not ever.

"If that's your attitude . . ." she began, "then I fear you shall live a short time. I've officially claimed my share in Thunder Mine by seeing my husband's lawyer. I've signed the necessary papers. Shamus willed his portion to me, because he wanted me to have it, though I admit I have a great deal to learn about mining. With your help I'll prove myself an astute pupil. Shamus promised me that you'd see to my welfare." She inclined her head. "Or was he wrong to think such a thing? Maybe he didn't know you as well as he thought he did."

Damon's face dissolved of color. His lips grew pale, and Eden wasn't certain if their pallor was from anger at her or dismay at disappointing his uncle. Either way, it didn't matter. Her words had the desired effect. Grabbing for the wide-brimmed hat which lay on a chair, Damon plunked it on his head. He turned away from her, leaving her with the impression of broad blue shoulders.

"Be ready to leave at sunrise tomorrow. If you're not waiting when I come to fetch you, I'm leaving for the mine without you." He'd spoken without looking at her, but now he twisted around to face her. "Understand?"

Eden nodded, and hoped he didn't notice the triumph glowing in her eyes. He did.

"Don't be looking so smug, Yank. New Zealand's not for fancy misses who lie abed all day, misses who dupe old gentlemen of their purses."

Her face grew crimson with rage. "I never did any such thing! Shamus was my husband. I loved—"

He broke off her heated words by pulling her toward him. "No need to lie to me," he whispered, his words fanning her face like wanton flames. "I'm not an old man who'll be taken in by a pretty face and figure. Your lies should strangle you, but I'm not swallowing them. I want to taste those sweet lips which lie so expertly."

Without Eden's even realizing it, Damon wrapped his arms around her. He brought her so close against his body that she felt his heart beating against her breast. Once again, as on that very morning, his face mesmerized her and stopped all conscious thought. She was aware of his musky scent, the way his eyes raked across her face. Drawn to his lips as if by a magnet, she soon found his mouth crushing hers.

Desire shot through her like an electrical current, sapping her of her resistance to fight. She moaned and leaned into him, simultaneously defeated and triumphant. Never had she felt this way, having no idea a man's kiss could make her flesh so tingly. Men had kissed

36

her in her short lifetime, and she'd pushed them away when their ardor became more than she could stand. Always images of her mother's rape would intrude and frighten her. Eden had begun to believe all men except for Shamus were animals. But the man kissing her now wasn't Shamus, an older man who'd been appreciative of a loving peck on the cheek, a pat on the hand. This man was young and virile, and Eden admitted she was attracted to him. For the first time she was willingly surrendering something of herself to another human being, and glorying in that surrender.

With her lips melting beneath Damon's, her body became a buttery pool. She heard his lusty moans and was very much aware of the way his hands slid across her breasts and down her backside to pull her into him, teasing her with his arousal. The blatant way he rubbed against her fueled Eden's latent desire, leaving no doubt in her mind that Damon Alexander was a very well-endowed male.

She made tiny mewling sounds of pleasure, unable to stop the magnificent sensations coursing through her. If he'd have laid her on the hard floor she wouldn't have stopped him, only rejoiced. Somehow she knew she'd come to New Zealand, not for the mine, but for Damon Alexander. Perhaps Shamus had known she was meant for Damon; maybe he'd wanted them to meet. The sudden insight that she wasn't being unfaithful to Shamus by responding to Damon's kisses made their newfound intimacy permissible.

Damon didn't see it that way.

He stopped kissing her and gazed down at her with frost-blue eyes. "What will you be charging me for sampling your wares, Mrs. Flynn?"

"What?"

"Your fee, woman. How much do I pay to bed you? I don't believe in getting something for nothing, at least nothing that's worthwhile. I've heard tell LaRue's whores are the most expensive, and from the looks of you, I'd guess you were worth a pretty price. So what's it to be? I'm willing to pay." Reaching into his shirt pocket, he pulled out a golden nugget.

Shock washed over Eden. At first she barely understood what Damon was saying to her, so caught up was she in the waves of passion engulfing her, the sensations and feelings she'd never known existed. Seeing the gold, Eden understood with startling clarity what he meant—and why he didn't like her. Somehow he'd learned she had worked at LaRue's and assumed she'd been one of her girls. A painful ache pierced her heart that he should think she'd sold herself for money.

Eden nearly laughed at her own musings. Well, why shouldn't he think she'd been a whore? She'd willingly worked at the brothel for three years and remembered how more than a few eyebrows had been lifted whenever she'd admitted her place of employment to people. However, she'd been quick to admit she was a bookkeeper. Not that it mattered. People still believed what they wished. She'd gotten used to the condemning stares, the chilly silences. She'd done nothing wrong, except support herself.

It seemed Damon Alexander was no different. He was ready to believe the worst about her, too. But somehow it hurt more to think he thought she'd been one of LaRue's girls. In fact, it hurt far too much. She silently cursed herself for being swayed by his good looks, his stirring kisses. She meant nothing to him. He wanted to be rid of her, and if she'd given in to her own feelings for him, he'd have adequate cause to truly believe she'd married Shamus for his money. For the first time she knew why Damon disliked her. He thought she was a gold digger, a woman who'd taken advantage of an ailing, older man. But couldn't he tell she wasn't like that?

Apparently not.

Eden hid her pain behind a tremulous smile. "So, you want to pay me."

Damon lifted an eyebrow. "Aye."

"I don't want your money."

"Am I to have you for free since you're in the family? I advise you to reconsider, because this is all you're going to get of Thunder Mine from me."

Eden broke away from him, wondering what had ever possessed her to want to be in the despicable man's arms in the first place. She made her way to her reticule resting on a nearby table. With trembling hands, she scooped up the purse and somehow managed to smile coolly. "You're very generous, Mr. Alexander."

"I always pay well for quality merchandise, and you're worth it. Shamus did have a discerning eye." He was smirking at her.

"Thank you for the lovely compliment, sir, but I'm not certain about the price." Making a mock pout, Eden went to where Damon stood like a marble statue. Placing a warm hand on his shirtfront, her fingertips found a button. Opening it, she placed a kiss upon the small expanse of fur-planed chest.

"How much is it to be then? Your teasing is driving me wild." The huskiness of his voice and the arm around her waist told Eden that Damon Alexander would have willingly offered a fortune in gold at that moment.

39

But Eden only laughed up at him and pushed away.

"You misunderstand," she said. "You see, I've been without male companionship for so long that I was ready for a bit of kissing. And willing I am to pay for it, too. So here, Mr. Alexander. You've earned your fee." She dug into the reticule and offered him a handful of gold coins. Damon backed away as if she held out a venomous snake to him. "What's wrong? My money isn't good enough for you? I admit it isn't worth as much as your golden nugget. I remind you that you aren't a professional, Mr. Alexander, but for a beginner, you aren't too bad. Perhaps in time, you'll improve."

"God, woman! You're worse than I thought to offer a man money for, for . . ."

"For a roll in the hay or the sack, or any other number of euphemisms which describe pure lust. Yes, I'm offering you money. What's wrong? Don't you like how it feels? Do you feel dirty, cheap?" Eden shrugged and put the money into the reticule. "You can't say I didn't offer to pay your worth."

Damon shook his head, seemingly unable to fathom the woman before him. "Shamus must have been insane to marry you."

His comment hurt, but Eden let it slide past her. She didn't see a reason to deny what he said, realizing it would do little good. Let him think what he wanted about her. She'd turned the tables on him, and now he must see she wasn't so easy to run off by attempting to seduce her or insult her. All she wanted was her portion of Thunder Mine. To hell with Damon Alexander and what he thought! "Shamus was insane with love for me," she told him. "Absolutely out of his mind with love."

"More like he was demented, Mrs. Flynn," he said

curtly, impaling her with those ice-blue eyes. He pulled open the door. "Be ready at five." It slammed noisily behind him.

Eden clutched her reticule until her knuckles whitened. Clearly he hated her, but she was safe from him as long as he thought she was a skilled whore. The arrogant man had taken great delight in stirring up her passions, and she'd have given in to him. She had stupidly thought that perhaps, just perhaps, Damon Alexander was the man of her dreams. Well, she'd been wrong. Alexander was more of a nightmare, and she must never let him discover her vulnerability. What a silly little virgin she was to think she could find love with such a heartless man.

Still, she wondered how he'd react if he knew the truth about her relationship with Shamus. What would he do if he knew she was a virgin?

"That's one thing you'll never know, Damon Alexander," she mused aloud. "You think you know about me, but you know nothing, and that's how I intend to keep it."

Throwing the reticule on the table, Eden started to pack for the journey to Thunder Mine.

Chapter 4

Eden was already waiting when Damon's knock sounded on her door the next morning. By the light of the gas lamp in the hallway, Eden noticed shadows beneath his eyes, a clear indication that he'd slept no better than she. He hadn't shaved, either; a thick growth of rough beard covered his face.

"I'm ready," she told him moments after he'd entered the room. "I do believe in being punctual." She gave him a curt smile, unwilling to mention what had happened the night before. She decided it was best forgotten.

Damon's gaze raked her petite form. From her wide-brimmed hat and down across her plaid shirt, snugly tucked into her pants, his eyes looked her over. Mostly they centered on her blue denim legs where the material disappeared into her sturdy brown boots. "You can't wear those pants," he told her matter-of-factly.

Eden glanced down at her pants and then at Damon. "Why not, may I ask? You're wearing them. In fact, most of the men I've seen so far in New Zealand wear them. Miners in America do, too."

"Aye, that's the point. *Men* wear them, not ladies. The

men here don't approve of females wearing pants. Don't you have a skirt or something else to wear?"

Eden clenched her fists, resisting the urge to bash in Damon's handsome face. "I'll wear what I choose. Pants are more comfortable than skirts."

"But you'll be the center of attention. The trail to the mine is filled with men who aren't gentlemen; the miners who work for me won't understand a female in pants. I won't take responsibility for your safety, *Mrs. Flynn.*"

She hated when he called her Mrs. Flynn. It somehow sounded disrespectful, almost like a dirty name on his lips. She also hated his high-handed attitude toward her. One night he practically seduces her because he thinks she's a whore, and the next day he's worried about keeping her safe from other men! What a strange man was Damon Alexander. But he wasn't going to dictate to her.

"I remind you, Mr. Alexander," she said, mimicking his tone of voice, "that the miners work for me, too. As far as the men along the trail, well . . . they'll just have to control their unbridled lust. And if I may remind you, sir, you don't think I'm much of a lady so I see no need for you to worry about my safety. Now, shall we go?"

A shrug of a powerful shoulder was the only indication that Damon had acquiesced. "I'm warning you," he proclaimed, "this country is wild and untamed. I'm not playing nursemaid to you. You'll have to learn to see to your own needs."

"I'm capable of taking care of myself."

"We'll see."

Seconds later, Nick appeared at the doorway, politely doffing his hat to Eden, and the two men carried her trunk to a waiting wagon outside the hotel.

The sun hadn't entirely risen, but the mountains in the distance held a glimmer of gold on their peaks. Eden found the morning chilly and bundled into a heavy coat which the man at the mercantile had insisted she purchase. She was glad now she had, delighting in the coat's warmth. She also delighted in Nick Patterson's warmth, his ready humor. He told jokes as the wagon trundled along the road which led out of Queenstown. Even though some of his jokes weren't that amusing, Eden laughed heartily because it seemed Nick's attention to her irritated Damon.

During the ride, they passed a number of men on the road. Blankets were tied to their backs and many of them carried shovels and tin pans, their intentions obvious. "Shamus told me the mines had played out," Eden noted. "Why are there so many people still coming this way?"

"They hope to strike it lucky," Nick spoke up. "Most of us are still hoping. Can't blame a bloke for wanting to make a find."

Damon snorted and urged the horse along. "If Sutherland has his way, no one will be free to pan at all. The bastard doesn't give a damn about any of us."

"Who is Sutherland?" Eden queried, wondering what person, other than herself, could elicit such a black scowl from Damon.

"Jock Sutherland," Nick filled her in, "owns a large and prosperous sheep station about five miles from Thunder Mine. He controls the water rights."

"So?" Eden asked, not understanding the problem and wincing when Damon turned to look at her like she was an ignorant child.

"I thought you said Shamus explained mining to you." Damon remarked.

44

"He did . . . some," she returned.

"If so, Mrs. Flynn, then he didn't explain about the water rights or you weren't listening, probably because you were too involved in your bankbook balance." Eden's mouth fell open in protest, but Damon continued smoothly. "Sutherland controls the water rights to a portion of the Shotover River, the same river that runs past Thunder Mine. The water is needed for placer mining and to operate the cradle, which helps separate the gravel from the gold. If Sutherland decides to dam up the river, the mine is done for and my people are out of work."

"I can't believe anyone would be so callous as to do such a thing," was Eden's innocent response. "Most certainly, it wouldn't gain this Sutherland person anything."

"You don't know Jock Sutherland," Damon finished dryly.

They continued onward for a few more miles and turned off the main road. Damon slowed the wagon to a stop. He jumped down and turned to Eden. "This is as far as we go. The rest of the trip is on foot."

"You're joking."

"No."

Casting an eye on her trunk, Eden looked helplessly about. "What am I to do with my things? What I'm wearing is all I've got. All my other clothes are packed."

Nick smiled at her. "Don't worry none. I'm going to take care of your things for you. A friend of mine is bringing a pack mule from Arrowtown and will meet me here at noon. I'll deliver your things to you in good condition, Mrs. Flynn."

"I'm certain you will," Eden said, but she felt uneasy

about not having her trunk. And realizing she'd be traveling alone with Damon for the rest of the journey didn't make her feel any better.

She made a move in Damon's direction, certain he'd help her off of the wagon. However, he stood there with a sacklike bag looped over his belt and a rough blanket slung over one shoulder and calmly surveyed her. When it became apparent that he was letting her fend for herself, she started to get off the buckboard, but Nick jumped forward and helped her down. "I'm pleased that some men in this backward country are gentlemen," she said loud enough for Damon to hear.

"If we're so backward, then you shouldn't have come," she heard him mumble. Striding up the steep pack trail, he didn't bother to see if she followed him.

Nick shot her an apologetic smile. Eden pulled her coat tightly about her and sunk her hands into the deep pockets. She forged ahead after Damon. More than once she almost called to him to wait for her, but she held her silence, knowing he'd most probably like for her to whine and complain. Still, she seethed with indignation because it wouldn't have cost him anything to be courteous and wait for her, or to ask her if she'd care to rest a while.

By the time they reached the top of the hill, Eden was winded. The coat was too warm and she pulled it off, tying the sleeves about her shoulders. Damon abruptly halted and Eden nearly bumped into him. He pointed to the twisting stone road below, interspersed with dry grass, and the abysslike ravine beside it. The mountainous countryside stretched endlessly before them. "That's the way to Skipper's Canyon. The road is going to get steeper as we go along. Are you up to it?"

"Yes," Eden lied. The ravine was a tangle of tussock

46

grass and spindly-looking plants, and they were up so high she felt almost dizzy. Perhaps descending it wouldn't be too bad—at least that's what she hoped. That Shamus hadn't mentioned anything about the treacherous trek to the mine caused her to feel betrayed by him. What else might he not have mentioned?

Damon took a canteen from the bag around his belt loop and handed it to her. Her throat felt as parched as the landscape, and she drank greedily from it. "You should have bought one for yourself," Damon said when she handed it back with her thanks.

Eden flushed and didn't reply. She couldn't admit that she had bought a canteen from the mercantile but forgot she'd packed it in her trunk. Wouldn't he just love to know that! She wasn't willingly going to give him more ammunition to use against escorting her to the mine. She watched while he took a rope from the same sack and tied it around his waist. When he came toward her with the other end of it, she took a step backward.

"Are you going to tie that around me, too?"

"Aye. The way is going to be dangerous and the road thins out in spots. With you tied to me, I can help you along. Just follow in my footsteps and you'll be fine."

"Thank you," she said, wondering if she'd been wrong about him. Perhaps he was a considerate person after all. But he dispelled any warm feelings a few seconds later.

"If you think you might fall over the cliff—"

"Yes?" The thought of such a mishap petrified her.

"Kindly untie yourself and don't take me with you."

Was he joking? Eden couldn't tell because Damon looked so solemn when he took the rope and began looping it about her waist. She could feel his agile fingers through her shirt, evoking the stirring memory of his kiss and the intimate way he'd touched her the night before. Her breath began to come in tiny pants she couldn't control.

"Goodness but the air is thin up here!" she exclaimed, not wanting him to think he was the reason for her gasps.

"I hadn't noticed," he said, and gave a hearty tug on the line, forcing her to brush against him. "But if your breathing is an indication of how you react when you're too close to a man, I'd better hope you don't attack me."

"You arrogant lout! My breathing has nothing to do with you. How dare you say something so uncouth to me!"

To Eden's surprise, Damon reached out and tucked a stray wisp of her hair beneath her hat. To her shock, he actually flashed her a heart-stopping smile. "Your eyes shimmer like greenstone when you're mad, Yank."

He was the most handsome man she'd ever seen, and the fact that he was actually paying her a compliment caused her legs to feel rubbery. But she wouldn't allow him to see he'd gotten to her again. She didn't need him to know she quivered each time he as much as glanced in her direction. Instead of smiling back as she longed to do, she stiffened her backbone and forced herself to sound like a haughty matron. "I've told you not to call me by that vile name. I won't answer to it, Mr. Alexander."

"Suit yourself, *Mrs. Flynn.*" He showed her his back, seemingly nonplussed by her icy demeanor.

For the rest of the day, they trekked through mountainous terrain. Damon had been right about staying close behind him. Eden was too frightened of the yawning canyon below not to follow in his every footstep.

48

Sometimes she almost grabbed his shirt for support when the road grew steeper and the climb more arduous. But she didn't. She was more afraid of touching him and being unable to let go than of losing her balance. His voice was a comfort to her. Each time they were forced to climb higher or descend the twisting turn of the road at an odd angle, Damon calmly warned her beforehand, then assured her she'd be fine. Which she was, but she still couldn't wait for this interminable trip to end.

Shortly after noon, he'd handed her a biscuit from his sack and they'd rested for a few minutes before continuing. By the time dusk colored the sky all purple and gold, Eden didn't believe she could walk another step. "How much farther?" she asked as she wiped the grime from her perspiring face, leaving a trail of fingermarks down her cheek.

"About another two miles, but with night coming, we should make camp."

The thought of sleeping outside hadn't entered her mind, and she wanted to balk. But her every bone ached and weariness was overtaking her. She barely gave him a nod of understanding. Once more, as she had done all day, she followed after Damon like a docile and trusting puppy.

Damon led her away from the road into a twisting and turning landscape of trees and bushes. Finally, they entered a clearing and stopped before Damon untied her. "I'll start a fire," he told her, placing the sack and blanket on the ground. "If you must tend to any personal needs, there are lots of bushes. I promise I won't peep."

Catching his meaning, Eden couldn't help but color a furious shade of red. She made her way into a copse of trees, hoping she wouldn't fall over the thick, gnarled roots or come across any dangerous wildlife.

When she rejoined Damon, she discovered he'd already started the fire and was warming a small pot filled with water over the open flame. "Thought you might like some tea" was his response to her unanswered question. She watched through tired eyes as he filled two tin cups with the water, then took a small pouch containing tea from the sack. The tea tasted warm but lightly bitter. Eden drank it nonetheless. The biscuit Damon handed her was left uneaten in her palm as her eyes started to close from exhaustion.

She was vaguely aware of Damon placing the blanket beside her. His voice sounded miles away when he gently told her to lie down and rest. And that was the last thing she remembered until morning.

Soft streams of sunlight filtered through the nearby trees. Eden was slowly brought to wakefulness by the early-morning cawing and chirping sounds in the forest. A dewy, fresh scent filled the air. Eden breathed deeply, not quite awake and believing herself to be at home again, before the war, in her own bed. As she hugged her pillow to her breasts, she felt safe and protected. Soon she'd hear her mother's lyrical laugh floating down the hallway and she'd join her parents in the dining room for breakfast. And, oh, she was suddenly so hungry!

"We've got to get a move on." A deep voice intruded into her twilight state. "The mine is still a good distance away."

Eden started and opened her eyes. At first she wasn't certain where she was. Then reality dawned and as she glanced around, she saw the nearby trees and realized she

50

was lying on the ground, half wrapped in a blanket, the rough material of which grazed her cheek. She turned her head back to find herself looking directly at Damon's handsome, smiling face. Not only was he grinning down at her, but she quickly discovered he was holding her in his arms. Her bottom was pressed intimately and shamelessly against him. Worst of all, she could feel his very evident arousal.

"What are you doing?" she mouthed, not hiding her shock.

"Waking up."

"How dare you try taking advantage of me in my sleep. You're a despicable man, a horrible—"

"Hold on now!" Damon thundered near her ear. "You're under my blanket, remember. I don't recall seeing you bring anything to sleep on, or eat and drink. I've fed and watered you the last day—"

"You talk as if I'm a plant!"

"That's because you are one. You're like a hothouse flower who needs care. You're totally unsuited to this way of life and the sooner you realize it, the better off you'll be."

Eden's eyes flared. "Oh, you'd like it if I gave up and turned back, wouldn't you? Well, I won't. And if you think to take advantage of me, you're sadly mistaken. I'll fight and scratch and bite. What happened to my mother won't happen to me!"

Damon assessed her with a look which contained both bafflement and anger. "If I wanted to make love to you, Mrs. Flynn, I'd much prefer you awake and alert. But you're sleeping under my blanket, and I didn't intend to shiver all night long just to play the gentleman with you."

"Which we both know you're not," she shrewishly taunted.

"Aye, I'm not a gentleman who wears fancy clothes and doles out good cash to impress a witch who thinks she's better than him." His eyes narrowed to slits and his voice lowered to an intimate whisper. "And if you're thinking you're a lady, think again. You were clinging to my arm around you, holding it against your breasts. And your delectable round bottom seemed to enjoy pushing against me. Nay, I'm not a gentleman, but a man. And you're the type of woman who could make a saint lose control with that kind of teasing."

Eden colored all the way to her hairline. "I was asleep. I didn't realize what I was doing."

"Ah, I see. So you're awake now."

"Yes, of course."

"Good." His mouth descended upon hers, stifling her surprised gasp. The kiss was firm and domineering, filled with a warmth that sent heat to her chilled bones. He'd caught her off guard, but Damon always seemed to do that to her. She wanted to push him away, but there was something about the way Damon kissed her which drove everything out of her mind. She wanted to lie unmoved in his arms, but she found she couldn't. Her arms wrapped tightly around the forearms which held her and, without meaning to, she pushed her buttocks into his aroused manhood.

It was Damon who broke away. He let her go and rose to his feet in one motion. His eyes never left her face. "Get yourself together. We've still got a long way to go."

"Damn you," Eden cursed under her breath when he began throwing dirt on the campfire. But she wasn't certain if she cursed him or herself.

Chapter 5

Eden's breath caught in her throat when she followed Damon to the edge of the cliff. Despite her resolve not to touch him, or even speak to him after he'd kissed her that morning, she couldn't stop herself from grabbing his shirt-sleeve for support. Her head swam a bit as her gaze focused on the tumbling waters of Shotover Point, some thousand feet below them.

Damon peered at her pale face and clasped her trembling hands. "You're not afraid of heights, are you?"

"No, I'm not," she told him, forcing herself to look at him and smile bravely. She'd never thought heights frightened her before now, but then again, she'd never climbed treacherous cliffs, either. It wouldn't do for Damon to see she was scared. They had passed other miners on the way up, and some of them had their wives with them. Damon had seemed to know all of them and had exchanged courtesies with them. Eden didn't recall seeing fear in the women's faces, and she remembered thinking they looked to be a hearty bunch with their stout bodies and plain gowns. A few eyebrows had lifted at her unusual attire, but no one had said anything disparaging. She truly envied the miners' wives for their fortitude in staying with their husbands. If it wasn't for the fact that Damon expected her to quit, she'd willingly turn tail and run back to Queenstown. But that meant a long and dangerous trek, and this journey was clearly proving her to be a coward. She contented herself with the hope that the worst part of it must be over by now. She'd simply forge ahead and make a new life for herself. After all, that was why she'd come to New Zealand in the first place.

Bestowing a brave smile she didn't feel upon Damon, she walked down the cliff beside him to a spot where a number of people were gathered. They seemed to be waiting for something. A few of the men kept an eye on a wire cable which Eden judged to be approximately three hundred feet above the rushing waters.

A man with shaggy, gray-streaked hair affectionately pummeled Damon on the back. Damon grinned and introduced the man to Eden as Tom Creig, one of Thunder Mine's employees. "So, you're Shamus's wife," Tom said to Eden, shaking her hand. "We all miss the old coot."

"I miss him, too," Eden responded, her eyes misting. It was so obvious to her that Tom and Shamus must have been good friends. Tom then called to a woman who stood nearby. Miranda Creig was a thin woman whose brown hair was partly gray and tied in a loose bun atop her head. She smiled at Eden upon learning she was Shamus's widow.

"You're a mite younger than we expected," Miranda said not unkindly. "But then Shamus was always known to have a way with the ladies, young and old. Just like Damon here. Huh, Damon." Miranda nudged Damon good-naturedly.

Eden noticed Damon was blushing like a schoolboy. An odd reaction, Eden thought, since she'd already seen him with a prostitute and knew he was suspicious of *any* woman, gently bred or not. Apparently he loved only his mine and money. Which was fine with Eden. She didn't need Damon Alexander ruining her plans to begin a new life.

"Here comes the Goose!" Tom's shouts broke into Eden's thoughts. He took off his hat and began waving in the direction of the wires above the river. It was then Eden saw something which made her heart nearly stop beating. Attached to the cable was a chairlike apparatus. It seemed to fly in midair like a large brown bird, and sitting inside it was a man who gleefully waved to the waiting group.

"My God, what is that thing!" Eden's words were nearly drowned out by the happy shouts of those nearby when the chair landed some distance from where she stood and the man disembarked, seemingly none the worse for wear. One of those who'd been waiting, a man whose largeness had given rise to joking earlier, took the vacated seat. The chair rocked precariously when it was lifted up and sent on its way across the river.

"Don't break the cable, Tiny!" someone called to the departing man. Tiny's happy laugh echoed back to them.

Damon was smiling when he turned his attention to Eden. "That's the Gliding Goose," he said, almost proudly. "Shamus and some of the miners rigged it up years ago. It's the only way across to the other side."

Eden's mouth went dry with fear. "You mean we have

to take that across the river? I have to get on that *thing* by myself?"

"Aye. It's good you're not afraid of heights," he told her. She saw a challenge in his expression, but at that moment she didn't feel up to meeting it, so she said nothing. Instead she watched as the Gliding Goose returned a number of times to ferry those from the other side of the river to where they stood, then picked up the people who waited with them. When it was Miranda's turn, she nimbly took her seat. The miner's wife didn't seem concerned at all, apparently finding nothing unusual about being in a chair that hung hundreds of feet in the air above a rushing river.

But Eden's palms perspired. She knew her time was coming soon, and she couldn't believe she actually was going to sit in that horrible, unsafe-looking thing and almost *fly* to the other side. What had she gotten herself into? Had she come this far only to fall to her death?

Damon came and stood alongside her. Tom had just departed and they were next in line. "There's nothing to worry about, Eden. The chair has never fallen, and the cables have never broken. Shamus and the other miners made certain of its safety when they built the Goose. If Shamus had thought there was any danger to you, he wouldn't have told you to come."

"I'm not afraid."

"You're lying."

"Yes, I'm afraid!" Her voice was a hiss. "I've never been so afraid in my whole life. At this moment, I wish I'd never left San Francisco and come to this primitive place. Is that what you want to hear, Mr. Alexander? Are you happy now?"

"If you want, I can take you back to Queenstown."

"Not on your life," Eden ground out from between her teeth. "The only place I'm going is across the river—on the Goose." Where that bit of false courage came from, Eden didn't know. Damon grinned down at her, and she could swear she saw some sort of pride shining in his eyes.

All too soon the Goose was back. Eden's courage deserted her, but she walked to the monstrous thing on rubbery legs while Damon spoke to the man in charge of the cable. The man nodded to her and doffed his cap.

"What's happening?" Eden asked.

"We're going together" was Damon's reply. Before she could ask how that was to happen, Damon sat on the chair and motioned to her to take her place on his lap. She shook her head; the shock of being so close to him frightened and excited her at the same time. Maybe she should go alone, even though she was afraid. That was preferable to letting Damon see her absolute terror, the stark fear which she knew would show on her face. But to have him hold her while they rode across the waters was so tempting.

Her decision was made when the people behind her urged her on. "Go ahead, miss," someone cried out. "We ain't got all day here."

Within seconds, she found herself on Damon's lap. He placed her legs at an angle and settled her against him. Then a large strap on the chair's back was buckled around them. When Damon wrapped his arms around her waist, the chair lurched forward and they were off. Eden closed her eyes.

The late-morning breeze blew vigorously, and Damon took her hat off to clutch it in his hand. Wisps of her hair, coming loose from her long braid, framed her cheeks.

Eden was aware of his breath upon her ear, the way her body fit so perfectly and snugly against him. She felt uneasy with her legs flying free in space and she couldn't gather the courage to open her eyes.

"It's really pretty up here," Damon told her. "You should look."

"I . . . can't."

"Aye, you can do anything you set your mind to. I know you can. I'm holding you, you won't fall. Go on. Take a peek, but don't look down."

What was there about him that always broke through her resistance? No matter how much Eden longed to balk, to refuse, Damon always managed to make her do those things she'd thought were impossible, the very things she feared doing. She almost refused again, but Damon whispered into her ear, "Open your eyes, Eden."

She did so and sucked in her breath at the majestic and untamed beauty. The mountains, gloriously green and purple, surrounded them on all sides. An azure sky, bluer than any blue she'd ever seen, was so close Eden thought she could touch it. The Goose flew swiftly through space, and Eden knew how a bird must feel to soar high and free above the earth. "Oh, Damon, how thrilling this is!" Glancing quickly at him, she saw a hint of a smile on his lips.

Eden didn't want to close her eyes again for the rest of the short trip, no longer afraid of the Goose but of missing something wildly beautiful. She found she enjoyed the feel of the wind as it rushed through her hair and stung her cheeks. The landscape enchanted her with its soft palette of misty colors. And now, for the first time, she could imagine why Shamus had loved this land. It seemed there was no finer way to see New Zealand than from above.

All too soon the Goose reached the other side. People gathered and waited while she and Damon disembarked. Eden felt a twinge of disappointment when the Goose took off with its next occupant.

"So you enjoyed yourself," Damon noted, keeping a protective arm about her as she made her way down the mountainside of Skipper's Canyon.

"Oh, yes!" Shining flecks of gold danced within the depths of her eyes when she looked at him. "It was wonderful. I can't wait to ride the Goose again." Her manner grew quiet then, and she masked her enthusiasm with a reserved expression. "Thank you, Mr. Alexander, for taking me across," she said quietly.

Damon stopped walking. He still held her hat, but instead of handing it to her, he placed it on her head. Brushing aside the stray wisps of red-gold hair, his sapphire orbs shone like cobalt. "You called me Damon up there. There's no need to be so formal. Eden."

Was this some sort of a truce? If so, Eden was wary. Damon hadn't wanted her as his partner. He still thought she had worked as one of LaRue's girls. Did he realize now she wasn't going to leave and must make the best of the situation? If that was the case, and he intended to accept her as his business partner, then Eden would relent. She disliked being so frosty, especially to a man as handsome as Damon. Besides, it wasn't in her nature to hold a grudge for long.

"You're right. After all, we're family," she admitted.

Damon flashed her a rich, warm smile. "How about some breakfast at the best restaurant in Skipper's Canyon?"

"You mean something other than stale biscuits and

59

weak coffee? Maybe some eggs and bacon, with grits on the side?"

"Aye."

"Then lead on . . . Damon."

Which is what he did.

The restaurant Damon chose was immaculate. Blue-checkered cloths covered the tables and matched the dresses worn by the waitresses. Joanie, the pretty young woman with fluffy blond hair who waited on their table, seemed to know Damon well. Eden soon learned she was Tom's and Miranda's niece. As she poured tea for Eden, Joanie's face dimpled into a becoming smile.

"I know you'll get used to New Zealand, ma'am," Joanie assured Eden. "I was raised in England, but my uncle and aunt took me in when my parents died. For a long time I didn't think I'd like it here—you know, with the Maori wars and the primitive living conditions. But times have changed. I can't imagine being anywhere else."

"Don't you want to travel, to see the world?" Eden asked after swallowing a mouthful of the best scrambled eggs she'd ever eaten. At least she thought they were the best; she was so hungry anything would have tasted wonderful.

Joanie clutched the teapot tightly. "Oh, no. My uncle hasn't the means to send me off anywhere. Sometimes I save enough from my wages to take a trip to Christ Church and visit my cousin, but really, I'm quite contented to stay here."

Joanie smiled at Eden as if she was a small child who didn't understand what she was being told. Eden, in turn, didn't understand why a young woman as pretty as Joanie had no desire to leave a mining town, why she seemed happy to work in a restaurant. All through the conversation Damon said nothing, merely wolfed down his breakfast. Joanie finally cleared her throat to gain his attention. "Have you seen anything of Mr. Patterson?" she asked. "He hasn't been in here for quite a while."

"I'm certain you'll see Nick soon," Damon assured her with a broad smile. "He's scheduled to bring Mrs. Flynn's things to the mine, so I'd bet he'll come in here for a plate of your best lamb stew before long."

Joanie giggled. "Yes, he does like the stew." Then she blushed and shyly smiled before departing.

Eden glanced from Joanie's retreating back to Damon. "What was that about?"

Damon finished his tea and threw her an assessing look. "What do you think?"

"I'd think Joanie was smitten with Nick Patterson, but he's old enough to be her father."

"She's more than smitten. Tom told me she's in love with Nick."

Somehow Eden couldn't imagine why someone like Joanie would consider herself in love with a man like Nick. Granted, Nick was gentlemanly and kind, but he was so much older than Joanie. Most certainly she could have her pick of any young man. But then she thought about herself and Shamus and realized she shouldn't judge others.

"Does Nick know how she feels?"

Damon nodded, a bit too briskly. "Joanie grew up calling Nick, Uncle Nick. He and Tom were very close. But one day things changed. Joanie was no longer the little girl who climbed upon his knee. She'd grown up and developed a crush on him. Nick couldn't handle her calf eyes, and Tom figured it was time Joanie left Thunder Mine to make her own way before . . . something happened. Miranda's cousin owns this restaurant, so Joanie was given a job and a room upstairs." Damon pinned her with a penetrating glance. "It was all for the best, I'd say. Nick's nearly forty-five, too old for a young woman like Joanie."

Nick was younger than Eden had originally thought, in fact he was younger than Shamus had been when they met. "Has anyone bothered to ask Nick how he feels about Joanie?"

Damon looked at her as if she were daft. "Why should they?"

"Perhaps he feels the same way."

A muscle twitched in his cheek, and his eyes grew frosty like blue ice. "Nick knows better than to fall for a young woman, unlike some people I could name."

"Shamus, for one."

"You said it, I didn't."

"But that's who you meant. I don't sit in judgment of Joanie—or Nick, if he cares for her."

"Hah! You *would* feel that way, but there's one big difference between Shamus and Nick, which I think you've overlooked. Nick is far from being the rich man Shamus was. He's safe from money-hungry females."

"Like me."

"I never mentioned you."

But he had, indirectly at least. Eden felt her temper flare but forced herself to remain calm. What was the use of raising her voice, of refuting Damon's accusation? Once more, he had allowed her to think he might accept her, only to throw in her face what he considered to be her blemished past. He thought she was a gold digger and would never know she'd married Shamus to see him through his illness. He'd never know because she'd never tell him.

She gave him a tight smile, hating his supercilious attitude. "I think there's something you've overlooked with your self-righteousness, considering what I saw at the Greenstone Saloon."

He cocked an eyebrow. "And that is?"

"Let he who is without sin cast the first stone." Eden threw down her napkin and stood up. "When you're ready to leave, you can find me outside. I think I need a breath of fresh air." And with that, she fled the restaurant.

Damon cursed himself for almost forgetting who and what Eden was. But the truth came back with a vengeance when he left the restaurant . . .

Eden stood on the boardwalk with a man Damon instantly recognized as an acquaintance of his uncle. Bert Carruthers, an Australian, had panned for gold alongside Shamus years ago. He'd made a modest strike very close to Thunder Mine. Ever since then he'd pretended to be a gentleman by wearing flashy clothes, complete with a diamond stickpin in his lapel, and reeking of cheap cologne and whiskey. He thought he had a way with women, but in truth they laughed behind his back while eagerly grabbing for his money. It seemed Eden was to be his newest conquest, but from the look of things, she wasn't interested.

"Aw, come on, duck," Bert cajoled Eden, standing much closer to her than Damon thought necessary. He chucked her chin, causing Eden to back away. Bert laughed. "I know you ain't as cold as all that. I mean you look like a dirty mess now, but," his eyes skimmed over her unladylike attire, "in a fancy red dress, I know you're a looker. What you say? I got a lot of money and can make things real good for you. Come on, my girl, give old Bert a try."

"Get away from me!" Eden hissed and turned, only to bump into Damon as he departed the restaurant.

"What's going on here, Bert?" Damon's greeting was affable enough, but his eyes held a warning. In a proprietary gesture, he took Eden's arm and led her to one of the two horses he'd hired early that morning.

Bert scurried behind them. "I'm tending business here, Damon. You ain't got no right to interfere."

"I've every right." Damon helped Eden onto the chestnut mare and stood alongside the animal like a protective mountain. "This woman is my uncle's widow. You're dishonoring his memory with what you're doing."

Bert chuckled and thumped Damon on the shoulder. "Hell, man, you mustn't know what she is." Bert shot Eden a telling look, but Eden didn't deign to glance in his direction. "She don't look like much now, but Damon, I've seen her in her gaudy finery at LaRue's. One night I was there, and she was sitting with Shamus like she was a perfect lady. But, well . . . she ain't one. Ladies don't work at a place like that. Shamus didn't seem to mind, and hell, I wouldn't have minded, either, if she'd paid me some attention. After all, we all have to have our fun."

Eden stiffened her back, unable to look anywhere but straight ahead. "Go on, ask her if she don't remember me," she heard him say. "I know she does, 'cause I went

64

to the table and introduced myself like the proper gentleman I am. Even offered for her, but Shamus wouldn't hear of it, told me he'd kill me first before I insulted her again. She knows me, don't you, honey?"

Damon glanced at Eden. The muscle in his cheek began twitching. "Is that true?" he asked her.

She found the courage to speak. "Yes, I remember you, Mr. . . ."

"Carruthers, duck," Bert told her and doffed his hat, seemingly pleased with himself. "Must be kind of hard to remember every gent's name." He grinned, displaying his uneven teeth.

Eden flushed. The insufferable man thought she'd been one of LaRue's girls. There was no point in denying it; he wouldn't believe she'd been a bookkeeper. Neither would Damon. But she'd scratch and claw any man who thought he had a right to her because he had money to pay her. Still, it hurt a great deal for Damon to come face-to-face with a man who believed she had sold herself.

Damon climbed onto his horse. His hands captured the reins. From his lofty perch, he cast a derisive grin in Bert's direction. "Mrs. Flynn is no longer in LaRue's employ, Bert. Don't come sniffing around the mine for her, or I'll have to carry out my uncle's threat. You got that, *duck?*"

Eden couldn't help but notice Bert's sudden pallor and the way he immediately lost his cockiness, seeming to be no longer interested in her. "Yeah, Damon. You won't get no trouble from me." He doffed his hat to Eden. "Good day, Mrs. Flynn." Then like a scared jackrabbit, he took off.

Damon urged his horse along the dusty street, filled with mules, loaded down with mining gear, and miners leading the mules. Eden cantered alongside him, and it was only when they were outside the town that he finally spoke. "I hope there'll be no further need for me to have to defend your honor, Mrs. Flynn. I don't relish having to shoot a man simply because he wants to pay for your favors."

Eden bit down on her lower lip. So, they were no longer on a first-name basis. She should have expected Damon's scorn, but somehow, she hadn't. She'd thought he'd put his judgment of her past behind him and she was touched by his defense of her honor. But then, he was only doing what was expected of him, what Shamus would have wanted as her due. Her heart lurched in her chest at the unfairness of it all. Her honor and maidenhood were both intact and Damon continued to believe the worst.

Eden's voice held a trace of bitterness. "Please, Mr. Alexander, don't feel obligated to defend me. I can handle pesky men. I've handled *you* quite well so far."

"Aye," he admitted, chuckling mirthlessly. "But that's because I haven't had to try too hard to break down your resistance. Each time I kiss you, you melt like a piece of taffy, so where's the challenge in it?" His eyes held a bewitching and vexing blue light when he rode on, seemingly forgetting her presence. Eden blushed to the roots of her hair at his words because they were true—undeniably true.

The ride to Thunder Mine was accomplished more quickly than Eden anticipated. For a number of miles they'd followed a trail that led alongside the Shotover River. Dark forests lay beyond, and every so often Eden would hear strange, warbling sounds from within the hidden depths.

Once Damon stopped to speak to men who waded knee-high in the sparkling waters, their tin pans clutched tightly in their hands. She watched as one man shoveled out a small portion of the river's bottom and placed it in his pan. With a swirling motion, he allowed the water and mud to fall over the pan's edge before dipping into the river again.

"He's panning," Damon explained, causing Eden to jump as he broke the lengthy silence between them. "He's getting rid of all the water and rocks. If there's gold, the pieces will sink to the bottom of the pan when the other debris is cleared away."

The man's measured movements fascinated her. Would he find what he sought? Sure enough, when he finished, the pan's bottom was lined with shiny yellow particles.

"Oh, how easy it is! No wonder people become obsessed with gold fever."

Damon made a snorting sound. "Might look simple, but panning is hard, backbreaking work. Sometimes a man finds a little, sometimes he doesn't. More than likely, he doesn't. It took Shamus years to make his first strike, and he was one of the lucky ones. Not everyone becomes rich."

Eden let out a long sigh. Damon always mananged to quell her enthusiasm with realities. "Maybe it isn't the gold which keeps them coming back," she found herself saying. "Perhaps it's the challenge of finding it. Sometimes the journey can be more interesting than the destination, Mr. Alexander."

She didn't miss his penetrating assessment of her and

was somehow warmed to the toes by his blue-eyed probe.

Half an hour later they cantered past a cluster of small houses at the foot of a large mountain. A dark opening in the mountain yawned before her and a sign which proclaimed Thunder Mine hung above it.

Damon rode past a small house, telling her it belonged to Tom and Miranda. He named the owners of the other five houses, but they meant nothing to her. They headed onto a winding road which led away from the ramshackle dwellings. They halted before a gray-colored dwelling which appeared sturdy enough but was in need of a new coat of paint. "This is my place," he said without a trace of pride in his voice. "Don't expect too much," he warned her when he opened the door.

Eden quickly discovered Damon's warning was accurate. The interior, lighted by the afternoon sun through a dirty-paned window, left much to be desired. There was one large room, consisting of a small table and two rickety chairs, a washtub, pot-bellied stove, and an oven on one side. On the other side stood two cots with a chest between them and a wall mirror.

This had been Shamus's home, the place he'd loved so dearly, the place he'd spoken about in such glowing terms? Eden could barely believe it. She'd expected something grander. From what Shamus had told her, she had received the impression of a much larger house, complete with Maori servants. This was far removed from her imaginings, and once again she felt Shamus had betrayed her, but was quickly consumed by guilt. No doubt his illness had caused this delusion, but she could have sworn he'd been lucid till the end.

Her disappointment must have shown on her face. "I told you not to expect much," Damon said.

"It's fine," she tonelessly responded. "Rather rustic

decor, however."

Her reaction apparently amused him. "You're a one, you are, Eden Flynn."

Eden's hackles went up, immediately sensing a confrontation in the offing. But she granted him an innocent and guileless smile. "Explain yourself, please."

"Because you lie so damned well. Here you are, fancy lady that you are, in a place barely fit for the pigs, and you're pretending it's to your liking. We both know you're used to better than this."

"You know no such thing!" she spat. "You have no idea about my life, how I've lived. Oh, yes, I could tell you stories about my past, but I won't bore you with them. I could make things up, too, and you'd never know if I was lying or not. So, I'll tell you nothing except one thing: don't attempt to judge me or believe you know what I'm thinking or how I feel. I can guarantee that you'd be very wrong."

Eden didn't know what caused this outburst. She was dirty and exhausted, tired of Damon's nasty comments. Why couldn't he just let her alone for the time being?

"I'd really appreciate if I could wash this dust off and take a nap," she admitted after the retort she expected hadn't come.

"I'll get you some water from the pump," Damon told her and went to the door. He stopped and looked at her. "I assume you'll rest and then be leaving."

Eden smiled a tight, weary smile. "Need you ask?" From his baffled expression, she knew he waited for a different response, but that was all the answer he'd get for the moment.

Bert Carruthers swallowed his whiskey at one of the

many drinking establishments in town. A dance-hall girl who would have been pretty except for three blackened front teeth smiled at him. Her invitation was obvious, but Bert wasn't interested. The altercation with the Widow Flynn and Damon Alexander still smote his pride. "Uppity bitch," he mumbled under his breath, and he didn't mean the black-toothed girl.

He got up and had his glass refilled by the barkeep, oblivious to the piano music and the other patrons, whom Bert considered rowdy and of an inferior social class. Certainly he'd been one of those dirty-clothed miners a few years ago, but now he had some money and was a fine gentleman. So why had a whore like Eden Flynn refused him? It didn't make sense to Bert.

Out of the corner of his eye, he spotted Jock Sutherland nursing a drink. Now, Sutherland was a gentleman through and through. That was obvious to anybody who saw him. Sutherland's sheep station, High Winds, was the most prosperous in the area, located a short distance from Bert's own home. Sutherland could have come into town in his work clothes, but each time Bert had seen him, the man was dressed like a real swell.

His light blond hair was always neatly trimmed, as was his mustache. The only flaw to his face was the long white scar running the length of his right cheek. It was a known fact Damon Alexander had cut him during a fight over a woman when they were younger.

Bert envied the fine cut of the man's coat, which was lined in real satin and not sateen like his own coat. Bert glanced down, embarrassed to notice the fresh whiskey stains on the coat. He'd bet Jock Sutherland never spilled anything.

Bert nearly turned away when Jock glanced in his

direction, not expecting the man to acknowledge him. Many times he'd dropped by High Winds to visit Sutherland and his crippled sister, but Sutherland hadn't seemed interested in conversing, and Bert always left with the impression he'd intruded. But now the man actually grinned at him and waved him over to his table.

Sutherland stood up, surprising Bert further with the offer of his hand. "It's been a long time since I've seen you, Carruthers. Join me for a drink."

Such a friendly greeting from an important man as Sutherland was too much to be believed. Bert sat down with a silly grin on his face, too complimented by Sutherland's attention to wonder at the sudden friendliness.

For a few minutes they exchanged small talk. Bert tried to emulate Jock's proper manners and refined speech. No doubt about it, Sutherland was a real gentleman—not like some of the scum who lived around here, Damon Alexander for one, who protected a whore he'd brought to Thunder Mine. He could learn a great deal about being a gentleman from Sutherland.

"How is Miss Sutherland?" Bert finally asked, his nerve sufficiently raised after a few more whiskeys. He would have liked to court Marjorie Sutherland, despite her infirmity. It didn't matter to Bert if the young woman limped or that she was as plain as cake batter. She was wealthy and her name meant a great deal in the area. Just being associated with a Sutherland could open doors of opportunity.

"My sister is well, thank you. She wondered why you haven't visited High Winds lately."

"Naw! You don't mean it. Miss Marjorie actually said that?"

71

Jock nodded. "Perhaps you'll take tea with us on Saturday?"

"I will, I will," Bert declared, excitement reddening his face. "I'll look forward to it." This was more than Bert had ever dreamed of. Marjorie Sutherland wanted to see him! He barely heard Jock speaking to him, and was brought back to reality by a hard thump on his elbow from the man. "What you said, Jock?"

"I asked you if what I heard about this morning is true. Did you have some sort of altercation with Alexander and Shamus Flynn's widow? The whole town is talking about it."

Bert reddened, embarrassed by the incident and the way he'd backed down before Damon Alexander. Alexander was known to be tough, easy with his fists, just like Shamus had been. He hadn't liked tussling with either of them. "I guess I got carried away by Mrs. Flynn. She's a real beauty under all that dirt on her face, and I know she ain't really a proper lady 'cause when I was in San Francisco—"

"I don't care about that!" Jock snapped, bestowing a warm smile upon Bert even though his brown eyes didn't hold any remnants of warmth. "I need to know if it's true about her being Alexander's partner. Did she inherit Shamus's portion of the mine? Does she intend to live at Thunder Mine?"

"I don't know."

Jock made a tent out of his fingers and perused Bert at such length that Bert fidgeted. "Find out for me. I'd appreciate the information."

"But Damon told me not to snoop around Mrs. Flynn or the mine. You know his temper if he's crossed."

Jock's face darkened and his finger lightly traced the

scar on his cheek. "Find out for me. If you can't, I believe my sister shall be otherwise engaged and forced to cancel the tea."

Bert gulped hard. He knew what that meant. "I'll find out for you, Jock."

"Good, Bert. I knew I could count on you." Jock rose and left the saloon, leaving Bert to ponder just how he was going to discover Mrs. Flynn's plans.

Chapter 6

Nick arrived at sunset just as Damon was pouring himself a large brandy. He placed the crystal decanter on the mahogany sideboard after offering Nick a drink, which the man readily accepted. "Shamus always did have the best taste in spirits," Nick complimented. Nick gingerly sat upon the peach-and-green damask Louis Quinze sofa, uncomfortably aware of his dust-covered clothes. He couldn't wait to bathe, but for the last part of his journey, his mouth had been watering for some of Shamus's fine brandy and when Hannah, a Maori servant girl, passed through the room, he eagerly extended his glass for a refill.

"Yeah, I'll say one thing for old Shamus, he sure did know how to live." Nick cast an appreciative eye around the parlor, letting his attention wander to the marbled terrace which spanned all three sides of the room to overlook the valley below. Nick knew the mine was visible from here; that was probably why Shamus had built the house on this spot. He'd wanted a bird's eye view of the entire operation.

Shamus's managerial ability had been one of his greatest attributes. The man had had a way of making people work for him and not mind it. Because of that ability, Castlegate existed. The house was a small-scale replica of the grand manor Shamus's family had owned in Ireland before the Potato Famine and hard times drove them away.

Nick remembered the way Shamus had labored on it, joining the Maori workers he'd hired. It had been a tiresome undertaking, but Shamus had loved every moment of it and probably had known the position of each stud. Indeed, Castlegate was one of the finest homes in New Zealand, with its Georgian architecture and four Doric columns in front. There were five bedrooms and indoor plumbing, a luxurious oddity considering the primitive way most people lived. The furnishings had been specially made to emulate those in the original Castlegate and shipped from the finest furniture makers in Paris, London, San Francisco, and New Orleans. Nothing was too good for Castlegate.

And now there was a beautiful and intelligent woman to grace its elegant rooms. Nick wondered what kept Eden. He knew it must be near suppertime, for he could smell the delicious aromas wafting from the kitchen and hear the clink of the expensive china as the housekeeper set the table in the dining room. Minutes later, he joined Damon at the Queen Anne-style table. "Will Mrs. Flynn be joining us?" Nick asked innocently before digging into the mouth-watering pork served on a mound of rice and peppers.

"Eden is resting" was Damon's terse reply.

"That's good. I'll bet she was tired. Will she come down later? I want to tell her I brought her trunk."

"I doubt she'll be coming at all, Nick."

Nick's ears picked up on something in Damon's tone of voice. He didn't joke with him, as he usually did. Instead, he appeared subdued, but Nick sensed an undercurrent of moodiness within Damon. And the food was practically untouched on his plate, a most definite sign that something was amiss.

"If you've got something to tell me, lad, then you better get on with it. I have a feeling your moodiness has to do with Eden. Why isn't she eating with us? Why haven't you fetched her to tell her I've brought her trunk? I'm certain she'd like to change her clothes." Nick cocked a wary eyebrow. "Or has Mrs. Flynn already departed Thunder Mine? Did you run her off, Damon? Dammit, man, if you did . . ."

Damon held up a hand. "No, I didn't run her off. She's quite safe. She's staying at the old cabin."

Nick's mouth fell open. "You're joshing me, lad."

"No."

"Why would a lady like herself be staying there? Damon, tell me what you've done."

Damon began eating at last. He appeared unruffled, unmoved by the fact that Eden Flynn was staying in the cabin Shamus had lived in when he first started the mine. Its last inhabitant had been gone for five months. Nick wondered what Damon was thinking of to do such a thing to a delicately bred woman like Eden.

"I'm testing her," Damon admitted. "She came here of her own free will; now I'm going to see if she wants to stay here, or if she's all talk. But I doubt she'll be staying. The cabin isn't any place for the likes of a *lady*, now, is it? I'm betting she gets her fill of the place, the mine, and

76

New Zealand before she even learns of the existence of Castlegate."

"Your uncle would be ashamed of you, Damon. *I'm* ashamed of you." At least Damon had the good grace to flush, a sign he wasn't as hardhearted as he wanted Nick to believe.

Damon nodded in agreement. "Aye, maybe he would be ashamed of me, but the gold-digging harlot he married took him in. She was no sooner in town today than Bert Carruthers was panting around her and bargaining for her favors. *He* knows what she is, now the whole town will know. Already she's disrupted my life, but I won't have her sashaying around Castlegate in her whore's finery, selling her wares under my roof. Castlegate is mine, free and clear. Shamus deeded it to me before he left for San Francisco. Eden Flynn doesn't own any part of this house, so she can stay where I put her."

"Ah, lad, you are a hard man."

"I've had to be hard, Nick," Damon burst out. "You know why better than anyone."

"Tessa." Nick's voice was low but Damon heard him.

"Aye. Tessa."

"Maybe the time's come for you to forget her and continue with your life. You can't live in the past forever. Find a woman, son, make a new start for yourself."

"I suppose you believe Eden Flynn is the woman for me. Wouldn't that be just laughable for me to hook up with Shamus's widow, a prostitute. Hell, Nick! Eden's worse than Tessa ever was."

"I doubt that, but you can't see what's before your eyes, so you refuse to believe Eden isn't what she seems.

She's a real lady, she is. And the poor girl has suffered. Haven't you ever noticed how solemn her face is, how her eyes very seldom light up? She's burdened under a great weight, I tell you. But I'm not blind like you, and I can see that the only time she gets a gleam in those green eyes of hers is when she looks at you. Eden Flynn is smitten with you—take my word on that." Nick watched Damon closely, expecting a volatile reaction.

"You're right about that," Damon agreed, calmly sipping his brandy. "I've already noticed she does get a certain look when she's around me."

"Yeah, and you get a certain reaction, so don't deny it."

"I won't deny it. No matter what she is, Eden is a beautiful woman. A man would have to be made of stone not to desire her. And you know, Nick, I've been thinking about why she married Shamus and then came all this way. She wants respectability. She wants it bad enough to give up the lucrative trade she left behind."

"Then that says something about her good character, I'd think."

"Aye, it does." Damon was almost affable now, and he began to eat with gusto. "I wonder what she'd do if she realized she wasn't able to get that respectability—if the very weakness she fled from was placed before her and proved too much to resist. You know what they say about old dogs and new tricks, leopards not changing their spots—"

"I know what *I'd* say," Nick interjected, not sparing Damon an accusing gaze. "You're determined to run her off by making her life intolerable."

"Don't condemn me, Nick. You want to be convinced Eden Flynn has a heart of gold. Well, I'm going to prove once and for all that her interest is purely in gold. When she sees herself for the trollop she is, then I'll be free of her. And good riddance, too."

Nick didn't say anything else. Damon's determination to be rid of Eden bordered on obsession. Or was it an obsession to possess her? Nick wondered if Damon even realized he'd already fallen under Eden's spell. He couldn't help but smirk. It would serve the young whippersnapper right to discover that fact for himself.

Eden woke to an inky darkness. Getting off the small cot, she stumbled around hoping to find a lantern, but there wasn't one. The dust in the room tickled her nostrils and she sneezed just as a flickering streak of light illuminated the cabin.

"May God keep *wahine* well" came a man's lilting voice from the open doorway.

"Oh, my!" Eden turned, unprepared for the sight of a Maori in native dress. Since arriving in New Zealand, she'd seen Maoris but not spoken to one except for the small boy who had helped her in Queenstown. The man peered at her in the soft glow of the light which emanated from the lantern in his hand. Except for a colorful loincloth, he wore only a large jade necklace. His hair was black and shiny and rather long. His complexion was a light-brown color, and when he smiled at her he showed straight white teeth.

"Boss told me to bring lantern," he explained, entering only when Eden gestured him into the cabin. She graciously accepted the lantern and nearly groaned aloud at the dusty ill-kept room which the light illuminated.

"I'm afraid I have a great deal of cleaning up to do." Eden spoke aloud more to herself than to the Maori.

"I can get you a broom and mop, Mrs. Flynn," the man offered gallantly.

"Would you? I'd appreciate it so much. I can't stay here with this place looking so horrible. I don't know how my husband and Mr. Alexander could abide living here without so much as a curtain on the window."

The man's smile faded and Eden actually saw him blush. "I will get what you need. Are you hungry?"

"I'm famished."

"I will bring you some food."

"What is your name?" she asked.

"Tiku."

"Do you work for Mr. Alexander?"

"Yes, Mrs. Flynn. I help him."

"Oh, then you must point out which house Mr. Alexander will be staying in now that I'm here."

"He, uh . . . he will show you himself when he returns. I'll be back shortly."

Tiku spun around and departed before Eden could question him further. She was curious about Tiku. He didn't look to be a full-blooded Maori and his accent was definitely British.

Eden surveyed the cabin in the lanternlight. It looked just as awful now as it had that afternoon. She wondered how Shamus had lived here, how Damon had. There were so few amenities, but men apparently didn't need as much as women to be happy. She looked at the washtub, longing for a bath. But first there was work to be done.

Tiku returned, bringing with him a tin plate of rice with pork and a large cup of a sweet-tasting juice. In no time at all Eden finished eating and turned her attention to cleaning the cabin with Tiku's assistance. From a nearby well, Tiku filled a bucket with water for Eden, who promptly began to sweep, then mop the floor.

The cleaning didn't take as long as Eden thought it would. When she'd dusted what little furniture there was, she noticed Tiku waiting in the doorway with her trunk. "Mr. Nick brought this for you," he announced.

Eden was pleased to have her trunk but disappointed to learn from Tiku that Nick had already left. She thought this odd, for she'd thought Nick liked her. Even odder still was not having seen Damon for hours. She shrugged. Damon had made it very clear he didn't intend to act as a nursemaid to her, so there was no reason for him to see if she ate, or even if she was still alive. Damon didn't care about her. No doubt he'd crow with joy if she decided to leave Thunder Mine.

I won't give you the satisfaction, Damon Alexander. I'll stay at Thunder Mine until I rot, she resolved.

"You require something else, Mrs. Flynn?" Tiku queried.

Eden grinned. "Yes, a bath. Could you help me carry in the water from the well?"

They went outside into the dark and loaded buckets with water, trudging back and forth from the well to the house until the wooden tub nearly overflowed. Assuring Tiku she wouldn't need him for anything else that night and expressing her gratitude to him for his help, Eden rooted through her trunk until she found her white nightgown. She couldn't wait to get out of her grimy clothes and bathe. It seemed like two months had passed instead of two days since she'd last had a bath. She looked forward to the moment when she could slip into the tub and forget all about Damon Alexander's dislike of her.

She washed her hair and body with violet-scented soap Shamus had bought for her in San Francisco. Settling deep into the tub, the soothing water loosened the tension in her muscles. What a great strain she'd endured since leaving Queenstown. Many people would have given up and not gone farther; as it was, the journey from Dunedin to Queenstown had been long and arduous. Most certainly anyone with sense would have canceled the journey after meeting a man as arrogant as Damon. Yet she'd endured his crossness and his insults. Now she was at Thunder Mine and determined to stay. Damon couldn't do anything to force her to leave.

On that self-congratulatory note, she must have dozed. It seemed hours passed but it was only minutes when she heard a noise and opened her eyes to see Damon standing over her.

"I didn't hear you knock." Feeling flustered and embarrassed, she sank deeper into the tub until the waterline reached just above her nipples. What had he seen when she'd been dozing? How long had he been watching her? Had he liked what he'd seen? She felt herself blushing to even think such wanton things.

"I don't knock to enter my own house," he maintained, sitting on one of the wooden chairs by the table. Extending his long, booted legs in front of him, he didn't take his cobalt gaze from her. She felt impaled with the heat of it.

"You don't live here now. I'd like you to leave."

"Would you, Eden, really?" His voice was low and melodious, containing a silken quality which caused her to shiver. "Or would you rather I'd stay and lift you from the tub and place your dripping-wet body against mine? I'll bet you'd be nice and slippery in my arms, so wet and

82

warm that your bottom would slide into the cradle of my hands."

His eyes held Eden captive. She felt unable to move, could scarcely breathe. Desire washed over her and lapped at her like the bathwater. She wanted to stop him from speaking, from conjuring up these wicked images floating inside her brain. But she couldn't. She wanted to imagine.

"And then," she heard Damon say, "my fingers would massage your delectable flesh until you quivered with need, until you'd be gasping for release. And do you know what I'd do?"

Eden's throat had gone so dry, she could barely swallow. Tousled half-wet strands of hair covered her breasts and framed her face with wispy tendrils as she shook her head. She held her breath when Damon leaned toward her, very much aware of an ache between her legs, which was part pleasure and pain.

"I'd do this." His hand dove beneath the water and found the pulsating spot between her thighs, grasping it with a feather-light touch. "And then I'd lick you dry—all of you . . . every warm inch of you."

A ragged groan threatened to escape from Eden's throat, but Damon prevented it when his mouth suddenly swooped down upon hers. Desire rippled through her every nerve cell, threatening to inundate her with delirious sensations she'd never known existed. What was happening to her? Why must Damon be the one to cause her this exquisite torment? Her mind posed these questions, but she couldn't answer them. All she knew was that she wanted Damon's complete possession.

She was aware he was lifting her out of the tub and didn't care. He was holding her wet and slick body against his, just as he'd said he'd do. His clothes grew wet. Beneath the material, his body burned like a bushfire with his growing need. His kiss deepened into a primitive plunder of her mouth and senses, his tongue finding hers.

Eden nearly swooned from the torrent of need building within her. She was all too aware when his hands caressed her buttocks and pulled her against the hard bulge in his trousers. Her eyes widened and glazed over with her own desire. Having had no experience with any man, the sensual feelings were new to her and more wonderful than anything she could ever have imagined. Any qualms that Damon might not want her fled like a mist. She was ready to give him her heart and her body.

When she found herself beneath him on one of the cots it seemed the most natural thing in the world. She reveled in his expert touch, his kiss. It was as if their being together had been preordained, almost as if Shamus had known they were destined for each other. How right and wonderful it felt when his lips traced a wanton path to her breasts to tantalizingly lick the water droplets from her heated flesh. She moaned and buried her hands within the depths of his hair.

"Ah, Eden, you've built a fire in me," he whispered in a ragged breath. He looked at her, his eyes glowing like twin bonfires. "I've wanted you since I first saw you on the street in Queenstown."

"You have?" It seemed almost unbelievable to Eden that a man of Damon's pride should admit such a thing. His revelation touched her heart. Could it be possible he might love her? At this moment, she knew *she* loved *him*. Otherwise she wouldn't be giving herself to him. Perhaps he no longer believed she was a whore or the gold digger he'd accused her of being. Oh, she hoped so! Since her mother's death, she feared she'd cringe if a man touched her. But she craved Damon's touch and didn't think any other man could make her feel this way.

She must love him and he must love her. He wanted her just as much as she wanted him. And so much wanting must mean love.

"Aye, my beauty." He kissed each of her nipples and cockily grinned when she moaned. "So you like that, do you?"

"Oh, yes, Damon. I do."

"Ah, Eden, you're so beautiful and passionate. I like the way you writhe beneath me. I like everything about you."

"I'm glad." She spoke with heartfelt simplicity and stroked his cheek. She blushed when she said, "I'm in love with you. I know it's a bit early to say it, but I do love you. And I'll make you a good wife, if you'll have me. No other man makes me feel like you do. I loved Shamus, but that wasn't the same as this."

Love? Wife? What in the hell was she talking about? He looked at her, seeing an innocent-appearing woman. But he knew differently. All he wanted was to bed her, to prove to her she was a whore at heart, only out to claim a fortune she'd duped from a sick old man. And now he saw that the innocent facade hid a shifty creature who was trying to lure him into marriage—and then, no doubt, she planned to bilk him dry of his interests in the mine. Was there no end to this temptress's manipulation?

His face held a frozen look. "Just how many men have there been, Eden, love? Tell me. Did you count them? Were they all satisfied customers? But of course they'd be satisfied with a lying whore, stroking their pride and pretending to be an innocent. Was that how you got Shamus to marry you? Or did you withhold the sex until after you married him?"

He was unprepared for her heartfelt slap and the stinging sensation it produced on his cheek. He should have expected she'd react this way. Eden clearly hated to hear the truth about herself.

"My life with Shamus is none of your concern." She pushed at him, freeing herself from him. Her green eyes held venom. If she'd been a snake, she'd have killed him with that look. "And as far as the other men I've known . . . well, let's say that I lost count." There were never *any* men, but she'd let him think the worst. Once again he'd nearly been her undoing and now she wondered if he had *planned* to seduce her. But no more. She was on to him now.

Getting up, she reached for her gown and held the flimsy garment in front of her. "Get out of my cabin and don't come back."

Damon didn't make a move. He leaned on his elbows, his cheek an angry red, and calmly smiled. "I'm not leaving my own home. This is where I live, where you'll stay unless you can find another place. Either way, I don't care. But I'm not letting some fancy woman throw me out of my own house."

Eden looked at him in dismay. "You can't mean to stay here. It isn't right or decent."

"Hah! You're worried about decent? My God, woman, you nearly let me bed you, and now you're concerned about decency. What about all the other men who've been with you? You didn't care about being decent with them."

"I hate you!" she cried, and meant it because she

86

thought he wanted to *make love to her*. "I'll find someplace else to stay." With that, she headed for the door and would have made it outside except Damon lunged off of the cot and grabbed her. He held her around the waist while she kicked at him, barely missing his shin.

"Calm down, Mrs. Flynn, and act like an adult. You can't go roaming around without your clothes on, and I won't allow you to beg a place to stay from the people who work here. No matter what I think about you, you're part owner of Thunder Mine. You'll have no credibility whatsoever if you go off half cocked."

Eden smothered a frustrated sob. Damon was right, as much as she hated to admit it. No one would give her a chance to prove herself. But why did he warn her? This would have been the perfect way to be rid of her. "If I embarrass myself enough, then you'd be free of me. Why do you care if no one takes me seriously?"

Damon wasn't certain, either. But he couldn't allow Eden, no matter who or what she'd been, to disgrace his uncle's name publicly. What she did in private was another matter, and what she did with Damon Alexander in private was definitely for his own eyes and ears alone. "Get your nightgown on," he commanded in a voice much harsher than he intended. He released her and found a rope in the corner. He began stringing it from one wall to the top of the doorway, until it hung between the two cots. Then he took a large blanket and hung it over the rope.

"For your privacy, madam. I'll sleep on one side of the blanket and you the other. It will be as decent as you want it."

This seemed the only solution for the time being, but Eden wasn't certain she liked it. Damon brought out the wanton in her, causing her to act recklessly. And she wasn't certain she could trust him, either. "Hah!" How do I know you won't come sneaking around to the other side and try to—"

"As decent as *you* want it, Eden." And that was all he said to her.

Chapter 7

Despite the odd living arrangements, Eden found herself getting used to sharing the cabin with Damon. Hoping to brighten the interior, she'd sewed curtains for the two small windows and plucked wild daisies from the nearby fields; yet she didn't feel at home. She cooked and cleaned for herself, but she decided she'd be damned if she'd pick up after Damon or cook a meal for him. Her side of the cabin was kept spotlessly clean, Damon's side was ignored by her. This slight on her part gave her a sense of grim satisfaction.

With Tiku's help, she gathered a supply of foodstuffs, but since Damon never appeared in the cabin until well after dark and never once inquired if she'd fixed supper for him, there was always plenty of food on hand. Still, she couldn't help wondering where he ate—or with whom.

She was thankful that no one ever came down the path to visit. None of the miners or family members seemed to know Eden shared the cabin with Damon. Or perhaps they did and were too discreet to say anything. No matter her odd circumstances, Eden was content and interested in the workings of Thunder Mine.

She asked Damon about the men who worked for them. Damon introduced her to the miners and their families, whom Eden discovered were as kind and considerate as Tom and Miranda. She was pleased that a portion of the mine's profits were split equally among the miners, giving them an incentive to work since most of the other mines had long since played out. Granted, they were a rough-looking lot, but no matter how ignorant they might have considered her questions about the workings of the mine, they always answered her politely.

Most puzzling of all was Damon. She'd expected he'd argue when she demanded to be shown the mine, but he willingly gave her a tour. If there was something she didn't understand, he patiently explained and showed her firsthand what mining entailed.

She became familiar with the rocker, or cradle, so named because it resembled an infant's cradle. While watching in fascination, she saw gravel shoveled onto a sluice that fit on the cradle's top. Baffles or strips of wood had already been nailed onto the sluice. While the cradle was rocked, one of the miners poured water into it so the gold would lodge behind the baffles when the gravel washed out. Though this method was still actively employed, Damon had built larger sluices so the chance of losing the gold during the washout was lessened. He'd also placed quicksilver behind the baffles and channeled the river to rush through the sluices at a rapid rate. Because of the quicksilver, the gold then clung to the metal and wasn't randomly washed away.

"I'm working on a newer process I'd like to try one day," Damon admitted, so absorbed in his own thoughts to pay attention to whom he spoke. "It's a sort of machine to separate the gold from the gravel, eliminating all of the excess time and man hours of placer mining. But it's years away from existence. Besides, there is something New Zealand needs much more than that."

"What?" Eden couldn't believe he spoke to her like an equal.

"Roads. Or have you forgotten your perilous journey so soon?" He shot her a most devastating smile. In spite of her resolve not to be friendly to him and still smarting from her silly admission of love, she smiled back.

"I believe it will take some time to forget it." *And you,* she found herself thinking as she gazed up at him like a silly, infatuated schoolgirl.

Eden had no idea how pretty she looked as she stood in the mine, the glow from the lanternlight illuminating the golden streaks in her hair. She'd chosen a forest-green blouse that day with a matching split riding skirt, and the color matched her glittering eyes. But the desire on Damon's face spoke more clearly than any words. He wanted her, she was certain of that. He hadn't forgotten what had transpired between them only a few nights past. Eden's cheeks grew red at the memory, but never would she allow him to know he could unnerve her so easily.

"Do you plan to build roads now, too, Damon?" she asked as she began walking out of the mine into the sunshine.

"Aye. New Zealand needs them if we're to continue to grow as a country. There are too many impenetrable regions, regions which, if developed, could have an enormous economic impact. And the only reason we won't grow is lack of roads."

"You sound almost like a politician."

"Politics is something I want no part of, not like some others I could name." Damon's jaw clenched, his bitter expression quite obvious now that they were standing in the bright daylight. "I want what's best for New Zealand and the men I employ. But there are others who think only of themselves, who worry more about money than people's livelihood."

Eden didn't know whom Damon meant, but his very passion for New Zealand gave her an opportunity to glimpse the man beneath the hardened exterior. She felt drawn to him again, but pushed down her traitorous feelings. No matter how noble or patriotic Damon could be where his country and employees were concerned, he didn't care for her. And she must never forget that.

That afternoon Eden visited Miranda and spent an hour conversing with her and another woman called Jessy, whose husband had worked for Thunder Mine but had now passed on. Jessy Bookman was a friendly and likable sort of woman. She seemed to wear a perpetual smile on a face which was surprisingly unlined for a woman past sixty. Eden liked her immediately.

"It's hard to imagine Shamus married, isn't it?" Jessy glanced at Miranda for confirmation, and Miranda agreed, indeed it was. "Not that there was anything wrong with him, mind you," Jessy hurriedly assured Eden. "But then again, honey, you'd know that."

Eden felt herself flushing to imagine what these women would say if they only knew the truth about her marriage. Instead, Eden nodded. "Shamus was a wonderful husband."

"And a great man," Miranda asserted, peering openly

at Eden. "But life goes on, if you know what I mean. And, Eden, no one would think it unfitting if you married Damon. The boy needs a good woman."

"He does" came Jessy's quick reply. "But Damon's a man now and has a man's needs, not like years ago when he was so young and fighting Jock Sutherland to marry that Tessa Quitman."

Miranda shot Jessy a warning look. Eden attempted to be nonchalant as she drank her tea, but her insides churned. Somehow she'd never thought of Damon as having been married. "Shamus never mentioned Damon had a wife." Damon had never mentioned it, either.

Miranda patted her hand in reassurance. "Now, dear, there was no need for anyone to mention Tessa to you. It was a very long time ago, and he's been a widower for almost five years, I'd guess. Damon did take her death hard. He started drinking and raising a ruckus until Shamus stepped in and set the lad straight."

"That's right, I remember. He was real upset about it." Jessy shook her head sadly.

"How did his wife die?" Eden's voice quivered. She shouldn't be so shaken by this news, but she was.

Miranda put a finger to her lips in thought. "I believe she went to visit relatives in Christ Church and died there. Sudden-like, you know. I never did discover what killed her, did you, Jessy?"

"No, but I'll tell you one thing. Jock Sutherland never got over her. Tessa was the reason he carries that scar on his cheek. Damon cut him in a brawl over the girl. As fond as I am of Damon, I did feel sorry for Mr. Sutherland. I still do. He's such a perfect gentleman and so kind. Have you met him, Eden?"

Jessy's eyes gleamed after Eden replied in the negative.

"I have a feeling you will. Jock Sutherland can sniff out a pretty woman a hundred miles away."

Eden finished her tea and then excused herself. She needed to be alone and think. Damon had been married. Of course she was being ridiculous; there was no reason for him to have mentioned his late wife. Still, she wished he had. She'd fancied herself in love with Damon and now she discovered she knew very little about his past, and even less about the man himself. Damon constantly threw her off guard. From one minute to the next she was never certain if he was going to snarl at her or kiss her.

But she now began to understand that losing Tessa must have been very hard for him. Perhaps he hadn't always been so brooding. Miranda and Jessy both liked him. As for his considering another marriage—much less considering marrying Eden herself—that was ridiculous. Still her heart went out to him. She knew firsthand how deeply a person could be affected by tragedy.

As she made her way back to the cabin, she decided not to mention to Damon that she'd learned about Tessa Alexander. He'd tell her in his own good time, if he wanted her to know. She hoped he would confide in her and share his grief with her, because a part of her ached to console him. Yet the other part, the survivor, hoped he wouldn't—because she didn't know how much pain she could tolerate to discover the intensity of his love for another woman—even a dead one.

"You're a fool, Eden," she berated herself as she walked along, so caught up in her own musings, she jumped when a horse whinnied nearby. Warily glancing toward the direction of the sound, she spotted Bert Carruthers on a large roan. He cantered toward her. Immediately she was on her guard, wondering what he wanted. No one was about, and she prayed the man wasn't coming to finish what he'd started in town.

Inclining his red head, he grinned lecherously. "Good afternoon to you, Mrs. Flynn. Hope you're having a nice day."

"What can I do for you?" Eden didn't waste useless amenities on him.

"Oh, I just came to apologize to you for my rude behavior the other day. I'm sorry about how I acted, what I said to you."

This was a surprise, but Bert didn't look the least bit sorry. "Thank you. I accept your apology." Eden began to move on, aware of his every gesture as he followed beside her on his horse.

"Yeah, it was real bad of me to act like I did. Don't know what got into me. If I'd known you were Damon's woman, I'd have backed off sooner. I don't like to tussle with the likes of Damon Alexander."

Eden stopped, frozen in her tracks. "I'm not anybody's woman."

"Is that a fact? Well, that's interesting to know. Tell me, ma'am, how long you plan to stay at Thunder Mine?"

"That's none of your business, sir."

"Just being neighborly."

"Nosey, you mean, but for what it's worth, Mr. Carruthers, I plan to stay in New Zealand and make a new life for myself."

"Then I'll be the first in the territory to welcome you. We're neighbors, you know. My land is between Thunder Mine and Sutherland's station." He pointed in a northerly direction. "In fact, I'm having tea this afternoon with Jock Sutherland and his sister."

"How very nice, Mr. Carruthers. Good day." Eden cut

him off with an icy, haughty demeanor which would have done Queen Victoria proud.

"Mrs. Flynn!"

Barely stopping in her stride, she glanced over her shoulder.

"Don't mention to Damon I've been here. He might take offense. I don't want no trouble with him."

Eden didn't reply but kept walking away. Bert Carruthers disturbed her, yet she wouldn't mention to Damon that she'd seen him. He'd only believe the worst and assume she'd invited him to Thunder Mine. But what disturbed her more was the man's assumption she was Damon's woman.

Eden sighed. If only that were true.

Jock Sutherland tolerated Bert's presence in his parlor. He'd already learned from Bert's eager lips what he wanted to know about Eden Flynn. She intended to remain in New Zealand, not really a great surprise, but a very pleasant one from Bert's description of her beauty. He really must pay her a visit soon and welcome her to the area. As a member of the New Zealand Parliament, he should extend his friendship. And if it were true that the Widow Flynn was tarnished, her past might work to his advantage. As a politician, he'd long ago learned not to overlook any fact or weakness about a potential adversary, and if that adversary happened to be beautiful, then so much the better.

And then there was his sister.

Poor, crippled Marjorie, who was far from beautiful. Her nose was a tad too long, her hair a mousey shade of brown, and she was very thin and pale. Almost unhealthy-looking, Jock decided. The sun never touched her face because she stayed mostly in the house, which was as it should be. Jock didn't wish his sister to embarrass him with her deformity. Oh, he knew she couldn't help having been born with one foot shorter than the other, but cripples made people nervous and ill at ease. He couldn't afford people to remember him as the crippled Miss Sutherland's brother—not if he hoped to make inroads in Wellington and one day become governor of New Zealand.

Still, he was proud of Marjorie. Never had she done anything to displease him, of that he was nearly certain. Even now, as she sat across from Bert Carruthers, her good breeding forbade her from expressing her displeasure. But Jock knew her well enough to realize by the thin compression of her lips she'd never come to like Carruthers. The man was boorish, his manners no better than a savage. But a chance to marry her off to the lout was too wonderful to pass by. A marriage to Carruthers was the only way he could get his hands on the property which acted as a buffer between Thunder Mine and his own High Winds. He'd offered Carruthers a good price for the land a number of times and been refused. Jock didn't give a damn about Carruthers's land. It was Thunder Mine he wanted and was determined to possess. It was one way to get back at Damon Alexander, and if using Marjorie was the means to an end, then so be it.

Truly, he didn't relish hurting his sister, but sometimes one couldn't always have what one wanted. He'd learned that lesson only too well. He lightly stroked the scar on his cheek. Oh, yes, one way or another, he'd get his revenge upon Alexander.

"Would you care for more tea, Mr. Carruthers?"

Marjorie was always polite, Jock noted with a certain pride.

"No, Miss Marjorie, thank you. I've eaten all the scones." Bert let out a hearty laugh, followed by a belch. "Excuse me, but they were tasty. It's not often I get such a nice treat, me being unmarried."

"Ah, yes. I understand." Marjorie twisted the tassels on her black shawl and cast a helpless glance at her brother. Jock stood by the fireplace with a humorous grin on his face. It was apparent she wasn't going to get any assistance from him. "I hope things are going well for you, Mr. Carruthers."

"They are, and please call me Bert. We're neighbors, you know—"

"Tell me, Bert . . ." Jock interrupted. "Just how long has it been since you've had a good home-cooked meal or a woman to mend for you?"

"Can't recall."

"Marjorie is an excellent cook. She can darn well and sew beautifully. And as a housekeeper, well . . . you can see for yourself how spotless she keeps the house. Do I dare hope you're here today because you have honorable intentions toward my sister?"

"Jock!" Marjorie jumped up, holding onto her cane, clearly horrified at the thought of being courted by Bert Carruthers, or worse, married to him.

Bert appeared almost humble when he gave a nod in Marjorie's direction. "I'd be honored to have Miss Marjorie for my wife. I'd treat her right good, I would."

"I'm pleased to know that, Bert." Jock extended a hand to him, which Bert took in all seriousness. "Then we'll prepare for a wedding. How about Boxing Day?"

"So soon?" Well, I guess so, if that's fine with Miss

Marjorie." Bert smiled at his bride-to-be, quite unaware that Marjorie was in shock.

"It is." Jock spoke for his sister.

Before he left, Bert placed a hearty kiss on Marjorie's cold, pale lips. She stood in the middle of the room, unable to move. All she could do was watch her brother stare dispassionately at her.

"You've a great deal to do before your wedding," he told her.

It was the coldness in his voice that brought her to life. She realized that Jock had been embarrassed by her all these years. Her deformity had prevented suitors. No healthy young man wanted a cripple for a wife, so she'd been stuck at High Winds acting as mistress while their father was alive, their mother having died ten years earlier. But once their father was gone, Marjorie assumed she'd remain there forever. She kept a decent house, overseeing the Maori servants. She'd made certain Jock was well fed, and whenever guests came down from Wellington, she was gracious, but stayed out of the way. Though her father had left her a bit of money, High Winds belonged to Jock. She loved High Winds, and she'd done her best to keep her brother happy so she could remain. He'd have no reason to marry her off to just anyone.

Her efforts, it seemed, were in vain. Jock wanted her to marry Bert Carruthers. A shiver slipped up her spine. She'd rather die than marry that swine. If only she could marry the man she truly loved, but that could never be. No one must ever know how she felt.

"Cold, my dear?" she heard Jock ask.

Her large brown eyes lifted to his face. "How can you do this to me?"

"What? Arrange for an expensive wedding for you? I assure you, Marjorie, that your wedding will be the most elaborate in the Otago."

"I don't care about the cost!" Her voice was a hiss, surprising herself as well as Jock with its vehemence. "I won't marry that horrible man. I won't." Marjorie clenched her fist, and her face grew pink with her outrage. "I'll run away before I do."

Coming closer to her, Jock's face looked like a chiseled piece of granite, and his eyes were cold, so cold that they looked dead. He grabbed her arm, hurting her, but she didn't cry out. "I guarantee that none of my horses shall carry you, so you'll have to go on foot. How far do you think you'll get, Marjorie? But if you do make it, I wager you'll end up at Thunder Mine."

Her heart thumped painfully in her chest. He couldn't know. He couldn't! "No," she hotly denied.

"Yes," Jock asserted. "That's where you'd go. I've never said anything to you, dear sister, because there was no cause to chastise you for your silly infatuation, and believe me, I know your love is one-sided. That Maori bastard you believe you love hasn't looked twice at you, has he?" He twisted her arm. "Well, has he?"

She shook her head as tears filled her eyes. She made a valiant attempt to blink them away, but one slipped down her cheek. So, Jock knew she was in love with Tiku. Tiku's mother was the Sutherland cook, and Marjorie had been in love with him for years, a hopeless love, she knew—not only because he was a Maori but because she was a cripple. A man as handsome and perfectly formed as Tiku could never love someone like her. And it hurt to know this, but for Jock to know, too, was a cruel pain.

Her brother moved away from her, examining her from head to toe with icy contempt. "Thank God for small favors. Carruthers will expect a virgin bride. At least you haven't disappointed me in that respect, or then again, you had no choice but to remain untouched. You'd like that Maori bastard to make love to you."

"Tiku is a fine man," she proclaimed. "Much finer than you'll ever be. And he isn't a bastard. His father married his mother in a Maori ceremony. You know that Tiku's father was a British explorer, that he sent him to England to be educated. . . ."

"Marjorie, forget him. Tiku doesn't know you exist."

That was the truth and it hurt. Tiku never once looked at her except to speak to her on the days he came to High Winds to see his mother. "I know that."

"I'm glad. Now, let's concentrate on getting you married to Carruthers."

"You want Bert's land."

"You're more astute than I thought, my dear. Yes, I want his land. You owe me for your care, and this is the way you'll repay me. And if you get it into your head to run away, whether it's to Tiku or someplace else, I'll make certain your Maori prince suffers for it."

Marjorie's eyes widened in fear. Jock hated the Maoris, though he pretended to be concerned about them because it was politically feasible to do so. "You couldn't hurt him, Jock. You wouldn't hurt Tiku. He doesn't know I exist—what would be the point?"

"The point is that you know what will happen if you don't go through with the ceremony."

Her knuckles were white as she held on to her cane. Part of her ached to bash in her brother's head, but she was a gentle person and violence didn't come easily to her. There was no other alternative but to acquiesce to Jock's wishes.

"I'll marry Bert Carruthers, but when he touches me, I'll pretend it's Tiku."

Jock didn't hide his scorn. "Whatever you must do, Marjorie," he replied.

Chapter 8

When Damon entered the cabin he realized something was different. The small table had been set with a cream-colored tablecloth and a lighted candle stood in the center. The two plates with accompanying utensils caused Damon to lift an eyebrow in suspicion. Was Eden expecting company? Could it be a man? A swift surge of jealousy rushed through him.

He saw Eden when she turned from the oven, holding a pan of freshly baked bread whose delicious aroma filled the cabin. In a pink-and-white checked gown with a white apron tied around her tiny waist, she looked very young and innocent. Her hair was braided, a pink bow at the end, and hung enticingly over her right shoulder. When she saw him, she smiled, enchanting him with her beauty and warmth.

"You're back early," Eden commented, placing the bread on the table.

"Aye."

"I can see you've bathed already."

"Aye." He couldn't tell her he'd been home for a bath.

"I bathed in the lagoon."

She stood ill at ease. "I see."

She didn't see at all. If she did, she'd stop staring at him with those beautiful, shiny green eyes and turn away so he wouldn't have to see her luscious pink mouth, which looked as if it were begging to be kissed. He'd seen prettier women than Eden Flynn, but no other woman could get to him as she could, without even seeming to try. Damn the wanton witch for what she was doing to him. "I wanted to get a good night's sleep," he said more harshly than he intended.

"Will we be going to church tomorrow?"

He peered at her as if she were daft. "Church?"

"Tomorrow is Sunday. I assume there are services in town."

"Aye, sure there are." He hadn't been to church since the day he and Tessa were married.

"Shall we go then?"

"I'm not one for going to church, but I'll take you if you want."

Eden beamed her pleasure. "Have you eaten yet? I've got roast chicken and potatoes for supper."

The food did smell good, and he hadn't eaten much at the house. "I don't want to spoil your supper. I can see you're having a guest."

"Damon, don't be silly." Eden laughed and took one of the plates from the table and began to spoon some chicken and potatoes out of a roasting pan onto the plate. "I'm not having a guest unless you consider *yourself* to be one. Come on, sit down and eat." She placed the succulent food on the table.

A sense of relief washed over Damon. No one else was coming. It would be just the two of them. She'd prepared the supper in the hope he'd join her. He was summarily overjoyed to know she'd gone to the trouble of cooking him a meal and suspicious, too. Why had she done this?

Despite his reservations, he sat down, quaffing his own guilt at already having eaten at Castlegate. He really should tell her about the house, but it was *his* house, not *hers*. He'd thought she'd have already fled Thunder Mine once she saw the cabin and realized it wasn't luxurious like her quarters at LaRue's had no doubt been. But she'd surprised him by cleaning the place without complaint, and she'd even sewn some pretty green curtains for the window. She'd won over the miners and their women-folk—not an easy feat since many of them were suspicious of strangers in general. She'd even straightened out the mess he'd made of the account books, which had been Shamus's job, but something Damon hadn't had the time to do after Shamus left.

Still, he didn't believe she intended to stay in New Zealand. He expected she'd sell him her share of the mine and head back to America. She'd be wealthy enough and wouldn't need to return to the "profession" she'd left behind at LaRue's. He wanted to be hard on her and force her to leave, but he knew he was softening toward her.

Each time he looked at her he couldn't believe what she'd been. There was something in her face and tempting body that went beyond sheer physical beauty. He sensed she was vulnerable, and this surprised him. He wanted this woman as he'd never wanted another. And he knew she wanted him, too. He didn't doubt he could have taken her anytime he wished, and he would have, except he'd seen another side to her now that they were partners.

Eden was intelligent, possessed of a quick mind.

During the short time she'd been at Thunder Mine, she'd made suggestions about the working conditions which Damon intended to implement. She might not be familiar with mining, but she caught on quickly and was as good as any man.

But she'd told him she loved him, and he was afraid of losing his heart to her. That was something he wouldn't allow to happen, and not only because of her past. He didn't believe he'd survive the pain of the desertion he knew was inevitable.

"I hope you like the chicken," Eden said.

"Very good," he praised. "I've never tasted better."

She glanced shyly at him. "It was my mother's special recipe. She fixed it every Sunday. I remember how the kitchen slaves would flee whenever she decided to do the cooking herself. Mama always made such a mess!" Eden chuckled at the memory, not having thought of it in such a long time.

"Slaves? Your family owned slaves?"

"Yes. We owned a plantation in Georgia." She bit down on her lower lip. "At least we did until the Yankees came through and burned us out." She shuddered. "My parents were killed by them. I later went to live with my aunt in Atlanta."

Damon felt like the biggest fool, and his face burned with shame. No wonder she'd hated it when he'd called her "Yank." And he should have realized she was a southerner from the soft twang in her speech. There was a great deal he didn't know about Eden because he hadn't thought to ask her. "I'm sorry. We'd heard of the problems here and read some accounts of the battles. But that was all. This Civil War your country fought was very bad then?"

Eden was incredulous. Evidently Damon didn't know how horrible the war had been. But there was no reason why he should have known about all the atrocities, not when he'd been thousands of miles away and a British subject. What happened in America must have seemed unreal to him. "Yes, it was very bad."

A long silence followed. When supper was over, Eden began picking up the dishes, stunned when Damon began helping her. She washed while Damon dried. Later, she went to her side of the room and undressed. In the candlelight she saw his powerful figure silhouetted against the thin blanket that acted as a buffer between them. She barely breathed when he started to remove his clothes.

Even as a dark shadow, Damon's physique was superb. Her heart hammered in her ears, and her mouth went dry. If only she possessed the courage to get up and go to him, to put aside her fear that he'd reject her for what he thought she'd been and for who she wasn't. She'd reached out to him with the supper, having felt sorry for the loss he'd suffered. He must never know she'd done it out of love—and desire.

The candle was snuffed out. She heard the cot creak with his weight. Her cheeks flamed knowing he slept nude beneath the covers. She imagined how absolutely beautiful he must look, if it was possible for a man to be beautiful.

"Thank you for the supper, Eden," he said, interrupting her flight of fancy. "I appreciate it."

"You're welcome, Damon." She smiled into the darkness. They were on a first-name basis again.

"And, Eden?"

"Yes."

"I'm sorry I called you 'Yank.'"

She couldn't speak because she was crying softly to herself.

The ride into town was pleasant. The December morning was warm, and Eden knew the day would grow progressively warmer, until by midafternoon the heat would be almost unbearable. The topsy-turvy seasons didn't bother her so much now. Little by little she was getting used to New Zealand.

She sat next to Damon on the buggy ride into town. Her hands smoothed down her prettiest Sunday gown, a white dress with small blue dots on the material. On her head was a white bonnet. She wanted to make a good first impression on the minister and congregation. It meant a great deal to her to be a part of the community, to have the chance to start a new life. Even if that life wouldn't include Damon.

They couldn't live under the same roof forever. In fact, she doubted the roof on the place would hold out if a good thunderstorm happened along. It wasn't seemly for them to share a house when they weren't married, and she worried what others would think. Perhaps she could move in with Miranda and Tom for a short while, at least until she found another place to live. So far, she hadn't broached the subject of her moving out to Damon, fearful she'd see the joy in his eyes to be finally rid of her.

She cast a longing eye over Damon, who was dressed in a brown suit with a white shirt. He looked quite dapper though uncomfortable. He tugged at his shirt collar. "Aye, it's going to be a hot day," he predicted, observing the sky. "I'll bet it rains."

The sky above them was a brilliant azure with no clouds in sight, a fact Eden mentioned. "Doesn't matter," Damon told her. "I can smell the rain."

About ten minutes before services were scheduled to begin, they arrived at a small white church. Eden couldn't help but notice Damon was nervous as they approached a group of people standing outside. He'd mentioned he hadn't been to church in years and must have felt out of place. She was pleased to see that Miranda and Tom Creig were there, with their niece, Joanie. Most amazing of all was the sight of Nick, who wore a blue suit and sported a tiny rose on the lapel. They were warmly greeted by Nick and the others. By the time the service began, Eden felt at ease and Damon didn't seem as nervous.

In a small pew to the side of where she sat with Damon, she couldn't help but notice a handsome blond-haired man with a mustache and a young woman who leaned upon a cane. It was obvious to Eden that he had noticed her, too. Throughout the service, she felt his eyes upon her and she was forced to look at him. He smiled at her, and she returned one of her own. There was no need to be rude to the man.

But Damon saw this exchange and stiffened.

Could Damon be jealous? She liked thinking he might care just a bit about her.

Later, after the congregation spilled outside and Eden met some other members, Damon took her arm to lead her to the buggy. Suddenly the blond-haired man and the limping young woman were beside them. The man addressed Damon, but Damon barely nodded at him. The slight didn't seem to matter to the man. His interest was centered on Eden.

109

"I take it you're Mrs. Eden Flynn," he said politely and offered her his hand. "I'm Jock Sutherland of High Winds, and this is my sister, Marjorie." Marjorie nodded, a tiny smile splitting her lips. "We're your neighbors."

"Yes, I know. Mr. Alexander mentioned you own a sheep station."

Jock laughed. "I'm shocked Damon thought to mention me at all."

Believe me, he has, Eden wanted to say. She gave him one of her brightest smiles, including Marjorie. "I do hope we all can become better acquainted."

"I'd like that," Marjorie admitted.

"Marjorie is going to be a very close neighbor of yours, Mrs. Flynn. My sister is scheduled to marry Bert Carruthers on Boxing Day."

"My best wishes to you and Mr. Carruthers." Eden couldn't believe that this young woman was going to marry that awful Bert Carruthers and that her brother approved the match. Apparently Damon was taken aback by the news because his face paled and then darkened to meet Jock's smug grin. Several moments elapsed before he offered his congratulations to the bride-to-be.

Marjorie stiffly accepted their good wishes. "It was very sudden," she said.

They began walking. Jock fell into step alongside Eden and Damon walked with Marjorie, who was a great deal slower because of her limp. Damon took Marjorie's elbow and made conversation, but his attention was on Eden and Jock. The silly female was laughing giddily at something Jock said to her, probably some stupid blue-blooded joke. But he should have expected someone like Eden to be taken with Jock Sutherland.

Until last night he hadn't known what sort of a

110

background she'd come from. Now he did. A southern plantation, for God's sake! Slaves and mammies, cotton fields and gallant young men to twirl her around a dance floor. From the day she was born, her every whim must have been indulged. No matter what she'd become at LaRue's, she'd been born a southern aristocrat, complete with the silver spoon in her mouth.

And now here was Jock Sutherland to make all of her dreams come true. He was wealthy and owned vast amounts of land. He was a member of the New Zealand Parliament, an exalted position. The man's ancestors had been dukes and lords in England. No wonder she was taken with him. Their backgrounds were similar. They were two of a kind.

Hell! he swore to himself, barely hearing Marjorie Sutherland speaking about the minister's inspiring sermon that morning. Eden was more like Tessa than he'd thought.

"Oh, Mr. Sutherland, how entertaining you are!" Eden laughed up at Jock, her eyes a glittering green. "You and your sister must pay a visit to Thunder Mine soon."

Jock took Eden's hand and kissed it. She didn't miss the cold fury on Damon's face and felt warmed by it. He *was* jealous.

"I doubt Damon would welcome me, Mrs. Flynn, but I should be most pleased for you to visit us at High Winds. Would you care to join Marjorie and me for luncheon tomorrow?"

"Oh, do!" Marjorie enthused, coming to stand beside them.

"I would be most pleased." Eden didn't dare look at Damon. She could sense his anger rising, especially when

111

Marjorie offered him the same invitation, which he refused with a polite and friendly smile.

"Until tomorrow, then," Jock told Eden, patting her hand. "And may I say, Mrs. Flynn, that your southern accent is most charming."

Eden acknowledged his compliment with a dimpled smile and allowed Damon to help her into the buggy.

So that was Jock Sutherland, she mused as they drove back to the mine. He didn't seem to be the ogre Damon had made him out to be. He was quite handsome; not even the scar detracted from his good looks. But she decided it was normal for Damon not like like Jock since they'd been competing for Tessa. Eden thought it odd that Damon still carried a grudge against Jock when Damon had wooed and won Tessa. Why did he still dislike Jock Sutherland to the point of absolute rudeness?

"I guess you think I'm a bloody fool." Damon broke the strained silence when they were halfway home. "Sutherland could tell you were an American southerner from your speech. And here I was insulting you by calling you 'Yank.'"

"You're upset over that?" Eden was incredulous. She'd thought his silence was due to jealousy. "What does that have to do with anything?"

"He one-upped me."

Damon set his mouth in a grim line and urged the horse along. Eden seethed in her seat. He was upset because Jock Sutherland had been able to tell what part of America she was from! What a stupid, silly thing to be angry about! But she now knew that Damon's ill temper didn't come from any feelings he might secretly harbor for her. He was more concerned because Jock had known

112

something he hadn't.

What peeved her more was Damon's not mentioning the lunch at High Winds tomorrow, which proved he didn't care about her. If he did care, he'd insist she not go—and she *wouldn't* have gone. But she knew now what she meant to Damon. Nothing.

When they reached home, she stepped off the buggy without Damon's help. Placing her hands on her hips, she tilted her chin defiantly. "You're right, Damon. Jock one-upped you, but not in the way you think."

"Just what does that mean?"

"It means you are a fool, a stupid, blind fool. And I'm a fool, too. But I won't be one any longer. I'm going to find another place to live. I can't stay here with you, I—"

"Thinking of moving into High Winds, then, are you? Moving onto more lucrative pastures after you heard Marjorie will be marrying."

She hated him at that moment, hated his smug, handsome face which couldn't see beyond what he thought she was. Well, let him think the worst about her. What he thought didn't matter any longer. "I haven't been asked yet," she drawled.

"You will be, I'm certain. Good day to you, Mrs. Flynn." Damon inclined his head and tugged at the reins. The buggy rolled away from the cabin and away from her.

Marjorie Sutherland was a gracious hostess. Though Marjorie didn't speak very much, Eden liked her. She sensed that Marjorie was intimidated by her brother, and that may have been the reason she chose to say little. Eden found her to be an intelligent and warm individual. But when Eden asked her about her forthcoming marriage, it was Jock who filled her in on the details. Marjorie sat like a wooden carving, her gaze trained on the window where Eden's buggy waited outside, with Tiku seeing to the horse.

"It's going to be a grand wedding," Jock declared. "Nothing is too good for my little sister."

"Or for you," Marjorie retorted suddenly, and then lowered her head in what appeared to be contrition.

Something was going on between these two. Eden sensed Marjorie didn't want to marry Bert Carruthers, and if not, she didn't blame her. He was definitely not the type of man for a shy, self-effacing woman like Marjorie.

"Would you care to see my station?" Jock invited, ignoring his sister's outburst.

"That would be lovely," Eden said, realizing Marjorie wanted to be alone. Jock extended an arm to Eden and they left the dining room.

Marjorie waited until Nonnie, Tiku's mother, appeared and cleared the table. Then she stood up and went outside into the bright sunshine. Rain the day before had dampened the ground and the air smelled fresh. Though it was still warm, it wasn't unpleasant, and Marjorie smiled, not so much because of the weather but because she heard Tiku speaking to the horse. His deep, lyrical voice could still thrill her to her very core. As a child, she'd watched him in secret, wishing he'd see her as a human being and not as plain, crippled Marjorie Sutherland—the unapproachable child of the owner of High Winds.

Because of her infirmity, other children shied away from her. Her parents invited neighboring children and the children of local station owners to her birthday parties and other special occasions. They'd come with their parents out of a sense of duty and respect for the Sutherlands. But after a few polite words to her, the children would begin playing among themselves, not once asking her to join in. And because Marjorie felt unwanted, she'd sit on the sidelines and watch, her heart breaking to be so ignored.

The only friends she might have made would have been with the Maori children, the offspring of the servants at High Winds. She envied them their beautiful brown skin and healthy bodies, the way they'd scamper up trees like small monkeys, so free and happy. There were times she'd join in a bit and find herself laughing, pleased they allowed her to play. But then her mother would appear and haul her inside with a stern lecture not to associate with the "savages."

The odd thing was, Marjorie didn't consider them to be savages. They were kinder to her than the white children and more accepting of her deformity. They never said awful things about her behind her back as the neighbor children did. But there seemed to be no hope of ever making a friend until Nonnie came to work at High Winds with her son in tow.

Marjorie liked Tiku from the moment she first saw him. He was taller and smarter than the other children his age. His features were more European, his skin a dark shade of bronze. Marjorie learned he was the son of an English explorer but that his father had returned to England shortly after Tiku's birth. Sometimes when he was in the kitchen with his mother, he helped her prepare the meal. Marjorie would hobble in and sit speaking to Nonnie, but it was Tiku she wanted to see.

Sometimes he spoke to her, and a liquid warmth flowed through her at the sound of his voice. She liked him, in fact she thought she loved him. Nothing would make her happier than to believe he cared for her, too.

But one day she watched from the porch as the Maori children and Tiku began playing blindman's bluff. Tiku was chosen as the blind man and a kerchief had been wrapped around his eyes. The other children ran away to hide, leaving Tiku standing in the center of the lawn with arms outstretched, and Marjorie was left on the porch. She felt herself drawn to him, and in a moment of uncharacteristic daring, she limped forward, purposely putting herself in his path so he'd be forced to touch her.

Tiku grabbed her. A large, pleased smile split his lips because he believed her to be one of his playmates. She could still recall how wonderful it felt to have his powerful arms around her thin waist, how she wished to melt against him, to kiss him. But when he'd pulled off the blindfold, his triumph turned to horror to discover his captive wasn't one of the other little girls but tiny Marjorie Sutherland. She felt chilled to her very soul. "So sorry, Miss Marjorie," he'd exclaimed in dismay. "Sorry, so sorry."

He'd run away before she could call him back, to explain to him she wanted to play, too. As fate would have it, her father had seen what happened and he marched out of the house. His face, a face which looked so much like Jock's, had been red with fury. For the only time in her life, he slapped her and warned her never to play with the savages again. From that day on, she wasn't allowed outside when the Maori children were nearby.

But she'd never forgotten Tiku or his reaction to her. Even after he'd left High Winds and gone to school in England when his father sent for him, she thought about him. She knew he'd thought of her as a friend because each Christmas he sent her a letter, wishing her a happy holiday season. But she couldn't forget how appalled he'd been when he'd discovered it was she whom he'd snagged as the blind man that she always wondered if he might have sent the letters to appease his mother.

But that was years ago, and now she was grown and so was Tiku. When he returned from England, he'd taken employment at Thunder Mine and the only contact she had with him was when he visited his mother. But she'd never forgotten him, and she never would. She loved him with a quiet passion which deepened each time she saw him.

Struck by her own boldness, Marjorie hesitated for a second. Perhaps he wouldn't want to speak to her. He was so handsome dressed in a blue-and-white plaid shirt and black pants with his ebony hair blowing gently in the summer breeze that she felt plain and dowdy. Her gown was a dark-brown calico, and she guessed she resembled a scrawny wren. But she felt better when she saw Tiku's feet. He was shoeless, and she found herself giggling in relief because the boy she'd loved for so many years hadn't disappeared entirely.

"Hello, Tiku." She moved forward, hating her limp and the ugly cane which brought her to his side.

"Good afternoon, Miss Marjorie." He smiled at her, and it seemed almost as if he'd expected her.

"My brother is showing Mrs. Flynn around the station. I assume they'll be some time. Why don't you join me on the porch and have a glass of lemonade?" She almost bit her lip. Why had she asked him that? She'd only meant to speak to him, not invite him to sit on the porch with her. But the idea of sitting with Tiku in the shade seemed too wonderful to dare hope he'd accept.

For a few seconds she thought he was going to refuse her. He looked uncertain; his eyes perusing the landscape were wary and watchful. Then he flashed her the most beautiful white smile and said he'd be pleased to join her.

When Nonnie delivered the lemonade minutes later, Marjorie noticed her frown of disapproval. Nonnie considered Tiku to be a servant, but he wasn't Marjorie's servant so there was no reason he shouldn't have a cooling drink when he'd been waiting in the warm sun all morning long—and there was no telling when Jock would return with Eden.

"My mother is upset," he candidly admitted to Marjorie when his mother departed.

"If you'd rather not stay, I understand."

She attempted not to appear downcast, but her relief was so great when Tiku told her he wished to remain that Marjorie giggled.

Tiku grinned. "I like to hear you laugh. It is a very pretty sound."

Marjorie felt herself flushing. No man had ever paid her a direct compliment, not even Bert Carruthers, except to say he thought she was a fine woman, and that could have been said of many women. But for Tiku to like the sound of her laugh meant so much to her that she was speechless. Yet it seemed he didn't need a response from her and went on speaking about how nice a day it had turned out to be, though large clouds were gathering above the mountains, a sure sign of more rain.

She nervously twirled the cold glass between her hands. Usually she was composed, and now silently berated herself for acting like a silly young girl with her first suitor. She was definitely not young and Tiku wasn't a suitor.

They sat in silence watching the vast vista of green grass and purple-blue hills in the distance. Finally she felt Tiku's gaze upon her. When she looked at him, something in the darkness of his eyes knifed through to her heart. "My mother told me you're marrying Bert Carruthers on Boxing Day."

"Yes, yes, I am."

"Do you love him?"

If anyone else had dared to pry into her private life she'd have risen to her feet and left without a reply. But this was Tiku asking her a question she hated to answer. If only he knew the truth, he wouldn't look at her in such a way as to cause her agony. But why was he bothering to ask? Her answer could make no difference to him.

"I hope to . . . grow fond of him."

"Your brother is pushing for the marriage."

"Jock is doing what he believes is best for me." *And for himself.* "Mr. Carruthers is the only man who has asked for me and I must marry soon. I'm not getting younger. I want children."

"Then this is what you want to do."

It wasn't, but it was her only choice. "Yes."

Tiku rose from his chair at the same time as Marjorie and placed his glass on the small wrought-iron table which separated them. Their hands touched, hers so white and fragile, his so dark and strong. Tiku drew away first, almost as if he'd been burned by the contact.

He cleared his throat. "I trust you will be happy, Miss Marjorie." Then he went back to the buggy to wait for Eden.

* * *

119

High Winds, Eden discovered, consisted of much more than a house and outbuildings on a few acres. Until Jock showed her his land, she didn't have a clear idea of what a station was. Sitting next to him on the buckboard, he pointed to the distant purple hills, emerald valleys, and an endless sea of golden tussock grass. Fat, fluffy sheep nibbled their lunch on the side of a hillock under the watchful eyes of the stationhands on horseback. Three collie dogs ran hither and yon, barking orders to those errant sheep who attempted to leave the fold.

"This is just a portion of the sheep," Jock explained. "There are thousands more on the eastern slopes and plains of the station. During the shearing season when we muster them all together, it seems that all the clouds in the heavens have dropped to earth. All a person can see for miles is a blanket of white." The pride was evident in his voice, and Eden couldn't help but smile at him. She shouldn't like Jock Sutherland, not when Damon hated him so much. But no matter what he'd done to Damon in the past, he'd done nothing to harm *her*. Besides, she remembered Damon's comment about Jock controlling the water rights to the branch of the river which flowed past Thunder Mine. If he wanted to cut them off, he was within his legal rights to do so. Damon could be rude to Jock, but she wouldn't be. Not if Thunder Mine's survival depended upon gaining Sutherland's good will.

"I'm quite impressed," Eden told him, and meant it. "Not everyone could run such a large operation so efficiently. I also understand you're a member of Parliament. Do you go to Wellington often?"

"Every few months. Perhaps you'd consider accompanying me on my next trip. Wellington is an exciting city. You must get bored staying in the hinterlands after coming from a place as bustling as San Francisco."

"I haven't been here long enough to be bored," Eden admitted, purposely avoiding mention of her accompanying him to Wellington. "Most of what I've seen so far has been fascinating, however."

Jock appraised Eden out of the corner of his eye when her attention was diverted to one of the dogs as it rounded up a stray ewe. Bert Carruthers hadn't lied about her beauty or done her enough justice with his feeble compliments. Eden Flynn was a rare jewel, made all the more beautiful by the afternoon sun which shone upon her hair, forming a golden nimbus around her face. The white lace at the neckline of her blouse made her look soft and feminine, something Jock appreciated in a woman. But it was her figure, demurely covered by a pink jacket and divided skirt, which made his fingers itch.

He longed to cup her perfect, round breasts within his palms, to knead her buttocks while he held her body against his own. He wanted to kiss every part of her, to hear her beg for his possession. And, oh, what a sweet possession that would be. There wasn't a more beautiful and cultured woman in New Zealand than Eden Flynn. He didn't believe Carruthers's idiotic ravings about her working in a brothel. And even if she *had* been a whore, her past didn't matter to him. The future was what mattered. He had enough money to silence those who dared say anything against her. With a woman as lovely as Eden for his wife, and the governorship of New Zealand a distinct possibility, he'd have everything he'd ever wanted.

Not everything. He frowned and stroked the scar. He still needed to settle the score with Damon Alexander.

An hour later, the robin's-egg blue of the sky changed

121

to an opaque shade of gray. Thunder rumbled in the distance, disturbing the stillness of the summer afternoon. A brisk warm breeze whipped over them. Jock immediately headed back to the house, assuring Eden they'd make it before the threatened deluge. They did make it to High Winds, but only seconds after they were inside, the heavens, which had turned an ugly shade of purple, broke forth in a riotous assault of wind and rain.

"Goodness but you're both lucky to have made it back without getting a soaking." Marjorie lighted the oil lamps in the parlor and called to Nonnie to bring in the tea.

"I really should return to Thunder Mine. I hope this clears before dark," Eden worried.

"If not, you can spend the night. There's no point in hurrying back." Jock puffed on his pipe, seemingly convinced the matter was settled.

Marjorie readily agreed. "Don't worry, Eden. We have a perfectly nice guest room. Tiku will stay in the servants' wing. And I'm certain Mr. Alexander will understand if you don't return. He'll know you're in good hands." Her plain face brightened. "How nice it will be to have a guest!"

As it turned out, the summer gale didn't relent. The storm's ferocity increased as the hours passed. Eden grew edgy, though she couldn't think of a good reason for her apprehension. Damon wouldn't miss her, most certainly he didn't care about her. But still she worried he might think she had no intention of returning.

She silently berated herself for caring what Damon thought. Her affections, she knew, were misplaced, but that thought didn't stop her from wishing he cared about her, even a little.

Dining on a supper of roasted lamb and freshly cooked

vegetables, Eden was glad of Marjorie's company and found herself forgetting about Damon as Jock regaled her with hair-raising stories concerning his service during the Maori wars. She was enjoying her unplanned stay at High Winds and almost regretted when the clock in the parlor chimed the hour of nine.

Marjorie rose and beckoned to Eden. "Time to retire," she told her. Eden nodded, suddenly realizing that her day at High Winds had exhausted her. With Jock's arm placed solicitously around her waist, he walked with her to the stairs. Placing his hands on her shoulders, he gently kissed her forehead. "Thank you for a memorable day, Eden. I hope we'll be able to spend more time together in the future." His eyes were bright. Gleaming slivers of lust danced within their depths. Eden was taken aback. She liked Jock but hadn't anticipated his desire for her. She felt unnerved by it, which was silly. Damon had looked at her in such a way many times and she'd never been uneasy. In fact, if this had been Damon standing before her, she'd have expected him to sweep her into his powerful embrace and kiss her until she was breathless. Jock's gentlemanly peck left a great deal to be desired, and she knew she was being unfair by comparing the two men.

"Eden, your room is ready," Marjorie called from the upstairs landing.

"I'll see you in the morning," Jock assured her, and watched her go to her room.

After Marjorie helped settle Eden into the guest bedroom, she provided her with a plain white nightgown. "I hope you'll be comfortable. My room is next door if you need anything." She limped to the window, gazing out at the darkness, the rain lashing against the glass.

"The view of the mountains from here is quite enchanting, especially at dawn or twilight. I shall miss High Winds."

"You'll be perfectly happy in your new home." Eden made an attempt to reassure her. When Marjorie turned to face her, her cheeks were streaked with tears. "You don't want to marry Bert Carruthers, do you, Marjorie?"

Marjorie dabbed at her eyes. "No, I don't love him, but he's the only man who wants to marry me."

"Is that cause enough to marry someone you don't love?" Eden gently pulled Marjorie down beside her on the bed and looked at her in concern. "Does Jock know how you feel?"

"Jock's the one who initiated the whole thing. Mr. Carruthers would never have approached me, if not for Jock offering me to him like a lamb to the slaughter."

"I don't understand."

"Well, I do!" Marjorie's voice broke on a sob. "Jock is marrying me off to get Bert's land. Somehow he feels he can gain control through me." She grabbed Eden's hands in her own, her face contorted with pain. "Oh, Eden, please don't mention to Jock what I've told you and don't think unkindly of him. I love my brother, but sometimes I'm fearful of him. He wields so much power around here and in Wellington. He's a good man deep down, but he's changed over the years into a manipulative one." Her tears stopped, and hope suddenly shone within her eyes. "Perhaps if he has the love of a good woman, a woman like yourself, then he'll become the brother I knew as a child. I know I shall have to marry Bert, for he is my last chance at having my own home and children. I do owe Jock something for providing for me all these years, and in the end, maybe the marriage will turn out for the best. Wouldn't it be grand if you married Jock one day and we were related? I should like that ever so much!"

Eden mutely stared at Marjorie. She didn't know what to say or what to think. She pitied Marjorie for having to marry a man she didn't love, yet she understood why she felt forced to do it, and why Jock had arranged it. Some people would say she'd married Shamus for monetary gain, and they'd be partially right. She *had* married him for security but also out of genuine fondness. A deep love had blossomed between them, and in that she'd been lucky. But she doubted Marjorie would ever feel the same emotion for Bert Carruthers. Still, she'd learned long ago not to judge others, and she wouldn't judge Marjorie or Jock.

"I hope everything works out for the best for both of us," she whispered to Marjorie.

A pounding rain pummeled High Winds the rest of the night. In the morning, it abruptly stopped. Eden woke to the sudden silence, followed by a dazzling sunrise above the mountains, just as Marjorie had promised.

After a quick breakfast and a fond farewell to the Sutherlands, Eden joined Tiku in the buggy. A swift feeling of anticipation washed over her. It was time to go home.

Chapter 9

Eden had barely alighted from the buggy before Damon was upon her. "Where in hell have you been?" he demanded, his indigo gaze sweeping angrily over her.

"High Winds, of course" was her perfunctory answer as she took in his wet clothing and general disheveled state. "Tiku and I were forced to spend the night. We were quite safe. And please watch your language. Cursing isn't gentlemanly." She wasn't certain why she was behaving shrewishly when it was apparent that Damon had missed her.

"How was I to know you were safe?" he ranted on. "You could have been accosted by bushwackers for all I knew. Then I would have had to search for your bruised and broken body."

"As you can see, I'm fine. There was no reason to be worried. The Sutherlands took good care of me, and Tiku is an excellent protector." The knowledge that Damon cared enough to be worried about her warmed her.

After giving her a long look, Damon was satisfied nothing horrible had befallen her. In fact, Eden positively glowed this morning. Her cheeks were rosy, her eyes sparkled. Never had she looked more beautiful or more desirable to him. Then he remembered what she'd said about his being ungentlemanly, and his anger sparked anew. Of course she'd say such a thing after spending the night at High Winds in the company of the most gentlemanly specimen on the face of the earth. He couldn't compete with Jock Sutherland's polished charm, especially not this morning after he'd been up all night worrying about Eden and what might have happened to her. And then, while he waited in the cabin for her return, the roof had buckled under the storm's assault. The final straw to a miserable night.

He was a sodden, disgruntled mess with his clothes still wet and damned lucky not to have been injured, or killed, when the roof collapsed. The cabin was uninhabitable in its present state and Damon didn't intend to repair it. Certainly that would be the *gentlemanly* thing to do, but if Eden wanted a gentleman, let her hightail it back to High Winds. Maybe Sutherland was the reason she didn't look any the worse for wear this morning. Jealousy ate away at him.

"Aren't you going to ask how things are here?" he snapped. "Or don't you care now that you've slept in Sutherland's fancy house?"

"Yes, I care," she shot back. "And, Damon, why are you so wet?"

"I'll show you why!" With that, he grabbed her arm and yanked her across the yard to what remained of the cabin. "If you weren't so blinded by the gold dust in your eyes, you'd see that the roof has fallen in. I was lucky not to be killed."

"Oh, no!" Eden clamped her hands over her mouth.

The entire roof was gone; some pieces of it lay strewn around the dwelling and some inside. "My trunk and my things—"

"Are all safe. I was inside when the roof fell, but I rescued your precious trunk, at risk of life and limb, I might add."

So that was why he was so wet. He'd been waiting in the cabin for her when the roof caved in. He could have been killed. She'd been worried about her trunk because it contained all she owned, but now she forgot about it in her happiness to find him safe. No matter what he thought about her, she wanted him to know she cared. "Oh, Damon," she burst out, "I'm so grateful—"

"For saving your trunk?" he interrupted her. "God, woman, how shallow can one person be?"

"I . . . you don't understand. That's not what I meant."

"Aye, I know what you meant; you've said it often enough to me. I'm not a gentleman with fancy trappings and fine clothes like your friend Sutherland."

"I never said that," Eden protested.

"And I'm supposing High Winds impressed you." He scowled blackly at her, raising her own ire to be treated in such a disdainful way.

"Yes, it impressed me. High Winds is a grand house."

"Ah, then, Eden Flynn, it's a grand house you're wanting."

She placed her hands on her hips and shot him a look just as black but filled with defiance. "Yes."

Damon moved closer to her, his breath fanning the curve of her cheek. "Then it's a grand house you'll get."

He scooped her up into his arms as she pushed ineffectively against him. "What are you doing, Damon?

128

Put me down this instant."

"I'm going to show you something which puts High Winds to shame, Eden, love. I'm going to give you what you want." Damon lifted her onto his horse which waited nearby, then climbed up behind her. His arms folded around her when he took the reins to urge the animal into a furious gallop.

Raw fear shot through her. She didn't know what Damon was doing, why he was acting so strangely. She'd done nothing to warrant this rough treatment. And where were they going? She'd never been farther than the cabin or the miners' houses. Twisting around, she found that his gaze was focused straight ahead, blatantly ignoring her.

They followed an uphill road through an area rich with beech trees, exotic palms, and tree ferns. It was a wild and untamed paradise, the sky sometimes hidden beneath tangles of greenery overhead. Sweet and cloying scents mingled in the air. Colorful birds flew from tree to tree, chirping their annoyance at the sudden disturbance. When Damon's horse entered a clearing, Eden saw the white-pillared mansion on the hilltop.

A pleased and surprised gasp escaped from her. Never had she expected to find something so elegant and imposing in this wilderness. At first the house seemed out of place, but with the sun layering a golden sheen across its ivory facade, it blended in with the cloud-capped peaks of the distant mountains.

"Where are we?" she asked Damon when the horse skidded to a halt in front of the house. Her voice held awe, her eyes were large and wondering, glittering like the greenstone Damon thought they resembled.

Eden's little-girl innocence was getting to him again,

but he wouldn't allow his heart to soften. He purposely decided to sound hard. He needed to humiliate her for preferring Jock Sutherland over him, for not caring that he'd risked his life to save her possessions. Lowering himself off the horse, he pulled Eden with him. "It's Castlegate, my home."

She didn't have a chance to reply before Damon picked her up and carried her through the pillared terrace into a large and exquisitely furnished parlor. Placing her on her feet, he didn't miss the astonishment on her beautiful face as she took in her surroundings. Finally, after a careful consideration of the room, she gave a sudden, shuddering breath. "This is the house Shamus told me about. I wondered if he'd been delirious, but this is the house he said he'd helped build with his bare hands, not that shabby cabin I've lived in for the last week." Trembling with rage, Eden's eyes accused him. "This is where you've been taking most of your meals, isn't it?"

"Aye, it is." He leaned against the mantel above the fireplace, his own eyes wary, his expression guarded.

"Well, I have been a little fool. I felt selfish for not fixing supper for you when I cooked my own. Goodness but you must have had quite a laugh at my expense."

"That isn't true, Eden."

"Oh, really?" She walked around the room, examining objects, gently stroking the soft velvet on the back of a chair. "I'd say you've been living in grand style. Not that I begrudge you anything. I know what it's like to have nothing but the clothes on my back, to be at the mercy of strangers. But as hungry as those strangers were, they shared their food with me and offered me a roof over my head. But you provided me with shelter, too, didn't you, Damon? And a roof—I mustn't forget the roof. If I'd been sleeping in my bed last night, I might not be alive today.

"You placed me in a dirty hovel and let me clean the filthy place, make curtains for it, and all the time this was here." She opened her arms in an encompassing gesture, a sad smile turning up the edges of her mouth. "Will you do me the courtesy of explaining to me why you didn't tell me about Castlegate when I'm your uncle's widow? I had a right to know."

Damon lifted his brows in puzzlement. "Did you now? You think because you married Shamus that all he owned belonged to you?"

"I never said that."

"But that's what you were thinking."

"Damn you, I want an explanation!"

"Eden Flynn, you're cursing. Shame on you. How unladylike."

"Tell me!"

Damon let out a long sigh. "Shamus turned over Castlegate to me before he left for San Francisco. The house is mine. You have no claim to it."

Eden winced. It was just as she'd thought. Shamus had mentioned the house, but hadn't told her that he'd turned ownership over to Damon. Really, she didn't care about the house. What bothered her was Damon's assumption that if she'd known about it she would attempt to wrest it from him. He truly did believe the worst about her. But worse than being accused of gold-digging were the memories of the nights he'd slept on the other side of the blanket when he could have remained at Castlegate in comfort and luxury. Had he stayed with her out of a sense of duty to Shamus? To protect her? No, nothing as noble as that, she decided. Damon didn't care

131

enough about her to think of her needs. He'd wanted to protect his own interests—and bed her in the process. Yes, that was the only explanation for why he'd stayed in the cabin. He'd hoped to get lucky with the whorish widow and then send her on her way.

Stupid tears burned her eyes, and Damon floated before her in a haze. Even now, when the truth was out, when she realized how much he must want her gone from his life, she found him undeniably handsome. Indeed, she was a foolish woman, but no more would she fall prey to Damon Alexander's rakish charms. She'd already made up her mind what she was going to do.

Taking a deep breath, her breasts heaved with the effort. She attempted to steady her voice. "I don't want your home. However, I do have something *you* want. I've decided to turn over my share of Thunder Mine to you. The price you quoted me in Queenstown was very generous and I accept your offer. I'd appreciate your sending Tiku to help me get back to Queenstown as I'll be leaving immediately."

"So, you're quitting."

"Let's just say I made a mistake in coming to New Zealand. I shouldn't have left San Francisco."

"Will you be going back to LaRue's?"

She'd never considered that for a moment. As Shamus's widow, she was wealthy in her own right, but Damon didn't need to know her plans. In fact, she didn't really know them herself. She just knew that a lonely future stretched endlessly before her. "What I do is none of your business, Mr. Alexander." Eden began to tremble so violently, she knew she'd be unable to stay in the same room with him. Moving a few feet to the doorway, he surprised her when he blocked her way.

"Is this some sort of a ploy, Eden? Are you pretending to sell me your share just so I'll beg you to stay?"

This was too much for her. "You damned idiot," she hissed at him, the emerald fire in her eyes matching her temper. "I don't care if you beg me to stay. If you got on your knees and crawled after me until they were bloodied, I wouldn't stay. To be free of you and know a moment's peace again, I'll *give* you my share." She jabbed at the center of his chest with her index finger. "The whole world doesn't revolve around you and your precious mine. I'm sick of the two of you, sick to death of your nasty remarks about what you think I am. Well, mister, maybe I have some things to say about you, too, and they aren't pleasant. But I am a lady and I won't tell you how unfair you are, how totally aggravating and—"

His lips upon hers broke off her words and her train of thought. The heat of his kiss singed her mouth and sent shock waves of rampant desire through her entire body. Her heart sang at the intimate contact, but her mind cried out that this was wrong. He was toying with her, as he'd done from the very beginning, and she couldn't allow him to use her again, to have a laugh at the expense of her own pride or to let the cad know she loved him—which would be the most awful admission she could imagine.

"Ah, Eden, I love your fire," he whispered as his lips descended to the rapidly beating pulse at the base of her neck. "I love how you feel in my arms. I want you, I do."

"No, Damon. No." With tiny fists, she pushed against the broadness of his chest, but his arms locked around her waist and drew her nearer to him until she could barely think straight. No matter what had transpired with them moments before, Damon had the power to mesmerize her, to block the events from her mind. It was unfair that

133

he should use this power to overcome her weakness. "Stop it. Leave me be," she insisted. "I hate it when you do this to me."

"You know you love it." She heard the amusement in his voice and cursed aloud because it was true. "Ladies don't curse, love," he reminded her.

His hands wandered to her buttocks, expertly stroking the flesh beneath her skirt. She gave a strangled moan of pleasure, hating herself for enjoying her own weakness. "I . . . I'm leaving."

"Aye, Eden," he breathed as his hand came around to the front of her dress to fondle the spot between her thighs. "You're coming with me to the bedroom."

"No." She barely found the strength to protest.

"Aye, you are." His voice was so dangerously low, she barely heard him, but his sensuous stroking was so seductively stirring that she found herself unable to speak. Taking her silence for acquiescence, he picked her up and carried her down a marble hallway, entered a bedroom at the end, and kicked the door shut.

She found herself on a large four-poster bed with Damon lying next to her. He helped her shrug out of her jacket. "Such a prim outfit," he noted with a grin when he began to undo the many buttons on the front of her shirtwaist. "But you look damn alluring in it . . . though I prefer you without clothes."

Eden's mind whirled with the tantalizing sight of his bronzed hand upon the stark white material, skillfully opening the small pearl buttons. He groaned when his hands parted the cloth to encounter her erect nipples through her chemise. His thumbs touched them and made a swirling motion before lowering the chemise to her waist. Her upper body was bared to his lusty gaze.

134

Eden felt vulnerable and unsure. She attempted to cover herself with her hands, but Damon pulled them over her head, holding her wrists together.

"False modesty is a bit late at this stage." He smiled at her. "But if you like pretending, then I don't mind."

"I'm not pretending," she blurted out.

"Shh, love, let's not argue now." He soothed her with his lips. Anything she might have said died beneath the quivering desire which erupted anew within her. A part of her hated this power he wielded over her flesh, another part of her reveled in it. She should demand he cease his kisses, allow her to leave in peace. But she knew she'd never have any peace until Damon's possession quenched the burning ache that threatened to consume her.

Her mouth parted to receive his kiss, naturally accepting his tongue with not the slightest bit of repulsion. The time she'd spent at LaRue's hadn't all been spent in the office. Many times she'd taken meals with LaRue and the women who worked for her. Their talk had been unrestrained and very candid about what men and women did in bed together. Eden had tried not to appear shocked when they openly laughed at or praised a particular man's prowess. But she put aside her squeamishness to listen to them and discovered she was woefully ignorant about men in general. She was grateful for these conversations and thought herself totally prepared for what would happen when a man finally made love to her.

But she'd never expected the flames which licked at her insides now, the warm, melting sensation between her legs. She knew this mating was preordained, yes, she knew it now for sure, and nothing would stop their joining. No matter Damon's low opinion of her, she wanted him and would have him.

Her hands twisted within his grasp. She writhed when his lips began a downward descent to her breasts. Automatically she arched toward his mouth, yielding herself to him. She was more than willing to feel his mouth tugging upon her nipples, to be driven almost insane with her own desire as he suckled. And when she finally felt his warm lips upon her, she moaned with supreme pleasure.

Past thought, past caring what he might think, she whispered to him to undress. He moved away from her and began to remove his wet clothes. Her mouth grew dry as each piece of his clothing hit the floor. In the golden haze of the summer afternoon, he stood naked before her. She couldn't stop staring at him, convinced he was the most beautiful man in the entire world, incredibly and powerfully formed. His shoulders were broad, his arms and chest composed of corded muscles, his legs were long and strongly built. And then there was that part of his anatomy at which she took more than a cursory glance. It was large, hard and swollen with need. She shivered from fear but also with her own raw need.

"Damon." He came to her when she whispered to him, but she wasn't certain what she wanted to say.

But he didn't expect her to talk. Bending over her, he silently went about taking off her shoes and stockings, quickly followed by the remaining skirt and chemise.

Then their bodies came together like magnets. Something hot and liquid stirred through her. With each caress, each tantalizing sweep of his hands across her body, Eden matched him. She loved touching him, discovering what gave him pleasure. When he guided her hand to his pulsing shaft, she didn't draw away as she feared she'd do when the time came. In fact, she wanted to touch him there, to hear him moan when she stroked him. It was important to her to know intimately this part of him, this powerful, primitive part that was going to enter her body.

And Damon enjoyed her exploration, she could tell. But he grabbed her hand and smiled at her. "My turn now, my lovely."

He lowered her onto the bed until she was completely beneath him. His hand slid to the sensitive spot between her thighs. She was wet and slick and aroused. His fingers stroked her and then filled her. Eden gasped at the sweet, inundating fire, unprepared for the waves of pleasure which lapped at her. The women at LaRue's had never mentioned how wonderful it felt to be fondled like this. In fact, they never mentioned pleasure at all. Maybe they'd never experienced this side of lovemaking—not love like this. And she loved Damon, loved him with her whole heart and soul. If only he could love her some, if only . . .

"Eden." His breath was a ragged whisper against her mouth. "Open your legs for me." He stroked the inside of her thighs until she willingly and wantonly parted them for him. She was mesmerized by his handsome face, a ruggedly beautiful face, she thought. His desire was reflected in his eyes, and knowing he desired her caused Eden to feel more alive than she'd ever felt in her entire life. She watched his face when he lifted himself over her and poised to enter. She wanted to see his reaction when he discovered the truth for himself.

Eden flinched when Damon pushed into her, unprepared for the pressure. Her hands clung to his strong upper arms; her fingers dug into his flesh because she knew there was going to be pain and she steeled herself for it. He thrust again, this time more warily, and it was this emotion that flashed in his eyes as he came into contact with her maidenhead. "What in hell is this?" he burst out.

She nearly laughed aloud at his shock, but she wasn't about to let him withdraw from her. "Don't stop. It's all right. Please, please don't leave me." She kissed him with longing, with love, and Damon was lost.

"Hold tightly to me, Eden. I don't want to hurt you, I don't, but—"

"I know, Damon." Her body was on fire for him, and though she feared the pain, she was more afraid he might actually reconsider his intention. To make it easier for him, she wrapped her legs tightly around his buttocks and gripped his arms. Then with a quick intake of breath, she arched toward him, impaling herself upon his shaft so the thrust tore the fragile membrane. She couldn't help groaning and stiffening, almost willing herself to pull away. But Damon moved his hands to her buttocks, holding her close against him.

"It's all right," he murmured softly into her ear.

"But it hurts so. I never expected becoming a woman would be so painful."

"Trust me, love. It gets better." Damon kissed her and kneaded her buttocks until Eden soon forgot her pain. Something else was happening to her, and whatever it was, it was wonderful. Slowly, ever so slowly, Damon began to slide his length in and out of her, building a rhythmic rhapsody of pleasure so intense that Eden felt her own desire flare like wildfire within the core of her femininity.

She emitted tiny, mewling sounds, writhing beneath him and urging him to take her more deeply by gripping him tightly with her legs. His lust matched her own as he plunged into her again and again, ravishing her with his body and his eyes.

She didn't know how much longer she could stand this sensual torment, not certain what would happen at the end. It seemed they couldn't stop touching, kissing. Her movements grew more bold and daring as the seconds passed, his more intense, but gentle at the same time. It was when her body seemed to dissolve into molten lava, growing hotter with his every thrust, that the moment came, taking her unawares and sweeping her away into a star-filled universe.

Eden dug her fingernails into his arms, holding onto him when the ecstasy washed over her. The very center of her body throbbed with her total release. She buried her face on Damon's shoulder to muffle a lusty cry. He pulled her head up, entwining his hands within the depths of her hair, and gazed down at her. His eyes were such a bright burning blue, they resembled the tips of flames, but then they turned almost navy when he kissed her and groaned into her mouth. Damon shuddered atop her, and she felt the quick hot surge of his seed.

For what seemed like hours, Eden lay beneath him. She didn't move and couldn't get up the courage to speak. What could she say to him? *Thank you for a very pleasant deflowering, but now I must run?* And what must he think of her now that he knew the truth? He must have questions, so why didn't he just ask her instead of lying so quietly atop her?

Finally he turned on his side, not breaking their

joining. Eden's face went crimson to realize he was still somewhat erect. Hadn't she been woman enough for him?

Damon tipped her chin up and looked at her in such a heart-stirring way, the breath nearly died in her throat. "So, I'm your first," he remarked, and there was wonder in his tone.

"Yes" was all she could say, overcome by their lovemaking.

"I think you'd better explain about LaRue's and Shamus. My uncle was getting on in years, but he was a lusty fellow."

Eden sighed. "Oh, Damon, he was sicker than you realized. The last few months of his life he got weaker and weaker until he could barely lift his head off the pillow."

"Did you marry him knowing he was so sick?"

"Yes," she admitted sadly. "Shamus met me at LaRue's where I'd been working as a bookkeeper. He was so kind to me and we were both lonely. We grew to care about each other. When he asked me to marry him, he knew he was dying and needed someone he trusted to care for him. I wasn't certain I could do that, you know, marry someone I didn't love. But he said he needed me, though he made it clear that he couldn't be a husband to me. Our marriage was a sort of business arrangement at first." Tears gathered in her eyes. "He promised to leave me his money and a share in the mine if I'd marry him and take care of him. I agreed because I was fond of him and I needed security. You have no idea how frightened and lonely I've been since my parents died—since the Yankees . . ." Her voice broke.

Damon stroked her hair. "Life was hard for you."

Eden nodded. "But then I married Shamus and I began

to love him. He was so good to me, so considerate even when he was in pain. He loved you very much, Damon. His greatest disappointment was not being able to see you again."

"Ah, Shamus, Shamus." Damon kissed the top of her head. "So it was Shamus who wanted you to come to New Zealand."

"He insisted I come. Sometimes I think he meant to bring us together." Eden touched the hard wall of his chest and gazed up at him with dreamy eyes. "And I know I'm happy to be here."

"Then you won't be going away?"

"Not if you don't want me to leave."

"I've been a foolish man, Eden. I misjudged you and I'm sorry. I meant to get rid of you, to use you. Forgive me, please. And stay with me."

"Here, at Castlegate?"

"Aye, this is your home now."

He meant what he said, she could tell. For the first time since the war's end, she felt she belonged to a place, to someone who loved her. Damon hadn't said the words, but she knew he did love her. He had to love her, otherwise he wouldn't want her to stay with him in his home. She felt certain he'd soon confide in her about Tessa, that he'd proclaim his love and ask her to marry him.

Eden wrapped her arms around his neck. "I can't think of anywhere else I'd rather be."

He shot her a devilish grin, but there was pain in his eyes when he said, "Even High Winds?"

"Aye," she parroted his Irish accent. "There's no one like you at High Winds."

His sudden and earth-shattering kiss stirred up the

141

vestiges of their earlier passion. His manhood sprang to life within her, igniting the flames once more. When he began thrusting, she was more than eager for him.

Later, right before she fell asleep in Damon's arms, she knew without a doubt that there was no one like Damon Alexander at High Winds or on the face of the earth. He was special, and he was hers.

And no one would take him from her, not even the ghost of a long-dead wife.

Chapter 10

Damon swallowed his pride and galloped across High Winds. Only a few more weeks were left until the water rights had to be renegotiated. He cursed under his breath. Sutherland hadn't approached him yet, and he surmised the man was playing a waiting game. He, too, could play games if he chose to do so, but what was the point? The rights to that branch of the Shotover were too important to him and the men he employed. Without Sutherland's agreement, Thunder Mine was doomed and the men out of their jobs. Damon couldn't let that happen. Whatever his personal feelings concerning Jock Sutherland, he had to appease him today, or at least give the impression of appeasement.

He'd been to the house, and Marjorie had told him he could find Jock on the range helping to muster the sheep, and that's exactly where Damon found him. Jock sat on his horse, in the midst of hundreds of sheep, and directed the stationhands in their work. When he noticed Damon approaching, he became perfectly still.

"I'd appreciate a word with you, Sutherland."

"As you can see, I'm occupied. I'm certain whatever it is can wait until another time."

"No, it can't," Damon persisted. "I need to speak to you about the water rights."

"Is that up for renewal again?" Jock asked innocently, a malevolent twinkle dancing in his eyes. "How quickly the time passes." Jock smirked and turned his horse away from the mustering activity. Damon followed, and soon they stopped at a quieter spot. Both men dismounted.

"What's your decision concerning the water rights?" Damon asked, deciding it wouldn't do any good to beat around the bush with polite conversation.

Jock stroked his chin. "I haven't reached a decision yet, but I'll certainly tell you when the time arrives."

"There's barely a month left. I have men with families working for me. They're anxious to know what's going to happen."

"We all have families," Jock reminded him. "I really haven't given your situation much thought right now, not with planning my sister's wedding to Bert Carruthers. But when the hubbub is over and the time draws nearer, I'll start mulling over this water-rights problem."

"Come on, Sutherland, you know damn well what you plan to do. Every two years we play this cat-and-mouse game, and always we negotiate at the last minute. Just sign the bloody papers so I can tell my men Thunder Mine is safe."

Jock grinned a bit too broadly for Damon's liking. Damn Sutherland! The arrogant bastard always forced him to lose his temper while Sutherland himself never raised his voice.

"You must learn not to be so volatile," Jock advised, touching his scarred cheek. "I really do owe you some-

144

thing for this."

"Then settle accounts some other way, not with my men's livelihoods."

"Exactly what I intend, Alexander."

Damon breathed deeply, his hatred for Sutherland all too visible on his face. "I'm to assume your sister's marriage to my neighbor has something to do with evening the score."

Jock inclined his head. "Maybe, maybe not. You'll just have to wait and find out. I do so like keeping you on your toes." He lifted himself into his saddle. "How is Eden?"

"Fine."

"I'm glad. We spent an enjoyable time that night she was unable to return home. She's a true lady, unlike some women I could name."

Damon grimaced and heaved himself onto his horse. "Don't be getting ideas about her, Sutherland. Eden belongs to me."

"Does she now? Then I assume a marriage is in the offing. After all, you've been a *widower* for quite some time."

"Leave Eden alone," Damon warned. "She belongs to me," he reiterated.

"I truly wonder about that. She doesn't strike me as the sort of woman who would want a man who wasn't well educated. Certainly she'd never consider marrying beneath her station. She's not like our beloved, departed Tessa who could barely sign her name and knew nothing of proper behavior. So, where does that leave you, Alexander?" Jock proudly lifted his head, and every bit of his aristocratic lineage showed in his bearing. "Marjorie and I are inviting Eden to High Winds for the wedding. You, too, of course. I believe that once Eden sees me in my element as master of High Winds, she'll make the proper choice between us. Now I must get back to my sheep. Good day, Alexander."

How Damon hated him! He longed to fling the arrogant son of a bitch from his horse and pummel his patrician face to a bloody mess. He hated Sutherland for all the opportunities he'd had—the fine education, the aristocratic background, the way people jumped to serve him. But he hated him more because he was right. If given the choice between the two of them, he worried Eden would choose Jock.

Eden. Eden. Eden. His heart thumped out her name. He'd never known a woman like her. His blood fired to think of the way he'd left her that morning. She'd been asleep in his bed with the covers twisted around her uncovered voluptuous body. He'd wanted to make love to her again, but he feared he had worn her out the night before. They hadn't fallen asleep until dawn streaked the sky.

He couldn't wait to return to Thunder Mine and claim her as his. Just imagining her kisses and her beautiful, smiling face were enough to spur him home again. Thinking about her waiting for him lightened his dark mood. She'd totally surprised him by being a virgin. He loved that he'd been her first man—and her last, if he had anything to do with the decision. But he feared he didn't . . .

There was Jock Sutherland in the background. He had wanted Tessa years ago, but Damon had fought him and won her as his bride. And now there was Eden, a woman unlike Tessa in every way, but a woman who was used to life's finer amenities. She longed for respectability and security. Things which Sutherland could give her.

146

Things which Damon couldn't.

"Damn it all to hell!" he swore, galloping swiftly across the countryside. He was worrying for nothing. Eden was in his bed, not Sutherland's. And when he got home, he'd love her until she was so completely satiated that she'd never give Jock Sutherland an extra look. Damon knew he excelled in the bedroom. Sex had nothing to do wth fancy schools and manners or respectability. When naked, they were simply a man and a woman taking pleasure in each other's bodies. He would make sure his prowess would keep her with him. It was all he had to offer her.

"Is something troubling you, Marjorie?" Jock sipped a brandy while Marjorie drank her tea.

She looked at him from where she sat on the porch. The fading light shadowed her face. "I had guests for tea this afternoon. You remember I told you that Mrs. Kensington and her niece were stopping by."

Jock remembered them. They were both prune-faced busy bodies. "Yes, you mentioned that to me yesterday."

"I'm rather worried about what they told me. Shocked, too, though I can't believe this gossip about Eden is true."

"What did they say about Eden?" Jock was on the alert, his body stiffened.

Marjorie hesitated a moment and then waved a dismissing hand in the air. "Oh, they're spreading this dreadful gossip about Eden and Mr. Alexander. One of the servants at Thunder Mine is a cousin to Mrs. Kensington's butler, and the rumor is that Eden is living openly with Mr. Alexander—not just inhabiting the

147

house as a guest, but goodness knows I can't believe she's sharing the man's bed, too."

Jock's blood ran cold. He hadn't expected news of this nature. Oh, he knew Damon wanted Eden, and perhaps guessed that she was attracted to the brawny ape, but to be sleeping with him? If that were the case, then things were clearly progressing too quickly for his liking. "It's just servants gossiping, Marjorie. Don't take it all so seriously," he told her, pretending he found the rumor to be absurd. But it stung a great deal to believe Eden preferred Damon over himself. He'd been through this dilemma once before and was growing damned tired of Alexander besting him.

"But, Jock," Marjorie continued, her eyes shining, "Eden must be warned about what people are saying. I should tell her."

"No, you mustn't do that. You shouldn't get involved. Remember, my dear, we have a reputation to uphold in this community. Besides, I doubt the rumor is true, and it would never do to tell Eden what's being said behind her back. She'd be truly hurt if you told her and might not consider you her friend."

Marjorie thought that over for a few minutes. "Yes, I suppose you're right. But what if she hears this awful gossip from someone else? Really, I should do something."

"Believe me, she'll appreciate your silence. And if she hears this from another person, then so be it. At least you won't be involved." And neither would he. If he knew Mrs. Kensington and that niece of hers well enough, then the scandalous news would be spread throughout the countryside before the week was out. He believed he knew enough about Eden to realize she wouldn't take kindly to the gossip but would demand Damon do the honorable thing by her.

And Jock knew Damon wouldn't do that.

A lingering smile curved his lips. Soon he'd have Eden where he wanted her—in his bed as his wife. He'd simply leave all to the town gossips.

Marjorie's groan disturbed his pleasant thoughts. Immediately he saw what caused his sister such distress. It was none other than Bert Carruthers behind the reins of his buggy. "Be sweet, Marjorie," Jock advised. "Your fiancé is here and it looks like you might be in for a moonlit buggy ride tonight."

"I'd rather swallow castor oil," she hissed at Jock.

"You can always call off the wedding . . . but remember what will happen to a certain person if you do."

Even with her sitting in the shadows, Jock saw Marjorie tense and knew he'd driven home his warning. Moments later he sent a beaming smile her way and graciously extended his hand to Bert.

Yes, Jock decided after Bert swept Marjorie away for a romantic ride, things were going well for the present, and they'd continue that way. All he had to do was wait.

Chapter 11

Eden had never been happier in her entire life. Damon, of course, was the reason for this newfound contentment. For the first time in years she felt she truly belonged, that the nagging insecurity which had plagued her was a thing of the past. Though Damon hadn't confessed his love for her, it was impossible not to believe he didn't love her. Each time he touched her, kissed her, or took her to bed, he gave of himself in more ways than just the physical. Their bond was emotional and mental, spiritual, too, though she knew Damon would have laughed if she'd told him she thought him spiritual.

Having accepted all these things about their relationship, Eden waited for the moment he'd tell her about Tessa. He knew all about her past, and accordingly she expected to know his. But the days passed and Damon didn't mention his late wife. Were the memories too painful for him? Had he loved Tessa so much that just to speak her name would have been unbearable? Eden didn't begrudge him the life he'd shared with Tessa, but she worried that Tessa's memory was interfering with the start of a new life for herself and Damon. She wanted to hear him tell her that he loved her. She wanted to be his wife. As long as Damon clung to his private pain, there could be no beginning for them.

They were in town one balmy afternoon, having just eaten at the restaurant where Joanie worked. Nick was staying upstairs, and to Damon's amazement, Nick was helping to run the establishment.

"You're giving up prospecting?" Damon asked Nick when he joined them at the table.

Nick nodded. "Aye, I have. I thought it was about time I started settling down." He shot a furtive glance in Joanie's direction as she waited on another table. "I like it here, I do."

Damon grunted. "I never thought you'd give up looking for gold."

"Well, maybe I've found something better than gold, something more lasting."

Damon didn't immediately understand what Nick meant, but Eden wasn't the least bit surprised when Joanie came over and Nick, beaming with joy, held out Joanie's hand for their inspection. She wore a ring with a small sapphire stone on her third finger. "We're getting married," he proudly announced, and Joanie blushed a becoming shade of pink.

Eden congratulated the happy couple, the three of them waiting expectantly for Damon's good wishes. But Damon sat there in stony silence. "Damon, aren't you going to wish us well?" Nick asked, growing uncomfortable but holding tightly to Joanie's hand.

"No."

"Damon!" Eden's exclamation slipped out, shocked that he'd purposely be rude to his friend.

"And why is that?" This question was posed by Nick whose tenseness was transferred to Joanie. She moved her hand away, a crestfallen expression on her pretty face.

"Don't make me say it, Nick."

"Aye, man, go on. Tell me why you can't wish me and my Joanie good luck."

"Nick, please don't," Joanie pleaded.

"Aye, I want Damon to tell me."

Damon's expression darkened with an unreadable emotion, his voice was low. "A man who marries is a fool, Nick. Joanie, as pretty and sweet as she is, is much too young for you. You're asking for heartache by marrying her. What's to prevent her from running off with a young fellow one day? And you'll be left a bitter and broken man. I can't give my congratulations."

Joanie let out a little cry and fled from the room. Nick stood up, the veins in his neck bulging with his anger. He balled his hands into fists. "If you weren't my friend, I'd bash your head in for what you've just done to my Joanie. Aye, I admit I'm older than she is, a great deal older, but I love her, man. And she loves me. That's all I can ask for the moment. And if by chance she one day runs off with a younger man—a richer man—then so be it. But I'll be damned if I become like you. You're the bitter, lonely man, Damon, not me." He leaned toward his friend, his words intended for Damon alone, though Eden heard them. "You can't make a new life for yourself, you're too frightened of being hurt again. You nurse old wounds because you want to, and you don't want anyone else to be happy. You have the opportunity to start over and you'd better do something about it, otherwise you're going to lose your chance." Nick directed a look at Eden. "There's a fine woman sitting next to you. Do the decent thing and make an honest woman of her. People are talking, you know." With that, Nick left them.

Eden felt her face flaming, unable even to glance at Damon who sat for a few moments in moody silence. Finally, he told her it was time they started for home.

Nothing was said during the return trip, but Eden's mind whirled with Nick's words. The man was right. Damon must put the past behind him, accept Tessa's death. He'd be so much happier if he could begin to live in the present and realize what a wonderful life they could have together.

And now it seemed people were talking about her living arrangements with Damon. Nick hadn't said that directly, but that was what he'd meant. If Damon cared for her, even a tiny bit, he wouldn't allow her to be hurt by cruel gossip. They'd recently attended church services, and now that Eden thought about it, she realized some of the people who'd been so warm and friendly the time before had been distant and cool this time. Jock and Marjorie Sutherland had been there. Jock, always the gentleman, had complimented her dress, but she'd been so caught up in her thoughts and feelings for Damon that she'd paid little attention to him. But it was Marjorie who had sent her a warning glance and said a bit too crisply, "Living at Thunder Mine is no place for a lady, Eden. Really, you should consider moving someplace else."

Marjorie had clearly learned about her living arrangements with Damon. She knew Marjorie hadn't meant to be unkind, that she wished to spare her embarrassment by warning her to think of living elsewhere. And Marjorie

153

was right. She shouldn't be sharing a house, a bed, with Damon. It wasn't right or proper. If he cared for her, he should want to save her reputation.

She didn't want to push him into a hasty decision, but she had to know where she stood with him.

Eden followed him into the house and then into the bedroom. She loved this bedroom with its magnificent view of the valley and the mountains. Each morning she awoke to a multicolored dawn lying in Damon's arms. He was so tender and gentle, so passionate in their lovemaking. She adored him. But now he eyed her, his face granite hard as he sat upon the bed.

"Come here," he demanded, and held out an arm to her. Eden sat beside him, finding herself nestled within the depths of his embrace. He still wanted her, a good sign, she decided.

Damon began kissing her roughly, pushing her down upon the bed. His hands were everywhere upon her, but instead of arousing her, she felt fear. She noticed his eyes were wide open, but it was almost as if he weren't seeing her but someone else. And her heart flipflopped to think he might be imagining Tessa.

"Stop, Damon. You're too rough." Eden pushed at him, breaking away from his kiss.

His eyes were hooded. "Don't push away from me, Eden. Never push away from me." Once again he captured her lips, but his kiss bruised her mouth. This wasn't the Damon she'd come to love, but a stranger, a man she didn't know, a man she was suddenly afraid of.

"Da-mon." She broke away. "What wrong with you? You're scaring me."

"Ah, Eden, give over. I'm not in the mood for a gentle wooing of you today. Come on, open your legs for me. I

154

want to bury myself inside you." He started kissing her neck and lifting her skirt at the same time. His hand snaked up her leg to the downy junction between her thighs, already probing inside her and readying her with her own juices.

There was something frantic and frightening about his efforts. It was as if he didn't care about her at all. She wasn't aroused; this was nothing like the other times they'd made love. Then, she'd felt loved and wanted for herself. Now she felt almost degraded, almost like Damon's whore.

And that was what she was.

The truth hit her and stung her with such force that she groaned aloud. Damon was treating her like a whore, because he thought of her as one, even though he'd taken her as a virgin. He had a willing woman to bed whenever the whim hit him. He wasn't married to her, hadn't promised her anything, but allowed her to live in his fancy house and share his big, soft bed. She eagerly came to him whenever he wanted her. So, in Damon's eyes, she was no better than his personal whore. And a man didn't marry a whore.

"We have to talk," she gasped when his mouth moved away from hers.

"I don't want to talk, I want to . . ." and he whispered in her ear what he wanted to do. Eden colored furiously, not because she hadn't heard the word before, but because it sounded so coarse, so callow—the way a man would speak to a whore.

She began pushing at him, her legs tangling with his. But he was far stronger than she was, and her frustrated efforts caused her to sob. "Let me go, Damon. Let me alone!"

155

It seemed that for the first time he really heard her. Thwarted desire shone in his eyes. "What's wrong, Eden?"

"You're being too rough. I don't want to make love now."

"Oh, aren't I being gentlemanly enough for you? I saw you talking to Gentleman Jock after services this morning."

"Stop being ridiculous and get off me! I want to talk to you."

Seeing he was getting nowhere, Damon lifted his weight from her. Eden scooted away from him, risking his black look. "Talk," he gruffly commanded.

"You insulted Nick and Joanie. I think you should apologize."

He shrugged. "Fine, I'll do that."

"But you still believe he's a fool for marrying her, though he loves her and she loves him."

"Good for both of them. What now?"

He stood up, his back turned to her. The fact that she didn't have to look directly at him boosted her courage. "Damon, what am I to you?"

She saw him stiffen, and she sensed he immediately knew the direction her question was headed. "What do you *think* you are?"

Eden didn't like her question thrown back in her face, but more than that, he hadn't answered her. But she was going to be honest with him, even if he wouldn't be the same with her. "Nick said people were talking about us. I don't like being the subject of gossip."

"Don't worry about gossipers. You know you're not doing anything wrong."

"But I am, Damon, though I'm living with you because

I love you."

"And you're ashamed of loving me."

"No, I'm not. Will you look at me, please? I hate talking to your back." Damon faced her, and there was something so resigned in the gesture that her heart twisted. He stared at her with an implacable expression, almost as if he were a statue. She clutched her hands in her lap and squeezed the fingers together. Her face was open and beguilingly beautiful. "I love you as I never thought I could love another person," she candidly admitted. "I want to know if you love me."

"You know how I feel about you, Eden. I shouldn't have to tell you." He winked at her. "Don't I show you in bed how I feel?"

She rose to her knees. "I recall seeing you with a whore at the Greenstone Hotel not too long ago. I suppose you touched her and kissed her, too. Am I to assume you consider me to be like her? Am I your whore, Damon?" Her voice rose higher with each word.

Grabbing her by her shoulders, he looked down at her anguished face. "You're my woman, Eden. You know I care about you, so stop it!"

"I don't want to be your *woman!*" she shouted at him. "I want to be your *wife!* I want you to tell me that you love me."

Damon shook his head. "I can't."

She nearly choked on her own sob. It was true. Damon didn't love her, he'd never marry her. "Let's go on as we've been doing," she heard him say. "We don't need to be married to prove anything to anybody."

But you must prove something to me, she thought miserably. He let her go, apparently deciding that the issue was settled. But as far as Eden was concerned, it

157

wasn't. "Damon, is the reason you don't want to marry me, the reason you can't admit you might love me—is it because of Tessa?"

Damon stood watching her in amazement for what seemed like a very long time. Then he wrapped a large, powerful hand around the bedpost and squeezed it. "Who told you about Tessa? Was it Jock?"

"No. Miranda Creig mentioned her. Why didn't you tell me about your wife . . . her death? I would have understood."

"No, you wouldn't have understood."

"Then tell me about her. Make me understand."

"No."

"Damon, please . . ."

He scalded her with his fury. "I never speak about Tessa to anyone—especially never to you, Eden. Not to you! Just leave it alone. I can't bear your prying or your tears. Either be satisfied with what I've offered you or—"

"Or *what?* You've treated me like a whore, don't care a damn what people say about me, so then I should leave Castlegate. Is that what you're telling me? Is that what you want? You want to be free of me?"

"Do what you have to do, Eden. You will anyway."

Damon seemed resigned that she would leave him, and it was true, she couldn't stay here now, not when she knew how much he still loved a dead woman, not when she knew that in his eyes she was only as good as a whore.

As she got off the bed, she was shaking so badly she stumbled. Damon reached out and steadied her, not taking his eyes from her face. His arm around her waist clutched her to him, and she ached to stay there forever. But she couldn't. He didn't love her.

158

"Let me go," she whispered hoarsely, wiping away the tears which spilled onto her cheeks.

He released her. "Where are you going?"

"I don't know, but I've changed my mind—I'm not giving up my share in the mine. Shamus wanted me to have that."

"Aye, he did."

She turned away from him and rang for one of the servants to help pack her clothes. Within the hour she was ready and Tiku was driving her into town. She never knew that Damon stood on the road and watched until the buggy disappeared from view.

Chapter 12

Eden took a room at one of the more fashionable hotels at Skipper's Canyon. Her new residence included a nicely furnished sitting room and a bedroom whose cheery yellow-and-white wallpaper did little to lift her spirits. She was miserable without Damon, hopelessly in love with him. But she foresaw no future with him, not if he couldn't tell her he loved her and intended to marry her.

She meant what she'd told him about the mine. Part of it belonged to her, and she intended to consult Damon on its operation in time. The thought of seeing him now, so soon after her departure from Castlegate, tore at her heart. Eventually, after she'd put time and distance between them, she'd return to Thunder Mine. Perhaps then she'd be able to speak to him without breaking into a gale of tears as she was presently doing when a knock sounded on her door.

Dabbing at her eyes with a handkerchief, she opened the door to Jock and Marjorie. Inwardly she groaned. She wasn't up to company now; she looked a horror with her eyes all red and swollen, her cheeks streaked with tears.

But she managed a weak smile and invited them inside.

Marjorie placed her cane beside her on the sofa and removed her gloves. Jock sat across from Eden, his smile soft and filled with pity. Evidently they must have an inkling of what had happened between herself and Damon, Eden thought. She flushed and presented a brave facade, not wanting or needing anyone's sympathy.

"We've rented rooms in this hotel and wondered how you were doing," Marjorie revealed. "Tiku dropped by to visit his mother, and it was through him we learned you'd left Thunder Mine." She patted Eden's hand affectionately. "You did the right thing by leaving. A mining operation is no place for a lady like yourself, Eden."

Eden straightened, maintaining her dignity under Marjorie's well-meaning scrutiny. She wanted to tell Marjorie that her place was wherever she wished, but she guarded her tongue. Marjorie had been protected all her life, sheltered from reality. She would never understand why Eden had gone to Thunder Mine in the first place and probably would have little inkling as to why she intended to keep her share in the mine. And as far as her love for Damon Alexander, Marjorie would never understand that either. Then, remembering the amenities, she offered them tea, pleased that Jock didn't feel the need to say anything.

"No tea," Jock proclaimed, and stood up to take Eden by the arm. "We've got shopping to do and you're coming with us."

"What?"

"Yes," Marjorie instantly exclaimed, grinning broadly. "I want you to come with me to the dressmaker's so I can choose a wedding gown. I do so admire your taste in clothes, Eden, and would appreciate your help in picking my trousseau. And I'd be most honored if you'd consent to stand up with me. Jock is Bert's best man and you're the only person I'd consider for a maid of honor. Please say you'll agree, please."

Marjorie's pleas and Jock's insistent tug on her arm left Eden no choice but to agree. She couldn't see any reason not to help Marjorie with her trousseau or to refuse her invitation as the young woman's maid of honor. The wedding would take her mind off Damon.

For the first time in days, Eden laughed. "Let me get myself together," she begged them.

"You look beautiful," Jock whispered in all sincerity.

She thought she looked wretched, but Jock's heartfelt compliment buoyed up her spirits.

Perhaps life wasn't so awful after all.

The gown that Marjorie chose was a light shade of pink, edged with white lace on the high neckline and long sleeves, a dainty cluster of roses on the bustle. Eden knew Marjorie would look lovely in the color and that the gown's design would cause her figure to appear fuller. They discovered how much fun it was to ooh and aah over the sheer lace undergarments the dressmaker showed for their approval, to touch the silk chemises and pantalets. But in the end, the ever-practical Marjorie ordered two cotton slips, one pantalet, devoid of decoration, and a blue nightgown which would show little more than her face.

"We're shopping for your trousseau," Eden reminded her. "You must buy something frilly and lacy and very feminine."

"Why?" Marjorie turned her attention from a gray

162

serge skirt she was inspecting.

Eden spoke to her in a whisper so the dressmaker and her assistant wouldn't hear. "Because your groom will expect you to wear something special on your wedding night."

Marjorie's cheeks paled. "I didn't realize. What . . . what do you suggest?"

"Choose whatever you like," Eden offered. "I'll make a present of it to you."

"Oh, Eden, I don't know what Bert would prefer. I've never ever thought about this."

Eden thought Marjorie was going to faint and led her to a sofa. From the window behind them, Jock was visible as he waited outside. "Should I call Jock to take you back to your rooms? You look ill."

"No, no." Marjorie took a deep breath and the color, little that there was, seeped slowly back into her face. "I'll be all right in a few minutes." She smiled sadly, her gaze fixed on the floor. "I'm a pitiful example of womanhood, aren't I?"

"Don't be silly. You're having an attack of nerves. All brides do."

"But not all brides are marrying a man whom they don't love." She lifted her gaze to Eden's and clutched frantically at her hand. "I don't believe I can abide being married to Mr. Carruthers. The thought of living in the same house with him is awful to consider, but . . . but I can't even think about—that other part." A shiver wracked her slender frame.

Eden pitied her. She couldn't imagine being intimate with someone she didn't love. "You've been married, Eden," Marjorie noted, and swallowed painfully. "Is that other part so very dreadful?"

How could she tell Marjorie that the very act she feared was wonderful and totally earth-shattering, but that the man who had possessed her body and soul hadn't been her husband? She doubted Marjorie would understand or forgive such a transgression, yet she had to put her friend's mind at ease. "Making love is quite natural and really very nice. Please don't worry. Everything will be fine, just wait and see." She gave Marjorie an affectionate squeeze. "Now choose something frilly and expensive and let's have lunch. I believe Jock's growing impatient."

Marjorie nodded and chose a sheer, lacy chemise of pale ivory. Soon they joined Jock but Marjorie begged off from lunch, declaring the heat had caused her to feel ill. She insisted that Eden and Jock dine without her; she would return to her room at the hotel.

Much to Eden's chagrin, Jock chose to eat at the restaurant where Joanie and Nick worked. She felt ill at ease for Nick to find her with Jock Sutherland, but he didn't say anything untoward to her, and Joanie was her usual polite and friendly self.

"You're upset because I brought you here," Jock noted, his eyes not leaving her face.

"No I'm not."

A smile appeared beneath his mustache. "You're a very poor liar. You're worried that Mr. Patterson will think less of you for being with me. But you're also upset that he'll tell Damon, which is exactly why I chose this restaurant. I want word of our luncheon to reach Damon's ears. Then he'll know I'm in serious competition for your affections." He sipped his sherry.

Jock's bluntness caught her off guard. "I had no idea I was some sort of a prize in a contest."

"You are, my dear, and you'd better get used to the idea of my winning you. I assure you my intentions are quite honorable where you're concerned. I want to marry you."

"Marry me?"

"Don't look so stunned." Jock grinned, and Eden realized he was really a handsome man—not incredibly handsome as Damon, but good-looking in his own right. "You must realize how I feel, how I've wanted you from the first moment I saw you."

"I didn't," she admitted, overwhelmed. "But I'd rather you *asked* to marry me. I don't like being told you intend to marry me."

"All right, then. Will you marry me?"

Eden's head swam. Jock Sutherland was proposing to her, here in a public place. It wasn't the most romantic of marriage proposals, she supposed, but it was a proposal all the some. If this man had been Damon asking to marry her, she'd have thrown her arms around him and immediately answered yes. But this wasn't Damon. And she didn't love Jock Sutherland. He hadn't even kissed her, but he wanted to marry her. This marriage proposal was all very sudden and baffling. Did Jock want to marry her because he loved her or was this a way of settling things with Damon because of a long-ago feud over Tessa Alexander? Eden wasn't certain about Jock's motives and she didn't have to accept him. There was no reason in the world to be saddled with a man whom she didn't love. She was wealthy and didn't need the security of marriage any longer.

"I've been married, Jock, and widowed. I'm not ready to commit to a relationship as permanent as marriage now."

A nerve jumped near his right eye. For a moment his affable, hopeful expression darkened, but in an instant he was smiling at her. "I'm not giving up, Eden. I always get what I want." He lifted his glass to her in a toast.

Damon would apologize to Nick and Joanie. He'd stupidly caused a rift with his old friend and must make things right again. He'd walk into the restaurant, say he was sorry for what he'd said, and wish them well. Granted, he didn't mean the apology, still believing Joanie would make Nick unhappy. Damon hadn't met a happily married man yet, but if lying meant he'd gain Nick's friendship, he'd do it.

And then he'd see Eden. Tiku told him where Eden was staying, and he'd decided he'd try to win her back. He missed her like hell, wishing to believe the very reason he missed her had nothing to do with loving her. Love was an emotion he couldn't feel any longer, having inwardly turned to stone when he'd lost Tessa. But he needed to feel Eden's soft, warm body against his again. His large bed at Castlegate was cold and empty without her.

He felt certain he could convince her to return home with him that day because she loved him. And it was this knowledge which caused him to whistle as he entered the restaurant.

As luck would have it, Nick was standing in the foyer looking into the large dining room where a number of patrons were eating lunch. He turned at Damon's voice seeming to be pleased to see him, but a panicked expression instantaneously overrode his delight. "I apologize for what I said to you and Joanie . . ." Damon began, not understanding why Nick was steering him away from the doorway.

"Aye, Damon, I'm sorry, too, for my angry words. All is forgiven, lad. Now let's go into the kitchen and I'll pour you a shot of the finest whiskey we have. Goes down your throat like silk."

"I'd like to apologize to Joanie first."

"She's got customers. I'll tell her what you said."

"Well, can I get some service here?" Damon laughed. "I'm hungry."

"The kitchen, lad. I'll fix you something there." Nick pulled at Damon, practically dragging him away, but Damon's gaze wandered for a second into the dining room and he halted in midstride, rooted to the spot. Nick sighed. "I was hoping you wouldn't see them."

But he *did* see them. Eden sat much too close to Jock at a corner table, looking much too beautiful and completely unaffected by her departure from Castlegate. A pretty smile lit up her face as Jock raised his glass to her. Damon would have sworn the earth shook at that moment.

He'd lost her to Sutherland. Only four days had passed since she'd left and already Jock had made his move. And it was apparent from the way Eden peered at the man from beneath those long, velvety lashes that she'd made her choice. Well, it was as he'd expected and he shouldn't be surprised. But he was more than surprised—he was shocked, and something in his chest hurt like hell.

"Are you all right, lad?" Nick asked in concern.

"Aye, I'm fine, man. No great loss, eh?" Damon moved off, blindly heading for the outside.

"How about that drink, Damon?" Nick offered.

Damon turned and sent Nick such a cold smile that Nick felt chilled. "I'll be having a drink, my friend, but not here. And don't worry about me being alone, for I

167

won't be. My heart's been bruised but a small bit. I'll get over it. There are lots of beautiful, willing women in New Zealand. No need to pine for just one and she not even one of us.''

Watching Damon depart, Nick sadly shook his head and thanked God he had his Joanie.

.

"I do so like happy endings," Marjorie gushed to Eden and Jock as they left the small theater that night. A traveling players' group had put on a play, but Eden didn't remember the name or what it had been about. During the whole performance, her thoughts had centered on Damon, even when Jock surreptitiously clasped her hand and held it against his chest.

Jock was trying hard to win her. An hour after Jock had left her at her room that day, a delivery person arrived with a box of purple orchids. The flowers were from Jock, something she'd known before she read the card. On the heels of this surprise came another delivery—this one from the local jeweler. Inside the silk-lined box was a pair of earbobs made from greenstone, fashioned in the form of teardrops. *To match your eyes*, the card read. *Wear these tonight. J.*

And that was the first she learned about the theater engagement.

When Jock and Marjorie arrived to fetch her, she wore an emerald-colored gown which would have perfectly complemented the earbobs if she'd chosen to wear them. But they were noticeably absent, causing Jock to direct a baffled and displeased look her way. However, she did carry the orchids.

Because the night was warm, they walked the distance

168

to the theater. On the return trip, they had to pass through a very disreputable section of town, but then most of Skipper's Canyon could be said to be disreputable with so many saloons and dance halls. Jock had just positioned Eden on his left side, away from the street, when out of a side alley came a man and a woman. She nearly collided with the pair, but Jock pulled her instantly back.

"Hey now!" he cried to them. "Watch out. There's a lady here."

The woman lifted her head from the man's broad shoulder. And the man, who had been kissing the back of her neck, glanced their way. His laughter faded as he did so, and Eden thought her heart had stopped beating when her gaze met those familiar blue eyes.

"Well now, fancy this," Damon muttered to the woman in his arms. "It's my neighbor, the high-and-mighty Jock Sutherland, and his sister." He bowed to the Sutherlands. It was quite apparent he'd had too much to drink. He stumbled over his words and very nearly his own feet. But he didn't bow to Eden. "And this," he said to the woman, "is the Lady Eden, belle of the Old South. A true repre-sen-ta-tive of American womanhood. Did you know, Sal, that she's a Yank?" Damon grinned. "But don't call her that. She practically bit my head off."

"Away with you, Alexander," Jock demanded, rushing Eden and Marjorie down the wooden boardwalk.

"Of course, Gentleman Jock. Mustn't dirty the ladies." He grinned at the woman. "Come on, Sal, give me a kiss."

Sal giggled, the low-cut gown she wore riding lower upon her breasts as she reached up to kiss him.

Eden watched in revulsion, totally disgusted by this

169

outrageous display but so jealous and hurt she couldn't tolerate another second of watching Damon make a fool of himself, of wishing she were the one he held in his arms and kissed. Taking Jock's arm, she turned away and flounced down the street. Her face burned with humiliation, and she was so relieved when they reached the hotel. Since the Sutherlands' rooms were on the first floor, she told Marjorie good night and allowed Jock to escort her to her own room on the second floor.

She couldn't look at him, could barely open the door. Jock took the key from her trembling fingers and she rushed inside, Jock behind her. It was then she felt his hands on her shoulders, turning her to face him.

He tilted her chin and forced her to look at him. "Eden, I'm aware Alexander has hurt you and I've heard the rumors about the two of you. Are they true?"

"Yes," she admitted wretchedly.

He took a steadying breath. "Thank you for being honest with me. Now I'll be honest with you. I meant every word I said today. You are going to marry me, and one day you'll laugh at how you felt about Damon Alexander. He'll mean nothing to you, will be nothing to you but a misty memory. He doesn't deserve someone like you and tonight proves it. A leopard can't change his spots, and what you saw on the street is the real Damon Alexander. He's had countless women and can drink larger men under the table. He's rowdy, uneducated— and Irish. That about says it all."

"Please, Jock, I don't want to hear any more."

"And I don't want to say anything else about him. I want to kiss you, Eden. I want to show you what you can have with me."

"Jock . . ."

But it was too late. His mouth swooped down, taking her lips like a greedy vulture. The kiss was filled with fire and daring, and it stirred something within Eden. She found herself kissing him back, her fingers clinging to his lapels. Then abruptly he ended it, and he grinned with satisfaction.

"Now I know you aren't cold. I think you could care for me."

He left her. For a long time she stood in the center of the room looking at the door. Then she went into the bedroom and took the greenstone earbobs from the box and put them on her ears. She examined her reflection, noting the way the stones flashed their brilliance, how they shimmered and matched her eyes. Damon had once likened her eyes to the fiery stone; she realized that was why she hadn't worn Jock's gift that evening.

But now she purposely didn't remove the earbobs. Somehow she must get over Damon and stop associating every little detail with him. Wearing the earbobs was a beginning, and she decided to wear them the next day when Jock picked her up for breakfast.

There were worse fates than marrying Jock Sutherland, she decided. Loving Damon Alexander was one of them.

Chapter 13

Eden accepted Jock and Marjorie's invitation to celebrate Christmas at High Winds. Since Marjorie's wedding was to be on Boxing Day, the day after Christmas, and there was no reason to stay in town, the arrangement worked out perfectly.

Garlands of greenery, interspersed with brightly colored wildflowers, hung across the doorway between the parlor and dining room. A freshly cut pine tree filled the house with its sweet scent. When Eden closed her eyes and sniffed, she smelled baked turkey and peach pie, part of the Christmas dinner at High Winds. She imagined she was a little girl again, at home with her parents before the war. A smile curved her lips because she felt safe and happy. She almost expected to hear her parents' voices, but when she came out of her daydream, she found herself staring into Jock's eyes.

"Woolgathering, Eden?" he asked, and extended his hand to her to help her from her chair.

Eden laughed. "Yes, forgive me. I was thinking about happier times."

His eyebrow shot up a fraction of an inch. "I'm sorry you don't consider your time here with me to be happy."

"Oh, Jock, please don't misunderstand. I've had a delightful visit. It's just that my family is gone. I have no one to share the holidays with, and this time of the year used to mean so very much to me."

He bent low and brushed a tender kiss across her lips. "Consider me your family, Eden. You know how I feel about you, what I want from you."

She knew only too well what Jock wanted. He'd asked her once more since her arrival at High Winds to marry him, but she'd been unable to answer him, telling him she couldn't come to a decision yet. The truth was, she couldn't forget Damon. The blasted man haunted her thoughts and filled her dreams. It seemed there was no getting away from him.

But Jock expected an answer soon. She sensed he wasn't about to be put off much longer. She was spared saying anything when Bert Carruthers arrived, bearing a Christmas package for Marjorie. Soon they went into the dining room for the traditional Christmas dinner. Despite Eden's preoccupation with Damon, she found herself enjoying the holiday and was almost beginning to feel that she belonged at High Winds.

Boxing Day, Marjorie's wedding day, dawned with a slight misting rain. By noontime the weather had cleared and a bright golden sun shone through the gray clouds. "Ah, Miss Marjorie, you are fortunate," Nonnie said, placing a cup of tea on Marjorie's bureau. "Sunshine on one's wedding day is a good omen."

"Yes, that's what I've heard." Marjorie sipped at the

173

weakly brewed tea but could hardly swallow. Cold, fluttering sensations nested in the pit of her stomach. She wondered if she was going to be sick. Maybe if she became ill Jock would be forced to cancel the ceremony. But no. He'd never do that. Jock was too eager for her to marry Bert.

Her fate had been decided for her, and she had no say in the matter. She wouldn't balk, wouldn't cry. Marjorie was used to obeying, and couldn't imagine not honoring her brother's wishes. Any other prospects were nonexistent. Marrying Bert Carruthers was her one and only chance to have a home and family of her own. No longer would she be dependent upon Jock. After today, she'd be dependent upon Bert, but she wasn't certain which was the lesser of the two evils.

Seeing Nonnie caused her to blurt out, "How is Tiku?" before she'd realized she'd asked.

"Oh, very well, Miss Marjorie. He's going to help me serve your guests this afternoon."

"But . . . but he's not one of our servants. And he shouldn't be serving at my wedding, Nonnie. Tiku is an educated man."

"Still he is Maori," Nonnie sternly reminded her. "Tiku must know his place."

Marjorie bit at her lower lip, unable to fathom Nonnie. The woman had given birth to a son who was part white, who had been educated in England by his father, yet she didn't want anything better for him than to continue his life as a house servant. And what about Tiku? Didn't he care about his future? Tiku wasn't like his mother or her people. He was destined for better things than working in a kitchen. Marjorie wanted to argue with Nonnie about her position, but she kept her own counsel.

174

The clock on the mantel chimed two times. One more hour until she married Bert. One more hour until her fate was sealed.

Marjorie's wedding attracted more than its share of guests. By the time three o'clock came it seemed everyone in the Otago area had arrived for the festive occasion. At least that's how it appeared to Eden when she glanced out of the upstairs window of her room shortly before Jock was to escort his sister downstairs. Swarms of people, many whom she recognized from town and Thunder Mine, milled about the grounds. Four long tables on the lawn nearly overflowed with food and drink, and there was more in the kitchen. Jaunty tunes drifted through the air, courtesy of three fiddlers who stood beneath the leaves of an ancient oak tree. Jock, as one of the wealthiest men in New Zealand and a member of Parliament, had spared no expense for his only sister's wedding feast. Which was as it should be—Jock Sutherland had a reputation to protect.

Eden took one last look at her reflection in the mirror. The gown she'd chosen, a dark-blue silk shot through with streaks of silver thread, shimmered like moonbeams in a dark heaven. The color accentuated her porcelain complexion and highlighted the reddish-gold tresses which tumbled down her back. Two sapphire combs pulled up the sides of her hair, and in her hands she carried a cluster of colorful summer flowers.

"God but you're beautiful."

Jock's voice caused her to turn. He stood in the open doorway of her room, dressed in a black suit and a white lace shirt. Never had Eden seen him so handsome or been

175

the object of such a hungry gaze. A not-unpleasant shiver slid down her spine to be so desired. She went to Jock and allowed him to kiss her with such savage force she moaned. Maybe she was finally putting Damon behind her.

Amid the strains of the wedding tune, Jock led Marjorie to a rose-covered trellis and placed her hand in Bert's. Marjorie's paleness was disguised by the heat of the day, which coated her cheeks the same color pink as her gown. She made a comely bride, if not a beautiful one. But it was obvious to all who stood nearby as the Reverend Kent united them in marriage that the poor girl was very nervous. Her thin frame trembled and she could hardly repeat her vows. Bert, however, bellowed his for all to hear, and when they were pronounced husband and wife, he planted a loud, wet kiss upon his bride's mouth.

Eden reached for Marjorie, steadying her with a hand when Bert suddenly released her to accept congratulations from well-wishers. She seemed dazed by the event. In seconds she was swallowed by a sea of guests and Eden was pushed aside.

Miranda Creig appeared at her elbow, dressed in a pretty gray gown with red stripes on the skirt. "Eden, dear, I've missed you," she said, and kissed Eden's cheek. "You must come for tea soon. Thunder Mine has been so different since you left." Her expression grew serious. "Damon is different, too. He misses you, I know he does."

"I don't want to hear about him," she responded calmly, but her stomach somersaulted to hear his name. They spoke for a few minutes until Jock whisked Eden away to introduce her to the secretary-general and other members of Parliament who were his associates. It wasn't until this moment, surrounded by these dignitaries and hearing the favorable comments they made to her concerning Jock, that Eden realized what immense power and influence Jock wielded.

"Jock will be Governor Sutherland one day," the secretary-general predicted to Eden. He's an astute politician and a gentleman. Any woman lucky enough to marry him will be the envy of many a female. Most of the unmarried ladies in Wellington have set their sights for him, but Jock doesn't want just any woman for a wife." The man lowered his voice to whisper. "He told me he intends to marry you and is waiting for your answer. I advise you to accept," he finished with a smile.

Eden felt she was being rushed to make a decision. First Jock and now the secretary-general of New Zealand!

The dancing started, and Jock claimed her for a waltz. He was a superb dancer, moving with skill and grace as he waltzed her across the lawn. Was there no end to Jock's accomplishments? She knew she should feel flattered that he wanted to marry her. A great many envious female eyes were now following them. But for all Jock's wealth and political influence and powerful friends, Eden didn't love him. Was she leading him on by not refusing his proposal? Or was she doing herself a disservice by not accepting? She was growing more and more confused.

Out of the corner of her eye, she saw a brown-clad arm tap Jock politely on the back. "May I have a dance with Mrs. Flynn?"

Eden froze and ended the dance, much to Jock's annoyance. Jock spun around to face Damon, his hand tightening on Eden's waist. "I doubt the lady wishes to dance with you, Alexander."

Damon grinned cockily. "I believe she does. "Eden . . ." He held out his arms to her, in a trance she entered them. Jock, not wanting to cause a disturbance, smiled falsely and moved out of the way.

What's wrong with me? she asked herself, unaware of anyone save Damon as he led her in the dance. She followed his every lead, twirling gracefully around the group of waltzers. She should have refused him, blatantly ignored him. He had hurt her terribly, humiliated her on a public street, and now the cad had the supreme gall to spirit her away from Jock. And she'd willingly gone!

But each time he looked at her, her heart skipped a beat and she grew weak. How wonderful it felt to be in his arms again, even for a few minutes. She couldn't stop staring at him, drinking in his face, memorizing every feature for those moments when she was alone. She was a fool, she knew. But her heart ruled her sanity.

"I've missed you," he murmured, his hand tightening around hers. "I've been sick with wanting you. Please come back to Castlegate with me."

"You can't be serious."

"Very serious. I want you in my bed, Eden."

His words sent shivers of desire right to her very toes. She desperately wanted to be in his bed again, but he'd hurt her too much. And nothing had changed.

"You want me only because Jock does," she maintained.

He leaned toward her, his blue eyes filled with cold jealousy. "Has he had you yet?"

"I won't answer that impertinent question."

Damon smirked. "I knew it. He hasn't."

"Oh! You're so full of yourself, Damon Alexander, so

178

sure you know everything—"

"I know you, Eden, love. I know all of you."

A flush consumed her. He *did* know all of her. Damon knew her body more intimately than she did. He pulled her hard against him, causing her to lose step. "Come home with me tonight," he insisted. "Wake up in my arms tomorrow. I know that's what you want, I want you so much that I'm on fire, literally aching for you."

Eden couldn't stand any more. If Damon continued in this fashion she was going to throw herself in his arms and forget how he'd treated her. She wanted a husband and respectability, and Damon couldn't offer her that. "Leave me alone, Damon. Please don't bother me again." She pulled away from him at the same moment the music ended. "I can't tolerate any more pain because of you."

"Eden, I don't intend to hurt you. I want to love you— forever."

"A forever without marriage?" She shook her head, her eyes wide and filling with tears. "I can't be your mistress."

"Then be my wife."

His voice sounded so low, so wantonly intimate that Eden thought she imagined the words. "Damon . . ."

"Marry me." He pulled her into his arms, and his words flowed over her like warm, thick honey. "I love you, Eden. I can't live without you. Forgive me for how I've treated you, the cruel things I've said and done. I've never wanted a woman as much as you, I've never loved anyone as much as you."

"But Tessa. You loved her so."

His eyes blackened; there was a finality to his words. "Tessa is finally dead to me. You're all that matters. I want to make you happy. Say you'll marry me. Say it."

179

Her heart sprouted wings. Pure joy exploded within her. People were staring at them, some with knowing smiles on their faces, others, like Jock, in condemnation. But Eden didn't care. Damon was hers, if she wanted him. She had only to say the words.

"Yes, I'll marry you," she softly whispered, not wanting anyone else to overhear. This was their moment, the moment in time when their life began. And no one would spoil it for them.

Damon placed a tender kiss upon her lips. She felt herself opening to him, all of the desire she'd buried the past weeks resurrecting in an instant. "Come home with me, Eden. Leave with me now."

She nodded eagerly but told him she must speak to Marjorie first. And then Jock.

Marjorie, like most of the people at the wedding, had observed Eden and Damon. Instead of the stern lecture Eden expected from her, Marjorie surprised her by embracing her. "You love Mr. Alexander very much. I see that now. Be happy." She sniffed back her tears, gulping hard when Bert approached and grabbed her hand.

"We better be heading home," Bert said, a leer on his face. "The sun's setting soon, and we have quite a bit to do before bedtime."

Eden noticed that Marjorie blanched but followed dutifully after her new husband. "There's a match made in hell," Damon commented.

And hellish was the word to describe Jock Sutherland. From out of nowhere, he suddenly materialized beside Eden. His face was red, and his eyes burned with such hatred that Eden cringed. But his hatred wasn't directed against her but against Damon. "So, Alexander, you

180

think you've won." His voice was deceptively smooth.

"I'm here claiming the woman I love. I consider myself to be a lucky man for Eden to still want me."

"So you should."

"Jock . . ." Eden began, her mouth suddenly dry. "Be happy for us. We're going to be married."

"Really? Damon's going to do the honorable thing and marry you. Is that what you believe?"

"Yes, I do."

"If that's what you wish to believe, Eden, then I won't be the one to disillusion you. Congratulations to you both."

Jock rushed off, leaving them holding on to each other, fearful to let go. Concern shone in Eden's eyes when she looked up at Damon. "Jock can't do anything to hurt us, can he?"

"No, my love, he can't." He squeezed her reassuringly. "Now let's get your bag packed and get you away from here. Castlegate is waiting for us."

Eden sat beside Damon on the front seat of the buggy. Overhead, huge, glittering stars gleamed and lighted their way along the road. It was a perfect night, and Eden was content. Damon held the reins in one hand and held Eden beside him with his other arm. Her head was nestled on his chest and she caught the wonderful musty male scent of him. She lifted her lips to his neck and kissed him.

"Better be careful, woman," he groused good-naturedly. "Castlegate is still a distance away. Keep on teasing me like that and I might be tempted to ravish you in the forest."

"Do you mean that?"

He smiled down at her, believing her to be joking, but something wild and burning in her eyes told him she wasn't. "Take me into the forest, Damon."

And that's exactly what he did, finding a small trail off the main road. The buggy rolled over deep ruts, heading deeper and deeper into the greenish-black wildwood. When the buggy couldn't go any farther, Damon took her hand and led her into an untamed paradise.

The silence surprised her. Nothing stirred. It was as if the wildlife had been duly warned of their approach and wished to give them this time alone. They entered a primeval world that belonged only to them.

Suddenly Eden heard the sound of water. She gasped with pleasure when they stopped beside a cliff where a waterfall cascaded into a clear, bubbling pool. "This is beautiful!" she said, her eyes twinkling with delight.

"*You're* beautiful," he told her. "So very beautiful that I want to make love to you now."

"Oh, yes, Damon, now." She moved to touch him, but he shook his head. Instead, he undressed while she watched. Her heart sounded like a hammer in her ears and her pulses raced. Her fingers ached to caress his superbly made body.

But his fingers found her first. They began unbuttoning the back of her gown, sensuously sliding down her warm flesh. When her gown lay in a blue puddle at her feet, his hands stripped away her chemise and underclothes. Standing before him in only her stockings and satin dancing shoes, she should have felt embarrassed. But she didn't. He laid her upon his jacket and lifted one of her legs. His hand caressed her foot as he took off her shoe, and then ever so slowly he peeled away her stockings. By the time he'd gotten to her other leg, Eden was moaning and writhing.

"Love me," she urged.

Damon, it seemed, had other ideas. "All in good time, my love. First I want to look at you, to make certain you're not a dream. I couldn't bear it if you weren't real."

To prove she was flesh and blood, he began touching her breasts, kneading them with the palms of his hands, then replacing his hands with his mouth. His tongue lapped at her nipples, swirling around and teasing the buds before his mouth engulfed each of her breasts in turn, sucking until the raw heat of desire devoured her.

"Damon, please," she begged, unable to stand any more. She wanted him with a fierceness which left her panting.

"Not yet, Eden. Lie still and stop wriggling. I need to taste all of you." She knew what that meant, and she moaned aloud.

His lips skimmed over her taut stomach to swirl across her abdomen and end at his destination. Gently he parted her legs. His breath, warm and moist, fanned over her. And then she felt his tongue, determined to claim the very essence of her. Her hands tangled in his hair, urging him on with her mewls of pleasure.

Beneath the canopy of glittering stars, Eden soared to the dark heavens and exploded into a thousand gleaming pieces. When she came blissfully back to earth, Damon was over her, sliding inside her. With each thrust, the burning embers sizzled and sparked anew.

She wrapped her legs around him and arched toward him, meeting each strong thrust with abandon. His lips found hers, drowning her blissful moans with a rapacious kiss that branded her as his own. Then Damon grew still, holding himself erect inside her. She made a mewling sound of protest. "Not yet, not yet," he raggedly whispered, stalling his movements to increase the pleasure. But Eden was wild, her body craving satisfaction and knowing how to give it. Somehow she knew to contract the muscles which enveloped him like a glove. Damon's eyes widened, taken aback by what Eden was doing to him, but he gave only half-hearted protest. "You're a wanton witch, you know that," he said to her, nibbling the lobe of her ear.

"I'm what you've made of me," she confessed, and continued her mind-drugging torture. Soon their moans echoed as one. Their ecstasy peaked when Damon drove into her with a powerful thrust which took her breath from her. Damon shuddered and groaned at the same instant Eden's body exploded.

Damon wrapped his arms around her and they both lay bathed in starlight. "Damon?" There was a hesitancy in Eden's voice when he felt her stir some minutes later. "Did you mean what you said—about marrying me?"

"Aye."

"What happened to change your mind?"

"My love for you."

She snuggled against him and kissed his chest. "I love you, too. I'll always love you."

"I'm counting on that."

Damon stood up and pulled her to her feet. "Want a bath?" he asked, his gaze sliding to the lagoon before coming to settle again on her face.

A seductive giggle escaped her. Wrapping her arms around his neck, she clung to him. "You know perfectly well it's not a bath you're needing, you wayward son of an Irishman. You just want to get me in the water and have your wicked way with me again."

"Oh, so you're protesting then?"

"Never that, Damon." The teasing play left her eyes and a wicked glow shone brightly within them. "I'm yours whenever you want me."

"Ah, my fair Eden, my love." He kissed her and scooped her into his arms, carrying her to the pool. It was nearly dawn before they finally arrived at Castlegate.

Chapter 14

Two days later, Damon entered the law office of MacKenzie, Marsh, and Timmons. The receptionist showed him into Mr. Ralph MacKenzie's office, and Damon shook hands with the gray-haired barrister. MacKenzie, who had handled certain matters for Damon in the past, frowned after Damon finished speaking. "What you're asking may take a bit of time to accomplish" was his response.

"I'm aware of that, sir, but I have to know."

"May I ask why you've waited five years to discover your wife's whereabouts?"

"I didn't care where Tessa was before now. I've fallen in love and want to get married."

MacKenzie nodded, his weathered face breaking into a gentle smile of understanding. "Yes, I've heard about you and a certain Mrs. Flynn. This is a small town with many ears." He suddenly grew serious. "You've led many people to believe you're a widower, that your wife died a number of years ago. Have you told Mrs. Flynn that you can't marry until we learn if Tessa Alexander is alive or dead?"

Damon sheepishly admitted he hadn't. "I hoped you might be able to get some information, that after all this time Tessa might truly be dead. Christ Church was where she was headed the last time I saw her." His eyes darkened to indigo. "As far as I'm concerned, she's dead."

MacKenzie scribbled something on a sheet of paper, nodding as he listened. "I can sympathize with you, Damon, but you've got to realize New Zealand is a large, remote country. The possibility exists that Tessa may have left Christ Church to follow after this other man. She could be anywhere, anywhere at all, even Australia or America. If she doesn't want to be found, then we've very little chance of locating her to serve her with the divorce petition."

Damon couldn't help but scowl. "Oh, she's somewhere civilized, Mr. MacKenzie. Tessa always liked luxury. You won't locate her in the bush."

"I'll send one of my investigators to Christ Church. I don't really see much of a problem if we find her. She *did* desert you."

The two men rose and shook hands when the conference was completed. Damon nodded his head to Miss Donner, MacKenzie's pretty clerk and quickly headed for home. Eden was waiting for him, and he wanted to hold her, to prove to himself that she was real and not going anywhere.

Beneath the hot sunshine, he broke out into a cold sweat. She might leave him if she learned the truth too soon. He was still a married man, though he'd told everyone Tessa had died. He cursed himself for not seeking a divorce when she'd left him for a wealthy man in Christ Church. She'd committed adultery so the divorce would have been settled quite easily at the time. But he'd been so distraught, so angry at her and despising her so much that he'd cut her out of his life, half convincing himself she really was dead. As the years passed, he thought she might truly have died, for he heard nothing from her. There wasn't a reason to seek a divorce then, to discover if she might have passed away.

Until now.

Spurring his horse, he raced for Thunder Mine. Somehow he must delay Eden from making wedding plans until he learned something substantial. He feared she wouldn't understand his situation or be willing to wait for him if he told her anything now. Worse was the thought that she might turn to Jock Sutherland for comfort, and he felt chilled to his very marrow to imagine how Jock would take advantage of her distress. But luckily for Damon, Jock, like everyone else in the area, believed Tessa was dead. So his secret was safe for now, and Eden was his.

The moment he arrived home, he swept Eden into his arms and took her to the bedroom where he imprisoned her in his velvet embrace for the rest of the day.

Jock groaned his pleasure and spilled himself into the writhing woman beneath him. When he'd finished with her, he sat up, not even bothering to hold the wench in his arms. Minny Donner didn't care for the fevered kisses before lovemaking or the tender caresses afterward. She was a strange woman, but he admitted she was adept at firing his flesh. And, hell, he didn't mind if she preferred only the sexual act. That was fine with him. Minny was a no nonsense gal, and he appreciated it. They both got what they wanted, and sometimes he received a bit more in the way of information.

Minny was a clerk true, but she had a talent for keeping an ear and eye out for juicy tidbits of information concerning conversations she'd overheard at the law office. She always passed on things which might be of interest to Jock, things she thought he might want to know about people in the area. One never knew when one might need to apply some pressure, and to a man in Jock's position it paid to be informed.

Minny put on a gauzy robe and got up to pour Jock a whiskey. "Have you learned anything interesting?" he asked her, taking the glass she handed him.

"Hmm, let me think." Minny fell onto the bed and lay on her stomach. "Not too much, duck, but that handsome Mr. Alexander paid a call yesterday morning to Mr. MacKenzie."

"Really? I suppose he wants MacKenzie to pressure me about the water rights."

"Naw, I left the door open enough so I could hear and I don't remember anything about water rights. But he did speak about locating his wife. It seems he wants Mr. MacKenzie's investigator to track her down so he can divorce her or find out if she might be dead. Now I don't know Mr. Alexander all that well, but he's a handsome one. That wife of his must have been crazy to leave him. You know anything about her, Jock?"

Jock was out of the bed and starting to dress before Minny could blink. "Where you going?" she asked.

"I have an appointment."

"At ten o'clock at night? I thought you'd be staying."

"No, not tonight. Here." He took a number of bills out

of his billfold and threw them on the bed. "Buy yourself a pretty hat or something you want."

"Sure, duck. Thanks." Minny grinned, not at all upset by Jock's sudden departure.

While fixing his cravat, Jock peered at Minny's reflection in the mirror. "Did Alexander happen to say if his fiancée was aware of his situation?"

Minny ceased counting the money to look up. "I think he said she didn't know. That's why he was in such a hurry to be free of his wife. He wants to marry this other woman."

"I see," Jock said, and smothered a smile. When he'd finished dressing, he lifted Minny's chin. "Don't mention what you've heard to anyone."

"Do I ever? You know, Jock, you're a suspicious type of person."

"Yes, my dear." He eyed the money he'd just given to her which more than doubled her monthly salary at the law firm. "And aren't you glad for it."

"Will I be seeing you anytime soon?"

"No, I'm going on a trip."

"Oh, where you going?"

Jock started for the door, his mind working as he spoke. "I'm leaving for Christ Church in the morning."

Damon was at the mine when Bert Carruthers arrived at Castlegate, uninvited. Eden, who'd been working along with the house servants, was busily polishing a large silver candelabra on the dining-room buffet. As one of the servants led Bert to Eden, she saw that Bert's shoes were muddy and that large black footprints tracked across the Oriental rug. Though dismayed, she kept a clamp on her mouth. Bert was a neighbor and Marjorie's husband, she reminded herself, and she should put aside her personal feelings about the man. She'd never like him, but she could be civil to him.

Wiping her hand on her apron, she offered him a cool smile. "Damon isn't here. He's at the mine," she told him, believing he'd come to see Damon. "May I get you something to drink while you wait?"

Bert refused. With his cap at a jaunty angle, he watched her, and the skin on the back of her neck prickled. "How is Marjorie? I haven't seen her since the wedding. Please tell her I'll visit soon." She purposely turned away from him, going around the other end of the dining table. "I'll have Tiku get Damon for you."

"It ain't Damon I come to see."

She barely made it to the doorway before Bert held her waist fast, pressing her backside against the lewd, hard bulge in his trousers. "I've come to see you, Eden," he hoarsely whispered. "I think we need to finish what we started in town a few weeks ago."

"Get your filthy hands off me!" Her demand fell upon deaf ears.

"Aw, stop teasing old Bert. You know you like men's hands upon you." His breath smelled of liquor and was hot in her ear. "You like pretending to be a lady, but LaRue's ain't no finishing school. Come on, take old Bert to your bedroom. I promise you I won't tell Damon, and neither will you—not if you don't want something bad to happen to him."

Eden felt genuine fear when Bert began dragging her down the hallway to the bedroom. She dug her heels into the floorboards, but Bert viciously yanked at her. "Stop it! Let me go!" she screeched, not about to submit to Bert

191

Carruthers. She looked frantically about her. If only she could get a hold upon something, but his arms pinned hers to her sides. He dragged her along, ignoring her screams. She felt herself choking on her own breath, fearing the worst. But she was going to fight him, fight him with every ounce of strength she possessed.

It was then she heard a hard, conking sound. Bert stopped, frozen to a standstill. Then his arms slid down the length of her and he fell unconscious to the floor. Eden lost her balance and tottered, grabbing at the wall. With clumsy hands, she pulled her skirt out of Bert's grasp, unable to focus on anything but him until she realized Tiku, clutching a thick, gold-plated wall sconce, loomed over them.

Gasping sobs of relief choked her. Tears threatened to overwhelm her. "Are you all right, Mrs. Flynn?" Tiku asked, supporting her with a steadying arm. She leaned against him for a few moments to get her bearings. At least she wasn't physically hurt. If not for Tiku, she'd be fighting off Bert in the bedroom right now— Shivers wracked her to imagine such horror.

"I'm just frightened," she admitted, "but I'll be fine once you remove this . . . this person." She couldn't think of a word awful enough to call Bert, who lay with a large gash on the top of his head where Tiku had struck him with the sconce. "I'd appreciate it if you could take Mr. Carruthers home."

"Yes, ma'am." Tiku bent down and draped Bert over his shoulders with little effort.

"Tiku, thank you for rescuing . . ."

Eden had trouble speaking, too overwhelmed by what had nearly happened. "You're welcome, Mrs. Flynn." He gave her a thoughtful look. "I think Mr. Alexander will want to know about this."

Eden nodded. She'd have to tell Damon. He'd make certain Bert didn't return to Castlegate to bother her again. Tiku disappeared outside with his burden. Eden went to the window to see him depositing Bert on the back of the wagon. She pitied poor Marjorie. The sensitive young woman didn't deserve such a pig as Bert Carruthers for a husband.

With trembling hands, she picked up the sconce from the floor where Tiku had laid it and hung it on the wall.

Marjorie had just finished brewing tea when Tiku drove into the yard. She let out a little cry of joy to see him again. With the bright sun shining upon his dark hair and skin, he resembled a Maori god. How handsome he looked to her with his broad shoulders covered by a snowy white shirt, his lean thighs encased in dark trousers. She chuckled aloud to see his feet were bare when he disembarked at the back of the house. Tiku would never change.

But Marjorie's happy expression turned somber when Tiku hauled her unconscious husband like a sack of lard from the wagon. She opened the door for him before he'd stepped onto the porch. "What happened?" she asked, instantly noticing Bert's head was bleeding.

"Mr. Carruthers had an accident" was Tiku's response. "I found him near Thunder Mine."

Marjorie's hands clutched at her throat. "Bushwackers, do you think?"

Tiku shrugged. "I can't say, Mrs. Carruthers."

Marjorie led him to the parlor where he deposited Bert on the sofa. Bert groaned but didn't open his eyes. His skin was ashen, but it seemed the only damage done to his person was the wound on his head.

Marjorie hurriedly limped to the kitchen and found a wet washcloth. She began to clean away the blood, but she grew pale and moaned. Tiku took the cloth from her and ministered to Bert. He told her after a careful examination that the wound wasn't very deep. "But he should be stitched," Tiku advised her. "If you have some thread and a needle I can close the wound."

A tiny smile played around Marjorie's mouth. "You sound almost like a physician."

"I am," Tiku said simply, looking at her from liquid brown eyes. "But not a people doctor. I'm trained to care for animals. I studied veterinary medicine in London under my father."

"I didn't know that." Marjorie was shocked to learn this about Tiku. She'd never guessed he was trained to do anything but cook. "I thought your father was an explorer."

"Yes. He came to New Zealand to study the animal life. May I have the needle and thread?"

"Oh, yes, of course. I'll get them immediately." Marjorie went to her sewing basket and found what she needed. In fascination she watched as Tiku took the needle and held it over the flame of a candle—to sterilize it he told her, and to kill the germs. Then he went about his work, stitching Bert's skin together with expert hands. So, she thought, Tiku was an animal doctor. In that case Bert's skull was in good care.

Tiku was skillful and graceful in his movements.

Marjorie liked watching him. She felt silly for growing weak when she started to clean Bert's wound, but that was because she hated touching the man, not because she couldn't tolerate the sight of blood. Bert was a horrible husband, and since their marriage she'd been living a nightmare. He didn't have servants, because he was too cheap to pay them a fair wage. So Marjorie had been forced to do all of the cooking and cleaning herself. And Bert had taken charge of her inheritance, so if she'd chosen to run away she would have no money to leave.

And she had considered running away, seriously considered it. The man was a beast, a loud, foul-mouthed smelly monster. Since she'd stepped into this house on their wedding night, he'd abused her by calling her names and backhanding her if she as much as gave the impression she was going to sass him. She could take the slaps and the ugly words, but she couldn't tolerate the way he vilely used her body, the unspeakable things he'd done to her and made her do to him. If being married entailed such pain and humiliation as this, then she wished for death. Sometimes she prayed Bert would die, but immediately she asked God to forgive her. He was a human being, but even as she tried to convince herself of this fact, she couldn't think of Bert as better than an animal.

"Mr. Carruthers will be in pain when he wakes up." Marjorie blinked as Tiku broke into her thoughts. "Give him a swig of whiskey for the pain."

Marjorie grimaced. "He'd take one anyway." She hobbled to the door. "Thank you for bringing him home."

For a moment, Tiku hesitated. "Are you all right,

Miss Marjorie?"

She wasn't all right, she was miserable, but she couldn't let on to anyone about her marital situation. It wasn't proper. "I'm well," she said, but bitter tears sprang to her eyes and she gave the only excuse she could think of to account for them. "Sometimes I get homesick for High Winds."

For a brief instant she thought Tiku was going to touch her face. Instead, he swung open the door. "If you need me for anything, Miss Marjorie, I'll be at Castlegate."

"I'll remember." How could she ever forget? Tiku was so close yet so very far away from her. "You're a very good doctor," she praised him warmly. "Why do you cook for Mr. Alexander when you could be tending animals?"

"I mustn't get above my station, ma'am."

His terse words came out like a harsh croak. Before Marjorie could say anything further, he'd climbed into the buggy and was gone. Yet there was nothing she could say. Tiku was right. The Maoris criticized him for his education in a white world. Most whites wanted him to remain with the savages and wouldn't accept him, though he was intelligent and educated. Both peoples tended to look down upon those like Tiku, those who were considered Kua-Pakeha—a Maori who was more European than Maori. It wasn't fair. Life had played a cruel trick upon Tiku, and had been cruel to Marjorie, too. She loved Tiku but couldn't tell him.

If only things could be different, if only he loved her like she loved him.

"Mar-jor-ie."

She stifled her groan at Bert's call and heartened to

note upon close inspection that he sounded weak and looked even worse than he sounded. The disgusting beast wouldn't hurt her tonight.

"Thank you, Bushwacker, whoever you are," she mumbled under her breath, pouring Bert a huge shot of whiskey. "You've done your good deed for the day."

Chapter 15

"It was a grand wedding, don't you think?" Eden asked Damon, cuddling next to him in bed that night. She was thinking about what a pretty bride Joanie made and how handsome and proud a groom was Nick Patterson. The couple had decided to get married quite suddenly, and after receiving Nick's note, Eden and Damon had rushed into town to attend the ceremony, which had been performed by the local magistrate. And now, after a lovely afternoon filled with sweet-tasting wine and a wonderful supper at the restaurant where Nick and Joanie worked, Eden and Damon had decided to spend the night at the finest hotel in town.

Damon placed a kiss on the top of her bright head. "Aye, I hope they'll be happy."

"Oh, they will," Eden insisted, tracing his jawline with lingering fingers. "We'll know how they feel as soon as we're married."

Damon gave a nervous cough and reached for his jacket which hung on the bedpost. He pulled a cheroot out of the pocket. In the darkness of the room, the match flared and Eden could very clearly make out his tanned features. His face appeared tense, his expression guarded. What was wrong with him? Each time she mentioned marriage, he froze up on her, leaving her with the impression that he didn't want to marry her. Whenever she broached the subject of marriage, he vacillated about setting a wedding date, though he insisted the wedding would be soon. She worried he had changed his mind about wanting to marry her.

Damon *had* to want to marry her. She hadn't mentioned anything to him, but she thought she was pregnant, and she'd be damned if she'd tell him before they were married. A shot gun wedding was the last thing she wanted.

"The water rights need to be resolved," he said. It seemed he was purposely eluding a response to her earlier remark. "But Sutherland is gone away on business, I've heard. Just like the bastard to dodge me when he knows how eager I am to get the papers signed."

"The water rights are very important, aren't they?" Eden asked, pulling the sheet across her bare breasts. "Since you aren't getting anywhere with Jock, perhaps I could speak to him when he returns."

"Over my bloody dead body you will!"

"Damon, I have a way with Jock. I know I can sway him."

"Aye, I'm quite aware of how Sutherland wants you to sway him, but no, Eden, you're not to speak to him. The water rights are my concern."

"Have you forgotten who owns half of Thunder Mine, you arrogant bully? I care what happens to it and the miners, too, you know. And I don't care for the way you're treating me, like I'm some sort of silly woman

199

without a brain in my head."

"It's not your brain I'm worried about, but the rest of you. Remember what happened two weeks ago with Bert Carruthers? You couldn't fight him off, and he was half drunk. What do you think would happen to you if Jock Sutherland takes it into his head to try something? Believe me, he won't be drunk and you can't rely on Tiku to help you or for me to punch the man's face in. I'm giving you one warning: stay away from Sutherland."

Eden seethed with indignation. She was his partner, but he didn't see her as that. He'd already made up his mind about the water rights, not even considering that if they approached Sutherland together the man might relent. And as far as approaching him on her own, he would have none of it. Clearly, Damon only wanted her to sate his sensual appetites, the very thing he accused Jock of wanting.

"I can make decisions, too," she persisted. "I don't just run the house. The miners respect what I say, unlike some person I could name whose stubborn streak runs the length of South Island."

"Hmm, you're a feisty little miss."

"I won't be a miss for long, I hope, and I'm not little."

Damon gently tugged the sheet from her fingers and gazed at her full, rounded bosom. He grinned. "I'll say you're not little." He put out his cheroot and pulled her down beneath him on the mattress to kiss and plunder her breasts with his tongue. "You're delicious, and as intoxicating as a magnolia."

"I didn't know you knew what a magnolia smelled like," she murmured, growing dazed by his mouth moving across her body.

"I don't, but I'm betting they smell sweet, like you."

Eden knew Damon was a true Irishman by the blarney he spoke. He wanted her to forget about Sutherland and the water rights. He thought that if he made love to her, she'd be so overcome by his prowess that she'd put it all out of her head. Well, she'd forget about it for now. It was hard to concentrate on what she'd say to Jock Sutherland when Damon was kissing her entire body and driving her wild with desire. But when her head cleared and her body was satiated by his lovemaking, she'd rehearse what she was going to say when she met Jock Sutherland again.

For the moment she reveled in Damon's hot need, eagerly welcoming him when he slid inside her. Tomorrow she'd worry about Jock and the water rights. Tonight she belonged only to Damon.

Jock waited in a hired carriage near Littleton Harbor, observing the house that stood near the waterfront. It was in disgraceful condition and he couldn't help but wonder if its outside mirrored the person who inhabited it. It was imperative in Tessa's line of work, for her to be attractive, but he didn't hold much hope. Being a whore probably had taken its toll upon her looks.

He grew alert when the front door opened. A young, robust man was leaving. His eyes followed him down the street. He decided it was finally time to call on Tessa Alexander but was thwarted when another man coming from the opposite direction went up to the house and knocked. Immediately he was admitted inside.

"Damn!" Jock's disgruntled curse echoed in the carriage. He threw himself against the cushioned seat.

201

How many men was she going to entertain before the night was over? This was the third one to arrive in the last two hours. He remembered Tessa as being insatiable. She was well suited to whoring, but he was tired of sitting here and waiting to catch her in between customers.

Jock sighed heavily. There was nothing to do but wait. He'd arrived in Christ Church some days ago, believing Tessa would be easy to find again, but he'd been wrong. The man she'd run away with, one Jacob Shelton, a wealthy local businessman, was no longer available to give Jock her address. Shelton had died almost two years ago, Jock learned from the firm he'd owned. No one there knew anything about Tessa Alexander, who'd been his mistress. But fate intervened in the form of Shelton's widow, who happened to be at the firm the day Jock made inquiries. Mrs. Shelton had informed him coldly that on the death of Mr. Shelton, his wife and children had evicted the whore, as Mrs. Shelton called Tessa. Since Shelton's will made no provisions for Tessa, she had to make her way the best she could.

Apparently a dingy, dilapidated house in one of the worst sections of Christ Church was the best Tessa could do for herself. Jock was shocked. He'd have thought she'd have latched on to another wealthy man by now.

Stupid bitch. She could have been Mrs. Jock Sutherland; but she'd stupidly chosen to marry Damon Alexander instead. Jock remembered being enraged beyond belief when he learned she'd decided to marry Damon. Only the night before had he held the deceitful tart in his arms. He loved her beyond caring that she was poor and uneducated, the daughter of a drunken miner. He'd have given her anything she wanted to hear her whisper she loved him. Instead, she wanted Alexander because the mine was unbelievably prosperous at the time, and Jock was just a sheepman. He'd found Tessa in town with Damon, shortly before their wedding. Damon and he had fought each other like bucks over a doe. Jock lost, the scar on his cheek a tangible reminder of how much he hated Alexander and Tessa. But he'd kept up with her, even after she'd run off with Shelton. And now he was going to put his knowledge of her whereabouts to good use.

Soon he'd wreak his vengeance on both of them.

Half an hour later the third man departed Tessa's house. Without waiting a second longer, Jock sprinted from the carriage and went to the door. He clearly heard Tessa's less than melodious cry at his knock. "Hey now, I'm finished for the night. Go on your way!"

"Open up, Tessa. It's Jock Sutherland. I want to see you."

It took her a long time to come to the door. When it opened a crack, he saw her peering at him. "Jock, is it really you?"

"Yes, and I've got the scar to prove it. Now let me in."

He moved to enter, but Tessa pushed her weight against the door. "I don't think I should. How do I know what you're about? I don't trust you, Jock."

He flashed her a less than pleasant smile. "Well, I doubt I'm about the same thing as the three men who have just left your most picturesque residence. But I think when I tell you I'm here about your most beloved husband, you'll let me in."

"Damon? What about him?" she asked in concern. "He ain't been hurt, has he?"

"Let me inside and we'll discuss it. I'm not telling you anything out here, Tessa. I have a reputation to protect.

203

If anyone should recognize me—"

"Oh, all right," she said grudgingly. "Get your bloody hide inside and shut up."

Jock laughed out loud. Same old Tessa. She always did have a way with words.

The house's interior was as grim as the outside. Paint was peeling off the walls and was so faded, he couldn't discern what color it had been originally. The parlor was a hodgepodge of unmatched furniture. Torn doilies hung over the backs of two shabby chairs and a couch. A small wood table stood in the center of the room and looked ready to fall at any moment. From the doorway he saw a bed, the dirty sheets on it looking less than inviting. He shivered to imagine the vermin which must inhabit it. How low Tessa had fallen.

Yet in the lamplight, she didn't look as awful as he feared she would. Granted, she wasn't beautiful as she'd been when she left Thunder Mine, but with a good bath and some proper clothes she might pass muster. Her hair was still as black as a bat's wings, and her face was unmarked. Thank God she hadn't caught the pox. And the figure beneath her tattered lace robe was still shapely—a bit of extra poundage on it but not overblown. Tessa would do nicely once he took over.

Suspicious brown eyes glared at him as Tessa sat on one of the chairs. Spirited still, he realized. A good sign. She'd need spirit for the coming weeks, and fortitude. He'd brook no disobedience from the tart, and Tessa had better understand the rules before she returned to Thunder Mine.

"Tell me about Damon," she said, wasting no time.

"Ah, Tessa, how pained I am that you haven't asked about my health, and after all the years we've known each other."

"I know how you've been. I read the papers, and more than once I've read about the great Jock Sutherland and his high and mighty Wellington post."

"You make it sound as if I hold but a lowly government job. I'm a member of Parliament, my dear."

"I ain't your dear. I never was."

Jock flushed. God, this woman could still get under his skin, but now his dislike for her was intense. How dare she belittle his position in the New Zealand Parliament, this whore who opened her legs to any fellow who'd pay her price. And from the looks of her and her pitiful surroundings, Tessa didn't charge very much. The place was a horror and he thought he heard a rat scratching in the wall. "When did you learn to read?" he asked, remembering her as almost illiterate.

"Jacob taught me."

"Oh, yes, your erstwhile lover. Too bad about his death."

Tessa shifted her position and leaned her elbows on her knees. "Yeah, too bad for me 'cause his hoighty-toighty family threw me out of the place Jacob had put me. Just came and threw me out into the cold like an old boot, not caring if I lived or died. And this is where I ended up, broke and flat on me backside . . . But then, I was always good on me back. You remember how good, don't you, Jock?"

He didn't say anything; he couldn't. Some of those times he'd spent making love to Tessa had been the most wonderful in his life. He didn't want to remember them, didn't want to connect this hardened and coarse creature with the young and ignorant Tessa whom he'd adored. Instead, he could only stare at her.

Tessa pierced him with a malevolent glare. "I think you're glad things turned out bad for me. You hated me after I married Damon. But you hated me worse 'cause the man I ran off with wasn't you. I'm right, ain't I? You sit there in your fancy clothes and look down at me. You're just tickled to death at how things turned out for me."

"Yes," he admitted softly, so softly that Tessa cringed. "I'm pleased you've sunk so low, damned glad to find you in a rat-infested hole, living with vermin and sleeping with them. You deserve every rotten, awful thing that's befallen you. I loved you, Tessa, loved you more than my own life. And, hell, I don't even know why. You were an ignorant little tart who slept with me, with Alexander—and who knows how many other men. But I believed you loved me until I found out you were going to marry Alexander. I'd be willing to bet he thought you'd been a virgin, too, when he first had you. You sure as hell fooled me. Do you still have that ability, Tessa? Is that how you keep all your men happy and coming back for more?"

She jumped out of her chair and tore across the room toward him. She went for his face, but Jock grabbed her wrists before she could do any damage. "Get out of me house! Get out of here or I'll call the constable on you!"

With very little effort, Jock pushed her down upon the sofa. His weight held her in place. "Listen to me, you screeching harpy, I'm not leaving and you're not telling me what to do. I told you I was here about Alexander, and you're going to listen to me if I have to tie you up. Or maybe the likes of you would enjoy being tied up?"

Tessa's eyes burned like torches. "Let me up."

"Will you behave and listen to me?"

"Yeah," she relented.

Jock released her from under him. She sat on the far corner of the sofa rubbing her bruised wrists. Tessa would be easy to dominate, he decided. She'd do as he wanted with little trouble. "Now, my dear, I'll tell you why I'm here. I think you should know that an investigator from a law firm is looking for you. I wanted to find you before he could present you with the necessary papers."

"What papers?"

"Why, the petition from your husband to divorce you."

"Divorce me?" Tessa's face turned deathly pale. "Damon would never divorce me. He loves me."

"You can't believe that he still loves you. God, woman, you ran away with another man. Don't you know he's convinced everyone that you're dead?"

"No . . ."

"Of course you know that. Why haven't you returned to him if you thought he still loved you? Tell me. Go on." When Tessa didn't say anything, only stared in mute disbelief, he continued. "Allow me to refresh your memory then. I was at the mine the day you told Damon you were leaving. I heard what he screamed at you. I know you remember what he said. What was it, Tessa? What did your beloved, betrayed husband promise to do to you if you ever got within two hundred feet of him? Tell me. You know what it was. And you know he meant it."

Tessa's hands trembled and she clutched them in her lap. "He promised he'd kill me."

"That's right. But now you're going to have to face his wrath if you hope to keep any portion of Damon's wealth. And from the looks of things, you need to claim your share. You are still his wife—for the time being."

"I'll fight the divorce. Damon will back down when he realizes I still love him, that I've always loved him. I was weak—."

"And greedy. Something you still are, my dear, but not an unadmirable trait if used to your advantage. I advise you to return home immediately and get on your knees to Alexander, beg him to take you back. I forgot to mention that he's met a woman, a very beautiful woman, and intends to marry her once the divorce is final. In fact, this woman is living with him in the mansion Shamus Flynn built before his death."

Tessa shook her head in disbelief. "That was going to be our house. Damon wouldn't let another woman live there with him."

"But he has," Jock finished on a triumphant note. He had her now. Damon was Tessa's weak spot, something he'd detested once but relished now. "And Eden Flynn is no ordinary woman, Tessa. Not ordinary at all. She was married to Shamus Flynn and is Damon's partner."

"She's old then?" she asked in a hopeful voice.

"Sorry to disappoint you. No, Eden is young and quite beautiful. She's gently reared, an American southerner whose family owned a vast plantation. Well educated and well read, very bright, a true aristocrat."

"In other words, she's everything I'm not."

"Exactly."

Tessa stood up and paced the room. In the waning candlelight the outline of her body beneath the thin wrapper was visible. The sight was strangely stirring to Jock. He remembered what beauty the robe covered. Was Tessa's body still lovely to behold even after all the hard living and the men who'd touched her? Did he dare find out?

She turned to him, her face a frozen mask. "I'm not going to let Damon marry this woman. I'm going to fight for him and win him back. Maybe I don't have fancy ways like she does, but I know what pleases him. And this time I'll be a good wife to him. I will."

Jock smiled sourly. "I'm glad, my dear." He walked to her and parted the wrapper. Tessa's breasts lay bare to his hot gaze. her nipples were pink like tiny rosebuds, and he sighed with joy. Tessa always did have the most beautiful, full breasts. He looked closely at the rest of her. She was still lovely. No wonder she could make her way through life as a whore. It wasn't often that a man came across a pretty one, so he guessed Tessa was kept quite busy. Perversely, he was aroused by the thought of Tessa with many men. But his lust didn't spring from his desire for Tessa but for Eden, who at the moment was unattainable. Ironic that it was Tessa who was going to make Eden his.

His arms encircled Tessa's waist and he kissed her moist red lips. "Don't be making promises to be a good wife yet," he told her. "I have something else in mind first."

Tessa moaned and succumbed to his kisses. She followed after him and lay down on the table in the parlor when he gestured for her to do so. The wrapper she wore was open and revealed her entire body to him, and for the first time since she left Damon, she felt a true surge of desire. Her legs dangled over the table's edge, and when Jock touched her between her thighs she was already wet and slick. "You whore," he said viciously, though he was smiling at her. He quickly took off his pants and her heart lurched when he entered her. She sheathed him eagerly and wantonly, driving him deep into her. The sheer bliss of their joining nearly drove her insane. She writhed beneath him, arching toward his every thrust until the moment came when her whole body shuddered with pleasure.

Jock climaxed seconds later.

"God, but you're a hot treat," he moaned. "I don't know when I've ever had better."

Tessa winced, her fondness for Jock dissolved. He was treating her like a whore, assuming she was this passionate and unreserved with all the men she serviced. She wouldn't give him the satisfaction of admitting that this was the first real pleasure she'd had since she left Damon. Even with Jacob, she hadn't felt very much; she was too guilty over hurting her husband. And none of her customers gave her any fun, though some had tried. She'd begun to believe herself incapable of pleasure, but thanks to Jock, she knew she wasn't. But now she *was* suspicious of his visit to her.

"Why did you come to tell me about Damon and this woman, Jock? What difference could it make to you if Damon divorces me? You hate me anyway and should be glad if I suffer," she said.

Jock buttoned his trousers. "Oh, pardon me. I forgot to tell you that when you show up at Thunder Mine and remind Damon you're his wife, Eden will leave him. And I'm hoping she runs right into my arms. If not, my visit to you has been a failed venture." He looked deeply into her eyes. "Please don't make me wish I'd never laid eyes upon you, Tessa."

She didn't like the way that sounded, but like it or not, his future was tied to her efforts, and she didn't want to disappoint him. She had to succeed, not only for herself but for the great Jock Sutherland. She blanched to imagine what might happen to her if she didn't.

She smiled to herself, confident that Damon would take her back willingly. She had a secret that not even Jock knew, for if he did, Tessa had no doubt he'd have confronted her with the knowledge. And it was this secret which would make all the difference. Once Damon learned of it he'd never reject her.

In the morning she'd see Mrs. Pinkham and pay her for this month's care. Tessa was overdue in paying the woman, but Mrs. Pinkham was the motherly sort, all forgiving and honest, the perfect person to care for little Collin. Most of the money Tessa earned went to the boy. She herself lived a pitiful existence to make certain he was well fed and clothed—and loved. Yes, definitely loved. Mrs. Pinkham loved the cherubic child, as did Tessa, his mother.

And once Damon got a look at the boy, Tessa knew he would love his son as much as she did. Collin Alexander was her way of gaining entrance into Damon's life again.

Chapter 16

Jock was back. Eden had heard one of the miners mention he'd seen him on the road that morning. So, when Damon went to the mine after luncheon, she quickly combed her hair and plaited it, letting the braid hang down her back. She finished dressing in a plain blue shirtwaist and a gray split riding skirt just as the clock chimed one.

She was ready to speak to Jock about the water rights and mustn't let anyone know what she was about, especially Damon. Instead of asking Tiku to escort her to High Winds, she saddled her own horse and headed down the road.

By the time she made it to Jock's, she felt wilted by the intense summer heat. Already, they were well into January and fall wasn't expected for almost two months. She wondered how much more of this hellish weather she could tolerate.

Nonnie opened the door to her, and Eden entered the parlor, which felt surprisingly cool. Jock was on the range, but Nonnie would send for him, she said. Until he showed up, Eden nursed an iced tea that Nonnie smilingly had handed to her.

Within half an hour, Jock was home and dusting off his wide-brimmed hat on his pant leg. His face lighted up when he saw Eden sitting on the divan. She accepted the polite kiss on her cheek.

"It's been some weeks since I've seen you. . . ." Jock began, pausing to sip at his iced tea. "You're more beautiful now, if that's possible."

Despite what Damon thought about Jock, the warnings he'd shouted, Eden couldn't dislike him. Whenever she saw him he was so polite, so extremely kind and civil, that she couldn't accept he was anything but a gentleman. She knew she must have hurt him by dashing his hopes of marrying her, but he didn't mention the incident at Marjorie's wedding. Surely, he must have felt embarrassment in front of his friends and associates when she left with another man after they had assumed she and Jock were considering marriage. Yet Jock was so friendly to her, and if he was still pained by her choice, he didn't indicate his feelings.

"You must be lonely here without Marjorie," she noted. I'm visiting her on my way home this afternoon and I'll send her your love, if I may."

"Please do. I saw the newlyweds a few weeks ago, and Bert's nose was wrapped like a mummy. He says he broke it." Jock gave her a knowing wink which Eden ignored. She wasn't about to comment on Bert Carruthers and her near rape at his hands, but it seemed Jock already knew Damon had been the one to land the telling blow on Bert's nose.

After making some more polite conversation, Eden placed her glass on the table. Her expression was candid;

213

her eyes glittered with hope. "I understand the water rights are to be renegotiated very soon. So far, nothing had been done. Jock, I'm here to ask you to consider signing the papers giving Thunder Mine the use of the Shotover."

He lifted an eyebrow suspiciously. "Did Damon send you her to plead with me? If so—"

"No, Damon doesn't know I'm here." Eden visibly stiffened. "Jock, you must realize that whatever you decide to do not only affects Thunder Mine but me as well. I own half interest in the mine, and the miners and their families are my concern. Thunder Mine is one of the few remaining mines that is still profitable. If you decide not to renew the rights, then we're done for. The miners will leave and Thunder Mine will close."

"Perhaps Damon should consider sheep farming. The gold will eventually play out."

Eden didn't care for his high-handed attitude, but she realized Jock probably would be proved correct in the future. But the veins ran deep into the mountains and so it might be a very long time before the gold was depleted, and she told him this. Jock nodded in understanding and scrutinized her for a long while until she squirmed uncomfortably in her seat. Finally he got up and took her hand, bringing her to her feet.

"I'll sign the papers, Eden. Thunder Mine can still prosper. But I want you to know I'm doing this only for you, not Alexander."

She flashed him a grateful smile. "Thank you so much, Jock."

He peered down at her, a frown lining his forehead. "Alexander will hurt you, Eden."

"Jock, please—" She attempted to break away, but

214

Jock cupped her chin and kissed her gently upon her lips.

"When he does hurt you, come to me. I'd do anything to make you happy. Anything."

Somehow Eden knew he meant what he said, but she also knew Damon wouldn't hurt her. He still hadn't told her to set a wedding date and she still hadn't told him about the baby she suspected more strongly each day she was carrying. And she wouldn't tell him until the date was set. But time was growing short and within the next two to three months her condition would start to show. She didn't want Damon to marry her because of the baby. She needed to know he was eager to marry her because he loved her. Though she felt certain he did love her and wanted to make her his wife, something was keeping him from going through with the ceremony. What Jock said caused her to feel uneasy. She feared he might truly be right, and if Damon hurt her again, she'd be unable to bear the pain.

Eden broke away only because Jock dropped his hold on her. She managed to smile confidently at him, hoping he didn't recognize her bravado as false. "You worry too much about me, Jock. Really, you must find yourself a good woman, someone you can fuss over. I'm so happy that I want everyone to feel as I do."

"I'll do just that," Jock promised with a smile. "In fact, I have the very woman in mind."

"Good, now I must be on my way to see Marjorie." Eden walked out into the hot afternoon and mounted her horse. Jock waved farewell from the porch, but as she rode out of the yard, she felt a sense of foreboding. Jock's words rang ominously in her ears. *Alexander will hurt you. Alexander will hurt you.*

No, she argued with herself, denying Jock's prediction.

Damon loved her. She must place her trust in that love and stop worrying. But her mind was in turmoil when she arrived at Marjorie's. Luckily Bert was in town, and from Marjorie's expression when she told Eden this news, it was also a great relief for her.

Marjorie offered her a cup of tea and a selection of scones. Eden was startled when it was Marjorie herself who put on the kettle to boil. The absence of house servants was strange, given the fact Marjorie was not only a married woman now but a wealthy one in her own right. Eden drank her tea when Marjorie placed it in front of her, but when Marjorie looked out of the window at the clothes drying on the clothesline and commented that she must take them in, Eden could hold her tongue no longer.

"Do you do all the housework?"

Marjorie's face went from a pale ivory to a deep crimson. "Yes, Bert pinches every coin. He says servants are too expensive." She grew quiet for a second. "But there is one Maori girl who comes every so often to give Bert some sort of a back treatment with special herbs. They go into the bedroom and he says I'm not to disturb him. But Eden, there's always so much laughing and then a strange stillness that I think they're doing something other than a treatment." Her eyes registered defiance. "Though Bert pays her with my money, still I hope they *are* doing something else. I pray that the girl drains Bert so dry that when night comes he'll be so tired he has no energy left for me. The money would be well spent and I can't begrudge her if she can keep him satiated." Her voice broke. "I hate him, detest him!"

Eden could well understand Marjorie's sentiments. She placed an arm around the woman's frail shoulders

216

and let her cry. When she'd finished, Marjorie looked so pitiful and distraught that Eden wondered why Jock hadn't thought to intervene. He must be aware of his sister's circumstances. But there was an unwritten code, it seemed, among most men that they look the other way and not interfere in another man's domestic life.

"How is it that Bert controls your inheritance?" Eden asked.

"That was my father's doing," Marjorie explained, sniffing indignantly. "He worried about what would happen to me after he was gone. He thought I might take it into my head to squander my fortune. As if I would! He thought women were stupid silly fools who didn't need to do anything but look beautiful. Well, I wasn't beautiful, but I did have a quick mind. And I was lucky he realized that and hired a well-educated woman as my governess." She heaved a long sigh. "But Jock was to inherit the bulk of Papa's wealth, along with High Winds. It was Jock's duty to find a decent husband for me if Papa was no longer alive.

"So, upon my marriage to a suitable person, my inheritance was to be bestowed upon my husband who was to see to all of my wants, my needs—and I was to rely upon him for everything for the rest of my life. Only now I fear for my life married to a beast like Bert Carruthers; at the very least I fear for my sanity! But Jock was glad to marry me to Bert, pleased to no longer have me underfoot. My deformity always caused him endless embarrassment."

"I don't believe that," Eden protested.

"It's true!" Marjorie shot back, contempt in her eyes. "I love Jock and he does love me, but that doesn't stop him from disliking me. He wanted me married to Bert so he could get a hold on this land. Bert wouldn't sell it to him, you know."

Marjorie had mentioned that. Why did Jock want the land at all? In comparison to High Winds the Carruthers' land was very small; and the mine Bert had started a number of years ago had played itself out rather early, from what Damon had told her of the area's history. The land was rich and fertile for grazing, but High Winds already boasted untold acres of land for sheep raising.

The Carruthers' land acted as a buffer between Thunder Mine and High Winds. Could Jock want the land only to torment Damon, to act as a thorn in his side? Eden resisted that assumption. It was Damon who constantly espoused his hatred of Jock. Jock had never been anything but gracious to Damon in her presence, and if Jock truly hated him, she doubted the man would marry his only sister to a monster to claim some land. Marjorie was overwrought, seeing hidden motives behind her marriage and blaming Jock for it. Eden couldn't believe what Marjorie told her. If it was true, then who was more of the monster—Bert or Jock?

"Come stay with me for a while," Eden suggested to her. "You can forget about Bert, then perhaps when you return, things will be different." Eden didn't truly mean that, but she didn't know what else to say. Marjorie didn't believe her, either.

"Bert would only show up and make a commotion. And we both know what happened to cause Mr. Alexander to come over here and break his nose. I'm sorry for what Bert did to you, Eden, but I won't have you placing yourself in jeopardy to help me. Somehow I'll figure this out for myself."

*   *   *

Eden reached Castlegate only minutes before Damon returned from the mine. They spent the next two hours eating supper, bathing together in the large indoor bath tub, and making love. Their bodies were entwined like ivy when one of the servants discreetly knocked on the door and slid a piece of paper underneath.

Damon reluctantly rose from the bed and took the paper. As he read it, his face broke out into a broad grin. "Sutherland's sent a message," he told Eden, joining her again. "He's decided to sign the contract for the water rights for another two years. Sorry for the delay, he says." Damon took her in his arms, but Eden sensed something wasn't right with him.

"Aren't you happy about Jock's decision? This is what you've wanted."

"Aye, it is. But I've known Sutherland too long, and he doesn't give an inch. The bastard would have kept me dangling until the eleventh hour and loved every second of it. There's still a week left before he had to notify me. It's odd, very odd for him to relent so suddenly. I'd have wagered he'd insist I sweat blood for the next seven days."

If Damon had looked at her instead of at the ceiling as he spoke, he'd have seen the guilt on her face. She hated deceiving him by not telling him she'd gone to speak to Jock. But there was no need to upset him. Jock had agreed to sign the contracts, living up to his word. Everything was going to be fine. Once the contracts were signed, they wouldn't have to deal with Jock again for another two years.

"Be grateful Thunder Mine is still operating," Eden said, snuggling more deeply into his embrace. "Stop thinking the worst of Jock Sutherland." Her hands began exploring the fur-planed area of his chest. "When you think so much about Jock, you don't think at all about me."

Damon grinned and lifted her atop him. "Then I'll concentrate only on you, you greedy wench." And he did.

By midnight, Bert hadn't returned home. Marjorie had long since changed into her nightgown and braided her hair. Bert would no doubt show up reeking of liquor and cheap perfume. She hoped his time in town had been spent with some willing whore, as she didn't feel inclined to Bert's slobbering over her. And she hoped he'd had enough to drink so he'd pass out and not awaken until late the next day. She liked her moments of peace, stealing and holding on to each second with greedy relish.

Other women whose husbands caroused and drank endeavored to curb their husband's vices. Marjorie encouraged hers. Whenever Bert declared he was going into town, Marjorie didn't protest. Not that it would have done any good since Bert was like a willful child and would have his way no matter her opinion. Many men who drank beat their wives, but Bert beat Marjorie when he was sober. When he was drunk, he was usually unconscious. And this was how she longed to keep him.

She'd begged God to forgive her transgressions, believing herself a sinful woman to encourage her husband's vices. Now she just begged God to let Bert pass out soon after supper so she could get a decent night's sleep. It seemed God heard her.

However much she hated Bert, she found herself constantly limping to the parlor window. Once she thought she'd heard a noise, but glancing out into the darkness, she saw nothing. Perhaps he wasn't coming home, she reasoned, and grew angry. It was just like the stupid lummox to stay in town and keep her up all night waiting. She was tired from her endless chores. Dark circles rimmed her eyes, and fatigue lined her face. She wasn't cut out for housework. Because she was forced to walk with her cane, the smallest tasks were hard to perform. Just taking the laundry off the clothesline meant she risked falling. It was difficult to balance herself with one hand on the cane and the other arm and hand filled with laundry, some of it dragging the ground and becoming so soiled she had to wash it again.

And then there was the dusting, not too difficult a chore in itself, but there were four rooms of furniture upstairs and the stairs were unusually steep, the banister rickety. Heights had always frightened her, but the stairs at High Winds had been broad and carpeted and the railing thick and sturdy. She'd never been afraid at home. But here, each time she went up to the second story, she felt she was taking her life in her very hands. Bert inspected the rooms once a week, and if his index finger showed so much as a trace of dust, he backhanded her.

Marjorie kept the upstairs immaculate, and the furniture shone like sunshine. She kept a clean house and cooked passable meals, and for what? Bert would only come home and dirty things up, animal that he was, and he'd demean her cooking but gobble it up as if he were starving. Oh, how she wished he'd choke!

"Forgive me, dear Lord," she prayed. "Make me strong, make me a good person. Help me to endure this marriage and not think such horrible thoughts. Please help me make a decent home and be happy. If not that, then let me be content with my life. That's all I ask.

Please hear me."

She lighted the oil lamp and sat on the couch to read. An hour later, her eyes began to sting and the words on the page blurred before her. The book fell to the floor with a thud as she started to doze. She awakened, startled, and bent to pick it up when one of Bert's dogs began barking furiously in the yard. Marjorie immediately lowered the light from the lamp and went to the window. She saw Bert's horse galloping up to the house and realized Bert was clinging to its mane. She rushed to open the door just as Bert slid off of the animal.

He's drunk, she thought with guilty glee. But she'd seen the effects of alcohol on Bert many times, and Bert was more times than not "a happy drunk" until he passed out. This time she heard no bawdy song or slurred words. In fact, he seemed to be almost stupified. When he tottered onto the porch and into the house, she noticed that he held his hand over his arm.

"Bert, what's wrong? What's happened?"

He stopped and looked at her, his eyes holding venomous hatred. He moved his hand away, and Marjorie saw it was bright crimson. "You've been shot!" She took his arm, but despite his wound, Bert shrugged her off.

"Don't touch me, woman! I want nothing to do with you Sutherlands." His face was pasty white.

"Bert, you must let me tend to you. Who did this to you? Was it bushwackers?"

"I'm going to get a gun. I'm going to kill your brother."

"Jock? What has Jock to do with this? Bert, you must be out of your head."

"Yeah, out of my head to have agreed to marry a skinny hag like yourself, Marjorie Sutherland." He winced with pain, but Bert was a strong man and he managed to walk to the stairs. "That brother of yours wanted to get his hands on my land. I figured that's what he was after, but since you were my wife, then it would be an even swap. But your brother is a greedy bastard, Marjorie. And I'm going to kill him."

"Bert! Bert! What does Jock have to do with your being shot? Jock wouldn't shoot you!"

"No, he wouldn't. He's too gentlemanly to do it himself." He began climbing the stairs, not looking at Marjorie. "Two of his stationmen waylaid me on the road. I recognized them when they shot at me. They wanted to kill me, but I have a fast horse, Marjorie. Now I'm going to settle things with that brother of yours."

"Bert, don't. You're bleeding," she cried at the bottom of the stairs, but Bert didn't turn around. He disappeared into their bedroom, and she knew he was going to get the gun he kept in the dresser drawer. He was going to kill Jock, and no matter what Jock may have intended to do, she loved her brother. Somehow she must stop Bert. Perhaps if she could convince him to lie down, she could see to his wound.

She made her way clumsily up the stairs. It seemed it took forever to reach the landing. When she finally got there, Bert was coming out of the room. He'd tied a red kerchief around his wound, and he held a gleaming silver pistol in his uninjured hand. Fear consumed Marjorie. Bert really meant to harm Jock and she must stop him!

"Please lie down," she pleaded, trying to coax him into the bedroom with a small hand placed on his shirt-sleeve. "I'll clean the wound, get out the bullet. You're losing blood, Bert."

His malicious gaze swung onto her face. "Yeah, you

223

want to help me, huh, bitch? You hate the very ground I walk on. I wouldn't be surprised if you'd known about what your brother planned to do tonight. You uppity Sutherlands are no better than skunks to want to do me in. But you're not going to get away with it, and neither is that stinking brother of yours. I'm going to kill him, and after I do, I'm coming back here. If you thought your life was a hell, think what it's going to be like from now on! No court will convict me if you hope to get rid of me that way. I'm within my rights."

Bert threw off her hand like it was a bothersome insect and started down the stairs. Marjorie made one last attempt to stop him by swinging her cane out in front of her. She meant to block him, but she realized her mistake almost immediately. Bert cried out when the cane contacted with his wound. She saw he was furious and genuinely feared for her life when he wrenched the cane away from her. But it was his own strength that caused him to lose his balance.

He held out his hand to her, grabbing for her wrist, but in her fear, Marjorie did the only thing she could. She yanked away from him. Bert let loose a foul curse and she knew he was going to come after her to make her suffer for what he thought Jock had done. Instead, he fell hard against the banister, and before Marjorie could give a squeal, the banister collapsed. Bert toppled off of the steps like a rock in a landslide to fall with a resounding smack against the hardwood floor below.

She waited on the landing, paralyzed, unable to move. She could only look with terror at the stairs, spreading black and fearsome before her, without a hand railing. Her fingers vainly clutched at her neck, and sounds of raw fear bubbled within her throat. How was she to get downstairs? Would she be trapped up here forever?

On the floor beneath her, she heard Bert crying raggedly in his pain. He called to her, but she couldn't seem to move her eyes even to look at him. She stood on the landing like a statue and knew she should go to her husband's aid, but she'd have to go down the stairs. . . . And she feared she'd fall to her death.

She waited there for what seemed like hours, cold and shivering, listening to strange, gurgling sounds. Then there was silence. Somewhere in the back of her mind, Marjorie realized Bert had died. The stairs, the very things she had feared, had ended her torment.

Her fear abated, and she found her body felt warm again and she could move her muscles. She didn't even glance down at her husband's body and she didn't go down the stairs.

Hobbling to her bedroom, she fell into an exhausted sleep. It wasn't until hours later when she heard a piercing scream from downstairs did she waken and realize Bert's Maori girlfriend had come to give him his backrub and discovered his broken body.

Even when Jock and the constable appeared to take Bert away, Marjorie remained in bed. She was free of Bert at last and could do whatever she wished.

She had earned a bit of rest.

Chapter 17

Bert's funeral was held two days later. The cause of his death was listed as accidental. As soon as Eden heard of the tragedy she hastened to Marjorie's side. The fragile woman she expected to find was gone. In her place was a Marjorie who surprised everyone by taking charge of the burial arrangements, a Marjorie who summoned the bank president to her home to discuss Bert's estate when he was barely one day dead. Jock, who'd stayed with his sister through the removal of Bert's body and the questions placed to her by the magistrate, scolded her in front of Eden for seeing to the monetary affairs when Bert was hardly cold.

"Bert is just as dead today as he will be tomorrow, next week, or next month," Marjorie curtly maintained.

"I can take care of the estate for you," Jock told her. "A woman shouldn't worry about legal terms or money. Not when she has a brother who'll take charge for her."

"That's just why I intend to look after my own affairs. Bert's estate and whatever of my money is left which the blackguard didn't spend is my business, not yours, Jock. I suggest you place your own house in order before worrying about mine."

And that was that.

Eden couldn't help admiring this new Marjorie. The timid mouse who'd docilely married the man whom her brother had chosen for her was only a memory. It was no surprise to Eden that Marjorie didn't mourn Bert. She had been candid about her feelings, but Eden wondered if somehow Marjorie had a hand in his death, and then hated herself for thinking such a horrible and traitorous thought. Marjorie couldn't harm anyone, even an animal like Bert Carruthers. Her story about Bert's having been wounded by bushwackers, arriving home to get his gun, then growing dizzy and falling from the stairs, was accepted by the magistrate. Eden believed her and if the story was a lie, she didn't want to know about it.

Shortly after the funeral services, Eden and Damon told Marjorie farewell and headed for Castlegate. Jock remained behind, intently watching from the porch as their buggy departed the yard. A sly smile hovered around his mouth to see Damon pull her close against him and plant a loving kiss on her forehead. "Soon I'll have you where I want you," he mumbled, and curved his lips into a sneer. "Eden will be mine and you'll be no more than a bad dream, so enjoy yourself while you can, you bastard."

He turned to find Marjorie staring at him from the doorway. "I thought you'd be resting," he stated. "The last few days must have undone you."

Shaking her head, she went to the porch and sat in a rocking chair. Jock leaned against the weathered railing. He noticed Marjorie didn't seem the least bit upset or tired. In fact, her entire face glowed with contentment and she didn't appear to be at all fatigued. He couldn't help but be glad she took Bert's death so well. The man had been abusive to her, but Jock didn't regret arranging the marriage. A moment's qualm of conscience stung him because Marjorie had witnessed Bert's death, and that was something Jock hadn't planned. The lummox was to have been killed on the road, but thanks to two of the blundering fools who worked for him, Bert had escaped.

But in the end, all had turned out well. Bert was dead, and Marjorie owned everything—just as Jock had planned from the beginning. Sweeping a critical eye over the front of the house and recalling the interior, he realized the renovations would be costly. The house was old and a travesty of architectural design. But the price would be worth it. He'd move in one of his foremen when he took Marjorie back to High Winds. The Carruthers' property wasn't extensive, but his own flocks would have new grazing land. Shortly he'd extend High Winds all the way to Thunder Mine—and beyond. Before the year was out, Thunder Mine would belong to him and Eden would be his wife.

Jock was eager to be free of Damon Alexander, to have him out of his life entirely. He yearned for the day when he didn't have to worry about the insolent son of a bitch, to the time when he didn't have to spare Alexander an extra thought. And that day was coming soon.

But first things first. He must deal with Marjorie.

His sister rocked quietly back and forth, back and forth. Her brown-eyed gaze settled on the rolling land before her. "You know, Jock," she said, a trace of awe in her voice. "It's pretty here. Peaceful, too. Strange how I didn't realize before now. But with Bert . . ."

"Don't think about him any longer," Jock advised.

You're a very wealthy woman. When you leave with me for High Winds, you'll be able to do whatever you want with your money."

"Yes, I will." Marjorie gave him an odd look. "But I'm not going to High Winds. I'm staying here."

"Don't be ridiculous. You couldn't remain here by yourself, even if I'd allow it. I've decided to have the house renovated for my foreman and his family. I'll need someone to look after this part of the station on a permanent basis."

Marjorie clutched the chair arms. Her mouth tightened into a thin, determined line. "This is my house, Jock, my land. You aren't putting anyone in it or on it. I don't recall you ever offering to buy this property from me."

"Oh, come on, Marjorie, stop being difficult." Jock shifted his position, his brows drawing together into a point. "You know I wanted this property all along and Bert wouldn't sell to me. So I'm offering to buy it. I'll give you whatever you ask."

"Even if I ask for more than it's worth?"

"Yes, I suppose . . ."

"No."

"No what?"

"I'm not selling Kia Ora to you."

"What in the name of God are you jabbering about?"

"I've decided to name my station Kia Ora, it means good luck, good health in Maori." Marjorie smiled softly. "I believe it's a perfect name. The gods will bless it and express their favor by happy times from now on."

"Have you lost your mind, Marjorie?"

"You'd like to think so, but no, Jock, I haven't." She laughed out loud, something she hadn't done in a very long time. "If you could see your face! Your expression is priceless. You're certain I must be insane, yet you're hoping in my dementia I'll sell to you or let you take over. Well, if anyone has the right to be crazy, I'm the one. I've lived in hell for nearly two months, and it's only by the grace of God I've still got my wits. And yes, I blame you for every moment of my torturous existence as Bert's wife. Perhaps if I'd asserted myself long ago, I wouldn't have allowed myself to be coerced into a marriage I didn't want."

"All right!" Jock's hiss filled the quiet evening. "I'm sorry for making you marry Bert. But you know why I did it, and I'm being honest with you. I want this property, I have to own it."

"I know. Damon Alexander is a thorn in your side, and you want to needle him, to make his life a hell. Think again, Jock. I'm not selling Kia Ora to you and you're not taking it from me. For the first time I have control over my life, and all thanks to you. Having lived at High Winds all of my years, I know a great deal about sheep. I plan to run a first-rate station here—not as large as High Winds, of course, but first rate, none-the-less. So, be happy for me. That's all I ask."

Marjorie rose from her chair, clinging tightly to her cane. She could see she'd made her point with Jock, but still he wouldn't admit defeat graciously. "Do you remember how I got you to marry Bert?" he asked softly.

Marjorie gave a sharp nod. "You blackmailed me, if I recall. Tiku would be hurt if I didn't do what you wanted, you said."

"The threat still stands."

A look of sadness crossed her face. "Jock, you disappoint me. I had hoped you would understand, but you don't, and I must set you straight. I am not leaving Kia Ora, and you will not harm Tiku. I haven't outlived the devil to bargain with you. I've learned from you what it means to have power, how to wield it at the right moment. I advise that you accept my decision, otherwise I shall tell the magistrate how Bert was shot by your men, how you arranged to have him murdered. He, as well as the rest of New Zealand, should find the details fascinating."

She'd never seen Jock so pale or so shaken. "That's a lie."

Marjorie shrugged. "I hope it is, but let's allow the magistrate to do some investigating. I feel certain that the only bushwackers he'll turn up will be two of High Wind's stationhands. And when faced with a prison sentence, I'd assume their loyalty to you will be short-lived."

She limped toward him, but he backed away as if she carried the plague. "I'm sorry to do this to you. No matter what you think, I love you, Jock, and if you'd plotted Bert's death to save me from him I'd do anything you wanted. But you didn't care about me, didn't try to help free me from that monster. All you wanted was the land to destroy Mr. Alexander, not to save your own sister. For that, I can never forgive you."

"I don't want your forgiveness, I don't need it!" Like a man possessed, Jock rushed from the porch and mounted his horse. His eyes burned with hate for Damon Alexander and unrelenting disgust for Marjorie. It was at that moment that she knew she'd lost her brother forever.

"Keep your precious Kia Ora, Marjorie. It seems you've found something which means more to you than I do. But know I won't be back to bail you out when your station idea turns sour. You can't possibly compete with High Winds."

"I'm not in competition with you. But I want you to know something, too." She took a deep breath, never allowing her gaze to waver from him. "Give me any trouble, and that includes harming Tiku or Mr. Alexander, and I shall report what I know about Bert's death to the authorities."

Jock grimaced and held tightly to the reins. "Perhaps if you believe me to be a craven killer, my dear, you should fear for your own safety."

"I'm not afraid of you," she stated with conviction. "You'd never harm me, Jock, because we're of the same blood. And I know somewhere deep inside, you care about me and that will prevent you from hurting me." She held out a forgiving hand to him. "You're my brother and I love you."

"Damn you, Marjorie! Damn you to hell!"

With those words ringing through the quiet twilight, Jock viciously spurred his horse and fled Kia Ora. Marjorie watched until he and the horse became a speck in the distance. Then she returned to the rocking chair and sat until the velvety night enfolded her with its warmth. She had a great deal to do, but things could wait until the morning, she decided.

Tomorrow she'd deal with her pain over Jock. Tomorrow she'd go to Thunder Mine and ask Eden and Mr. Alexander if they'd help her employ stationhands and buy flocks. She could use their help, since she couldn't purchase any of High Wind's flocks. And she'd ask Tiku if he'd consider taking a position as animal doctor for Kia Ora. His talents were being wasted as a cook. But for tonight, Marjorie would think only about Marjorie. She must learn who and what she was. No longer a Sutherland or a Carruthers, she was simply herself, and maybe that wasn't such a bad thing to be.

The warm afternoon caused perspiration to dampen Eden's brow as she walked to the dressmaker's shop. She'd left Damon with Marjorie at the newspaper office, where the editor had tacked a notice for stationhands on the bulletin board hanging outside the doorway. Damon had expressed confidence that Marjorie would have no trouble recruiting men; someone was always in need of a job. Upon leaving the newspaper office, he was taking Marjorie to other stations to inquire about buying sheep. He'd told Eden to buy whatever she needed in town and head home, as he didn't know how long Marjorie's business would take.

Before Eden left him, she'd placed her hand on his arm and gazed up at him with hope in her eyes. "May I choose the material for my wedding gown?"

For a moment she thought he was going to say no, but he smiled at her and her very insides felt lighter. "Aye, that sounds like a good idea."

And it was a good idea, in fact Eden thought it was the best one she'd ever had. On swift feet she made her way to the dressmaker's where she busily glanced through pattern books and fingered materials, all the while aware of a woman who kept eyeing her. When Eden looked up, the dark-haired customer met her stare head on. "There are some lovely materials from which to choose," Eden noted with a friendly smile. "It's quite difficult to make a selection."

The woman didn't return the smile. "I overheard the dressmaker's assistant call you Mrs. Flynn earlier. Are you the same Mrs. Flynn who owns Thunder Mine, the widow of Shamus Flynn?"

"Yes, I am. Do I know you?"

"No—not yet." The woman turned away and flounced out of the shop.

"That's an odd one," the dressmaker said to Eden, having noticed what transpired between the two women.

Eden suddenly felt uncomfortable. The woman was a stranger to her, but it seemed as if she disliked her. "Who is she?"

"I don't know" was the truthful response. "She showed up here last week and bought a large number of readymade clothes. Every day she's been in here and buys something—not that I'm complaining, but she won't give her name, won't talk about herself at all. But she pays for everything in cash, which is unusual. Most of my customers buy on credit." The dressmaker placed her spectacles on her nose. "Now, let's see what you've got here," she said to Eden, and considered the material Eden had chosen for her wedding gown.

For the remainder of the afternoon, Eden immersed herself in the design of her gown, her hat, gloves, and shoes. She was having a grand time when she suddenly noticed Tiku and the buggy outside the window. She hurriedly left with the promise from the dressmaker that the gown would be finished in two weeks' time. Eden could hardly wait to wear it, but more than anything, she prayed for Damon to set the wedding date. Perhaps his telling her to choose the material meant he had made up his mind. She hoped so. With each passing day she grew more certain of her pregnancy.

When she sat beside Tiku and they headed for home, her entire face glowed. She'd tell Damon about the baby that night. Her instincts led her to believe that the wedding was going to occur soon. And it had to be soon. She couldn't wait another moment.

Tiku noticed the love and joy shining on her face. "You're very happy with the boss, Mrs. Flynn."

She giggled out loud like an infatuated schoolgirl. "Yes, very definitely happy."

"I'm glad. Mr. Alexander deserves a good woman to love him. He's been alone a long time now."

"Did you ever meet his late wife?"

He shook his head. "No. I was in England when they were married. After I returned, I was told she had died."

"Damon took her death very hard, didn't he?"

"Yes, ma'am. He drank and didn't take an interest in anything or anybody for a long time. Until he met you, that is. You've changed his whole life."

Eden couldn't help but flush under Tiku's complimentary gaze. "I hope I can make him happy. I don't want him to be sad or think he made a wrong choice after we're married."

"He'd never think that. He loves you. Don't try to compare yourself to the first Mrs. Alexander."

"I know I shouldn't. This whole afternoon when I've been so happy, I've been thinking about her, wondering what she was like. I guess it's normal to wonder about the woman who went before you." Eden gave a small laugh. "Forgive me, Tiku. I'm being a silly goose and boring you in the process. Let's talk about your plans. Damon told me you're going to work at Kia Ora for Marjorie. I didn't know you were an animal doctor."

"Not many people do know," he admitted. "I find it

difficult to admit to people that I was trained in England only because my father wanted to relieve his guilt in siring a bastard son by having me educated."

"I'm certain he didn't do it for that reason. Your father must love you very much."

Tiku grinned sadly. "He cares for me some, I think, but by educating me abroad he's shown me I'll never fit in there or here. I'll always be treated differently because I am different—not able to live among my father's people and no longer able to live among the Maoris. His gift of an education has branded me. My mother's family has disowned me."

Eden's heart went out in sympathy to Tiku. How unfair and cruel people could be.

"I know someone who thinks a great deal of you." Eden tried to offer him some comfort. "Mrs. Carruthers told me just this morning that she believes you'll do her and Kia Ora proud. And Mrs. Carruthers is a very discerning woman."

She'd have sworn Tiku blushed but she wasn't certain because of the deepening shadows. "Mrs. Carruthers is too kind."

When Eden arrived home she made certain that the Maori cook who had taken over Tiku's job had prepared supper. The lamb was already done, and upon tasting it, the piece of meat melted in her mouth. Making sure the dining-room table was set just right and pleased to see how the candles in the opulent chandelier bathed the room in a romantic light, she hurried to wash and dress before Damon returned. She changed into a green-and-blue-striped taffeta gown. The bodice was a deep royal-blue

236

and fit so snugly across her bosom, she found she had to hold her breath while a servant did the tiny buttons on the back.

There was no doubt about it. Tonight she had to tell Damon about the baby. Before too long, he'd be able to see for himself that she was carrying a child. A secret smile curved her lips. Tonight would be a special night indeed.

Just as the sun was dipping behind the mountains, she heard voices in the parlor. Believing Damon to be home, she practically ran down the hallway, only to stop in stunned silence when she saw the woman from the dressmaker's shop sitting on the divan. A small boy, next to her, clutched her hand. The woman didn't rise when Eden entered the room.

"I could not keep the lady out," the servant woman, Lanu, apologized to Eden, and shot the stranger a chilling look.

"That's all right. You're dismissed, Lanu." Eden waited expectantly, offering the child a friendly smile when he scooted closer to the woman, whom Eden assumed to be his mother. "I'm sorry," she said, realizing the woman wasn't going to say anything and unnerved by her contemptuous stare. "Today at the dressmaker's I failed to ask your name. I do apologize. If I'm supposed to know you—"

"You're not."

"Then how may I help you?"

The woman rose. Her eyes contained such venomous loathing that Eden's skin crawled. "You may leave me house, that's what you can do!"

Eden's mouth fell open in utter shock. She was speechless for a moment. Who was this woman? Was she insane? How dare she come into Castlegate and act as if she owned it. "I suggest you leave right now, madam," she finally said. "I fear you've made a great error in coming here." Eden spoke calmly, concerned the woman might be a bit mad and realizing the little boy, who was about four years old, was clinging in fear to his mother's skirts.

"The only one who'll be leavin' is you, you strumpet, you Jezebel!"

"Now just one moment..." Eden would have stood her ground, would have called for Tiku if the woman became more unruly, but the child started to cry. The woman bent and patted his back to comfort him, and Eden suddenly felt like the interloper, which was ridiculous. Castlegate was *her* home.

A movement from the veranda doorway caught her eye. Eden breathed a relieved sigh to see Damon standing there, assured the strange situation would be put to rights. But there was something about his very stance, the chilling way his gaze was riveted on the woman and the child, that paralyzed her into silence. The hand gripping his hat brim trembled violently, and she'd never seen his bronzed complexion so ashen in color. The haunting, pained expression in his eyes shook her to her very soul.

She made a slight move to go to him but stopped. Damon didn't seem to see her or hear her when she whispered his name. It was as if she'd died, and death would have been preferable when she saw him take a step forward and, without removing his gaze from the dark-haired woman hoarsely exclaim, "Tessa!"

Chapter 18

"Yes, Damon, it's me."

Tessa sounded almost proud, too haughty for Damon's liking when she faced him. He couldn't help but admire her courage. The bitch didn't even falter, didn't quake with fear. He was the one who was shaking, and not only because Tessa had the audacity to turn up at Castlegate, unannounced, uninvited, and most definitely unwanted. It was because of Eden his legs could barely carry him now. He couldn't look at her, so filled was he with embarrassment and humiliation.

Eden must be puzzled, more than upset. Worst of all was the disgust and utter contempt he knew she'd later feel for him. God, please let her try and understand. He prayed for the first time since he was a little boy. *Let Eden understand why I didn't tell her about Tessa. Don't let her leave me.*

But for now, he couldn't take care of Eden; first, he had to deal with Tessa.

But he was aware of Eden standing as still as a Maori wood carving. He took a controlling breath and spoke to

239

the woman who was still his wife. "I suppose you're here because Mr. MacKenzie's investigator found you and told you I'm petitioning for divorce."

Tessa made a helpless gesture with her hand which resembled a bird's attempt to flutter a broken wing. "No-o, no investigator contacted me. You can't mean to divorce me, Damon, me love. We've traveled all this way. I've come to plead with you to take me back." She appeared sufficiently distraught. "I've had a change of heart about us. I know now how much I love you."

"What a lying bitch you are!" Damon raked his hair and tossed his hat to the floor. "After what you put me through, the way you left me, you now say you love me. Tessa, I want no part of you! Get out of here!"

"Momma!"

It was then Damon took notice of the frightened child who stood behind Tessa. "Man's gonna hurt me!" he cried. "Momma, man's gonna hurt me."

"There, there, Collin," Tessa soothed, bending down to scoop up the child in her arms. "No one's gonna hurt me baby boy." She patted him on the back and shot Damon a hostile glare. "All your blusterin' has scared Collin. Lower your voice, he's a sensitive child." Her eyes narrowed toward Eden. "And tell your whore to get out."

Damon lowered his voice, but glowered at Tessa. "Don't you dare to call Eden that. I think it's time for you to be leaving."

Tessa laughed. "I won't be the one to go, Damon. I need to talk to you about our son." She stroked the dark-haired child's head. "He *is* yours."

Eden watched Damon's reaction. It was as if a thunderbolt hit him from the heavens as he jerked forward and cursed under his breath. "You're lying." But Eden could see even as he spoke that he was watching the little boy, carefully examining him, looking for features in the child's face to determine if the boy was his son. And Eden knew then with a clarity which caused her heart to nearly stop beating that Tessa was telling the truth. The physical similarities couldn't be denied.

This child was Damon's son.

She clutched at her throat just as Damon looked at her. For the first time since he entered the room, he seemed to truly see her, and she knew he'd already reached the same conclusion about the child. "Eden, sweetheart . . ." He started across the room toward her, but she backed away. "I have to explain about Tessa, about the divorce . . ."

"I don't want to hear about it. I can't bear to hear about it." Her voice cracked and tears glistened within her eyes like diamonds within emerald pools. She wanted to collapse at the unfairness of it all. Within her body grew Damon's child, but not ten feet away from her was a little boy whom she knew Damon couldn't desert—not if Collin was truly his son. She wouldn't tell him about the life growing within her. Not now, not when he had a wife and child. Dear God! What lies he had told her.

But she held herself erect. Her mother's training all those years ago about the importance of behaving like a lady came back to her. "There must be a great deal for you to talk over, so I'll leave you alone with your son and—your wife." She could barely utter the words, but grabbing a handful of taffeta skirt, she pirouetted and proudly walked through the veranda doors to head past the stately columns until she was outside. Then she ran until she collapsed, breathless and spent, upon a hillside.

Beneath the glittering stars, Eden screamed to the heavens and pounded her fists upon the ground.

"Damn you, Shamus Flynn, damn you for making me promise to come here! Damn you, damn you, damn you!" Burying her face within the cradle of her arms. she wept.

"Your woman is a fancy one," Tessa commented, checking the envy in her voice. "But she ain't your type." She managed a tremulous smile at his black scowl. "What do you think of our little Collin?" she asked, and kissed the boy's cheek. "He looks like you, don't you think?"

Damon ignored her, calling for Lanu, who immediately appeared. "Collin . . ." He addressed the little boy and smiled at him. "Lanu will take you outside to the stables to see my horses. I have a pony you might like to sit on."

The child's face brightened, and he wiped away his tears. "A real pony? I never saw a real pony before." Looking to his mother, he said, "I want to see the pony."

"Go on then." Tessa waved him away. "And be a good boy."

Collin assured he would be very good, and eagerly left with Lanu. Damon waited until they were out of the house. The only sound was the rhythmic ticking of the pendulum clock, and it reminded Damon of the many years he'd wasted being married to this woman. He should have divorced her long ago. Now he feared he'd lost Eden because of his stupidity in not freeing himself permanently of Tessa. He'd wanted to forget her very existence, but that was impossible. She sat before him a triumphant expression on her face because she thought she had him where she wanted him—and all because of an innocent child.

"Is the boy truly mine?" he ground out, unwilling to admit Collin was his.

"Of course he is. You're not blind, Damon. You can see he resembles you."

"Why didn't you tell me you were having a child when you left here?"

"I didn't know then. And, well . . . what would you want me to do after the horrible things you screamed at me? I couldn't very well come back, now could I?"

"So your lover accepted you and the boy."

"Aye. He loved me very much, and was good to Collin."

"What happened to your wealthy businessman?"

Tessa's voice shook. "He died."

"So now you've returned to Thunder Mine and me in search of greener pastures."

Tessa shook out her skirt. "Ah, Damon, I'd figure you'd think the worst. Can't you accept I've returned because I still love you, that Collin needs his father? We were good together once, you haven't forgotten that." Taking a step toward him, she wrapped her arms around his neck. "I think I came back just in time."

Damon glared down at her languid expression. Suddenly he laughed. "What a wanton creature you are. I don't love you. In fact I'm disgusted by you. Go back to wherever you came from and leave me be." He didn't miss her baleful stare as he disentangled her arms. "I'll take you into town, so be ready when I return. I have to find Eden and explain things to her."

Tessa indignantly placed her hands on her hips. "What is it you're sayin' to me, Damon Alexander? That you don't want me as your wife anymore, that you want to marry that slut who took out of here like her lace drawers were afire? Well, I'm not goin' noplace."

Moving toward her, Damon didn't miss the fear that suddenly blossomed on Tessa's still-pretty face. He grabbed her, his fingers digging into the flesh of her upper arms. "Never call Eden such a name again. You're that—and other names so vile I won't repeat them. I wish to God I'd gotten a divorce and not waited so long. I'd be free of you then, blissfully free."

"Why *didn't* you divorce me?" Tessa asked, grimacing with pain. This was the first time in five years that Damon had touched her. She enjoyed the feel of his hands upon her, even if it was to hurt her. "Did you love me so much, Damon?"

Damon sighed and shook his head. "Same old Tessa you are, always thinking too much of yourself. But, no, I hated you enough that I lied and told people you'd died accidentally. It seemed the quickest and least painful way to put you out of my mind forever. And it worked. Do you know that no one thought to tell me what a tragedy your death was. Not even Sutherland."

"Oh, that's because Jock already—" Tessa broke off, clamping her lips together.

"There's something you want to tell me about Sutherland?" Damon eyed her suspiciously, his fingers digging more deeply into her arms.

"Stop, Damon. You're hurting me!"

He let her go with such violent force that Tessa spun around and found herself clinging to the back of a nearby chair for support. "Be ready to leave," he reminded her.

She caught her breath. Her eyes were large, her tone combative. "If I leave, Collin goes with me. You'll never see your son again. I'll make bloody certain of that."

244

"The boy stays."

Her dark curls bounced when she shook her head. "He won't stay without me. I'm his mother, and he needs me. You can't be gettin' rid of me and keepin' him."

"Like hell I can't."

Rushing around to the other side of the chair, Tessa knew genuine fear. Perhaps it hadn't been a good idea to come here like this, but if she hadn't arrived unexpectedly, then she'd never be allowed into Castlegate. She gambled Damon would relent and want his son—and herself in the bargain. "Touch me and I'll scream to the top of me lungs. I'll bring your house down upon your head. I'll tell anyone who'll listen, you tried to kill me so you could marry your whore. Now who's goin' to deny that ain't the truth? You?

"I saw a barrister before I come here. I have me rights. Legally, we're still married and this is my house. If you know what's right and proper, you'll cart your precious slut into town. Besides, from what I been hearin' in certain circles, Mrs. Eden Flynn is considered to be the whore, not me. So, think long and hard about what you plan to do, love, 'cause her reputation is the one in shreds around here." Tessa cast a proprietary eye over the parlor. "If the rest of the house is as fancy as this, I'd say I've done pretty well for meself. Too bad I can't thank old Shamus personally."

She was determined to make his life a hell, he could tell. She'd returned for some other reason than love for him or wanting the boy to know his father. And he'd already accepted Collin as his own. The striking resemblance between them was too great to be ignored. But why had she come back? For his money? Perhaps. He had plenty of money, true, but she was up to something else, and she planned to use an innocent child to worm her way back into his life. He wanted to get to know his son, but he wouldn't allow Tessa the upper hand. She and the boy would stay at Castlegate for the time being, but not at the price of his sanity.

Damon clenched and unclenched his fists to control his rage. He hated the scheming witch, but until he could get the child from her, he'd be forced to put up with her. And then there was Eden. What would she say when she learned Tessa and the boy would be staying on? Dread filled him because he already sensed what her answer would be. And now he must convince her not to leave him.

"Somehow, some way, I'm going to be free of you. Forever free of you, even if I must pay a king's ransom to earn my freedom."

A satisfied smile ringed her red, painted mouth. "Ah, me darlin', you always did say the sweetest things to me."

Damon strode from the parlor, nearly bumping into his housekeeper and the child in his haste to find Eden.

"I rode the pony," squealed Collin to his mother.

"It was fun then?"

He nodded in reply.

"Then you want to stay on here? You can ride the pony every day."

Collin laughed in delight, and took his mother's hand. The Maori housekeeper coolly assessed Tessa, who appeared nonplussed by the scrutiny. "You're called Lanu?" Tessa asked, and the woman grunted. "I'm Mrs. Alexander. I'd like me bags which are on the porch brought inside and placed in the master suite, seeing that me husband didn't think to do it. And I'd like a nice warm bath for me and me son. Traveling is dirty business."

"But Miss Eden sleeps in the master's room," Lanu protested.

"Not anymore she don't," Tessa archly replied. "I'm Mr. Alexander's legal wife and will be treated like the mistress here. I doubt my husband's whore will be stayin' on much longer."

Tessa thought the little woman was about to refuse her command, but minutes later, the bags were in Damon's bedroom. She found herself lying on the softest and largest bed she'd ever sampled. From down the hallway, she heard Collin playing in another room. Despite the scene in the parlor with Damon and his whore, Tessa was certain everything would work out for her. In time Damon would accept Collin and then turn to her. All she had to do was get the Flynn woman out of Damon's life, and if she knew anything about properly bred women, Eden Flynn would be gone before morning.

She laughed out loud, heady with her own sense of accomplishment. Life was going to be good for her. She was certain of it.

Eden lifted her head from the sweetly scented grass, aware of Damon's presence before he dared whisper her name. Falling to his knees, he protectively wrapped his arms around her trembling shoulders. His stubbled cheek grazed hers, his lips kissed away her tears. "Eden, forgive me." His voice was a hoarse croak in her ear. "I should have told you the truth about Tessa."

Damon tilted her face so he could see into her eyes, but what he saw gave him no solace. The shimmering orbs, so much like precious greenstone when she gazed at him with trust and desire, laughter and anger, now regarded him without any trace of emotion. He was losing Eden, and above all things, he couldn't allow that to happen. Without Eden, he was half a man. She must understand, and *had* to understand why he'd lied about Tessa.

"I know you're hurt," he continued, and felt inane for even saying it. Certainly, she was hurt. What had he expected? "But I need for you to listen to me. I've got to tell you how it was after Tessa left me." Damon expected some reaction from her. He got none, but decided her shocked state might be for the best. As long as she allowed him to hold her, he could be certain she wouldn't run away. He could tell her the truth.

"I'm a proud man, Eden. You know that. I won't lie to you and tell you I didn't love Tessa when I married her. I did love her, I was mad for her. And Jock Sutherland wanted her, too, which made winning her all the more rewarding." A sigh ripped through his chest. "But I should have let Sutherland have the bitch, for she caused nothing but misery. She'd married me believing me to be the wealthiest man in the area, and aye, I admit I had money, but not as much as she thought I did. You see, Shamus was the one who controlled the purse strings for a long time. It was only as Shamus grew older and Tessa was gone that he gave me more responsibility in running Thunder Mine. Shortly after Tessa left the Otago with her rich businessman, Shamus admitted he'd purposely withheld most of the mine's wealth from me because he'd always disliked Tessa and thought she was a conniving witch who was after anything she could get."

"Shamus was a better judge of character than you," Eden unemotionally observed, fidgeting in Damon's embrace.

"Aye, you're right," Damon sadly admitted, stroking

248

her hair. "He loved you, sent you here to me, but I wanted to believe the worst about you rather than trust Shamus's judgment in marrying you. You see, it hurt to know Tessa had fooled me but Shamus had seen through her. My pride suffered when she left me for an older man. I figured she'd rejected me as a man, and afterward I began spending time with women who weren't decent. I didn't want to marry again, and I convinced everyone Tessa was dead, even going so far as to believe it myself. To me, she *was* dead. *I* was dead until I met you."

"Oh, Damon, don't!" A sob spilled from Eden's mouth and she pushed at him. "I don't want to hear any of this. Not now!"

Damon held her fast against him. "But I want you to hear, Eden. You have to know how much I love you. I love you so much, my darling, that for the first time in years I wanted a wife—you. I contacted Mr. MacKenzie to have Tessa found and petition her for divorce. I prayed she'd be dead, or so guilty over what she'd done that she'd consent without a fuss. I never expected her to turn up here. I hoped we could be married soon. If I'd have known Tessa would brazenly walk into Castlegate and claim her rights, I wouldn't have bothered trying to find her, I'd have gone ahead and married you—"

"Married me when you had another wife! And a child! Haven't you humiliated me enough without adding bigamy to the list? I can't bear to hear you say another word. Let me alone, let me be!" She struggled out of his grasp when Damon voluntarily loosened his grip. There was no point in holding on to her. Eden was lost to him. He knew that now.

He stood up when she did. The moonlight illuminated her, and he allowed his eyes to roam across her tousled hair with the grass clinging within its golden-red depths, to memorize every line of her tear-stained face. Even with her eyes red and swollen from crying, Eden was heartbreakingly beautiful, but no longer his to cherish and love. She was going to leave him, and nothing he could say would stop her. But he would try one last time.

"I'm going to divorce Tessa. I'll *make* her give me a divorce. Then, Eden, we can be married." Damon made one final attempt to hold her against him. He ached to feel her body melt into his, to know she still loved him. But she jabbed at his chest with tightly balled fists.

"I don't want to marry you!" she shouted. "I want to be free of you, and wish to God I'd never met you. I'm leaving here tonight and hope never to lay eyes upon you again."

"Eden, please, don't be leaving me." He held her fast, refusing to give in to her struggles by releasing her. "Tell me you still love me. I know you love me."

Suddenly she grew very still. Her heaving bosom was the only indication of her anger. "Let me go, Damon. I won't take you from your son." **Her words, spoken** softly and with chilling solemnity, sent a painful chill through him. She broke away and turned her back to him as she started back to Castlegate.

"Eden," he called, uncertain as he did so what he could say to convince her to stay.

Without looking at him, he heard her voice. "Don't come after me. I want nothing to do with Thunder Mine or you ever again." And those were the last words she spoke to him. When he returned to the house hours later, he sensed a loneliness and knew Eden was gone. Lanu padded quietly into the parlor where he stood and handed him a piece of faded parchment.

"Miss Eden said to give you this, Mr. Damon." Lanu's face expressed her sadness and she choked back a sob as she fled from the room.

Damon read the missive, not the least surprised to discover he held Eden's deed to Thunder Mine. His heart gave a jolt when he saw her finely scripted signature finalizing that she had turned over her portion of the mine to him. If this had been a few months ago, he'd have been ecstatic to have Eden Flynn out of his life. Now he felt such pain he didn't believe he could tolerate it. She was gone, and the ache which consumed his entire body was a hundred times greater than when Tessa had left him.

He went to the bedroom, hoping against hope that this was all a nightmare, that he'd open the door and there would be his Eden, waiting for him in the big bed and holding out her arms to him. And when he entered the bedroom, he could see a woman's figure on Eden's side of the bed. Hope filled him. She hadn't left after all. Perhaps things could still work out for them—

Damon froze in his tracks, his eyes wide and viciously blue as he gazed down at the woman who slept so peacefully. It wasn't Eden at all.

It was Tessa.

Chapter 19

Kia Ora was beautiful when the sun rose above the mountains and gilded the peaks with golden fingers of sunshine. Eden couldn't help noticing how the inside of the Carruthers' house glowed now, too, since Marjorie had employed a carpenter to rebuild the stairs and carpet them in an attractive peach-and-green floral pattern. The heavy, ominous paneling was gone, replaced by a white-and-peach striped wallpaper on the parlor walls. Elegant mahogany furnishings replaced their spartan predecessors in every room of the house.

Under Marjorie's expert eye, Kia Ora was slowly coming into its own.

Eden sipped an iced lime drink which was prepared for her by Marjorie's new housekeeper, an Englishwoman named Bonnie Day, who Marjorie had hired in town. In fact, Kia Ora bustled with servants, which was as it should be, but Eden was to discover that each day of the last seven since Eden arrived during the dark of night and begged Marjorie's hospitality, Marjorie lifted herself onto a horse's strong back and rode into the open countryside. "I must tend to my flock," she'd say to Eden and grin from ear to ear as she rode off with her long brown braid flying in the breeze to join Tiku on the plains.

It was clear that Marjorie was happy, and since Tiku joined the household, her plain face beamed until she no longer looked anything but pretty. Marjorie was in love with Tiku, Eden could see that, any fool could tell. And it was just as obvious to Eden that Tiku returned that love. His eyes constantly followed her, seeming to drink in her every movement, seeming to know what she wanted before she asked for it.

However, Eden doubted Tiku would act on his desires. From her conversation with him, he felt he was beneath most people, and she realized this included Marjorie. Thus, he'd hold himself away from her—which was regretful. These two people loved each other but couldn't openly admit that love because of society's rules.

And here was Eden Flynn, a woman in love with a married man, a woman having that man's child. She wondered what would be said about her when she bore Damon's child. She wondered what Damon would say. A chilling fear suffused her body and she shivered. She must leave the Otago area before her condition became too apparent. Damon mustn't know about the baby or he'd find some way to keep her here. Never would she stay and bear a baby out of wedlock, never would she allow her child to become a victim of cruel remarks and treatment. Soon she'd leave. Maybe Tiku could escort her back to Queenstown and then she'd return to America and make a new life for herself and her baby. She'd simply tell people the truth about her widowhood. No one would know the child wasn't her husband's. Her wealth allowed her to give her baby everything, to make a decent life for them both.

But a lump formed painfully in her throat. A new life meant she'd be without Damon, and not all the wealth in the world could alleviate her suffering. Today was the day she'd start her new life. She was going to see Mr. MacKenzie and officially receive her money for her share of Thunder Mine from Damon.

Today she'd sever all ties with Damon Alexander— except for the smallest but most significant one growing in her womb.

A knock at the door barely intruded into her thoughts until Bonnie appeared in the doorway. "You have a guest, ma'am. Mr. Sutherland is here to see you."

Eden instantly rose to her feet as Jock approached her and Bonnie departed. Dressed in a dark suit of clothes with a snowy white shirt, Jock looked every bit the gentleman, but it was the sympathetic smile on his handsome face which caused a sob to escape from her. Jock must have come because he knew about Tessa. Eden alternately felt affection for him but also humiliation. If Jock knew, then everyone else in the area must know Tessa had returned.

Clasping her hands between his large, warm ones, Jock gave her a brotherly peck on the cheek. "I heard about what happened. I've been worried about you."

Eden managed to smile. "Thank you, Jock. You're a good friend to visit me."

"You're looking a bit pale," he noted worriedly. "Have you been outside the house since your arrival?"

"No, I haven't felt like leaving my room until this morning. Marjorie has been such a gracious hostess, such a wonderful friend to me." She glanced around the room.

"Don't you like the changes she's made in the house?"

"We're not discussing my sister, so don't try and steer from the subject, Eden."

"And what might the subject be?" she asked.

"You, and you know it. Now, why have you buried yourself inside? Wait, don't tell me. I'll tell you. You're afraid you're going to run into someone who knows about the return of Damon's prodigal wife and child."

Eden bit down upon her lower lip. Just to hear Damon's name hurt. "Jock, please don't go on." She broke away from him and went to stand by the window. The early-morning light touched her face in a golden haze. "The last week hasn't been easy for me."

He was behind her, placing his hands upon her shoulders and turning her toward him. "I can imagine what you've been going through, my darling. But now that you know what sort of a person Alexander truly is, you can forget him. No one blames you for his lie. You can't hide yourself away from people forever, Eden. One day you'll have to confront them with your head held high like the aristocrat you are."

"I'm aware of that, but—Damon isn't a bad person, Jock. I can understand why he lied to everyone. What that woman did to him was unforgivable."

"Can you forgive him for lying to *you?*" Jock ground out from between his finely chiseled lips.

Jock hit at the heart of the matter. She'd considered the circumstances of Damon's marriage, even going so far as to think she could forget Tessa ever existed if he divorced the woman. Damon had shown up at Kia Ora the day after her arrival, but Eden had told Marjorie to tell him she wouldn't see him, that he had nothing to say which might change her mind. Instead, he'd given

Marjorie a note for her, and Eden still kept it. Damon had told her that he loved her, and he'd somehow free himself of Tessa, to please wait for him, that he was anxious to hear from her.

She hadn't replied. She couldn't because she didn't know what to tell him now that she knew he had a son who needed him. But she couldn't write to him or forgive him. He'd lied to *her*.

Jock cupped her chin. "I'm sorry for causing you more distress. I can see the subject is a painful one. I came to offer you a ride into town. Today is the day you see Mr. MacKenzie?"

"Yes. How did you know about that?"

Jock gave her a mysterious smile. "There's very little in the Otago that I don't know, Eden. Just say I have my way of discovering things." Minny, MacKenzie's clerk, had passed on the news to him, once again proving to be an able source of information. "Allow me to escort you. I can't bear imagining you riding into town with a servant."

Eden couldn't think of a reason to refuse Jock's request, and why should she? He'd more than proved he was her friend by always coming to her aid, and he'd granted Thunder Mine the water rights to please her. She couldn't forget his kindnesses and was deeply indebted to him. "I'll be ready to leave shortly," she told him, and started out of the room but stopped and shot him a grateful smile. "You've been my champion, Jock. Thank you for caring about me."

Jock bowed low to her, and Eden felt as if she'd been transported into her parents' drawing room on the night of a large ball when young gallants danced attendance upon her. As she went to her room in search of her parasol, she willed herself not to think about Damon, the man she loved. He wasn't a gentleman like Jock, he'd never treated her like the true lady she was until he'd discovered she was a virgin. But Jock always had. And she was grateful to Jock Sutherland because not once had he rubbed salt in her wounds by telling her "I told you so. I told you Alexander wasn't a gentleman." He'd always been supremely patient and kind.

He was the sort of man who would be a good husband to her and father to her child.

"No," Eden mumbled out loud and grabbed for the yellow-and-white parasol matching her gown. "I don't want to marry anyone—not Damon or Jock." But the seeds of a marriage were planted, and she wasn't quite certain how.

The silence in Mr. MacKenzie's office was oppressive. There was no need for Damon's presence since he'd already signed the necessary papers, buying out her share of Thunder Mine. But there he sat across from her, his long, booted legs thrust out in front of him. He hadn't had the courtesy to wear a formal suit on such a serious occasion as this, but wore a light-blue shirt, unbuttoned at the neck, and a pair of tightly fitted, brown corded pants. It was almost as if he intended to flaunt his physique at her, to watch her beneath those hooded blue eyes until she squirmed in her seat. She couldn't help but think how different he was from Jock, who was always a gentleman; Damon could be so very uncouth in manners and dress. What he'd chosen to wear today proved he didn't give a damn about what anybody thought.

But Eden thought he looked magnificent.

"Mrs. Flynn, your signature." Mr. MacKenzie's voice turned her attention away from Damon. The man held out a quill to her and she daintily dipped it into the ink container, and after a moment's hesitation, she signed her name on the parchment. "I trust all has been to your approval," Mr. MacKenzie said to her. "Now, where shall I have the funds deposited?"

"What do you mean?" Eden asked, unable to think clearly in Damon's unnerving presence.

"At which bank should I have the funds deposited?"

"I don't know." Eden's mind whirled. Where was she going when she left New Zealand? She had absolutely no idea. "I'll be leaving shortly, probably for America," she admitted. "Maybe San Francisco, but I can't say." For a second she couldn't speak because tears suddenly choked her. This was going to be the last time she'd ever see Damon, and they sat across from each other like adversaries. "Must I make a decision now?"

Mr. MacKenzie sympathetically patted her hand. "No, my dear, you can take as long to decide as you wish. But before you leave New Zealand, I should like to know where you're going so the necessary arrangements can be made. You're a very wealthy woman, Mrs. Flynn. Extremely wealthy."

Eden stood up. "Yes, thank you, sir." She started to leave the office when Damon was suddenly beside her, his hand on the doorknob.

"I have to speak to you," he whispered. "You can't mean to leave New Zealand. I won't let you go."

"Damon, I'll do what I please."

"I love you. Doesn't that please you enough to want to stay?"

Her face flamed a vivid shade of scarlet. She threw a

258

quick glance at Mr. MacKenzie, who pretended to be absorbed in his paperwork. "Damon, please don't go on. I don't want to hear what you have to say. Anyway, this isn't the place to discuss . . . our problem."

"This is the perfect place," he persisted. "Mr. MacKenzie is taking care of my divorce. He knows everything there is to know about us."

The blood pounded in Eden's head. "Has Tessa agreed to a divorce? Has she left Castlegate?"

Damon dashed her hopes of ending their misery by sighing and shaking his head. "No. If I want a divorce, a court will have to decide, and from what Mr. MacKenzie told me, Tessa deserted me and the chances are good that I'll be granted one. But . . ." he shook himself, "I'm not going to do that, even though it means a shorter wait than getting her to sign the necessary papers, which she claims she'll never do. Otherwise, she'll take Collin away with her."

From his attitude she knew something was wrong. "Why can't you directly petition the court?" she asked, almost not wanting to discover the truth.

"Because of you, Eden. You'll be named as correspondent, and your name dragged through the mud; our love will be made out as tawdry and cheap. I won't allow that to happen to you—even if it means losing you."

"Then there's no hope for us, no hope at all." She stood very still, her gaze taking in his face. Then she touched his hand which was still on the knob, feeling all the warmth and power it contained. She knew she'd never be able to touch him like this again. "Good-bye, Damon. I wish you well." How she spoke without breaking down would always remain a mystery to her, but she'd cried so often and so long the past week that she didn't have a tear left to shed.

"I'm not giving up on us," he whispered into her ear before he opened the door. "I love you and I'm going to have you."

Anything else she might have said to him was forgotten when Jock, whom she'd forgotten was waiting in the outer office, placed a proprietary hand on her elbow. "Is everything settled, my dear?" he asked Eden, who missed the triumphant smile he threw at Damon.

"Yes, I'd like to return to Kia Ora now."

"Certainly," Jock told her, and began to lead her away when Damon's voice stalled both of them.

"So, Gentleman Jock has come to the damsel's rescue, I see. I should have known you wouldn't waste any time, Sutherland."

"You're quite correct in that." His grip tightened on Eden's arm. "But you're notorious for wasting time—say five years of it. Now good day, Alexander. Eden is eager to leave."

Damon noticed the pleading expression in Eden's eyes not to cause a scene, and he deferred to her. As much as he hated Sutherland and would delight in beating the haughtiness out of him, he didn't wish to humiliate Eden further. He loved her so much that he knew he must free her, at least until he thought of some way to force Tessa to sign the divorce papers and gain custody of Collin. He needed to get to know his son and wouldn't give him up.

But he felt chilled to his very soul to imagine that Eden might actually marry Jock Sutherland. The two of them made a striking couple, and their backgrounds were similar. And knowing how persuasive Jock could be, Damon anticipated he'd press Eden to marry him.

Would she accept his proposal? God, he hoped not! If

260

only Tessa would leave Castlegate of her own volition, if only she'd agree to the divorce. But Tessa was a stubborn woman and not about to be coerced into doing something she didn't want to do. The deck was stacked in her favor—and all because of an innocent child.

"Something wrong, Mr. Alexander?" Minny asked. "You look like you've lost your best friend."

Damon smiled sadly and put on his hat. "I've lost much more than that, ma'am, much more."

On the return trip to Kia Ora, Eden humiliated herself by falling ill. Jock hastily stopped the carriage and she scampered out of it to lean over a small gully where she vomited that morning's breakfast. She was mortified to find Jock standing beside her, and offering his handkerchief.

"I'm sorry," she sobbed aloud, almost on the brink of tears.

"Don't apologize," he told her, clasping his arm around her waist to help her to her feet. "You didn't look well this morning. I told you I was worried."

Eden's hands were shaking when he helped her into the carriage and took his seat next to her. She expected Jock to start for Kia Ora, but he barely moved a muscle. He looked at her for what seemed a long time until he cleared his throat. Eden immediately tensed, on the alert and praying Jock believed she had only a stomach upset.

"Eden, are you having a child?" Her wince at the question didn't go unnoticed by him. "I presume Alexander doesn't know."

Why deny her condition? Jock wasn't a stupid man. "I didn't want to tell him until he'd set a wedding date, but there won't be a wedding now, so . . ." Tears trickled down her cheeks. "I'm in disgrace. I can't bear to imagine what people will say if I stay here and have Damon's baby. That's why I must figure what to do with my life, where to go."

Jock grabbed her around her waist and pulled her close against him. "I forbid you to go anywhere, Eden. You'll stay here and marry me. I'll take care of you and your child. No one will ever need to know that I'm not the father. Say you'll marry me, tell me you will. I love you so much, Eden. I'm in torment with wanting you!" His mouth swooped down upon hers, drowning her protests.

The kiss blazed with passion, and Eden felt herself responding to Jock but was horrified by her body's awakening desire. If this had happened before she saw Damon in the law office, she'd be tempted to give in to Jock, to agree to marry him. But she had seen Damon, and she knew without a doubt that no matter what he'd done to her, she still loved him. And if she couldn't marry Damon, she'd not wed another man—especially Jock—whom Damon hated. Such a marriage wouldn't be fair to any one of them, least of all Jock. She simply didn't love him.

Pushing at him, Eden broke the kiss. "Don't make this more difficult for me than it is already. I can't marry you, I won't marry you."

"Why? Tell me one good reason why."

"I don't love you, Jock. That's all the reason I need. If I married you, you'd only be hurt because I can't forget Damon. I'll never forget him."

"Then we'll live in Wellington. You'd never have to set foot here again. You could learn to love me."

"Oh, Jock, I don't want to marry a man I have to learn

to love. What sort of a marriage would that be?"

She saw he struggled to compose himself. When he let her go and picked up the reins, his scar stood out white against his tanned skin. "I won't give up on you, Eden. You'll marry me." His response numbed her to silence. Damon had said the very same thing to her earlier—but somehow she believed Jock.

Tessa paced the veranda, the swishing of her taffeta gown breaking the silence of the afternoon. Where was Damon? He should have been home yesterday after going into town on business. It was just like him to keep her waiting, making her wonder if he would ever return. Damon was quite capable of upsetting her with his blatant disregard for her feelings. She always made certain he knew how she felt, and sometimes she screeched at him like a fishwife when he paid her no attention. But that was the problem.

Damon didn't care about her.

Many times she'd attempted to strike up a friendly conversation, even going so far as to entice him to bed her. She realized he might not want to speak to her, but for him not to desire her as a woman hurt her unbearably. Men paid money for her charms, and her own husband couldn't stand the sight of her.

Tessa blamed Jock for her current dilemma. She'd foolishly listened to him, believing Damon would fall prey to her feminine wiles, but whenever he was at Castlegate he moped around with a long face. He didn't need to admit he was pining for Eden Flynn, and Tessa was insane with jealousy. Never had she begged a man to want her, but if begging was required to get Damon to bed her again, to truly be his wife, then she'd gladly sink on bended knee. If only Damon would want her again, then her future would be secured. She couldn't use Collin as a leverage forever.

The servants barely tolerated her and she was alone most of the time. What was the point of being mistress of a fine house and wearing fancy dresses with no one to care about her or see her in all her glory?

Her gaze strayed to the mine, causing her to remember the miners and their families. Since her arrival, she hadn't paid a visit to her former acquaintances. Now seemed the perfect time. She was so bored when Collin napped that even the thought of spending time with the same people who'd sneered at her father and herself years ago would be preferable to her own company. Some of the women had looked down their noses at her and whispered behind her back when Damon had started courting her. They'd thought she wasn't good enough for him, her being the daughter of a drunkard. Well, she was living in a mansion now, while they still inhabited small run-down cottages. Maybe it was time to rub their noses in her success.

Twenty minutes later, Tessa halted the buggy in front of Miranda Creig's house. Miranda was the head busybody, and all the women gravitated toward her. Recalling Miranda as having been kind to her, Tessa realized her kindness hadn't been genuine. She'd pretended to be her friend, all the while she tried to talk Tessa out of marrying Damon because she thought they weren't suited. Tessa had married him anyway.

Now she was a proper lady. Just let Miranda try to tell her she wasn't good enough to be Damon Alexander's wife.

At Tessa's polite knock on the door, Miranda peered at her and gave a strained smile. "What a surprise, Tessa. I hadn't expected to see you. Your return from the dead was quite an accomplishment."

Tessa preened in her green lace gown, ignoring the remark because she didn't know how to respond. "I figured it was time for a visit, since I'm mistress of Castlegate now. Ain't you goin' to invite me in for a spot of tea, Miranda?"

Miranda hesitated and glanced back into her tidy parlor. "This isn't a good time for me."

Suddenly not wishing to impose, Tessa nearly turned and left except she heard women's laughter coming from inside the cottage. Her face turned a bright shade of red to think Miranda had guests and wouldn't invite her to join them. After, all, Damon owned the very cottage to which Miranda refused her entrance. She wasn't going to allow the lowly woman to snub her. "Oh, a party you're havin'," Tessa exclaimed. "I've come just in time."

Brushing past Miranda with a pasted smile on her face, Tessa wasn't prepared for the sudden silence which ensued upon her abrupt appearance. The women sat around a table, their teacups poised in midair. Tessa recognized Joanie, Miranda's niece, and the other miner's wives. But her smile froze on her face to discover Eden Flynn within their midst.

She felt betrayed by the very people who had scorned her years ago, the very people she now wished to impress. They were more in Tessa's social class than Eden Flynn, this well-educated woman whom Damon loved. It wasn't fair for Eden to be here, to be invited for tea, when she'd been blatantly ignored. Her hurt turned to fury and she directed it against the person she now hated the most in the world—Eden.

"So, you ain't happy at Kia Ora with the fancy Marjorie Sutherland? Now you've come to hobnob with the lower end of the social scale, Mrs. Flynn."

"Mrs. Creig was kind enough to invite me to tea," Eden stiffly but politely responded.

"Oh, aye, you came all that distance to take tea with the ladies. More than likely you came to get an eyeful of my husband."

"Tessa, I think it's time you left," Miranda firmly stated.

Tessa sent Miranda a baleful glance. "Aye, I'm goin', but I want the whore to know my husband's not interested in her. He has me to warm his bed at night and don't want no fancy tart. Damon still tells me I'm the best he's ever had." Her malevolent gaze swept over Eden's pale face. "Even better than you."

Joanie's audible gasp was the only sound in the room. The women glanced nervously at each other, and then from Eden to Tessa and back again. Tessa wanted to get a rise out of the proper Mrs. Flynn. She ached to tear the very hair out of her head, because this was the woman who kept Damon from being a proper husband. But Eden's face was a mask of politeness. "I'm very pleased you and Mr. Alexander are getting on so well," Eden calmly stated. "It is rather odd, however, for Damon to have told everyone you were deceased. I wonder why he did that. Have you an answer for such a strange behavior, Mrs. Alexander?"

Tessa didn't know how to reply, certain everyone already knew she'd run away with another man. Her mouth dropped open and her face turned the color of beets. Like a whirlwind, she flew out of the cottage and scrambled into the buggy. "I hate Eden Flynn," she groused aloud as she headed back to Castlegate. "I hate her, hate her!"

The woman had mortified her with a few well-chosen words. The biddies must have been talking about her when she'd arrived. The gossip would never die down as long as Damon stayed away from home. If only she could obliterate Eden from Damon's mind—if only she could take back those five years, forget they ever happened. If only Damon would forget and love her again.

She couldn't stand being ignored by him, aching for him to touch her. She was still a young woman and in love with her husband. Her body had certain urges and needs that only a man could fill.

And Damon was the man she wanted to fill her.

But like the wanton creature she was, she needed release until Damon wanted her again. There was only one man in the world she could seek out to end her torment, the one man who always knew how to give her pleasure, the one man she'd turned to so many times in the past.

Turning the buggy around, Tessa headed for High Winds.

Chapter 20

The confrontation with Tessa had unnerved Eden. When she'd accepted Miranda's tea invitation, she never expected to see Tessa, but now that she had and learned Damon was sleeping with his wife again, she knew she'd done the right thing by leaving Thunder Mine. Perhaps he'd never loved her at all. Maybe his hurt at losing Tessa had been so great he hadn't realized Tessa was the woman he'd wanted. Now that she was back, and the little boy with her, he must realize he still desired his wife and must put the past behind him.

Which was as it should be, Eden decided. Yet she couldn't stop the torturous ache that gnawed at her heart. By giving in to Tessa, Damon had betrayed her own love for him. No matter what he'd told her in Mr. MacKenzie's office about obtaining a divorce, it was plain to Eden that Tessa was back in his life to stay.

Despite her pain and the mixed emotions about Damon, when she neared the tiny trail down which Damon had once led her to make love to her in the forest, she turned her horse onto the rutted road. The late-afternoon sun vanished beneath the canopy of foliage as she made her way into the wild, verdant paradise. Soon she found herself by the lagoon and the cascading waterfall. Pictures of the hours she spent in Damon's arms flashed through her mind. If only she could forget, but she wanted to remember; maybe it was that very night, here in this place, that their child was conceived. Every precious moment of that night must be remembered and stored forever in her heart.

The afternoon was dreadfully hot, and Eden decided to take a quick dip in the cooling water. She stripped off her riding skirt and blouse, entering the lagoon in her thin chemise. The water rippled over her when she dove beneath the silvery depths to surface at the other end near the roaring waterfall. The sound deafened her, and she didn't hear her roan whinny when a brown stallion was reined in beside the animal. So engrossed was she as she stood beneath the translucent cascade that she had no idea she was being observed.

It was after she'd swum back again and was standing in ankle-deep water that she saw Damon. Her heart literally skipped a few beats to find him casually sitting on a large boulder, his arms resting on his bent knees. His eyes were shadowed by the brim of his hat, and Eden instinctively sensed they were filled with dancing sapphire flames.

"Cooling off, are you?" he said, a husky sound to his voice.

"I . . . yes," she stammered, flustered at seeing him. "Have you been here long?"

Damon lifted his hat from his forehead. His fiery gaze raked over her, scorching her half-naked body with its heat. "Long enough, beauty."

An unwelcome flush consumed her face as she became

horribly aware that her nipples, clearly visible beneath the wet chemise, were pebbly hard and thrusting toward him. Worst of all, the goldish-red down at the juncture of her thighs was not lost to his roving, hungry stare. Eden attempted to cover herself with her arms and made a dash for her clothes on the bank of the lagoon, but when she started past Damon, he reached out and wrapped his arms around her waist.

He pulled her slick body between his legs, settling her against the obvious bulge in his trousers. She squirmed in protest, not wishing to be so close to him, hating him for betraying her with Tessa but delighting in the very intimacy she fought.

"I thought you were a water nymph when I first saw you," he whispered, nuzzling her neck. "I couldn't believe it was you, Eden, waiting for me."

She pushed ineffectively against him, feeling herself melt at his expert assault of her senses. "I didn't know you'd be here." Swallowing hard, she found herself barely able to speak when Damon's hand brushed against her breast to knead the soft flesh beneath the gauzy material which clung so tantalizingly to her curves. Despite her brain pounding out the message that he should stop touching her, she moaned as his hand wandered across her hip. His fingers trailed wanton fire as they neared their destination. She caught her breath when they finally discovered the silken slit between her thighs. "Oh, don't," she pleaded. "Don't touch me."

"But you love it, my darling. You love for me to touch you." Damon pulled her head down to meet his lips. The kiss was filled with a sweet passion which caused Eden to grow dizzy with desire. She wanted him so much; every inch of her cried for his caresses. But she couldn't give in to him, she wouldn't. Tessa was his wife, not Eden. He'd forfeited a new life for both of them because of his lie about Tessa. And now he had a son, a child who needed him.

No matter how much Damon's very touch could stir her to distraction and desire, they weren't free to love.

Her hands pushed at his chest and she managed to break the kiss. "What is it, Eden? Don't deny me. You want me as much as I want you. I've been through hell thinking about you. I lie awake at nights, imagining you're in my arms. I love you, I need you. Don't leave me. Spend the night with me under a blanket of stars."

God, she was tempted to stay with him! Did he think about her when he was with Tessa? Or had he sought her out because he was simply an insatiable lover? Did Damon want her because he sincerely loved her? Or did he want her as his mistress? He'd lied to her about owning Castlegate, he'd lied to her about Tessa. Could he be lying about loving her? Had he *ever* loved her?

As much as she wanted to stay with him, she didn't need any extra pain because of her love for Damon Alexander. He'd caused her enough anguish already.

Lowering her head, her hair spilled across her face like a brilliant banner. Then she lifted her gaze to his. "If you love me as you claim, Damon, you'll let me go. And you'll understand why I can't stay with you. Our being together isn't right. We said our farewells in Mr. MacKenzie's office. I've decided to return to America." She hadn't reached that decision until this second, but it was seeing Damon again, being in his arms, that caused her to realize she'd never know any peace. Loving him the way she did, she couldn't be near him and not desire him. Perhaps if she wasn't tempted by his virile presence,

271

she could start to live again.

"You can't be meaning that."

Slowly, she nodded. "I do."

Damon's grip tightened on her waist. "I won't let you leave."

Eden gave a trembling smile. "What are you going to do to keep me here? Will you tie me to a tree, keep me hidden in a cave somewhere? I assure you I won't make a willing prisoner. I'll complain like a shrew . . ."

"I don't care, Eden. Without you, I'm not whole."

She choked on the lump that formed in her throat and gently brushed an errant curl from his forehead. How had she ever thought this man was crude? Maybe he hadn't been educated as extensively as Jock, but he possessed the soul of a poet. At that moment, she loved him more than she had ever loved another person in her life. Her lips touched his, drinking in the sweetness of the man, telling him good-bye.

Eden moved away from him and started to dress. She turned her back so he wouldn't see the tears gathering in her eyes and know she was weak. If Damon had touched her at that moment, she feared she'd relent and become his mistress with no thought to his wife and son.

When she faced him, she was sufficiently composed to walk the distance to her horse. Damon followed her and helped her mount. For the space of a heartbeat his hand clasped hers. "I love you, Yank," he said in such a hoarse voice that she trembled.

"I love you, you wayward son of an Irishman." And then she spurred the horse, unable to look at him again. It was a blessing that the animal knew the way to Kia Ora, for Eden's eyes were so blinded by tears she couldn't see.

* * *

"A toast to you, my dear. Returning with the boy was a stroke of genius." Jock lifted his brandy snifter to Tessa, who lay nude upon his bed. "How'd you think that up all by yourself?"

Tessa grew uneasy. "I got me a brain, Jock. I can be crafty when I want, but Collin is me son. And I'm not lyin' about Damon bein' his father."

Jock's brows lifted in surprise. "Are you certain?"

"Of course he's not Jacob's lad."

"I didn't think he was. Could I be Collin's father?"

"No!"

"Good, just checking, my dear." Jock joined her on the bed and slid his hand along her thigh, his eyes watching her face. "Has Damon bedded you yet?"

"Heavens, Jock, do you need to know everythin'?"

"Hmm, by your touchy response and from the way you nearly attacked me when you arrived here, I'd say he hasn't. What's wrong, Tessa, are your charms not appealing to your husband any longer?"

Tessa sniffed. "Damon's makin' me suffer, that's why he won't bed me."

"Maybe he doesn't want you."

"He does—he will . . . as soon as he gets that uppity American whore out of his system."

"Tsk, tsk. Don't demean my future wife."

"You'd do well to marry someone else, Jock," Tessa advised, not bothering to hide her jealousy of Eden. "She ain't one to be tamed by the likes of you. She's got claws, she has."

Jock laughed and pulled Tessa on top of him. His manhood sprang to life at the contact. "I'm partial to the tigress type myself. Now play the kitty and purr prettily for me. Pretend I'm your errant spouse, if you must, but when you finish with me, I suggest you return home and seduce your husband. The sooner you get him to bed you, the better off we'll both be."

"I don't have to pretend with you, Jock."

"I know, Tessa, you never did." Jock suckled one of her nipples and closed his eyes, because he *did* have to pretend that the woman in his arms was Eden.

Thunder rumbled across the gray sky, disturbing the tranquil morning. After finishing Bonnie Day's delicious breakfast, Eden and Marjorie sipped tea in the dinning room. Marjorie's face showed her distress at Eden's news that she would be leaving for America soon. "I'll miss you terribly," Marjorie admitted. "You're the closest friend I've ever had."

Eden patted Marjorie's arm. "I feel the same about you, but I have to resume my life. There's no reason to stay in New Zealand any longer. Thunder Mine is what brought me here. Now that I've sold my portion to Damon, I must go."

"Because you can't stand being near him."

Marjorie's astute assessment of the situation caused Eden to nod sadly. "I love him so very much."

"I know that, but, Eden, don't you think you might find Jock an acceptable husband? He has his faults, but I know he loves you."

Eden shook her head in disbelief. "I thought you and Jock were estranged. Why would you plead his case for him?"

Marjorie stared at her from over the rim of her teacup. "Jock is lonely, and he's my brother. No matter our differences, I still want the best for him."

"You never told me why you cut your ties with him."

"And I won't, Eden. You don't want to know." Her tone grew frosty. "Sometimes I can't believe he's capable of certain things, but he has a brilliant future in Wellington. One day, he might even be governor. Any man so intelligent and charming can't be all bad." Her face softened. "Please reconsider staying so my brother can charm you into marriage. You'd be so good for him, I know your love could change him."

Eden stood up and walked to the window. Outside, lightning streaked a jagged line across the distant sky. A brisk breeze stirred the leaves on an elm tree. "There's a bad storm coming this way," Eden said, not wishing to discuss Jock with Marjorie. Her mind was made up; she was going home to America. She dreaded saying farewell to Jock, knowing he'd attempt to change her mind. When they had seen each other the past week, Jock had proposed but told her he'd wait for her answer. Jock expected her to accept, but she didn't love him enough to marry him. Why wouldn't he realize she'd never marry a man with whom she wasn't in love? She'd married Shamus without being in love with him, but she'd been young and naive, content to go through life without passion and desire.

She was older now, and she knew what physical love entailed. Damon was the only man she'd ever love in that way. He was the only man who knew how to make her heart sing, her flesh quiver with need. Being intimate with Jock—or any other man—was unthinkable. She wished she was already on the ship, headed for home. Maybe then she'd be able to stop tormenting herself with thoughts of Damon.

Marjorie gulped down her tea and rose to her feet, grabbing her cane. "I have to find Tiku. He's on the

275

plain, seeing to a sick ewe. The poor little darling may not make it."

"The weather looks horrible. Stay inside, Marjorie."

"No, I have to tend to my sheep, see for myself that every one of them is all right." Placing her oversized hat on her head, she tied the string beneath her chin. "They're my children, they're all I have."

As Marjorie limped away, pity and love for the woman swelled in Eden's breast. Marjorie was living for her sheep, treating them like the children she'd never bear. She was alone except for Tiku, but she wouldn't reach out to him. For all Eden's unhappiness, she felt blessed for the life growing within her. She might not have Damon, but she'd never be alone.

An hour later, the wind howled outside the house like a banshee. The trees swayed and branches broke, dropping heavily to the earth. The pale gray sky had turned a dark purple. The thunder grew louder as each jagged strike of lightning split the heavens.

Marjorie knelt beside Tiku as he buried the ewe. None of his ministrations could save it. "You did your best," she told him. "Let's be grateful the rest of the flock is healthy." Her braid whipped around and stung her face as a vicious gust of wind pushed her slight frame against him. Tiku felt so strong when he caught her in his arms, a bulwark against the approaching storm.

"We better head back to the house," Tiku advised, but it seemed he held her longer than necessary before finally helping her to her feet. They mounted their horses and rode into the path of the storm. But with each streak of lightning and thunderous roll, the horses became harder to control. Finally Tiku pointed to an outcropping of rock. Marjorie couldn't understand what he was saying to her above the wind, but she urged her horse to follow behind him.

The rain broke before they reached their destination. Cold drops of water beat mercilessly upon them, instantly soaking their clothes. Tiku grabbed Marjorie's reins and quickly tethered the horses to a tree. Then he lifted her down from her horse and carried her into the small, dark cave. Placing her on the ground beside him, he realized Marjorie hadn't broken her hold around his neck. She was shivering and her teeth chattered uncontrollably.

"I'm so, so cold," she told him.

With her small face just inches from his, the feel of her body pressed close against him, Marjorie stirred the passions within his soul. He'd never wanted to be near to her, ashamed of the way his body always responded to her, frightened she'd sense the pent-up longing inside him. To have Marjorie laugh at him or pity him for loving her would be terribly humiliating. As long as he held himself aloof from her, he was safe. But now, Marjorie, his pretty and sweet Marjorie, was trembling in his arms and he was more afraid then he'd ever been in his life.

She lifted her beautiful brown eyes, the dark lashes fringing them like sable. Tiku caught his breath, unable to look away. Some people might call Marjorie plain, and many did. Some called her a cripple. Tiku had never thought of her as either plain *or* crippled. In his heart, Tiku knew Marjorie Sutherland was special. To him, she was a lovely, fragile doll he feared to touch, because he worried he'd hurt her. Yet now she stared at him and touched his wet face with gentle fingers, tracing the lines of his mouth, and he felt as if fire danced across his lips and ignited the flame inside him.

"Kiss me," she pleaded in a soft whisper, drawing closer to him. "Kiss me just once."

Lost beyond caring, Tiku claimed Marjorie's mouth in a kiss that expressed all of the longing and devotion he'd secretly harbored for this woman. Wild desire swirled through him when she arched against him, expressing a need to be fully loved in return. But he broke away, breathing raggedly and afraid to see the contempt on her face for a momentary weakness. His body ached to possess her, but he wouldn't dishonor her, couldn't live with her hatred.

Marjorie made a startled cry and she buried her face on his wet shirt. "I'm sorry," he heard her say. "Forgive me for—for making you . . . kiss—me."

Tiku lifted her face and discovered her face was pink and she no longer was shivering. He'd never seen her more beautiful. "You didn't *make* me kiss you. I wanted to kiss you," he admitted.

"Oh!"

He smiled at her startled reaction. "It's natural to want to kiss a beautiful woman."

Marjorie's eyes grew large. "Do you think I'm beautiful?"

He might as well be truthful. "Yes."

"But . . . but I'm a cripple and I'm plain, everyone knows that. Why would you want to kiss me, why do you think I'm beautiful? Why don't I repulse you?"

"You're not repulsive, don't ever say that about yourself again," he commanded. "And as far as your limp, you can't help that. But you're a graceful woman and so very lovely that I could sit and look at you all day.

You're not plain, not at all plain. And as far as what everyone thinks, they're wrong, and not in love with you. I am."

"You're in love—with me?"

His hand smoothed down the wet strands of her hair. "Very much, but I shouldn't tell you. Perhaps it's because the wind and rain have made us prisoners for a short time; maybe I'm telling you how much I love you because it seems as if we're the only two people in the world for the moment. But, Marjorie, I do love you. Don't hate me for admitting the truth to you."

For a few anguished seconds he thought he had insulted her. She was so quiet, her eyes so large and filled with what he thought was pity. Then amber specks like gold dust began to dance within them, and she did the most unexpected thing, the most endearing thing. She kissed the tip of his nose and smiled at him. "I love you, too. I've loved you since the day you first came with your mother to High Winds. For the rest of my life, I'll love only you."

"Really?"

"Really, truly, sincerely," she whispered. "I want to make love to you. Would you mind—if I made love to you?"

How unexpectedly daring she was, how much he loved her! "Only if I can make love to you at the same time," he said, and breathed in the intoxicating sweetness of her hair. "But when we leave here, nothing will have changed as far as society is concerned."

"I know, but I don't care," she admitted, and began kissing his neck. "Everything though, will have changed for us. And we're all that matters."

We're all that matters . . . we're all that matters. Tiku's

279

heart thumped out the words like a chant. Marjorie was right. They were all that mattered.

Eden rode across Kia Ora, unprepared for the harsh weather conditions. She knew searching for Marjorie was a foolhardy thing to do, but she'd been worried when Marjorie hadn't returned at the storm's imminent approach. She started after Marjorie before the first raindrops but found herself caught in the driving downpour. Marjorie was a good horsewoman, but in weather as vicious as this, she didn't believe the frail young woman could control her mount. The fact that Tiku was nowhere to be found, either, gave Eden some consolation that Marjorie might be safe. Deciding that both of them must have taken refuge from the storm, Eden started back to Kia Ora.

Large raindrops streamed down her hat, and she couldn't see where she was headed. The strong winds pushed her horse in the opposite direction. It wasn't long before Eden realized she was lost. She glanced frantically around her but, blinded by the deluge, she didn't have a clear idea of where she should go. The landscapes were no longer familiar. She'd have attempted to find cover, but she was on the open plains, without benefit of a tree or protection of a ramshackle hut the stationhands sometimes used for refuge.

There was nothing left to do but hope the horse found the way to Kia Ora.

After Eden rode for what seemed like hours, the unthinkable happened. Lightning struck the ground very near to where she rode. Her horse reared up in terror, and Eden, frightened also from the blinding bolt, couldn't control the animal. Without warning, she fell from its back and hit the ground with a painful thump. Somehow she lifted her head to see the horse running away, and then everything grew black.

"She's a mightly lucky young lady. All she got was a bad bump on the head, but she'll be fine." A man's voice brought Eden out of the fog shrouding her brain.

"Are you certain, Dr. Putnam? Her face is so pale and she's still running a fever." Eden recognized Jock's cultured tones. "She isn't fully conscious yet."

"Mrs. Flynn will be coming around soon. Don't worry, Mr. Sutherland. Now if there's any trouble with the pregnancy . . ." Putnam's voice lowered, "get me at once. But I don't foresee any problems."

The sound of heavy footsteps leaving the room caused Eden to finally open her eyes. She'd thought she was alone, but Jock was bending over her, intensely watching her. "Thank God!" he muttered seeing she was awake. "That old sawbones said you'd come around, but I was beginning to doubt it. Eden, love, you gave me an awful scare." He sat beside her on the bed and took her hand.

Eden was totally confused. The last thing she remembered was being on the ground after the horse threw her. Now she found herself in a large bedroom with Jock Sutherland beside her. "Am I at High Winds?" she asked him.

"Yes, poor darling. You don't know what happened to you after your accident?"

"No," she mumbled. It seemed like speaking caused her head to pound furiously, just to move her eyes was an ordeal.

"Well, as near as I can discover . . ." Jock began, "you left Kia Ora and somehow stumbled onto my property during the storm. Apparently your horse threw you. The animal showed up at the stables. He'd been one of my horses before Marjorie took him with her to Kia Ora. My groomsman notified me, suspicious that a saddled horse would suddenly appear. I realized something must have happened to you or Marjorie. A group of us went out to search and we found you." Jock affectionately squeezed her hand. "I'm grateful all you suffered was a bump to the head."

"What about Marjorie? I was looking for her, but I couldn't find her."

"She's fine," he ground out. "Tiku is with her at Kia Ora. I told her you were here, and she said she'd bring over some of your things."

Eden began to sit up but fell back down when the room whirled around her like a top. "Oh, my head!" she complained.

"You're not to move," Jock advised, gently rearranging the covers about her.

"But I can't stay here."

"You can and you will. Dr. Putnam was very explicit in his instructions about that. Remember, you suffered a horrible fall and you're carrying a baby. Allow yourself sufficient time to recover. I insist on that, Eden. You're not going to be a balky patient while you're here, are you?"

She was struck by Jock's solicitous ministrations, overcome by his kindness to her. The man had probably saved her life and that of her child. She owed him a great deal. "I'll be the perfect patient," she promised, and managed a grateful smile though it hurt.

Jock planted a kiss on her forehead. "Just rest, my dear Eden, and regain your strength. If you need anything, ring the bell on the nightstand and Nonnie will answer. I'll check on you later."

Eden barely realized Jock had left the room as she drifted off to sleep again.

Jock went downstairs and lit his pipe. He sat in a large overstuffed chair, triumph glowing on his handsome face.

Fate had intervened in his behalf by causing Eden's accident to occur on his property. He'd been waiting for some reason to bring her to High Winds but none seemed adequate enough to cause her to leave Kia Ora. She was set on sailing away to America, on leaving New Zealand and Damon Alexander behind her. But Jock had other plans, plans even now he'd set in motion with a letter to Mr. MacKenzie. Soon he'd be free of Alexander, and Eden would forget he ever existed.

She was at High Winds, where she rightfully belonged, and Jock intended to keep her there—by hook or by crook.

Chapter 21

"I hope I've brought everything you'll need," Marjorie told Eden the next day. "You have no idea how upset I was when I received Jock's note saying you'd been injured at High Winds. What were you doing out in that abominable weather anyway?"

"Looking for you. I was worried about you." Eden sipped at her tea. Her head still ached, but the pounding wasn't as bad as it had been the previous day, and her fever had broken. Her legs felt rubbery, and each time she got out of bed to use the water closet, the room would spin. A few days' rest was what she needed, she assured herself, and then she'd be on her way—back to America.

Marjorie lowered her gaze and toyed with the large blue bow on the front of her gown. "I was in good hands. Tiku was with me."

"I figured that, after I'd foolishly rushed into the rainstorm."

"I'm sorry about causing you distress." A tiny smile lifted the edges of her lips. "But that afternoon was the most wonderful of my life."

Eden stopped herself from asking her the reason why. From Marjorie's pinkened cheeks and the gleam in her eyes, Eden knew something had happened between Marjorie and Tiku, but since she'd never confided to her that she loved Tiku, Eden didn't press her friend. "Jock will take excellent care of you," Marjorie espoused. "He loves you quite deeply . . . in fact, he told me he's asked you to marry him."

"I don't love him, Marjorie."

Marjorie appeared crestfallen. "I had so hoped . . . I mean, you'd be so very good for him and maybe he'd change his ways of dealing with people."

"What do you mean by that? This isn't the first time you've alluded to a flaw in Jock's character. Marjorie. Is there something I should know about Jock?"

Shaking her head, Marjorie limped to the door. "I have to leave now. Tiku's waiting for me downstairs." As she turned, Eden noticed that her eyes were a bit too bright, her smile a trifle forced, almost as if she were trying to convince herself of something when she said, "Please consider marrying my brother. Truly, he's a decent man."

After Marjorie's departure, Eden was more than puzzled, but it seemed her friend had scarcely been gone five minutes when Jock poked his head into her room. "Could you stand some more company?"

Eden smiled a smile she didn't feel. Something gnawed at her, an uncertainty about Jock pricked at her. Why must Marjorie constantly assure Eden that Jock was a good and decent man? Why did she believe that a marriage would change him? Change him in what way? The man who now sat on the chair next to her bed and presented her with a bouquet of wild roses didn't appear to be in need of changing. His bearing, his manners, and attitude were perfect. She'd be foolish not to marry such a man, but she couldn't help wondering if Jock Sutherland was too perfect.

"The flowers are lovely, Jock. Thank you." She breathed in their scent. "You're spoiling me."

"I hope so. Maybe when I succeed in spoiling you so rotten, you'll consider marrying me."

Another proposal. Eden found herself tensing, her body growing rigid as she waited for the inevitable question. But he surprised her by not asking it. Instead, he sat back in the chair and steadily assessed her. What was there about Jock that caused her to squrim sometimes?

"I wish you wouldn't look at me like that," she blurted out when she couldn't take another second of his perusal. "You make me uncomfortable."

"Oh, I hadn't realized. I'm sorry, Eden." Eden didn't believe he meant the apology, because he once again took a long look at her before reaching for the pipe in his shirt pocket and lighting it. As he sat there, wearing a pair of brown, corded pants and a checked shirt and puffing on his pipe, he resembled the typical farmer. But there was nothing typical about Jock. "You know, Eden, I've been thinking about that day you came here and begged me to sign the papers for the water rights to the Shotover. I fear you may have caused me to act hastily."

She clutched at the bouquet. One of the roses pricked her finger, but she didn't feel the sting. Why did Jock bring that subject up now? The issue about the rights had been settled. "Explain what you mean, Jock. I don't understand how I caused you to do anything in haste."

His smile was cold. "Certainly you do, my dear. You

wanted Alexander to be happy, so you came begging me to sign the necessary papers. And I agreed, not because I care a damn about Damon Alexander. I said I'd grant the rights only because you owned part of Thunder Mine and could benefit. Well, since your departure from there, I've discovered that you've sold your share to your partner."

"Yes." She didn't like where this conversation was headed, and she made a silent prayer that she was wrong. But she wasn't, and Jock's smug expression told her the truth before he even spoke.

"I didn't sign the contract."

"But you said you were going to sign. You sent a note to Damon and told—"

"Yes, yes, I did." He patiently puffed on his pipe, driving Eden insane with waiting for him to finish. "Yet a clerical error at Mr. MacKenzie's office kept the paperwork in limbo. The contracts had to be prepared over again, and when he sent them to me the other day for my signature, well . . . I didn't see the point in signing over the water rights any longer. I only agreed to sign because of your pretty plea, Eden. And now, since you don't have a vested interest in Thunder Mine, I feel it would be foolhardy to grant the water rights to Alexander and wrote Mr. MacKenzie this. You must understand that since you're going to be my wife, I can't in good conscience grant that loathsome lummox permission to use the Shotover."

"You lied to me!" she cried, making a move to get out of bed. Suddenly she wanted to strike the arrogant smile from his face. Jock was using her against Damon, and silly twit that she was, she'd unwittingly fallen in with him by selling her share of the mine away. "You're a dishonorable man to go back on your word and . . . and I haven't agreed to marry you. I won't marry you— ever!"

With a lightning-quick movement, Jock got up, and his body pinned hers upon the mattress. "I don't care for honor," he sneered. "Honor accomplishes nothing. Do you believe I've achieved anything because I'm honorable? Hell, no, Eden! There are too many things in life to grasp for, too many things honorable men don't strive to take. It's their very honor which is their undoing. But I'm not like those men, and I thank God I'm not honorable, because if I were such a person, I'd let you leave here in a few day's time and sail away. But I won't. You're not going anywhere. You'll agree to marry me, you will, and your honor will be as bedraggled as my own."

"I'll never marry you," she protested, trying to push him off her. But she was as weak as a newborn puppy. Jock easily held her in place as he kissed her, and it was apparent to Eden that he wanted her to respond to him. She wouldn't give him the satisfaction. Holding herself rigid, her lips didn't open to him, and when he looked at her, her face was a mask of indifference.

He laughed in amusement, his reaction infuriating her. Like a rag doll, Jock moved her closer to the top of the bed and proceeded to arrange her pillows. "You're a wonder, Eden, if you think I didn't anticipate your cold response. I know you're still in love with Alexander, but get used to the idea of marrying me."

"I won't be forced into a marriage to feed your pride, Jock!" she shot back at him. "Your hatred of Damon is behind this. It goes back to Tessa."

He stopped and peered down at her. "Yes, Tessa did have something to do with it—originally, until you came

288

into the picture, Eden. I'm in love with you, but you love Alexander, who's unworthy of your love. My fights with him up to now have been small ones, but now I'm fighting for my future here. I'm going to fight dirty to keep you." Jock bent down, his face came very close to hers. "And I'm going to win."

Physical weakness and her own fear for Damon caused her to tremble, but she slipped her hands beneath the covers so he wouldn't see he frightened her. But she wouldn't allow him to browbeat her, to think he had the upper hand. "I won't barter away my freedom for you, Jock, or for Damon. You won't force me to marry you. I won't be like Marjorie who married a man she didn't love because you commanded her. I don't need your wealth and I don't want you to raise my child. As far as the water rights, you can hash that out with Damon, but if I know him, Thunder Mine will operate with or without your signature on the contracts."

"You think so?"

"Yes!"

"Ah, my love, how gullible you are." Kissing the top of her head, he smiled tolerantly at her. "Get some rest. You'll soon be busy with our wedding."

She didn't turn her face away, as she longed to do. Instead, she glared at him, her eyes burning with reproachful rage. But Jock only laughed out loud and left her alone.

Tears of anger and dismay choked her. She'd been so wrong about Jock. He wasn't a gentleman at all but a villainous man, and she must get a message to Damon. He had to be warned that Jock didn't intend to sign the contracts. But then she remembered Jock had written to MacKenzie that he wouldn't be signing them. He'd even explained her part in it, and MacKenzie would tell Damon. So there wasn't any point in bothering to inform him. She'd bet anything he'd make an appearance at High Winds to confront Jock.

And when he showed up, she'd explain she had tried to help him by begging Jock to grant Thunder Mine the rights to the Shotover. Damon might misunderstand why she was at High Winds, believing she had caused Jock to renege on the rights out of spite. She'd tell him about her accident and would assure him she was innocent of any duplicity. Damon would understand, she knew he would. He loved her and trusted her.

But she feared he hated Jock Sutherland more than he loved her. Damon might not understand at all.

Damon understood. He understood only too well. Eden had deceived him, from the very first she'd deceived him. She allowed him to believe she was a prostitute who'd married his uncle for his money. And she'd been a virgin. Then he'd fallen in love with her and trusted she wouldn't beg Sutherland to sign the contracts. But she had done exactly what he told her not to do. According to MacKenzie, Jock had granted the rights only because Eden begged him to. Now, since Eden couldn't benefit directly from Thunder Mine, Jock wouldn't sign.

Rage caused Damon to whip his horse into a lather as he covered the distance to High Winds in record time. He was going to have it out with Sutherland once and for all. Granting the rights was one thing, but the last straw had come that morning when Tiku arrived to tell him that Sutherland was preparing to dam up the Shotover at the point where Kia Ora met Thunder Mine.

Damon had been disbelieving but had ridden to investigate and discovered Tiku was right. Some of Jock's stationhands were even in the process of building a makeshift dam. Why was Sutherland doing this now? Why did he feel he had to take such strong action? If he hadn't granted the rights, the miners would have continued using the river water just the same, whether it was illegal or not. Their livelihoods depended upon it.

Damming up the Shotover was a desperate act. Damon realized Sutherland hated him enough to risk alienating the miners and their families. Only a few men would lose their jobs, but word would soon filter back to town and other areas in the Otago. Sutherland's name, his word as a gentleman, wouldn't be worth beans. The very people who'd placed him in Parliament would cry out against him. What could the man hope to accomplish by this deed?

Had Eden somehow contributed to the damming up of the Shotover? Had her hurt and anger about Tessa been the reason Sutherland changed his mind? Damon couldn't believe she'd do this to hurt Thunder Mine. She had claimed to love the mine, to love him. The woman knew he *was* Thunder Mine.

"She had nothing to do with this," Damon reasoned out loud and galloped up the long drive to the large brown house. Eden couldn't be involved. She was due to leave New Zealand shortly, and he couldn't imagine this would be her parting gesture to their love.

Not surprisingly, Damon discovered Sutherland was waiting for him. Jock answered the door at his furious knock.

"Alexander . . ." Jock began, and grandly waved

Damon into the house. "How pleasant to see you again. Your visit isn't totally unexpected."

"You're a contemptuous bastard," Damon spat out, more than infuriated by Jock's elegant display of calm. "I should have known you'd renege on the water rights, but to dam up the river is the dirtiest trick you've ever pulled."

"I doubt that." Jock puffed on his pipe, appearing thoroughly amused by Damon's loss of temper.

"Open the river, Sutherland, or I'm going to do it for you."

"Really. Well, my men have orders to shoot anyone interfering with the building of my dam, especially you. The authorities won't lift a finger, for I'm well within my rights—and you know it, Alexander."

"Maybe you'd like another scar to match the one you've got."

A nerve jumped in Jock's cheek. "Your bullying doesn't threaten me. I've won the great prize and you don't realize it. But you will."

Damon's hands ached to bash in Jock's face, to strangle him. "And what prize is that, Sutherland? You've nothing I want . . ."

A sound from the top of the stairs caused Damon to glance up. Eden stood there in a silk robe and holding onto the railing. Her long hair flowed like a red-gold sun around her shoulders. Apparently she'd been standing there for some time and overheard everything. "Jock means me, Damon."

Damon stood rooted to the spot, not expecting to see her here at High Winds and most certainly not in a state of undress. Waves of jealousy washed over him, and for a few seconds he grew weak in the knees. "What in the name of heaven are you doing here?" he cried out and almost started up the stairs but stopped. There was something in her face, something cold and calculating, that made his heart thump with dread.

Her southern drawl sounded low and velvety soft. "High Winds is a grand house, you said that yourself. I could do worse than marry Jock Sutherland—which, by the way, was being made to look like a fool by you."

He gulped down his pain. "So you're going to marry Sutherland."

"Yes, I am. But don't worry about the dam. I'm certain my fiancé will open the Shotover and sign for the water rights." Eden glanced to Jock. "Won't you, darling?"

"Of course, my dear. Anything you want."

Damon very nearly rammed his fist into the wall, the ache inside him was so intense. Was Eden crazy to marry Sutherland or was she as loathsome as Jock? Perhaps he'd never known her as well as he thought. But all he could do was shake his head in disbelief at this woman who he loved like no other person in the entire world. "Should I kiss the hem of your robe, your ladyship?" Damon jeered, his eyes shooting blue fire slivers at her.

He noticed her hand squeezed the railing until her knuckles turned white. Eden shot him a smile of haughty disdain. "I don't require your thanks. Good-bye, Mr. Alexander."

Her very attitude chilled him. God, she was just like Jock! Backing down the stairs, he didn't stop looking at her. When he reached the bottom, he permitted himself a withering stare. "My condolences to you on your engagement, Mrs. Flynn."

Jock's hearty laugh floated over him, and Damon impaled him with a warning glance. "I trust you'll keep

293

your word about the dam and the water rights."

"Certainly. I have what I want now." Jock seemed more than pleased when he showed him the door.

Damon lifted himself onto his horse. The ride back to Thunder Mine passed in a haze of anger and pain.

At High Winds Jock ascended the stairs and helped Eden back to her room. "You did the right thing," he praised and settled her into bed. "Shall I start the preparations for our wedding? I think late March would be adequate time to give you to regain your strength. Also, I need time to invite my constituents in Wellington."

"Do whatever you want," she said icily. "The wedding plans aren't important to me."

"Eden, don't think of going back on your word to me. I will dam up the river and then nothing you say or do will sway me."

"I won't go back on my word, Jock," she spat at him like a venomous reptile. "You knew I'd find out about the dam and you knew I'd agree to marry you to save Thunder Mine. I'll marry you and we'll live in Wellington. For all I care, we can be married in Wellington . . ."

"No," he disagreed with a smarmy smile. "We'll be married at High Winds. I want Alexander to know you're mine, then we'll move to Wellington."

Eden shrugged, unable to say anything else. The matter was settled—she'd sold her soul to the devil to save Damon and lost his respect in the bargain.

"You'll like Wellington ever so much, Eden. I visited there once with Jock, when he was first elected to Parliament," Marjorie gushed two days later, after Jock had gone to Kia Ora to personally inform his sister about

294

the marriage. "The houses are set on hills and overlook the harbor. There's a lovely view from the house Jock owns."

Eden sat on the porch, her hands lying idly in her lap, while Marjorie crocheted a pretty green-and-blue afghan. She didn't feel like doing anything; in fact she'd begun to resent Marjorie and the way she constantly espoused Jock's good points and the wonderful life Eden would lead as Jock's wife. It was almost as if Marjorie was attempting to convince herself that Jock was truly worthy of that love. But Eden didn't believe Jock was worthy of any loyalty or love. Now she knew why Marjorie hoped marriage would change Jock. The man was a monster.

"I'll never love him," Eden flatly stated. "He's hateful."

Marjorie's needles stopped clicking and she glanced up with tears in her eyes. "I know."

"Don't defend him to me any longer."

"I won't, but, Eden, if you ever have need of me or Tiku, don't hesitate to send for us. I know Jock loves you and will make your life tolerable."

A frustrated sob welled within Eden's throat. *A tolerable life.* She'd wanted a brighter future than that. If not for the child growing within her, she'd feel that her life was over. From now on she'd live only for the child, Damon's child, and hope Damon might forgive her and come to understand why she agreed to marry Jock. Maybe she'd forgive herself for not telling him she carried his baby. But until that time arrived, she must make the best of what life had to offer—even if that meant appeasing Jock Sutherland.

Chapter 22

Eden's wedding to Jock was fast approaching. The bump on the back of her head had long since gone down and her health was restored. She should feel wonderful, she knew. Soon she'd be Jock's wife, the envy of any number of women. Eden, however, dreaded her wedding day. But Jock didn't give her the time to sit and sulk. The last week had been a whirl of social activities in town and at High Winds. They'd taken tea at the house of prominent citizens, attended dances and suppers. Just the previous night High Winds had been the scene of an elegant ball, and the house now echoed with the happy chatter of overnight guests from Wellington.

With Nonnie's assistance, Eden finished dressing. Her organdy gown was the color of daffodils in a summer meadow, and the high sheer bodice and elbow-length sleeves were trimmed in green satin. The dainty bonnet atop her flame tresses matched the gown, and the satin slippers on her feet were yellow. When Jock knocked on the door, Nonnie handed Eden a frilly lace parasol.

"Beautiful," Jock complimented her with a large smile

and held out his arm to her. He affectionately squeezed her hand. "You'll do me proud as my wife when we get to Wellington. I'll be governor in no time."

Eden couldn't bring herself to say anything to him. Her face was tired from the false smiles she'd pasted upon it when people were present. Jock knew how she felt about him so there was no point in pretending when they were alone. "One day you'll love me," he promised with a slight edge to his voice.

"One day pigs will fly," she drawled prettily. Seeing his sudden glower, Eden sighed. "I'll behave myself in front of your friends, Jock."

"Please do. The secretary-general is watching me and I need his support if I hope to ever be governor. No one must suspect anything is amiss between us. No one," he emphasized. "Today's horse race is important to High Winds and to me. For the past twenty years the Sutherland Meet had brought together the people in the Otago. For the good of my family name, a name which shall soon be yours, too, I suggest you put aside your hatred of me. Can you do that for me, Eden?"

Eden realized Jock could have coerced her into behaving properly at the race course today, but for some odd reason he asked her to comply with his wishes. The thought struck her that he hoped to capture her heart with kindness rather than bullying tactics. "I'll do you proud, Jock."

A smile twitched beneath his mustache. "I knew you would come around. Everyone is waiting for us to join them on the race course."

They left the house and went outside, nodding and speaking to their guests and the general populace who streamed into High Winds on foot, by horse or buggy.

Jock had told Eden days earlier about the Sutherland Meet. His father had started the annual event, and only the best horseflesh was entered into the race. Each rider who entered wore a favor bestowed upon him by his sweetheart or wife, and the winner's trophy was always presented by the mistress of High Winds with a congratulatory peck on the cheek. There were very few years when Jock's father or Jock himself hadn't won. It was a known fact throughout the Otago that the Sutherland men were excellent horsemen and almost impossible to beat. This year Jock expected to win again, riding a large white stallion named Ice. He grinned at Eden in anticipation when they stopped near the finish line. Since she was to soon be mistress of High Winds, he'd informed her she would present the trophy to the winner. "Of course I shall win," he said confidently. "I look forward to claiming a kiss from you."

Eden opened her parasol. Standing next to the secretary-general and his wife she smiled to keep up appearances. "Mr. Sutherland," the lady proclaimed with a grin, "you are a scoundrel."

"Yes, madam, I admit I am, but I'm also very much in love with my fiancée and I will win today. I couldn't bear her to kiss any other man."

"Now you must beg for a favor from your lady," the secretary-general advised Jock.

"Ah, yes, a favor." Jock looked directly at Eden. "May I have a favor from you, my love? Something for good luck."

Eden had been prepared for this and handed him a white lace handkerchief. He grinned and tied it around his wrist. "Now I'm assured of a win." Jock left to join the other riders.

"Mr. Sutherland is such a fine gentleman," the secretary-general's wife praised. "You're so very lucky to be marrying him, Mrs. Flynn," she sighed.

"Yes, I am lucky," Eden agreed, and swallowed the bile rising in her throat to tell such a lie. She didn't feel lucky, not lucky at all.

Her gaze wandered around the crowd, and she noticed Nick and Joanie with Tom and Miranda Creig. She waved to them, and she knew they saw her, but they didn't return the acknowledgment, merely looked away. Eden was hurt by the snub, but she should have expected it. No doubt Damon had told them what had happened, and they, too, believed she'd been in league with Jock. But it was because of her that he removed the dam on the Shotover. Didn't they realize she'd never willingly hurt Damon or Thunder Mine? She colored to imagine what Damon must have said about her. Dwelling on how he must hate her increased her pain and strengthened her resolve to leave the Otago and move to Wellington with Jock.

Marjorie joined them minutes later. Eden noticed how pretty she was in her pale-pink dress, how her cheeks glowed with color. Tiku stood a respectful distance away, but they constantly glanced at each other and smiled. Eden envied Marjorie, who knew in her heart that her love was returned.

"There's Mr. Alexander with his wife and son," Marjorie blurted out, then blushed furiously. "I'm sorry," she whispered to Eden, contrition on her face. "I didn't mean anything . . ."

"I know, Marjorie. There's no harm done." But there was, and not because of Marjorie's unthinking outburst. Eden hadn't expected to see Damon at the Sutherland

Meet, but there he was across the way, mingling with the Pattersons and the Creigs. Collin was held securely in Damon's arms and her heart melted to see him affectionately rumple the boy's hair and notice the genuine love between them—which was as it should be. They were father and son and should love each other.

But then Eden saw Tessa, and nearly choked on her own hate for the woman. Tessa looked lovely and was respectably dressed, her arm securely locked in Damon's. The Alexanders seemed to be a perfect, loving family. Eden wanted to glance away but was unwillingly drawn to the happy scene. She stared in spite of herself, wanting to be the woman beside Damon, aching to rush over to him and convince him she'd known nothing of Jock's plan. Her heart burst with her love for him and she wanted to confess her pregnancy to him. Would he want her if he knew she carried his child? Would he leave Tessa for her? The hope inside her died when Damon finally caught her eye.

Curtly, he nodded in her direction and impaled her with blue frost. Eden shivered and turned her attention to the couple beside her, pretending she heard something they'd just said. But she heard nothing except the hard pounding of her own heart.

The riders were mounting up, and Jock waved to her. Sitting atop the large white horse dressed in his brown-and-buff riding attire, Jock held himself like a nobleman. The other men, though also from good families and not unattractive, couldn't compete with him. There was something about Jock that caused people to notice his princely bearing. He was the center of attention until another rider reined in alongside of him.

Eden held her breath to see Damon, seated upon his

300

large black stallion. She remembered the horse, War Dance, was his pride and joy. He'd bragged to her once that he was the fastest horse in Otago, and this year he'd prove it.

Now she knew what Damon had meant. He intended War Dance to win the Sutherland Meet, to beat out every horse, including Jock's Ice. Especially Jock's Ice.

From the way Jock's face resembled chiseled marble, it was apparent to Eden that he hadn't expected Damon to enter the race. In contempt, his gaze raked Damon's attire of a plain blue shirt and pants. Jock made a snide comment but Damon only shrugged his shoulders and laughed.

"Isn't that the man who left Marjorie's wedding with Mrs. Flynn?" the secretary-general's wife asked her husband in a loud whisper.

"Uh, yes, my dear, but please . . ." His reply to his wife was lost within the titters behind Eden.

"Ignore everyone," Marjorie begged Eden.

Eden gave a tiny laugh of assurance that she didn't care what people said and wasn't hurt by their knowing winks. But everyone knew what had happened between herself and Damon and nothing could change the past. Her hands clung to the stem of her parasol and she wished to lower it in front of her face. Would this horrendous race ever be over?

Finally the riders took their places and the secretary-general went forward with a pistol in his hand and discharged it when the crowd grew quiet. The horses took off from the starting point with lightning speed. Their hooves dug up the earth, leaving clumps in their wake. Raised voices urged on the riders, people were still betting on the winner. It seemed the competition between Damon and Jock transferred to the crowd, for the other riders were forgotten when both riders moved to the front of the line.

"Sutherland!" someone exclaimed.

"Alexander!" another proclaimed.

"Come on, Ice!"

"Rush to it, War Dance!"

And so it went. As they made their way into the turn, Eden lost sight of them. Her loyalty was for Jock, but her love for Damon, and she dreaded the moment one of them crossed the finish line. *Please let someone else win,* she silently prayed.

"Here they come!" Marjorie shouted, jumping up and down.

Thundering hooves brought Damon and Jock into view. Jock was in front, his body hunched low as he whipped the horse ever forward. Damon was coming up fast behind him, and it seemed Jock was going to win. But in the twinkling of an eye, Damon allowed the horse his head. Horse and rider surged forward like an ebony-and-blue streak. The crowd went wild, their cheers deafening as War Dance took the lead and crossed the finish line before Ice.

Within the din that followed, Marjorie pressed a hand on Eden's arm. "You must present the trophy to the winner," she reminded with a wan smile.

"Yes, I must," she mumbled and took the secretary-general's arm as he led her to the winner's circle.

For the moment everyone was watching Damon, congratulating him as he trotted the horse toward her. But Jock watched from the sidelines, not a flicker of an eyelash betraying his feelings. Eden knew he was nearby, yet her perverted gaze drank in Damon's handsomeness and she attempted to hide her pride at his win. He mustn't know how she felt, she mustn't embarrass Jock in front of his friends and the people here. She'd simply present the trophy to Damon and that would be it. After today she'd never have to see him again or be subjected to people's scrutiny and less than kind comments.

Closing her parasol, she picked up the trophy and waited for Damon to dismount. He slid off of War Dance and bridged the distance between them with three large strides until he was on the platform beside her. His towering presence and the many curious eyes trained upon them caused her to falter. She didn't know if she could speak, her throat was so dry. But Jock stared at her, and she sensed he waited to see her reaction. Gathering her wits about her, she held out the gold trophy to Damon and congratulated him in a voice that sounded detatched and unemotional.

His fingers brushed hers when he took it from her, and he waited expectantly. Why didn't he leave the platform? she wondered. What was he waiting for?

"I believe the winner deserves a kiss," he said to her and grinned.

"Oh, yes, you do." Her face was horribly warm and she knew her cheeks must be red. She swallowed and lifted herself onto her toes to reach the side of Damon's face. She dutifully pecked his cheeks, and found herself trembling when she finished. But Damon's eyes flared, and without her realizing what was happening, he jerked her to him.

"You can do better than that, Mrs. Flynn."

His mouth, warm and moist, descended upon hers, drowning out her words of protest. Damon's kiss deprived her of breath, but she didn't fight him. Instead, her body melted into him and began to respond the instant he touched her. She hadn't a clear idea if the kiss lasted two seconds or two minutes. When he broke away, her knees were shaking and she was pale.

"Thank you, Mrs. Flynn," he said in a husky, suggestive tone which rushed the blood to her face. And then he left her standing there until Jock took her by the elbow and led her away from the silent, stunned crowd.

"My fiancée is recovering from an illness," she heard him explaining to someone. "The heat is wretched and has made her ill."

Somehow, though she didn't remember the walk, they were inside the cool house and she was sitting on the sofa. Jock plunged his hands into his jacket pockets and gazed out of the window. It was some time before he spoke to her. "You humiliated me."

Eden became aware of him at last. She shook her head to drive out the image of Damon's face, but the feel of his kiss still clung to her mouth. Without meaning to, she had humiliated Jock and herself. If only she hadn't responded to Damon, but from the very first second she'd looked up from the ground at the man atop her all those months ago in Queenstown he had mesmerized her. Jock was hurt and embarrassed, as was she. Damon had meant to humiliate her and he'd done an admirable job.

Eden rubbed her head with her hand. "You saw what happened, Jock. Damon overpowered me."

"And you liked it very much. Admit it." He turned from the window. "Every damn person in the Otago knows how much you liked it!"

She'd never seen him so angry, but Jock wouldn't make her feel worse than she already did. Eden rose to her feet, ignoring his vicious expression. "Yes, I liked it.

In fact I loved it! I love Damon and I always will. Why can't you understand my feelings for him? Why do you want to marry me when you know I'll never love you? This incident today spoke louder than any words. People won't forget it, certainly not any of your Wellington friends. If you marry me, feeling as I do about another man, I'll only be a detriment to your career."

"Everyone will forget in time."

"But *I* won't forget! For God's sake, Jock, I'm having Damon's baby!"

The anger disappeared from his face, and he gently grasped her by the shoulders. "Believe me, people will forget and so shall you."

He was so chillingly calm, that a shiver of apprehension slid down Eden's back. "I don't want to forget," she admitted with a hint of defiance in her voice.

"You will, Eden. You will."

With an unruffled air, Jock left her and went outside to join his guests.

Tessa was quiet, much too quiet for Damon's liking. After they arrived home from High Winds, Damon carried a sleeping Collin to his room and settled him in bed. He stood over the child and felt a strong surge of love rush through him. Collin was perfect in every way. He'd never known a more lovable and affable little boy. Collin was the only good thing which had come out of his marriage to Tessa.

He knew she seethed with anger, and it was only Collin's presence in the buggy which had prevented her from unleashing it. When he entered the parlor he found her pacing the floor, the steady swish of her gown the only sound coming from her. He'd embarrassed her, as he knew he would, but the kiss was meant to humiliate Eden. Yet now that he'd kissed Eden again, touched her again, he couldn't stop thinking about her. If he took Tessa to bed, perhaps his ache for Eden would go away. He discarded the notion. He didn't want to bed Tessa. He didn't want any part of her.

He wanted Eden.

Tessa heard him enter the room and she twisted around to survey her glum-faced husband. "Proud of yourself, Damon? Did you have to make a laughingstock of me in front of the whole Otago with your whore?"

"You're the whore." He calmly took a cheroot from a silver box on the sofa table.

"Ain't you ever goin' to forget the past?" Tessa pleaded. "I want to be your wife and you better consider yourself damn lucky that I still want you at all, after the touching scene between you and the Widow Flynn at High Winds this afternoon. People were snickerin' behind their hands. And believe me, Jock Sutherland ain't goin' to take kindly to what happened."

"Since when do you worry what Jock thinks?"

"Since . . . since never," she spat out. "I don't care about Jock. It's you I want, Damon. I want you to bed me."

He lit the cheroot and sat on the divan. Tessa had that look about her again, the sort of look a mare in heat gets when a stud is put in the paddock with her. She had that same wild gleam in her eyes a few weeks back. She'd pleaded with him then to bed her and he'd refused. Then one night he had noticed a sense of contentment about her and she hadn't begged since.

The thought passed across his mind that she'd been

with another man. Could Jock have been that man? More times than not she brought up Sutherland in the conversation, and always she worried about Jock's reaction to something Damon had done or said to him. It would be just like Jock to bed Tessa as a means of manipulating her. But what would controlling Tessa gain him?

Unless Jock had discovered Tessa's whereabouts and brought her to Thunder Mine so Eden would marry him!

Perspiration broke out upon Damon's forehead. There was no other explanation for Tessa's sudden appearance.

He grew still and observed his wife, seeing her for the first time not as the conniving whore he thought her to be, but as a desperate woman. She'd tried every trick to gain entrance to his bed. Damon slept in another bedroom on the opposite side of the house. One night she'd sneaked into his room while he slept and slipped naked beneath the covers. He awoke to fiery hands stroking his shaft, and he'd thought for a few fuzzy moments in the dark it was Eden beside him. He instantly hardened, only to lose his arousal to find Tessa beside him.

Tessa's curses rent the air when he lifted her from the bed and placed her in the hallway, locking the door behind him. Other men desired his wife, but she repulsed him. It was then he'd heard her shrill shriek. "Jock Sutherland wouldn't turn me out!"

And Damon bet he hadn't. But would Tessa go to Jock again for satisfaction? Was this the way to get his divorce, keep his son, and then claim Eden for his wife? Tessa paced like a lioness in a cage, and if he kept refusing her advances, she'd break out of her prison and find a willing man. And if that man was Jock . . .

"Go to bed, Tessa. You're overwrought."

"Aye, I'm overwrought," she spat at him. "What would you have me be after you kiss that Flynn woman in such a way, and me standin' there with egg on me face, tryin' to pretend there ain't nothin' to it? A fellow behind me commented that you seemed ready to tear the gown off her." She pointed to the trophy on the mantel. "I wish you wouldn't have won the bloody thing."

"I'd say Sutherland wished the same thing, and speaking about the contemptible bastard brings up something I need to ask you. Did he bring you back here from Christ Church?"

Tessa's mouth fell open and she stopped pacing. "Why would you be thinkin' such a thing?"

"Because I wonder if he knew where you were all these years and decided to make my life a living hell when I thought I'd found heaven, that's why."

Tessa sneered at him. "Ah, because of your precious Eden, you think he needed me to break you up. Well, you're mistaken, me love. But if he had found me and talked me into returnin' to Thunder Mine, then he did you a favor. Your wonderful lady friend hightailed it, she up and left you." Tessa bent down, hissing into his ear. "Now if she loved you like she claimed, she'd have fought for you. Wouldn't she, duck?" A smug smile lifted her lips and she went to her bedroom, slamming the door soundly behind her.

Damon couldn't argue with her forthrightness.

Jock finished reading the message from Tessa which he had found on the desk in his study earlier that evening. The crafty bitch must have sneaked into the house

308

sometime during her visit. Leaning back in the large, comfortable chair, he swirled the brandy in his snifter and his mouth twitched with amusement at what she'd written. Her spelling was so poor as to be laughable, her grammer atrocious; but she had made it perfectly clear she was in need of some physical attention. It seemed her virile husband wasn't performing his husbandly duty by her.

"Never fear, dear Tessa, I shall come to your rescue," he muttered and downed the brandy. She was falling right into his hands, and all because of her own wantonness. It was her greatest weakness which was going to destroy Damon, the man she so desperately loved but couldn't convince to bed her.

Jock hoped she'd enjoy their tumble together, really he did, because it would be her last.

Chapter 23

High Winds buzzed with anticipation. On the morrow Eden Flynn would marry Jock Sutherland, and a constant stream of guests arrived for the festive occasion. Happy chatter wafted through the ceilings and drifted down the hallways as the visitors from Wellington were shown to their rooms, many of them to sleep four to a bed, as space was limited. Some of the locals from town had set up tents on the lawn. No one wanted to miss this wedding, it seemed. The wagging tongues had wagered it would be just as entertaining—and surprising—as the Sutherland Meet only two weeks before.

Some individuals bet that the beautiful Mrs. Flynn wouldn't marry Jock Sutherland but would run off with Damon Alexander. Rumors were flying that Damon and his wife weren't getting on well, and that Eden Flynn was the cause of the dissension.

Not a chance, others espoused, and deciding they were in the know, upped the ante. Damon Alexander might not care for his wife, but he wouldn't dare put in an appearance. They knew for a fact through the servant grapevine and High Winds's stationhands that Alexander was to be barred if he approached Sutherland property. If he was unlucky enough to trespass near the house, Mr. Jock Sutherland had ordered the man shot. And it was a known fact that no one disobeyed Gentleman Jock—ever, not when the secretary-general himself was staying at High Winds for the wedding and counted upon Sutherland for protection. Why, the local magistrate was to attend the ceremony, and what an embarrassment it would be for him if Alexander broke through and caused a ruckus.

For all the betting and joking, Eden didn't find any of it amusing. She thought High Winds looked like an armed camp with the stationhands riding the borders and instructed to shoot Damon if he attempted to approach the house. It was ridiculous, something out of a medieval romance, for Jock to believe Damon might stop the wedding. He'd gone so far as to forbid her to go no farther than the copse of trees around the house.

But Jock didn't take into account Damon's hatred of her. Eden had, and knew Damon wanted nothing to do with her. She was also made more humiliated by Jock's overprotective attitude. With the armed stationhands nearby, no one forgot what had happened at the Sutherland Meet. Jock had made her a virtual prisoner, and sometimes she thought the guards were there not so much to keep Damon out but to keep *her* in.

The night prior to the wedding, Jock led her downstairs into the candlelit dining room where they dined with the secretary-general and his wife, and other Wellington dignitaries. As usual, Jock was a charming host and he complimented her later that she'd played her part of hostess well. He was proud of her. Drawing her close to

311

him when he brought her to her room, he kissed her with such pent-up passion that Eden grew dizzy, not with longing but repulsion.

"Tomorrow night you'll finally be completely mine," he whispered, fondling her breast. "I've waited a long time to possess you, Eden."

She realized Jock had given her time to come to care about him. He could have forced her into submission, but he wanted her to come willingly to him. If only she could do that, if she could love him and block out his faults. But she'd never forget how he'd manipulated her into this marriage and would never forgive him.

When she went into her room, she lay on the bed and stared up at the moon-streaked ceiling. After tonight she'd never have to sleep alone again, but the man whose arms she ached for wasn't Jock.

"It's about time you were gettin' here," Tessa groused to Jock. She peered at him from the bushes along the Shotover River as he reined in his horse. "I gave you my note long ago, and now you're just gettin' around to meetin' me. I've got other things to do besides waitin' out here in the dead of night for you."

"Your time must be taken up with bedding your husband," he snidely remarked as he led her deeper into the woods.

"Shut up, Jock. I ain't here to talk about him. But after you're married to that Flynn bitch, he'll be wantin' me again."

"Tessa, my dear, if a mating is imminent between you both, then why have I been hounded by you to meet you here?"

Jock halted, and Tessa stopped behind him. The moonlight gave her face a translucent glow, and she looked so vulnerable to him, like the sweet young girl he'd loved all those years ago. She licked her lips. "Because I need me a man, and I want you, Jock."

"I'm second best, eh?"

"No," she hastily reassured him, wrapping her arms around his neck. "Tonight you're the only one." Tessa wantonly pressed her body hard against him. Jock felt himself swelling with lust and need. Just for a short while, he'd forget her past and be transported back to a time when he loved her. This one last time would be sweet for them both. He'd see that Tessa enjoyed his lovemaking. He'd take her slowly to the summit. In fact, he'd make love to her more than once and when he had finished with her, she would be so satiated that she'd fall fast asleep in his arms beneath the stars and wouldn't awaken.

She'd never know he had killed her.

A shooting star soared through the glittering firmament. Marjorie grabbed Tiku's shirt-sleeve and pointed to it. "How breathtaking it is! she cried, leaning closer to him as he guided the buggy along the road from town. "I'll wish upon it," she said, and closed her eyes.

Tiku chuckled. "You're superstitious."

"Yes, aren't you?"

"Not really."

"Don't you want to know what I wished for?"

"I can see you're bursting to tell me, so I'm listening."

Marjorie smiled, and a feeling of love washed over her. No matter how strange other people might think her to

313

be, Tiku never laughed at her. He always listened to her. "I wished we'd always be together."

Her fingers stroked his cheek as she gazed up at him in adoration. "I also wished to give you a son," she whispered.

Stopping the buggy, Tiku stared down at her. "Are . . . are you having a child?"

"Yes."

Instantly she was in his arms and he showered a myriad of kisses upon her face. Marjorie giggled. With others, Tiku was always so restrained and serious, but with her he was playful and constantly expressed his love for her. But then his kisses ceased and his face was so solemn that her heart threatened to break. She knew what he was thinking.

"We can't be married, Marjorie. People won't accept us."

"Pooh on them. We love each other; our baby was conceived in love. I don't give a fig what anyone says about us or our child. And . . . and I love you so much that I want to tell everyone I'm proud to be having your child."

"Ah, my pretty Marjorie, I am indeed blessed." He sighed his contentment when she laid her head upon his chest.

She was truly happy now, truly complete.

The buggy started rolling down the road toward Kia Ora. Jock's wedding was tomorrow afternoon, and the hour was late. They must get home and go to bed, but Marjorie doubted they'd get much sleep. Too many mornings both she and Tiku were exhausted from their lovemaking and stayed abed later than they should. Bonnie Day, whom Marjorie guessed didn't approve,

314

never expressed by word or deed that she thought her employer was living in sin with a savage. But Marjorie didn't need Bonnie's approval—or Jock's. After tomorrow, Jock and Eden would leave for Wellington, and though she'd miss them, her life was now to be lived only for Tiku and their child.

Marjorie snuggled next to Tiku and smiled to herself. But her happy musings ended abruptly when a rider on a white stallion rushed from a trail near the Shotover, some two hundred feet ahead of them. By the light from the moon she was able to identify the rider as Jock. Apparently he hadn't noticed them.

"What in the world could Jock be doing out this time of night near Thunder Mine?" Marjorie glanced in bafflement at Tiku. "He should be at High Winds, preparing for his wedding tomorrow."

Tiku laughed. "You sound like his mother. Your brother is a grown man and can come and go as he pleases."

"Yes, you're right," she agreed, clasping her hand over his. She must stop worrying about Jock, but the habit of many years standing was hard to break. He'd been responsible for Bert's death, she knew that, but she couldn't hate him. He was her brother.

She comforted herself with the thought that Jock was taking a late-night ride because he might be nervous about marrying. Though this endeared him to her, his midnight ride still causd her a strange uneasiness.

"Where's my momma?" Collin inquired of Damon the next morning.

Gulping down his coffee, Damon hauled the child onto

his lap. "Sleeping, in her room."

"No. I was in there and Momma's not sleeping."

"She must have gotten up early and gone outside." But that was highly unlikely, Damon realized. Tessa never rose until noon.

"Lanu said she wasn't outside."

Damon placed the child on a chair and served him his breakfast. They spoke about the pony in the stables, and Collin insisted that Tessa be found since she was to watch him ride the pony without the help of the groomsman. "All right, you nag," Damon teased. "I'll go find your mother. Finish up your breakfast."

Collin nodded agreement and Damon went into the kitchen to ask Lanu if she'd seen Tessa. Lanu and the servants all claimed they hadn't seen her since bedtime the night before. Damon checked the master suite and discovered the bed hadn't been slept in.

So the tart had slipped out on him. He'd expected Tessa would eventually sneak away to meet someone, and he wasn't surprised. However, he *was* surprised that she'd been gone all night. Tessa was the sort who took her pleasure swiftly and then wanted a long night's sleep alone.

Had Tessa been with Jock? Damon tensed to believe she had been and wished to beat the devil out of Sutherland. It would be just like the unprincipled man to bed Tessa on the night before his marriage to Eden.

Eden.

Days ago he'd promised himself he wouldn't think about her, but she invaded his dreams at night. Today was the day she was to marry Jock, and he would lose any chance to claim her again. As it was, even if he believed she still loved him, he'd be unable to take her away. Jock had turned High Winds into a veritable fortress to keep him out, which caused Damon to wonder even more why Sutherland feared him.

He'd lost Eden but gained a son. From this day on, Collin would be his life.

"Ah, how beautiful you are," Nonnie exclaimed, clapping her hands. "Such a pretty bride."

"Yes," Marjorie agreed, misty-eyed. "Eden is the loveliest bride I've ever seen. My brother is so lucky to be marrying her."

The object of their heartfelt compliments barely acknowledged them. Eden stood in the center of the bedroom in her ivory satin wedding gown. Summer daisies decorated the crown of her upswept hair, and Nonnie smiled as she competently arranged the gauzy veil. Eden wanted the ceremony completed, not certain she'd hold up under the strain of waiting. But as the time drew near to the moment when she'd go downstairs to be united to Jock, the secretary-general, who was to give her away, hadn't put in an appearance.

She glanced out the window and noticed the guests weren't assembled. People spoke to each other in small groups, others straggled off, but their voices carried up to the second floor and she swore she heard someone mention "Alexander." Just when she decided to have Nonnie check and see what was the cause of the delay, a knock sounded on her door and Jock entered.

"Jock, it's bad luck to see the bride!" Marjorie admonished.

Jock ignored her, training his eyes on Eden. "I have to leave, my dear. Something has come up and it's imperative I ride off for a while. As soon as I return, the ceremony will take place."

"What happened?" Eden asked, fearing that if she waited another moment she'd go mad but more than grateful for the short reprieve. "You're dressed, the guests are growing impatient . . ."

"I'll explain later. Under no circumstances are you to leave the house. The magistrate's men shall be nearby" was his terse declaration and he was gone.

"What do you suppose that was about?" Marjorie went to the window. "There are a number of men mounting up."

Looking for herself, Eden saw not only the station-hands and law officers but some of the guests on horseback. They all carried guns. They waited until Jock came out of the house and mounted Ice, then they departed in a whirlwind of dust and thundering hooves.

"I think it's a posse," Marjorie remarked. "I wonder what happened."

They didn't have long to wonder, for a moment later the secretary-general's wife flew into the room. Her face was bright with excitement. "There's been a murder!" she cried. "The men have gone to hunt down the killer. He made it onto High Winds and was shot! Heavens, what a day!" She fanned herself with her handkerchief. "He escaped the men and now is a terror to the countryside."

"Who was killed? Who are they after?" Eden questioned before Marjorie asked the same thing.

The woman opened her mouth to speak, but faltered. "Oh, my dear, Eden, I'm sorry. Forgive me, I had forgotten about you and Mr. Alexander."

"Tell me! What about Damon?"

"He's wanted for the murder of his wife. Her body was

318

found along the Shotover this morning, strangled, I believe. The rumor is they constantly argued and he was heard to threaten her a number of times. When the constable went to question him, he bolted away, but before he could be captured he'd made it to High Winds. One of Mr. Sutherland's stationhands shot him. No one knows how bad he was hurt, but he managed to escape."

A cry of anguish erupted from Eden's throat, and she fell to the floor in an ivory satin heap. "Damon didn't kill Tessa! He couldn't kill anybody!" she screamed for the whole house to hear. "I don't believe it! I don't!" But even as Marjorie hovered around her and tried to quiet her, Eden wasn't certain she believed her own rantings.

Could Damon be capable of murder? Had he killed Tessa? He wanted a divorce, and he'd told Eden that somehow he would be free of his wife. . . . Quivers of alarm and suspicion overpowered her.

Eden. He must save Eden. Eden. Eden.

Damon's mind whirled with images of her and Jock Sutherland, and he knew he had to rescue her from High Winds. He couldn't let her marry Tessa's murderer. And Jock had strangled Tessa, he knew it. But no one would believe him. The constable had arrived that morning with three of his men and approached Damon at the mine with news that Tessa's body had been discovered by a placer miner along the Shotover. They'd questioned him about Tessa and the rumors they'd heard about his wish to divorce her. He'd answered them truthfully, why lie when he'd done nothing wrong? But it seemed they were convinced he was guilty and decided to arrest him for Tessa's murder. Their proof of his guilt was a letter found by her body, the letter he'd written to Eden in which he told her he loved her and would free himself of Tessa.

Damon's mind had been working while they questioned him, and he'd come to the realization that Tessa must have met Jock someplace and that he'd killed her. There was no other explanation for her to have left the house other than to see Jock. He was the only friend she had in the Otago, and Damon knew it had been Jock who'd brought her from Christ Church. Jock had murdered her and now was framing him with a letter he'd written to Eden. Jock wanted him out of the way— permanently.

God, his shoulder hurt! Luckily, the bullet had gone straight through, but he was losing blood and a strange weakness threatened to overpower him. He was riding on War Dance across the open plains of Kia Ora, having eluded the constable's men, but the bullet had come from one of Sutherland's stationhands. Damon knew it was only a matter of time before a posse was on his trail.

He needed help and knew of only one person who would freely offer it.

Tiku saw him on the plains before Damon spotted him. Immediately the Maori rode toward him, scattering the sheep in his wake. No words were necessary, as he immediately discerned Damon was in trouble. He grabbed the reins and led War Dance to a more secluded spot where no one would see them.

"I owe you my thanks," Damon groaned when Tiku helped him from the horse. His breath came heavily and he was unable to sit up.

"Don't thank me yet." Tiku pronounced each word distinctly. "The blood flows freely, and I must stop it. But you can't remain here. Word travels fast, Damon.

You must hide."

"The lagoon. Take me there."

Tiku nodded, and tried to stop the bleeding by applying pressure. "I'll get the wagon and place you beneath the freshly sheared wool. If anyone sees me, they'll believe I'm headed into town to sell it."

"Tiku, wool makes me itch."

"Better to itch than to die, my friend."

Jock had been gone for three hours. Dusk was descending and Eden's nerves were stretched taut. There wasn't going to be a wedding that day, and Eden didn't care. Her thoughts centered on Damon and she couldn't stop the kaleidoscope of images twirling around her brain.

She saw Damon, hurt and bleeding, left to die somewhere or be captured by the constable, if not killed. Jock was the driving force behind the posse, she knew it. Everyone looked to him because he was a member of Parliament, perhaps one day to be appointed governor of New Zealand. If Damon were captured, no one would lift a hand to save him, not if Jock decreed his death. The bullet from the stationhand's gun was proof that men did whatever Jock wanted.

More than anything, she prayed Damon would escape. She paced her room, rushing to the window each time she heard voices in the yard. But now all was strangely silent, the yard empty. The townspeople must have realized the wedding wouldn't occur and had gone home.

Marjorie knocked on her door and peered inside. She quietly entered the room and shut the door. "Eden," she whispered. "Tiku's waiting behind the house. He knows where Damon is and will take you to him."

"Oh, Marjorie, did he say how Damon is?" Eden started ripping open the buttons on the front of her wedding gown, not wasting a moment.

"He's lost a great deal of blood, but Tiku stopped the bleeding and sewed up the wound. He won't tell me where Damon's hiding because of Jock." Marjorie placed a pleading hand on her friend's arm after Eden had changed into a riding outfit and boots. "Damon is innocent, Eden. Stay with him and don't come back here, even if you both have to run away."

Eden kissed Marjorie's cheek. "Take care of yourself . . . and Tiku."

Marjorie flushed but didn't apologize for not telling Eden she and Tiku loved each other. "Be as happy with Mr. Alexander as I am with Tiku, Eden. That's what I want for you. And here, wear this . . ." Taking off her lace shawl, she placed it over Eden's head and then handed Eden her cane. "The house is overrun with guests and the magistrate's men. Jock gave orders that you're not to leave, but I am free to do so. If anyone sees you, pretend to be me. No one will stop you if you're seen leaving with Tiku. They'll assume we're returning to Kia Ora."

Tears of gratitude and love for Marjorie blinded Eden. She wasn't certain she'd see Marjorie ever again after tonight, and already she missed her. But Damon waited for her and she had to go to him. He was her life.

Slipping out of the room, she managed to make it to the back stairway, ready to give a convincing imitation of Marjorie's limp, if someone should happen by. No one was in the kitchen and she made it outside without trouble, then was pulled aside by Tiku, who stood near the back door. He pointed to the buggy and Eden started to run for it, but his arm on hers warned her to be still when Jock and a group of riders galloped into the yard.

They'd already been spotted by Constable Vickers. "Going home, Mrs. Carruthers?" he called out.

Eden pulled the shawl tightly around her face, making certain her hair was well hidden beneath it. With a halting limp, not unlike Marjorie's, and Tiku guiding her to the buggy, she muffled an affirmative answer and returned the wave. The blood pounded in her ears, and she dared not look directly at any of the men, especially Jock, who now dismounted nearby. She could see Jock was disgruntled and that his wedding attire was a mess of dust and dirt. Indeed, there wouldn't be a wedding that day. She could only pray he wouldn't go in search of her too soon.

Eden and Tiku got into the buggy, and she held her breath and prayed. *Please don't let Jock look this way, don't let him look at me.* But almost as soon as she'd finished the prayer, Jock called out, "Marjorie, how is Eden faring?"

"Dear gracious God," she whispered.

"Answer him," Tiku prodded.

Eden swallowed and attempted to imitate Marjorie's British accent. "Fine, Jock. She's resting."

Her heart nearly stopped beating when Jock started walking in their direction. "Are you ill? Why is that shawl about your face in this warm weather?"

"Mrs. Carruthers has taken a chill and needs to return home," Tiku swiftly responded, and began urging the horse forward. "Today has been trying for her."

"Marjorie, let me bid you a proper farewell," Jock shouted.

Panic swelled within Eden, and her blood turned to ice

323

with each of Jock's approaching footsteps. He was within twenty feet of them when the secretary-general came out of the house and called to him. Jock, ever suave and courteous, lifted his hand to the buggy's occupants in semblance of a wave and joined the man on the porch. The horse and buggy sauntered from the yard but broke into a full-scale trot when on the road.

"Hurry, Tiku," Eden cried, and allowed herself breath again. "Take me to Damon."

Chapter 24

Darkness enfolded the forest in a velvet warmth. No stars glittered overhead as Eden followed Tiku and the lanternlight along the trail to the lagoon. With each step, her heart thumped in anticipation to see Damon again, to hold him in her arms. She'd beg his forgiveness, that's what she'd do, for allowing him to believe she knew about the damming of the Shotover, for deserting him when he needed her.

A small outcropping of rock shielded Damon from view. Eden saw him, lying on a soft nest of ferns, only after she'd come around the other side of the lagoon and nearly stumbled upon him. From the lantern's light, Eden saw Damon's eyes were closed and he lay so still, she worried he was dead. But Tiku bent down and gently touched Damon's shoulder. Damon stirred and came awake. "How do you feel?" Tiku asked him, examining the bandaged wound.

"Hurts like hell," Damon admitted.

"You've a fever, too, so I'm going to have Eden give you the elixir I've brought."

"Eden?" He sounded disbelieving and blinked a number of times when Tiku moved out of the way and Eden came forward.

She didn't immediately go to him as she longed to do, but stood watching him with a wary expression. What if he didn't want her? He seemed so surprised to see her that she suddenly wondered if he'd asked Tiku to bring her here in the first place. She surmised correctly when Tiku explained. "Someone needs to care for you. I have duties at Kia Ora, so Eden is the best choice. I've brought blankets and enough food to last a few days—until you're able to travel. I'll check on you again in a day or so." Tiku glanced from Damon to Eden and back again to Damon. "I trust I won't need to referee." Tiku positioned the lantern on the top of a rock, bade them farewell, then silently, he left them.

Eden held a flannel blanket and absently fingered the fringe. She felt so unaccountably foolish, so embarrassed to realize Tiku had arranged for her to come to Damon. Damon hadn't asked for her at all.

Finally, she got her bearings. Damon needed her care.

"Are you cold?" she asked in concern, falling to her knees beside him.

"Aye, 'Tis chilly I am."

She couldn't help but smile as she laid the blanket over him. Damon always reverted to his brogue when uncertain or nervous. Did her presence make him nervous? That would be better than making him angry.

When she would have moved away, he caught her wrist in a surprisingly strong clasp for a feverish man. "Did your husband allow you to leave his bed and nurse me?"

"I didn't get married today."

"Ah, of course, my shooting must have prevented the happy occasion. Will there be a wedding tomorrow?"

Eden shook her head. A long strand of hair spilled out of a pin and fell across her shoulder. "I'm not marrying Jock or returning to High Winds. I'm staying with you, Damon, for better or worse. I should never have gone in the first place. Because I left you, Tessa took over Castlegate. It's because of me that you're lying here now, hurt and hunted down for murder. I shouldn't have run away but stayed and fought for you."

"Aye," he agreed with a quiet firmness. "You should have stayed."

Choking back a sob, she fought for control of her emotions. "Tiku came for me. I realize now you didn't ask for me, but I'll stay with you until you tell me to leave."

The grasp on her wrist loosened and he brought her hand to his lips. He placed a small, warm kiss within her palm. "Stay with me forever, my beauty."

"Oh, Damon, do you mean that? Can you forgive me for letting you believe I supported Jock in damming the river? I didn't. I only agreed to marry him because you and the miners would suffer if I didn't. None of this would be happening, except for my stupidity—"

"Eden, if you don't stop your jabbering, how am I, a sick and wounded man, ever going to get you to bend down and kiss me?"

She sucked in her breath at the realization he did love her and somehow knew the truth. Golden lights shimmered within his eyes and mesmerized her. Stretching out and lying against the hardened length of him, she felt his arms go around her and bring her against the warmth of his chest. Their lips touched of their own accord and the kiss was filled with a bright fire, a sweetness which caused the tears to spill from her eyes and roll down her cheeks.

"Woman, what are you crying about?" he asked, wiping one tear away with the pad of his thumb. "Aren't I doing a good job of kissing you?"

Her fingers trailed sensuously across his stubbled chin, and she nestled her head on his shoulder. "I want you to do more than kiss me, but, Damon, I don't deserve your love or forgiveness. How can you want me, ever again?"

"Ah, my beauty, we've both made our share of mistakes, and mine was the worst. I'm hoping that one day, *you* can forgive *me*."

The sadness in his voice touched her like nothing else, not even the kiss he placed on the top of her head. "I forgave you long ago," she replied in an aching whisper.

"Then you really will be staying with me, Eden? I should make you go back to America, because until I can prove Sutherland killed Tessa, there's no life for us."

"You think Jock killed Tessa?" She sat up and peered closely at Damon. Perhaps his fever had unbalanced his thinking, but no, she could see he meant every word he said and was perfectly lucid. "Why would he do such a thing? I can't believe he's capable of murder—"

"He is! And I have to prove it. But you're not thinking of going back to him are you?"

"No, never."

"Eden, he's framing me for Tessa's death with the note I sent you when you were at Kia Ora. It was found by her body."

Her shocked expression was all Damon needed to know she hadn't given it to Sutherland. "Jock must have searched my room," she said, and her anger grew. "How dare he do such a thing."

"That's not all. Jock went to Christ Church and persuaded Tessa to return. From the very first he wanted to hurt me, and he knew that by bringing her back, you'd leave me. But apparently he was afraid you'd change your mind and wanted me out of the way permanently. So, because everyone knew how much I hated her, he's made it look as if I killed her to be free of her. After I realized Jock was behind Tessa's death I rode to High Winds. It was a stupid and unthinking thing to do, but I wanted to get you away from him, to save you from marrying him. Instead, I get a shoulder full of lead and I'm running for my life."

"And you have me," she reminded him, sinking down next to him and circling her arm around his neck. "You'll always have me—and Collin. We have to get Collin, Damon." Her face filled with apprehension. "Suppose Jock decides to use him as a leverage."

"I thought about that already. Tiku went to Lanu and she's hiding Collin at her *pa.*"

Eden breathed a relieved sigh. The *pa* was a fortifed village and Lanu's home. Jock wouldn't look for the boy there. "Then we have only ourselves to worry about for the moment."

"Eden?" Damon asked after a few minutes as they snuggled together. "Do you think I could take some of that elixir Tiku brought?"

"Are you feeling worse?" she questioned in alarm.

"No, but not any better. Tiku swears the elixir will make a sick person as good as new, and I'm eager to be feeling better again."

"I know. You must regain your strength as soon as possible and clear your name."

"Aye, but there's another reason I need to regain my strength and it doesn't require running after Sutherland."

A sly grin surfaced on his tired face and his hand started up her riding skirt to stroke her inner thigh. She gasped in surprise and melted against him, waiting for him to continue, but he didn't. "I'm afraid that's all the fun you're going to get for now" was his apologetic admission.

"Then you'd best be swallowing your elixir right away." Teasing emerald sparkles glowed in her eyes when she reached for the bottle.

"The son of a bitch has kidnapped her! He stole her out from under your men's very noses!" Jock stalked the parlor, his face blazed with crimson fury. Constable Vickers and Magistrate Anderson could only stand in sheepish silence.

"We're at a loss as to how Mrs. Flynn was taken away . . ." Anderson began but immediately quieted beneath Jock's mask of rage.

"Get out, get out, both of you, and take your flunkies with you! My stationhands are better watchdogs than the lot of you." Jock slammed the front door behind them with such vehemence that the windows shook.

"God, where is she?" he cried, and threw himself in an armchair. He should be searching for Eden, but it was too dark to see now. But by the morning's first light, he'd head out and find her by himself. He blamed the bumbling law enforcement officers for this. They were to be watching the house, keeping a sharp eye to make certain Eden didn't run away or that Alexander gained entrance. But she was gone just the same. How in the hell had she escaped with Alexander?

Or had she escaped on her own?

That possibility hadn't dawned upon Jock until this second. Had she learned about Alexander's shooting and sneaked off to find him? He wouldn't put it past her to have found a way out of the house. But how had she left the property without anyone seeing her? The guards had told him the townspeople had dispersed shortly after he and the posse had ridden off that afternoon. No one was seen either entering or leaving High Winds except for Tiku and Marjorie. And Jock had told them good-bye himself.

Or had he?

He now remembered the incident clearly. There was something about the way Marjorie had acted. She didn't speak or look directly at him when he asked her why she wore the shawl so near to her face. Tiku had been more rigid than usual. Jock realized something wasn't right and had gone to question his sister but had been interrupted by the secretary-general. For the next hour and a half he'd been forced to give an accounting of Alexander's shooting and what precautions were being taken to secure the countryside. The secretary and his wife left soon afterward, relieved to return to Wellington and civilization. Jock had begun to fear the shooting and the confusion afterward might eventually cost him the governorship.

If not for the lengthy exchange, he'd have realized earlier that Eden was gone. But when had she left? Could she have sneaked away while he was out hunting down Alexander? No, Nonnie had said Eden was in her room with Marjorie the whole time. Then had she left while he spoke to the secretary-general? No, of course not.

331

Someone would have seen her leave and according to the magistrate, no one had left the property during this time.

So that meant one thing. Eden had left the house and been clearly observed doing it. That hadn't been Marjorie in the buggy beside Tiku at all. It had been Eden!

"Where's my sister?" Jock bellowed at the top of his lungs and went to the kitchen in search of Nonnie. The Maori woman would know where Marjorie was, he had no doubt. Tiku was her son, and apparently she didn't give a damn if he despoiled an Englishwoman.

But it wasn't Nonnie he found in the kitchen, seated at the table and calmly sipping a cup of tea. It was Marjorie.

"Shall I pour you some tea?" she asked, smiling at him.

With his back against the door, he peered intently at her and scowled. "So, you've tricked me. Should I congratulate you?"

"I'm sure I don't know what you mean."

"Lying, fornicating bitch! You know damn well you helped Eden to escape with your savage. Now where is she? Tell me where she is or I'll—"

"Kill me? Is that what you'll do to me, Jock?" Marjorie stood and raised herself to her full height. "Will you murder your own sister? But, yes, I think you might consider it. I've heard that after the first one or two killings, murder becomes easier. Is that true?"

Jock eyed her cockily. "Don't think to blackmail me with that absurd business about Bert's death. No one would believe you."

"I'm not thinking so much about Bert but of Tessa. Tiku and I saw you on the road the other night, very near where Tessa's body was found. And Ice was racing down

332

the road like a windstorm. Constable Vickers and the magistrate might be interested in what we saw, but I trust you can explain your presence at Thunder Mine, Jock."

His face lost all color, and for just an instant Marjorie saw panic flare within his eyes. Then a guarded expression crossed his features. "I offer no explanation other than I took a late-night ride."

"So near to where Tessa was found. Did you hear or see anyone, anything suspicious?"

"You are the little inquisitor, aren't you?"

Marjorie sighed and her voice broke. "You killed Tessa."

Jock nonchalantely examined his fingernails. "No one would believe your outrageous tale, my dear. What credibility can you, a woman who sleeps with a savage, offer?"

"I'm honest and everyone knows it. Everyone also knows how much I love you. I have no reason to want you harmed, so why wouldn't I be believed? I suggest you turn yourself over to the authorities."

"Marjorie, you're a simpleton and a pathetic cripple." He laughed, seeing her wince. "I've tolerated you all these years because you were my sister, but as of this second, I disown you. I never want to see you again."

"I pity you, Jock. You've lost everything."

"I've lost nothing, but I'll have it all when I find Eden."

He stalked from the kitchen, leaving Marjorie a trembling mass of emotions. Jock might be her brother, and she'd always love him, but she knew what she had to do.

Damon was much better two days later. Eden

diligently tended to his wound, cleaning it and changing the bandages which Tiku had left. He was even able to move his arm without grimacing in pain. "It's loosening up a bit," he said, grinning at her as she bent industriously over him. "You're the best nurse a man could ever want—and the best medicine." His hand brushed against her breast.

"Don't be so cheeky or I'll have to slap you."

"Cheeky, am I? I'm thinking more like stinky. I need a washing, Eden, and the lagoon is just waiting for me."

Eden looked at him, a doubtful expression in her eyes. Damon's fever had broken yesterday morning, but she worried he'd have a relapse if he went into the water too soon. But the day was warm and dry and the flesh on his naked chest was cool to her touch—and he *was* in desperate need of a bathing. "All right. I give you permission to bathe."

"Thank you, Mum, I do appreciate it," he whispered in jest, and placed a feather-light kiss on her lips. It was meant to be a playful kiss, but the instant their mouths touched, the pressure deepened. Desire shot right through Eden and she smothered a groan against his lips. Damon wasn't in any condition for the sort of play she had in mind.

She broke away and cleared her throat, glancing at the lagoon. "You better get your bath."

"Then I'll need some help undressing."

"Oh, yes, you do, but that's all, Damon. Don't get any other ideas. You aren't entirely recovered yet."

"What sort of ideas would those be?" he innocently queried, his face appearing guileless.

"If you haven't thought of any, then I won't put them into your head." With her attention riveted on unbuttoning Damon's trousers and working them down his long legs, she moved her gaze to that part of him which was large and hard. "It seems you've thought up some ideas of your own."

"Aye, and they're not all in my head." Damon pulled her toward him with his good arm and Eden didn't resist. He trailed hot, stirring kisses along her face and neck to seek the valley between her breasts. "Wouldn't you like to take off your shirtwaist?" he invited in such a husky voice Eden's body felt like jelly.

"But you're not well yet, I don't want to get you riled up—"

"I'm good enough for a man who survived a bullet wound," he contended. "And, woman, you've already riled me, so do the honorable and decent thing by having your wicked way with me. There's only so much teasing I can stand."

"I've never teased you."

Damon nuzzled the lush valley. "But you have," she heard him say. "You teased me into wanting you from the first second I saw you. Those greenstone eyes teased me into giving you my heart. And now you've taken my soul from me, too. Eden, I love you."

Damon held her by the waist and she knelt before him. When he looked up at her, she nearly cried because she suddenly knew she could never have married Jock, even if he hadn't turned out to be such a monster. She'd always belonged to Damon. For the rest of their lives, they might have to run because of something Damon hadn't done. But they'd be together—and that was all she'd ever wanted.

Sliding down the length of him, she began to unbutton her shirtwaist and riding skirt. With Damon's assistance, she was finally naked and clapsed within the circle of his arm. Tenderly he settled her hair around her shoulders and smiled a melting smile, filled with love and desire. "This is how I always see you in my mind, with your hair all tousled and gleaming like a sunset, your naked body quivering against me. And I'm a happy man because you belong to me, wild Eden."

"Oh, Damon, I love you so."

As one, they stood up and waded into the lagoon where they washed each other and kissed until passion won out.

Leading her out of the water, Damon fell beside her on the soft ferns. His mouth touched hers in a crushing kiss which tore the very breath from her. Eden felt herself opening to him, body, mind, and soul. Her heart hammered against her rib cage as his hands swept over her breasts, her waist, her thighs, then came to rest between her legs. Damon wanted to touch all of her at once, and she lost herself in the same frenzied wanting.

He groaned in pleasure as her hands explored him, sliding across his chest and down the lean expanse of flank until her silken fingers closed around his throbbing, warm shaft. "Eden my love, I'm aflame already. Don't do that." But it was too late, for she stroked him with long, leisurely strokes, reveling in the unabashed esctasy on his face. Finally when he was in such an aroused state that the end to his tender torture would be swift, Damon grabbed her by the waist and pulled her atop him. "Ride, my wild Eden, ride," he coaxed in a ragged whisper that burned at her core.

She sheathed him with the hot glove of her femininity, straddling him as he held her hips in place to meet his thrusts with a downward plunge of her own. The very heavens opened to her with each of Damon's tormenting strokes. She felt her body melting upon his engorged manhood, rushing toward fulfillment. So long a time had passed since they last made love.

Damon, too, was on the precipice. He held her tightly and began a swift rhythm which threatened to undo her. Then he suddenly grew still and arched toward her in one glorious possessive thrust. Eden fell into a star-filled chasm the second she felt his hot, throbbing release and barely realized Damon had captured her mouth to quiet her cry of wanton pleasure.

Afterward, she lay in the crook of his arm while he stared down at her, his hand gently massaging her stomach. She felt so wonderful, so alive and loved. For the moment she could forget that Damon was a hunted man. She began to drift into sleep when Damon's voice brought her back to instant wakefulness.

"When are you going to tell me you're having a child?"

Damon, as always, had taken her unawares. She'd meant to tell him but had never found the right moment. It seemed now was the perfect time, if only he didn't stare at her with those eyes which were now a darkened shade of blue, expressing his dismay.

"I wanted to wait until things were more settled."

"Were you ever going to tell me? You would have been married to Sutherland and having my child—at least I assume its mine."

"Yes, Damon, the baby is yours. And to be honest, I didn't ever want you to know about it. You were married and already had a son. There was no need to burden you with my baby."

"*Our* baby," he empahsized. Damon rapidly blinked away tears, and Eden knew she had hurt him deeply.

She wrapped her arms around him. "Forgive me, but I couldn't tell you. I expected to leave New Zealand by myself. Jock blackmailed me into agreeing to marry him. I told you why."

"But Jock knew about the baby?" He gave a short, raspy laugh at her nod. "What a perfect revenge against me. He'd marry the woman I loved and would raise my child."

Eden stared into his eyes, fear filling her own. "Have I lost you again?"

A deep, shuddering sigh ripped through him, but he clamped his arms about her in an iron grip. "Never, my beauty. I don't like that you didn't want to tell me about our baby, but I can understand your reluctance. But I need your forgiveness, too."

"You have that already."

"And you?"

"And me."

"Then all we need is Collin with us and for me to clear my name to be at peace."

"Damon, you're not thinking of going after Jock—"

"Aye," he answered in such a bone-chilling tone that she feared it would be foolhardy to try to stop him.

Chapter 25

"So you're certain about these facts, Mrs. Carruthers. Before his death your late husband admitted that Mr. Sutherland wished him killed?" Constable Vickers sat across from Marjorie, his hands on his desk, while Magistrate Anderson stood nearby.

"Yes. Bert was quite certain of it. My brother wanted Bert's property and forced me into marriage with him. Then, if Bert died, the property would revert to me. Jock, however, offered to buy Kia Ora from me after Bert's death and I refused." A wracking sigh shook Marjorie's shoulders. "I didn't want to believe my brother was capable of such a crime, but now I do."

"Why? Is there something else you need to tell me?"

She swallowed hard, and tears welled within her eyes. "The night of Tessa Alexander's death, Tiku and I were coming from town. We noticed a rider ahead of us shoot out of the forest, near where Tessa's body was found. We both recognized the rider as my brother."

"Couldn't you have been mistaken?"

"No, sir. He was riding Ice, my brother's white

stallion, and no one can control the horse but Jock. I confronted him with what we saw and he told me no one would believe me. I know Jock killed Mrs. Alexander but is making it look as if her husband did it. He wanted to marry Eden Flynn, but she was in love with Damon Alexander, and this was Jock's way of getting rid of him."

"Why didn't your brother just kill the man instead of the woman?" asked the magistrate.

Marjorie shook her head sadly. "Jock detests Mr. Alexander and wants him to suffer. You must believe me." Her eyes implored them and her voice broke. "I . . . don't want to harm my brother, but justice must be done. Mr. Alexander is innocent of the crime."

Both men glanced in concern at each other and told Marjorie they'd investigate the matter. After she left the office, Vickers leaned back in his chair. "What do you think?" he asked Anderson.

Anderson rubbed his chin in thought. "I think Sutherland has gotten too big for his trousers and needs to be brought down a number of pegs. After Mrs. Flynn's escape from High Winds, and with the secretary-general in residence, we've looked like complete bunglers. Can't do any harm to investigate Mrs. Carruthers's claims."

"You're correct," agreed Vickers, and grabbed for his hat. "And you know what? I think Sutherland killed Alexander's wife and should be tried for her murder. Just let the bloody bastard make us out to be fools in front of his fancy friends when he's brought to trial in Wellington. I could write quite an informative book about some of his unscrupulous dealings. I've overlooked them in the past, but no more, Anderson. No more."

With that determined comment hanging in the air,

Vickers put on his hat and went to round up his men for the ride to High Winds.

"Damon, please reconsider going after Jock. There's nothing to be gained by it. We can get Collin and run away to America or Europe. No one will ever find us." Eden's pleading fell upon deaf ears. Damon had made up his mind.

"I'm not running forever," he pronounced and loaded his pistol. "We'd have no life. I want better than that for you and Collin—and the new baby."

At the sight of the gun, Eden's eyes widened. "Are you going to shoot Jock?"

"Not if I can help it. I want to bring the bastard into the constable alive and only hope he confesses."

Throwing her arms around his neck, Eden sobbed into his shirtfront. "I don't want to lose you. I love you."

Holding her close, Damon smiled down into her hair. "I'm too much in love with you to consider being killed."

They walked hand in hand as they meandered through the forest. Terror clutched at Eden's heart to imagine what waited for Damon on the other side. He was doing the honorable thing, she knew that. But she remembered what Jock had screamed at her about honor. Damon was an honorable man, Jock wasn't; he played by his own rules.

They'd gone half the distance when Damon stopped short and poised the pistol at a movement within a cluster of bushes. Eden tensed but breathed a relieved sigh when Tiku appeared. "You gave me a start," Damon chided, and lowered the gun.

"Damon, you can put the gun away for good," Tiku

informed him as he flashed a brilliant smile. "The constable has just been to High Winds and is taking Sutherland in for questioning about Tessa's death and that of Bert Carruthers. I spoke to Constable Vickers before the arrest, Marjorie, too. We saw her brother on the night of Tessa's murder, very near to where her body was later found. And Marjorie told him that Bert was shot by Sutherland's men, at Jock's command. You're free, it appears."

Eden let out a wild, joyous cry, and Damon picked her up and swung her around. Tiku's news seemed too wonderful to be true. Damon needed to hear it with his own ears. They left the forest to find Tiku had brought War Dance and a horse for Eden. Catching up with the constable on the road back to town, they reined in beside Vickers and some of his men.

"I understand I'm free."

"Yes, Mr. Alexander, you are. Sutherland is your wife's murderer. Of course he denies he killed her, but Mrs. Carruthers and that Tiku fellow claim they saw him near Thunder Mine the night of her death. There is one thing that puzzles me, however. Where did the note next to Mrs. Alexander's body come from? It was addressed to you, Mrs. Flynn." Vickers turned his attention to Eden.

"I received the note at Kia Ora," Eden explained. "When I stayed at High Winds, Mrs. Carruthers had my things sent to me. Apparently Jock went through my belongings and found the note. He must have placed it beside Tessa."

"Yes, ma'am, I'm certain that's what happened." Vickers shot her an encouraging smile. "Sutherland is up ahead, guarded by my men. You've nothing to worry about now, but I think it would be a good idea if you didn't ride into town with us. A lady like yourself doesn't need to be gossiped about in a situation such as this. For your best interests, I'd advise you go home and wait until Mr. Alexander returns."

"Constable Vickers is right," Damon agreed. "Return to Castlegate and wait for me."

"But I want to be with you."

"It's better that you don't. Please go home. I want to think of you there, waiting for me. And when I get back, we'll have a great deal of celebrating in store." Damon said, winking at her.

She couldn't help but bubble over with laughter. "All right, I'll wait for you."

"Like a proper wife," Damon finished. His eyes roamed over her body in a way that caused her to tremble with anticipation. She was actually going to be his wife!

"Yes, just like a proper wife, your wife."

With a happy smile on her lips, Eden turned her horse and started for Castlegate.

They neared town and spotted the group of men whose job it had been to guard Jock Sutherland. Damon was shocked to learn Sutherland wasn't to be found. The men were scattered hither and yon, riding into the bush and coming up empty. "Sutherland has escaped, sir," a young man advised Vickers.

"How in the name of God did he do that!" thundered Vickers. "You men are trained not to be given the slip. What's the matter with the lot of you?" Vickers's face was so red, it looked ready to burst.

"Well, it's that bloody horse he insisted he ride," the young man explained. "Seemed harmless enough to let

343

Sutherland take his horse, looked like an ordinary horse, it did. But when we got near town, the thing rose up on all fours. I've never seen a more powerful animal. I was holding the reins the whole time and I tied the knots on the rope that was tied around Mr. Sutherland's hands. But the man somehow undid them and jerked the reins from me when the horse reacted to some sort of a command from him." He gulped and lowered his eyes. "The horse bolted and Mr. Sutherland took off. We gave chase but couldn't catch him. I've never in my life seen a faster horse. It was like trying to catch the wind."

Vickers muttered a profane curse. "Fan out and find Sutherland!" he shrieked to his men. "Find the bloody cur now! . . . Where are you going?" he shouted at Damon, who had spurred his horse to a gallop back down the road.

"Eden may be in trouble!" he shouted over his shoulder, unaware that Vickers had realized the same thing and rushed after Damon. But War Dance was faster than the constable's horse and Vickers couldn't keep up the pace.

Elation soared through Jock at his escape. The stupid bungling fools had been left behind. He was free and no one would catch him. Somehow he'd make it home and quickly gather a few things together and leave the Otago for now. There was no other choice but to leave. He blamed Marjorie for this mess. She'd ruined his life, as she'd promised to do if he interfered with Alexander or Eden. One day he'd make Marjorie pay for this, now he must flee, must think of himself.

Ice easily ran the path which traversed the length of

the Shotover. Vickers and his bunglers wouldn't catch him. By the time they arrived at High Winds, he'd be long gone.

Turning Ice away from the path, he took a small trail which cut through the forest but would force him to cross Alexander's property, Kia Ora, and then his own High Winds. Not many people knew about the trail and Jock felt assured that the authorities were probably moving in a westerly direction, while he was going east.

"Jackasses!" he grumbled, and gave Ice a vicious kick to spur him along at a speedier pace. Ice instantly responded and Jock soon neared Castlegate. The ivory-colored facade glistened like a fairy castle in the sunshine, but Jock didn't notice. He wanted to reach High Winds in record time, and he would have, too, if he hadn't seen the woman on horseback ahead of him.

Her hair flew behind her like a blazing comet, her very posture in the saddle bespoke breeding. It was Eden, and she was alone. She was his for the taking.

His loins ached with longing for her. God help him, he still desired the wanton witch, the betrayer of his trust. And he would have her.

With cunning skill and agility born of years in the saddle, Jock rushed alongside her and in one fell swoop, he plucked her like a wild daisy from her trotting horse.

Eden sputtered, fear and bafflement in her eyes as she clung tenaciously to Ice's mane to keep from falling. She was confused, but Jock didn't give her a chance to get her bearings. His laugh, rich and filled with menace, reverberated through the woodlands.

"Let Alexander find you now!" he triumphantly crowed.

Chapter 26

As the magnificent horse bolted onto the plains of Kia Ora, Eden realized Jock's destination was High Winds. Somehow she must swallow her panic and think what to do when they got there. She'd beg for help, but perhaps no one would come to her aid—not when a man as determined as Jock held her captive.

He rasped into her ear. "You're coming with me. Alexander will never find you."

"I'll fight," she vowed, attempting to appear brave.

"The challenge of making you want me is the thing, my dear."

Terror gripped her in its thrall. She must get away from Jock before he got to High Winds. Since they were on Kia Ora, Eden realized Marjorie's stationhands would be somewhere close by, tending to the flock. Perhaps she'd see Tiku . . . anyone who might help her. With her gaze ever vigilant, she'd wait until she saw someone and could make an escape.

But it seemed this section was deserted. Nothing but open plain stretched before them, and Eden's hope of escaping sagged. A strangled sob rose in her throat. No one could help her if they did see and realize something was wrong. They'd be unable to catch up, even on horseback. There wasn't a faster horse in the Otago than Jock's Sutherland's Ice.

Except for War Dance.

The abrupt appearance of the black stallion with Damon atop him barely registered in her mind before she heard Jock's vicious curse. Damon pulled alongside them, his pistol trained at Jock, and he grabbed the reins, jerking Ice to an abrupt halt. The horse reared up, his front legs flailing wildly to maintain his balance and coming back to earth with a thud. Eden fell to the ground, the soft grass cushioning the blow, with Jock beside her.

For a few seconds she felt dazed but was aware of Jock's arm still gripping her by the waist. The sky above her seemed to spin and reel and then settled into place. Her breath came in tiny gasps, partly from the fall but also from the pressure of Jock's arm. Somehow she managed to quickly glance his way and saw he was dazed, too. A thin red gash streaked his scar-free cheek, and when he brought his hand to it and felt the blood before he saw it, Eden anticipated his reaction.

She went for his pistol at the same moment he did. His target was to be Damon, of that she was certain, but she wouldn't allow Jock to hurt him. Their hands grappled with the gun and Jock, who was stronger, viciously pulled it from her. In one movement he pointed the gun at Damon, who had dismounted and was coming toward them, and yanked Eden unceremoniously to her feet, her body partly blocking his.

"I'm going to kill you, Alexander. I've waited for this moment, lived for it. Drop your gun or I'll shoot Eden."

347

Damon stopped in his steps. "You don't want to kill her."

"You're right, I don't. But unless you drop the gun, I'll shoot her where she won't suffer permanent injury. Still, she'll be hurt and in pain. I know you don't want Eden harmed."

A nerve twitched beside Damon's right eye, as he assessed the situation. His gaze moved over Eden and then behind her, coming again to shoot Jock a withering stare. "You're a bastard, Sutherland."

Jock gave a triumphant laugh when Damon threw down his gun. "And you're a weakling. I have you exactly where I want you now, Alexander, and I'm going to have your lady, too." Jock pushed Eden away from him and she fell to her knees. The cocking of the trigger on Jock's gun sounded like a tiny explosion in Eden's ear. A terrified scream was torn from her throat when a gun fired, deafening her with its roar and causing her eyes to close as cold shock waves pounded through her brain. She was transported back to the day her parents were killed, remembered the sounds of the cannons, the guns, the screams of her mother. But it wasn't her mother who screamed again and again until she couldn't stop. It was herself.

In a corner of her mind she heard her own voice shrieking. Damon! Jock had killed Damon! She couldn't live without him, she wanted to die, too. There was nothing, no one left for her. The man she loved was dead!

Jock's hands grabbed for her arms and she struggled, cried out against him. "No! No! I hate you, hate you!" But it was when she heard her name being called and found herself wrapped in a familiar embrace did she stop crying and slowly opened her eyes.

Damon gazed down at her, his concern deeply etched into his beloved handsome face. "Eden it's over," he told her in a comforting tone of voice.

"You're all right! Where's Jock?"

He inclinded his head. "Dead."

"But how?"

"Constable Vickers."

Damon helped her to her feet, and Eden finally understood what had happened when she saw Vickers standing over Jock's body. The constable had come up behind Jock and shot him in the back before Jock's gun discharged at Damon. "Oh, God!" she cried, and turned away to think how Marjorie would react to her brother's death. Damon's arms never left her as he helped her mount War Dance and climbed up behind her. Then they headed for home.

Ice galloped wildly across the plains and found his way back to High Winds, but there was no doting master to greet him.

Epilogue

Eden placed her infant son in his cradle and took Collin by the hand. She quietly closed the door to the nursery. Collin put his finger to his lips when Damon appeared in the hallway. "Shh, Papa. Baby Shamus is sleeping."

Damon grinned and ruffled the boy's hair. "Shouldn't you be asleep, too?"

Collin nodded slowly, not happy about going to bed. "Can't get to do nothing round here," he mumbled but hugged his father good night and kissed Eden. "I love you, Momma," Collin said.

"I love you, too, baby," she told him and hugged him tightly. The hug was broken when Lanu came to take Collin to his room and get him ready for bed. "We'll be in to check on you later," Eden promised and blew him another kiss.

With her arm tucked in Damon's they walked onto the veranda. Thousands of brilliant, twinkling stars filled the night sky and cast a silvery counterpane across the valley below. It was a perfect night, a night when everything couldn't be anything but wonderful. And everything *was* wonderful.

Marjorie and Tiku had married and inherited High Winds. Recently Marjorie had given birth to Tiku's son. The baby was beautiful with a coffee-colored complexion and deep blue eyes which one day would darken to a walnut-brown like his father's. So far, he bore little resemblance to Marjorie, but she'd proudly told Eden he was a quiet and happy baby—so perhaps his personality would be like his mother's.

Joanie Patterson's first child was due in three months, and Nick strutted around town like he was the only man to ever be a father. Eden guessed Nick would be a wonderful father, because he was kind and considerate— a great deal like Damon.

Damon. Her heart was in her eyes for him to see when she looked at him. After being married for nearly a year and bearing him a child, Eden still reacted the same way to him each time he touched her. She wondered if other women felt this melting sensation for their husbands and pitied them if they didn't.

Damon's warm lips claimed hers in a kiss which caused her to cling to him in wanton response. His mouth moved to the slim column of her neck. "We better tell Collin good night soon," she heard him say in between breathless kisses. "Otherwise I'll have to carry you to bed and by that time he'll be asleep."

"Oh, yes," she moaned, and arched toward him, desire flaring deeply within her. "We must tell Collin good night."

"The lad loves you, Eden, like you were his own mother. *I* love you."

Tears gathered in Eden's eyes and spiked her lashes.

She loved Damon and the children so much she ached. Gazing up at him, she whispered, "I love you, more than I ever thought I could love anyone. You've given me so much—"

"I've given you nothing but love, my beauty."

And that was a great deal.

Lanu coughed discreetly, interrupting them. "Master Collin is ready to say good night."

"We'll be there in a second," he told Lanu. "Ready to go in, Mum?" he asked Eden.

Eden wiped her eyes. "Yes, in a minute. Go on. There's something I have to do."

Damon raised an eyebrow in perplexity but started into the house without her. She turned her attention to the sky above and fastened her eyes on the largest and most glittering star. "Shamus..." she began, her whisper lifting and floating toward the heavens. "I hope you can hear me, I need for you to hear me. Know how grateful I am to you for loving me and insisting I come to this wild land. You gave me more than your wealth. You gave me Damon and my children." Her voice broke. "Thank you for giving me back my life."

Eden suddenly grew quiet, realizing Damon watched her from the doorway and waited for her. Holding out his hand to her, she started for him but cast another look at the bright star, shining like gold dust in the black velvet sky, and she stopped because she could have sworn it winked at her.

Then she took Damon's hand and went inside.